The Benevole

"Goodman skillfully blends mystery, adventure, and a dash of romance."
—*The Washington Post*

"The book's story elements . . . are rooted in historical fact and recounted with convincing realism—and wit. Ms. Goodman's ill-mannered ladies are delightful company."
—*The Wall Street Journal*

"If you love Georgette Heyer, you'll love *The Benevolent Society of Ill-Mannered Ladies*. Smart and sassy and featuring heroines of a certain age, this is the Regency I've been waiting for. Adventure! Mystery! A touch of romance! This delightful novel has it all!"
—Jenn McKinlay,
New York Times bestselling author of *Fatal First Edition*

"A refreshing new arrival on the historical mystery scene! A wise, kind, and sharp-tongued sleuth solves crime in a well-portrayed Regency England. A must-read for lovers of the Regency and historical mysteries alike."
—Jennifer Ashley,
New York Times bestselling author of *Speculations in Sin*

"A rollicking feminist romp—think Jane Austen meets James Bond—that breaks the shackles of period genre fiction and liberates women from the forces arrayed against them."
—*The Sydney Morning Herald*

"For fans of historical fiction, romance, and ladies tired of being restricted by society!"
—Book Riot

"A truly delightful romp through the Regency period. Alison Goodman has crafted a feminist adventure story that will have you cheering on the unconventional Colebrook sisters in all their exploits."

—Stephanie Marie Thornton,
USA Today bestselling author of *Her Lost Words*

"Fans of Georgette Heyer's Regency novels will savor this mystery. . . . Well-developed characters, a touch of romance, and cases involving social issues of the period enhance the experience."

—*Library Journal* (starred review)

"If you love historical fiction, thrilling adventures, women who don't follow society's rules, and witty romance, you need to read *The Benevolent Society of Ill-Mannered Ladies*. Add it to your TBR ASAP!"

—Culturess

"Fresh and fearless, Alison Goodman's exquisitely written, impeccably researched, genre-blending novel shines a light in the darkest corners of Regency England. *The Benevolent Society of Ill-Mannered Ladies* is part heart-racing adventure, part gothic mystery, part tantalizing romance, and wholly wonderful. I can't wait for the next installment!"

—Joanna Lowell, author of *A Shore Thing*

"Well plotted, with emotionally rich characters. This novel should delight those readers [who] enjoy Regency mysteries with a bit of romance that have strong female characters."

—*Mystery & Suspense Magazine*

"The book is well paced, excellently researched (with several fun historical characters like Fanny Burney), funny, romantic, and action-packed."

—*Historical Novels Review*

"A rollicking and joyous adventure, with a beautiful love story at its heart, about two rebellious sisters forging their own path in Regency London."   —Smart Bitches Trashy Books

"Fierce, funny, and often dark, this is an eye-opening portrait of a colorful yet misogynistic period in English history. Readers will be eager to return for the duo's next adventure."
                                                —*Publishers Weekly*

"All three adventures are marked by successively mounting complications that fans of either the Regency period or take-no-prisoners feminism will cheer. Think of the Bridgerton novels with the steamy sex replaced by female-forward action sequences."
                                                —*Kirkus Reviews*

"This feel-good romp comes with a little bit of everything—endearing heroines, adventure, romance, mystery, and the promise of more stories to come."   —*425*

"A joyous romp through Regency England that is equally entertaining, revealing, feminist, heartbreaking, and humorous. . . . This book would be loved by anyone looking for a historical adventure that breaks the bounds of convention to feature women 'past their prime' taking matters into their own hands."
                                                —Books+Publishing

"Goodman's ladies are the undercover Regency heroes we've been waiting for! This is sparkling, thrilling, romantic fun."
                    —Toni Jordan, author of *Dinner with the Schnabels*

"Witty and poignant, this is a clever twist on historical romance and mystery. The Colebrook twins are the Regency's answer to Holmes and Watson!"
                    —Belinda Alexandra, author of *The French Agent*

"Heroines can appear out of nowhere and soon become indispensable, and such is the case with Lady Augusta Colebrook, who, with her twin sister Lady Julia, is at the heart of this compelling, enthralling, unforgettable novel. You will be very glad you've let Gus into your life, then wonder how you ever did without her."
—Sophie Green, author of *The Bellbird River Country Choir*

The Ladies Road Guide to Utter Ruin

ALISON GOODMAN

BERKLEY PRIME CRIME

NEW YORK

BERKLEY PRIME CRIME
Published by Berkley
An imprint of Penguin Random House LLC
1745 Broadway, New York, NY 10019
penguinrandomhouse.com

Library of Congress Cataloging-in-Publication Data
Names: Goodman, Alison, author.
Title: The ladies road guide to utter ruin / Alison Goodman.
Description: First edition. | New York : Berkley Prime Crime, 2025.
Identifiers: LCCN 2024043319 (print) | LCCN 2024043320 (ebook) |
ISBN 9780593440834 (trade paperback) | ISBN 9780593440841 (ebook)
Subjects: LCGFT: Detective and mystery fiction. | Novels.
Classification: LCC PR9619.3.G62 L33 2025 (print) |
LCC PR9619.3.G62 (ebook) | DDC 823/.914--dc23/eng/20240924
LC record available at https://lccn.loc.gov/2024043319
LC ebook record available at https://lccn.loc.gov/2024043320

First Edition: May 2025

Printed in the United States of America
1st Printing

The authorized representative in the EU for product safety and compliance is
Penguin Random House Ireland, Morrison Chambers, 32 Nassau Street,
Dublin D02 YH68, Ireland, https://eu-contact.penguin.ie.

For all the women out there
whose ideas and opinions have been talked over,
interrupted, denigrated, or dismissed.
Ladies, it is time to roar.

The
Ladies
Road Guide
to Utter Ruin

The Trouble
with Brothers

1

The gentleman riding on the bridle way in front of me had not noticed his horse was lame. The gray mare's head bobbed excessively and her gait was short and choppy on the compacted sand of Rotten Row. Clear signs of distress. It was no wonder; the man jerked upon the reins and his seat was deplorable.

"I think we must intervene," I said to Leonardo, leaning forward in my sidesaddle to stroke his chestnut neck. "Otherwise, he may ruin her."

My hunter tossed his head as if in agreement. A whimsical notion, perhaps, but I have always held that horses are creatures of great sympathy.

"Thomas, I am riding ahead," I called to my groom, who followed at a discreet distance on his own mount.

"Aye, my lady," he answered.

I shifted my weight in the sidesaddle and gently urged Leonardo into a trot, the sound of his hooves dull thuds upon the damp ground.

The dawn light had broken through the dense autumn fog, and the trees and paths of Hyde Park were finally visible around us. Most of the other riders on the bridle way were grooms exercising their highbred charges. Only a few members of the bon ton, including myself and the two men ahead, were flouting the royal order that allowed grooms—and only grooms—to gallop upon Rotten Row at daybreak. Since anything above a trot was forbidden at all other times, it was worth the early start and slight risk. Although if I rode as badly as Mr. Deplorable, I would not have bothered.

"Ho, ahead," I called, my breath misting in front of my mouth. "Stop! Your horse is lame."

I drew Leonardo alongside the two riders and matched their slower pace. I did not know Mr. Deplorable, but I certainly recognized the compact athletic man mounted on the bay beside him: Lord Milroy.

Damn, one of the most contrary men I had ever met. He had a reputation as a Tory kingmaker—always avoiding the forefront of politics, but highly influential nonetheless—and was well-known for his view that women had no place in the political sphere, even at the social periphery where we were relegated. Ironically, we came into each other's orbit quite frequently at the Berry sisters' soirees— the heart of informal political discourse—and he and I had clashed twice in the debates. So far, the score was one all, but I believed the money was on me to win the next bout.

"Lord Milroy, your friend's horse is lame," I said in greeting. "He should dismount before he does any more harm."

"Lady Augusta," Milroy said, saluting me with a bare nod, his voice a rumbling baritone of disdain. He liked to dabble in the theater—imagining himself, no doubt, another Kemble—and had learned to use his voice to excellent effect. "I see you do not confine your lectures to the debating ring."

The swords, it seemed, were already drawn. "This is not a lecture, Lord Milroy, it is a fact: the mare is lame."

He and his companion reined their mounts to a halt. I did the same, settling more firmly into my saddle. This was not going to be an easy rescue after all.

"We are most fortunate, then, to have your eagle eyes upon the situation," Milroy said, casting a droll look at his friend. "I had heard you liked to ride with the grooms, Lady Augusta—so singular for a lady of your rank. What is the attraction, I wonder."

I ignored his sly innuendo and the fact that he did not introduce his smirking companion to me as etiquette demanded. "I imagine it is the same as for yourself, Lord Milroy: the chance to gallop. However, your friend should dismount now."

My suggestion went unacknowledged. Instead, Milroy surveyed the impressive dimensions of Leonardo. "Such a large hunter for a woman. One wonders who advised you to purchase such an inappropriate mount." He touched his forehead under his beaver hat in a theatrical gesture of recall. "Ah, but of course, you are sadly without the guidance of a husband."

I matched his silky tone. "I think it is always best to ride a horse that matches one's skill." A glance at his smaller gelding brought home my double meaning. His mouth tightened. A pleasing result, but the mare had cocked her lame hoof and the suffering was plain in her eyes. Time to move this conversation to its goal. "You have not introduced your friend to me, Lord Milroy," I said firmly.

Upon such a blatant prompt, he had no choice. "Lady Augusta, allow me to introduce Mr. Charles Rampling, lately of Hertfordshire, who is currently my guest here in London."

"Lady Augusta, enchanted," the man slurred, and made a clumsy bow in the saddle, sending his poor horse into an unnecessary step upon her lame foreleg. It seemed Mr. Rampling was still quite foxed from the night before.

"You should dismount immediately, Mr. Rampling," I said briskly. How many times did I have to repeat myself?

"Dismount?" Mr. Rampling echoed. "Good God, no. I'd have to walk if I dismounted."

Perhaps he did not understand the urgency of the situation. "That would be the case, certainly, but if you do not, you could damage your mare permanently."

Mr. Rampling squinted at me, then giggled, a ridiculously high-pitched trill. "So, are you a horse physician, Lady Augusta?"

"Of course not," I said, pitching my voice over Lord Milroy's laugh. "Anyone with an ounce of knowledge would see—"

Rampling shrugged. "Then, begging pardon, my lady, this is my animal and I'll do with her as I please. I am not about to walk upon the Row like some Johnny Raw."

"Perhaps the effects of last night's revels are still with you, Mr. Rampling," I said sharply. "Only a fool would disregard such an injury to his horse and by doing so compound it. Surely you do not wish—"

"Are you scolding my friend, Lady Augusta?" Lord Milroy asked with mock jocularity. The angle of his long chin, however, held the jut of battle. "Perhaps it is not only this mare that needs a bridle."

I stared at him, taken aback. "I beg your pardon?"

"He means a scold's bridle," Mr. Rampling slurred helpfully. He giggled again, his rocking mirth pressing the poor mare into another pained shift upon her lame hoof.

I drew a steadying breath. Every fiber of my being demanded that I tell Milroy exactly what I thought of him, but that would not help the horse. I had to get her away from these men at any cost.

"Mr. Rampling, I will give you seventy guineas for her if you dismount and hand her over now."

It was twice the amount the mare was worth, but I did not care.

Rampling's eyes widened. "Seventy? Well, I—"

Milroy quelled Rampling with a glance, then leaned forward in his saddle. "Too easy, Lady Augusta. How about a wager instead? Your horse and skill against mine. A race along the length of the Row. Winner takes the mare. Surely a lady who rides with the grooms will not balk at a race."

Even in a world where fortunes were regularly won and lost on the flip of a card or the roll of the dice, Milroy was famed as a hard gambler. I had heard that he had once wagered he could find a man to eat a cat alive. The tale was most probably—and hopefully—apocryphal, but the message was the same: the man would wager a great deal upon anything.

A hot rush of competition surged through me. Leonardo was the superior horse and my own skill was easily a match for Milroy's. I could beat him. Even so, he was asking me to race for money on public ground. A whole new level of impropriety. Moreover, such a wager in front of the grooms would inevitably bring gossip. I could not afford to attract any attention to myself. Not with what was currently at stake: Julia and I had two fugitives hiding in our house, and Lord Evan—my dear absent Evan—was being hunted by the Bow Street Magistrate for absconding and robbery. Any eyes upon us could put them all at risk.

"I think you are well aware I cannot accept such a wager, Lord Milroy," I said. "Mr. Rampling, would you consider one hundred guineas?"

A ridiculous price, but we were in competition now and I was not going to lose.

From the corner of my eye, I saw a handsome black horse approach at a stately pace, its elegantly dressed rider instantly recognizable: Mr. Brummell.

Good God, what was he doing here? George Brummell did not usually emerge from his rooms until midday.

"Lady Augusta," Mr. Brummell called. "Well met."

I collected myself enough to raise my riding crop in greeting.

George reined in his mount beside Leonardo and made a bow in the saddle to the two men. "Good day, Lord Milroy, and Mr. Rampling, is it not?"

Rampling straightened from his lolling slump. It was not every day that a man of his ilk was recognized by the king of fashionable society. "It is, Mr. Brummell. It is, it is indeed," he stammered, returning my friend's salute with vigor.

George glanced at me with a lift of his brow. It was plain he knew I was fuming.

"I have just offered Mr. Rampling one hundred guineas for his mare," I said, as evenly as I could manage.

George raised his quizzing glass—hanging around his neck on an elegant black riband—and considered the gray with some authority. In his youth he had been a cavalryman and he knew his horseflesh. "That is rather exorbitant, my dear Lady Augusta, since she is quite lame." He shifted his scrutiny to her rider. "You should take it, Rampling. You will never get a better price."

"Of course I'll take it," Mr. Rampling said. He dismounted—an untidy affair that forced a huff of pain from the mare—and offered me the reins.

Clearly, he had agreed only because George had told him to sell; a man's advice was always worth one hundred times more than a woman's. Moreover, if that man happened to be "Beau" Brummell, then there could be no refusal. I gritted my teeth and took the reins. A hollow victory, but at least the horse was safe.

I turned in my saddle and waved to Thomas, waiting nearby on his mount, to join us. Upon his arrival, I handed him the reins. "Walk her back to the mews and ask John Driver to start poulticing her right foreleg."

"Yes, my lady." He hesitated. "Shall I return?"

"No. I will be along presently."

With a nod and a bow, Thomas rode slowly toward the Hyde Park Gate, leading my new mare behind him.

"What is the horse's name?" I asked Rampling.

The man shrugged. "I just call her the old gray," he said from the ground, which, frankly, summed up the worth of the man.

"I had thought you were made of sterner stuff, Lady Augusta," Lord Milroy said, a false smile on his thin lips. "Perhaps we will have that race one day. For a different wager."

"Certainly," I said, meeting his smile with my own. "I would relish defeating you again."

Milroy straightened in the saddle.

George cleared his throat. "Will you ride with me awhile, Lady Augusta?" he asked, casting me an amused glance.

"I would be delighted." I looked down at Rampling. "I will send my groom to return your tack, and my man of business will be in contact with you directly. Good day." I met Milroy's hard look. "Good day to you, too, Lord Milroy."

George touched the brim of his hat in polite farewell and we turned our horses, quickly settling into a matched pace.

"Did I hear correctly? A wager with Milroy?" George asked when we were well out of earshot. "I would not recommend standing against him. He plays to win—no regard for the cost—and between you and me, I do not think he always plays fair."

I glanced at my friend; the warning was odd enough, considering George's own penchant for hard gambling, but I would never have expected him to impugn another man's honor. Still, I could believe it of Milroy. He was in politics, after all. "He challenged me to a race down the Row for the mare, but of course I could not take him up on it."

George smiled. "Yet you were sorely tempted, no doubt, despite the scandal that would have ensued."

I returned the smile. "Oh, George, you have no idea how tempted."

"I have some idea. You do like to push boundaries, don't you?"

I snorted: that was definitely the pot calling the kettle black. George Brummell had risen from a common birth and a mediocre cavalry career to become the king of fashionable society, all on the strength of good looks, good taste, and a great deal of wit. He had not just pushed boundaries; he had vaulted over them.

He raised his quizzing glass and surveyed me. "So, you took my recommendation and went to Weston."

I looked down at my riding outfit: a habit styled along military lines in blue superfine wool with four rows of black braid across the bodice and epaulets à la Hussar. George, of course, was the epitome of riding elegance, his own superfine blue jacket—also made by the great tailor—cut precisely across his shoulders, with immaculate buff breeches, a pristine cravat, and well-shined riding boots.

"Indeed. Thank you for the introduction. I had not expected Weston to make it himself."

George dropped the quizzing glass back upon its riband. "But of course he did. I introduced you." He surveyed the misty bridle way, a frown upon his handsome profile. "It is a pity there are not more riders to see our matched splendor."

I laughed at his pained tone. "I must admit I was not expecting to see you here at this hour."

"Alas, my own lost wager at Watier's," George replied.

"I did not lose the wager," I said. "I just could not accept it. Now or ever, unfortunately. I thought you had vowed never to appear in Watier's wager book again after that last loss."

George had told me about the famous wager book—all gentlemen's clubs had them, apparently—where bets, from the frivolous to the extraordinary, were recorded.

He shrugged. "I could not resist. Alvanley bet me that Lord Dannerby would not wear his usual repulsive puce this Friday past. The man had not deviated from the color for months. Alas, he arrived wearing chartreuse, and so I must accompany Alvanley here for a week. He finds galloping down the Row at this godforsaken hour the height of enjoyment, whereas he knows it is my worst nightmare."

He lifted his chin to indicate another rider, near the Hyde Park Gate, watching us. I recognized the portly figure of Lord Alvanley, astride a big roan. I bowed in his direction, and he returned the greeting, but he did not urge his horse forward. Not joining us, then. Apparently, this conversation with George was to be private.

"I am glad to have found you here alone," he said, compounding my sense that our meeting was not just happenstance. "I have come across some information that may involve you and your sister."

"Indeed?" I prompted, trying to keep the wariness from my voice.

"Is it true that you have Lady Hester Belford staying with you?"

I had not expected such a blunt question. I stared at him for a long moment—too long—then busied myself with my reins. I had thought we had managed to keep the existence of our guests quiet, since most of society had already left the city for their estates. Then again, the Prince Regent had delayed going to Brighton due to the war with America and so a small number of his cabinet and entourage were still in London. How much did George actually know? Had he heard about Julia and me rescuing stolen children a month ago or liberating women from an asylum?

"Whoever told you that?" I finally asked.

He smiled across at me but said nothing.

I had always had my suspicions about George Brummell: a man so close to the Prince Regent would be in a prime position to gather intelligence. I also knew for a fact that underneath all that frippery and pleasure-seeking was a fine, strategic mind. The Home Office would, no doubt, pay well to know the activities of an unpredictable royal and the factional lords around him. And since the idea of informing upon one's own regent and nobility was far too French for any British official—the bloody Terror being still so raw in all our minds—I was sure such a role would be designated "custodial" rather than espionage.

We walked on. Leonardo leaned his big head over and mouthed at the black's bridle but got no response. He shook his head, snorting. I understood his frustration.

"What if Lady Hester was in fact staying with us?" I finally asked in my best nonchalant manner.

"If she were," George said, "then I would mention that Lord Deele, the lady's brother, is aware that she is no longer in the town of King's Lynn and is making inquiries."

I digested this for a few paces. George seemed to know a great deal about Hester's situation. Did he also know about the illicit return of her other brother, Lord Evan, from the penal colony in Australia, and his involvement in our activities? Tempting to ask, but a question would be offering up information to a man whose motivations I did not fully understand.

"Has Deele heard where Lady Hester might be?" I asked instead.

"Not yet," George said. "Nor has anyone else to my knowledge, but . . ."

"He will eventually," I supplied, and received a nod from my friend.

Another problem to add to my list. When the Marquess of Deele did find Hester, he would, once again, attempt to remove his sister from her beloved Miss Grant and incarcerate her in an asylum, or find some other way to keep the women apart. At least until Hester turned thirty-five, in five years, and was no longer under his vindictive guardianship.

"Do you and Lady Julia go to the Berry sisters' drawing room tonight?" George asked. The subject of Lady Hester was clearly at an end: information imparted and received. "Those of us still in attendance to His Highness will be present. I believe Lord Sidmouth is speaking."

"Indeed, my sister and I will be there," I said.

"Excellent. I look forward to your dismantling Sidmouth's argument." He sent me a glinting look. "And perhaps Lord Milroy's too."

I bowed in my saddle. "Thank you, I will do my best." I paused, knowing that my next, more serious gratitude would no doubt be brushed aside. "And thank you for the warning about Deele and your continued goodwill."

"You may always count on my goodwill, Augusta."

I smiled. "Considering your cultivated capriciousness, I wonder why."

He laughed and gestured to his Weston ensemble. "It is simple. You and I are cut from the same cloth."

One of his puns. Yet there was another meaning behind it.

He straightened in his saddle. "Well now, if Alvanley and I are to gallop, then we should do so and get it over with. Adieu." He saluted with his crop and turned his horse.

Did I dare ask him about Evan? It was a risk, yet I had to know.

"George," I called.

He reined his horse in again and looked over his shoulder.

"Have you heard any other whispers about the Belfords? About the older brother?"

He raised his brows. "I hear many things, Augusta. Do be careful, my dear. Some boundaries are too dangerous to cross, even for us well-dressed people."

And on those cryptic words, he clicked his tongue to his horse and trotted away. I watched him rejoin Alvanley at the gate, the two men immediately in deep conversation.

Did his parting words mean Julia and I should be careful about aiding Lady Hester, or was he referring to my dealings with Lord Evan Belford? Whatever the case, he seemed to know a great deal about our illicit activities.

Upon that uneasy thought, I narrowed my eyes and searched the gloomy tree line alongside the Row. It had been three long weeks since we had heard from Lord Evan, and I half hoped to see him, despite the fact that it would be madness for him to risk London. It seemed a new lover's heart was always full of hope. And, as I was quickly discovering, doubt too. Three weeks felt like a long time to go without some kind of message, and I could not help but wonder if he still felt the same as I did. We had parted on our first kiss—a giddy, wonderful moment for me—but perhaps not as memorable for him. Had he come to his senses?

Of course, there was no sign of his lean silhouette in the remnants of the silvery mist.

I did, however, see the inevitable Bow Street Runner watching me in case he did appear. A lone figure standing at the fence—mid-height, slouch shouldered, and clad in a sober dun greatcoat. At least I hoped he was a Bow Street Runner. The other possibility crawled across my nape: could it be Mulholland, the thieftaker? He had, I believed, once worked for the Runners but had been dismissed for egregious corruption. We had heard he was hunting Lord Evan, too, and did not care if he brought his bounty in dead or alive. The descriptions of him reported sandy hair and red whiskers. I peered at the slouched figure, trying to distinguish his coloring, but the brim of his beaver hat was pulled down low and the distance between us too far for detail.

Seeing my attention upon him, the man turned and walked into the last of the low-lying mist, leaving a knot of disquiet in my innards.

I turned Leonardo and stroked his neck, preparing to gallop. I needed to outrun these megrims and ghosts. At least for the length of Rotten Row.

2

By the time I trotted Leonardo into the mews behind our new Grosvenor Square home, my thoughts had shifted back to the mare I had bought and how I was going to justify the price to my sister. Perhaps if I asked Julia to name the horse, she would overlook the fact that I had paid three times the market price for a broken-down mare that we now had to stable in London at exorbitant cost.

John Driver, my coachman, emerged from the tack room.

"How was he moving today, my lady?" he asked, taking Leonardo's bridle and receiving a muzzle nudge in the ribs for his pains.

"Very well, as you can see," I said. "No more hint of that stiffness."

"Good," John said gruffly as he rubbed Leonardo's forehead, then led him to stand beside the mounting block. "We were lucky on that score. Forgive me for saying so, my lady, but I don't know what Lord Duffield was thinking, selling him like that to a man who rode heavy."

I knew exactly what my brother had been thinking: *How can I cause Augusta as much pain as possible?* He had managed to do so, too, by selling the horse that had been my last precious gift from our late father. By God, I had been furious, and in truth I still could not forgive Duffy for such high-handedness. At least his perfidy, in the end, had not denied me my horse. Leonardo had been mysteriously delivered back to me. A gift—in absentia—from Lord Evan. Now my beautiful hunter was doubly dear to me: a gift from my father and my beloved.

"Have you had a chance to look over the gray?" I asked as I dismounted onto the block.

"I have," John said. "Thomas told me what happened. It's going to take some time to bring her back. She has a sweet nature, though."

"Will she be sound again?"

"Aye. Although no thanks to the fool who nearly rode her into the ground."

At the corner of my eye, I saw Thomas leading the limping gray toward the stables and, beyond him, two other figures, both female: one tall, bone thin, and swathed in shawls, the other smaller and in a print dress too fine for a maid. Good God, was that Lady Hester and Miss Grant? I gathered my habit skirts and hurriedly stepped down onto the flags.

What was Miss Grant thinking, bringing Lady Hester outside?

Over the last three weeks it had slowly transpired that Miss Grant was not only devoted to Lady Hester but also exceptionally stubborn, making our cohabitation increasingly strained. As I said to Julia more than once, if Miss Grant would just do as I asked instead of questioning me at every turn, then we would all be much happier. Julia had laughed and said that looking into a mirror could often be a discomfiting experience.

Miss Grant saw me crossing the flags and, with a reassuring touch to her beloved's emaciated hand, hurried to meet me.

"What are you doing out here?" I demanded. "It is too dangerous for you to be wandering around. What if you are seen?"

Miss Grant bobbed into a curtsy but lifted her decided chin.

"We are being careful, Lady Augusta. She just needed some air." She looked back at Lady Hester leaning against the stable wall—sunken eyes closed, thin chest rising and falling in deep breaths—and lowered her voice. "In truth, now that she is strong enough to walk, she cannot abide being shut in a room too long. I think it brings back too much of the horror of her incarceration."

I could readily believe it. I had seen her shackled to the asylum bed. Yet George Brummell's revelations were still loud in my ears. And perhaps a little too sharp upon my tongue.

"I understand, but it is dangerous to be out here. You must return. My sister and I are doing everything we can to keep Lady Hester safe, but you must do your part."

Miss Grant drew herself up to her full five foot five inches. Still a good four inches below my own height, yet it felt as if we were standing eye to eye. "That is unfair," she said. "It is a half hour past dawn and I made sure only your servants were about. Or would you prefer Hester to stay in her room and scream with the horror of her memories?"

"Of course I do not want that," I said. "Even so, you and Lady Hester are now our responsibility, and it is hard enough to keep your presence a secret without you wandering around outside." I paused. Should I mention what George had told me, to drive home my point? No, she would tell Lady Hester, and the last thing that poor woman needed was more anxiety. I would not let any harm come to Evan's beloved sister while she was under my protection. And that included bad news. "Please, come back inside now. Both of you."

I ushered her toward Lady Hester, but she resisted, boots firmly planted on the ground.

"We are, of course, eternally grateful for your assistance," she said. "But we are not your responsibility. When Hester has recovered some more strength, we will be on our way. I have every belief that Lord Evan—now that he has elected to stay in England for Hester's sake—will help us find sanctuary. We do not wish to impose upon your and your sister's hospitality or goodwill."

"You are in no way imposing, nor do we want you to go," I said hurriedly. Julia would not be pleased if our guests left prematurely on my account. And perhaps more selfishly, I did not want Evan to leave the country on their account, for I could see no possible sanctuary other than outside England.

"Thank you. However, when I have a plan for our safety, we will take our leave."

I knew from experience that keeping loved ones safe was no easy task, but I refrained from airing my wisdom. Instead, I extended an encouraging hand toward the house. "Shall we?"

Miss Grant gave a stiff bow. "In a few minutes."

I watched her walk back toward Lady Hester, the unease I felt at the Row now a definite sense of foreboding.

*T*wo hours later, after regaining my composure and changing into a new blue gown, I went down to breakfast. I had, in fact, spent more time than usual choosing my ensemble. Later in the day we were expecting a call from Colonel Drysan, who had been present, twenty years ago, at the duel between Lord Evan and Mr. Sanderson that had sent Evan to the penal colony for murder.

I had organized this meeting with the colonel three weeks ago, but he had been forced to cry off due to an attack of gout. Well, that was the excuse he had alluded to in his note of apology, but I could not help wondering if he had, in fact, been avoiding the visit for some other reason. Whatever the case, I had reissued the invitation twice and he had finally agreed to make his call today.

I had high hopes for the visit. All accounts of the duel, including Evan's own, reported that Mr. Sanderson had been fatally caught across the chest by the tip of Evan's sword. Even so, I was not convinced that he had killed Sanderson. If there was any justice in the world, Colonel Drysan would provide some clue as to what had really happened and so set us upon the path to clear Evan's name.

Julia was already installed at the breakfast table and intently reading a letter as she sipped her tea. She had, it seemed, dressed for the impending interview, too, for she wore a new white lace cap and a white gown with a dusky rose over-tunic—a heartening departure from the sorrow-drenched grays and purples she usually wore in memory of Robert, her late betrothed.

I was glad of the change, but I could not help noting that it had occurred after Mr. Kent, the Bow Street Runner, had visited us. Admittedly, the man had risked his policing career by obscuring the facts about Lady Hester's rescue, and then compounded that risk by coming to warn us that the thieftaker Mulholland was now pursuing Lord Evan. Even so, it was clear the real reason he had called upon us was to see Julia. There was no doubt he was a charming man, but, as I reminded my sister, he was also a Runner who would have no compunction about arresting Lord Evan if given the chance. A rather awkward situation, all round.

Julia looked up from her letter and smiled as I took my seat. "Oh, you do look nice," she said, then lifted the thick packet she was perusing. "I have received a letter from Miss Sarah Ponsonby."

"Sarah Ponsonby? One of the Ladies of Llangollen?" The surprise of my sister's correspondent temporarily overtook my own news. When we were very young, the Ladies of Llangollen were still one of the biggest scandals in society—two ladies of quality who had run away together to live in Wales. Time, however, had taken them from scandal to oddity, and their singular arrangement was now more or less accepted by the bon ton. "I did not know you wrote to Miss Ponsonby."

"You do not know everything about me," Julia said.

I refrained from answering. We used to share everything, but lately something had changed, creating a greater distance between us. Perhaps it was the advent of Mr. Kent. Or maybe it was our disagreement about the best treatment for the tumor in her breast. She firmly claimed faith in her doctor and her God. Whereas I had faith in neither.

"Miss Ponsonby and I have been writing—on and off—since the year of the French truce," Julia added. "We met at that dinner Lord and Lady Davenport hosted at their estate. Do you remember? The two little ladies in the somber gowns with white ruff collars?"

I did not. It was, after all, ten years ago, and I had not been gifted with the same phenomenal memory as my twin.

"Anyway," Julia continued, "since Miss Ponsonby and Lady Butler have gone against all convention and the wishes of their families to live together as close companions, I thought maybe she would have some wisdom to share in regard to Lady Hester and Miss Grant."

"Good God, Julia, you did not tell Miss Ponsonby about Lady Hester, did you?" I asked. "All of society visits them in Wales on their way north. They know everyone. If they mention us and Lady Hester in the same breath, it will get back to Lord Deele. I wish you had consulted me before you did such a thing."

"Of course I did not tell her. I am not a fool," Julia said, frowning over the top of the letter. "You are not the only one in this house who can think strategically."

"Well, what did you write, then?" I asked, somewhat ungraciously.

"I described, in only the vaguest terms, two ladies of our acquaintance who wished to set up a home together against the wishes of their families. Miss Ponsonby's reply is quite touching, Gus. She says that it will be hard for the ladies to withstand the coaxing and coercion of family and friends, not to mention the scorn of society, but if it is truly what they wish, then to stand firm. I can only imagine what she and Lady Butler went through to find their happiness."

At least Julia's letter seemed vague enough not to have raised any singular interest. And we had never been socially linked to Lady Hester before she had been incarcerated. Perhaps no harm had been done, after all.

Biting back further remonstrance, I said, "Lady Hester and Miss Grant do not need any advice to stand firm. It is all they have done for the past three years." I looked across at the empty chair opposite. "I see Miss Grant is not yet down for breakfast."

Was she avoiding me after our confrontation?

"She is taking a tray with Lady Hester," Julia said. "She seems somewhat out of sorts."

So, that was a resounding yes.

I waited until Weatherly, our butler, had finished pouring my cup of coffee, then shifted a small vase of sad-looking Michaelmas daisies out of the way of the imminent sweep of my newspaper. Ever since we had moved in, Julia had made a point of sending one of our maids out every morning to buy a posy from the old flower woman who sat at the gates of the square's central garden. According to our neighbors, the old woman had been there nigh on thirty years, scraping a living. Julia was now on a campaign to make every house in the square buy a daily posy. A challenge, since our neighbors were not generous and the flowers not particularly well-kept.

Julia put down the letter from Miss Ponsonby and opened her

gold pillbox, choosing one of the blue mass pills prescribed by Dr. Thorgood for the breast tumor. She took one every day, as instructed, but frankly I could see no benefit from them. In my view it was well past time for a second opinion.

"Oh, and I have asked Cook to make a pound cake and a selection of biscuits for Colonel Drysan's call today," she added.

"A good thought. Cook's baking does seem to put our male guests into good humor," I said in a bland voice. Mr. Kent was particularly fond of Cook's almond macaroons.

Julia placed the pill in her mouth and took a sip of tea, a toss of her head doing service both to wash down the medicine and to answer my jibe.

"Do not expect too much from Colonel Drysan, Gus," she said, snapping shut her pillbox. "Twenty years is a long time. He may not remember anything."

True, but I could not help hoping for some revelation. Julia picked up the next letter on the small stack, made a small sound of surprise, then broke open the wax with a flick of her thumb. I caught sight of the direction on the packet: written in Duffy's impatient scrawl. What did our dear brother want now? Well, he would have to wait; I had a confession to make, as well as Brummell's troubling news to impart.

"I rode the Row this morning, at dawn," I said into the silence.

Julia looked up from the letter. "You rode with the grooms? Oh, Gus, really? At least tell me you took Thomas for propriety."

"I did. It was exactly what I needed, my dear. A good gallop." She opened her mouth to continue her protest, but I hurried on to the meat of the matter. "I came across Lord Milroy. He was with a Mr. Rampling, who was riding a lovely gray mare. The thing is, Julia, he was riding her lame, and even when I told him, he would not dismount. So I rather saw red and ended up buying her."

"You bought her?" Julia echoed. "Gus, you cannot save everything in the world. Last week it was that cat with one ear, and now a horse? We have enough on our plates at the moment dealing with our new friends." She glanced upward to the next floor, where Lady Hester and Miss Grant were situated. Although considering Miss Grant's recently aired thoughts, perhaps they were not.

"The fool was going to damage her just because he did not want to walk, Julia. I could not bear it. John Driver says she will come good. You would have done the same."

"I doubt it," Julia said dryly. "You are rather formidable when you 'see red.'" She eyed me with resignation. "Perhaps we can use her for the servants' gig."

"A good thought," I said with conciliatory enthusiasm, although the mare would be the most expensive gig horse in history. Before Julia thought to ask what I had paid, I added, "You will never guess who else I met there. George Brummell. And he had some rather disquieting news."

With a glance, I gathered Weatherly into the conversation. He had accompanied us on all our missions of rescue and had proved himself as capable with his fists as he was with a wine inventory. I suspected he enjoyed an adventure as much as I did.

They both listened intently as I reported my conversation with Mr. Brummell, including his odd warning at the end.

"You trust Mr. Brummell's information, my lady?" Weatherly asked when I had finished.

"I do. If anyone would know what is happening within society, it is the Beau. I think we will have only a matter of a week or two before Deele discovers his sister is in London and takes action."

Julia sighed. "I do not know what is to be done with Lady Hester. She is still far too fragile to be moved. Besides, where would we move her to?"

"She may be fragile, but at least she is up and walking now. I saw her and Miss Grant in the stables." I paused, letting that information settle. "I spoke to Miss Grant and she is adamant that once Lady Hester is recovered, they will be on their way."

Julia frowned. "They were in the stables?"

"Indeed. Miss Grant told me Lady Hester cannot abide being shut in a room for too long. It brings back the horror of the asylum. Even so, it was very reckless. Particularly since I think the Runners may still be watching us."

Or someone worse, but I had no evidence of that other than my own fear.

Julia shook her head. "I cannot imagine what she went through. We must work out a way for her to be more comfortable while she is here. Did you tell them about Mr. Brummell's warning?"

"No."

"Whyever not?"

"For Hester's sake; she does not need that burden upon her recovery. And I rather think it would propel them into premature action."

Weatherly offered me the bakery basket. I chose a dark baked roll and nodded my thanks.

"If I may say," he said, "I concur with you, Lady Augusta. If you wish it, I could arrange for myself and the footmen to ensure they do not go outside. Politely, of course."

"Absolutely not!" Julia said. "They have suffered enough anguish over Lady Hester's incarceration. We must not add to their distress by incarcerating them here in our home, even in a polite manner."

Although it worried me that someone might happen upon them outside, my sister was right. I nodded my agreement.

"That is a relief," Weatherly said. "I thought I should offer the obvious solution, but I would not be easy with the task."

I saw the memory of the asylum and its pitiful inhabitants in his face. He and Julia had not seen the worst of it, but there had been enough anguish in that experience for us all. Moreover, the mistreatment of the women must have brought back memories of his own early, brutalized years, before he was a free man. He had not told me much about his youth, but I had read Mr. Wilberforce's abolitionist reports.

"We would never want to place you in a position that compromised your principles, Weatherly," I said firmly. Although considering the last few months, that was rather a grand promise.

"Goodness no," Julia added vehemently. "But as it stands, we must come up with a plan to find a safe haven for them that is close enough that the journey will not harm Hester's recovery."

"It will not be easy." I tilted my chin at the letter on the table. "What is the news there? If Duffy and Harriet are still on their honeymoon, perhaps we could tuck Lady Hester and Miss Grant at Duffield House for a week or two."

Julia picked up the letter again. "Alas, they have already returned, somewhat prematurely, it seems, due to . . . well, you will hear their reasons."

She read from the letter.

We were disappointed in the Peak District and Harriet cannot conceive why it is lauded so much. Nor did we find the Lake District to our liking—the environs cold and the society disappointing. We do so dislike the accents in those parts—Harriet declares she cannot understand a word anyone says and believes that they speak so on purpose. Not

to mention the boorish manners. We considered traveling to
Scotland, but in truth it held no lure and, since I have given
up the Bath let as the city no longer appeals to Harriet, we
have returned to Hanover Square to settle in properly. We
will then repair to Duffield House for Christmas.

"How could they not be pleased by the Lake District?" I demanded, ignoring the fact that Duffy had ceased letting the house in Bath, a residence our father had taken for our health and enjoyment. I also did not remark upon the fact that he and Harriet were now in London but not inclined to relate their adventures—or, rather, lack of adventures—to us in person. Purely, I knew, to snub me. I had figured I would be persona non grata with Duffy after I absconded from his wedding, and to be perfectly honest, it did not sting as it probably should have. However, I would sorely miss the Bath residence.

"I rather think Duffy and Harriet are incapable of being pleased by anything," Julia said, uncharacteristically tart. She tapped the letter. "Duffy goes on to invite me to Christmas at Duffield, but . . ." She trailed off and I could read the next in her face.

"Does not invite me." I crossed my arms. "I suppose it is to be expected."

It did hurt to be barred from Duffield House at Christmas too. A lifelong tradition ripped away.

"I will not go either," my twin said staunchly.

"Thank you, my dear, but I rather think you must. I do not wish to drive a wedge between you and our only remaining family." I saw Julia about to resist and added, "One thing is certain: I would not trust Duffy to keep Lady Hester safe. He would more likely hand her over to Deele."

"Sadly, that is true," Julia said. "Let us think on the problem. In the meantime, I will speak to Miss Grant and apprise her of Mr. Brummell's warning."

"Do you really think that is wise?" I asked. Behind her, Weatherly's face held the same dubious expression as my own.

"I think it is right," Julia said.

Wise and right were not always the same, but I did not voice the thought. Instead, I broke open my bread roll and settled in to eat and wait—impatiently—for Colonel Drysan to make his call. Maybe he would impart something useful, or incriminating, that might hold the key to my beloved's exoneration. And that restoration of Evan's good name might, in turn, provide Lady Hester with a brother-guardian who did not seek to rip her from the arms of Miss Grant and incarcerate her in an asylum again.

A lot to place upon a polite interrogation held over tea and pound cake.

3

Colonel Drysan, retired, eyed Cook's elaborately iced creation set on the low table between us and said, "Thank you, Lady Julia. Most kind, most kind. I would not say no to a slice."

A circuitous way of saying yes, but I was quickly discovering this was how the colonel expressed himself: every thought in his head uttered, the words often circling around the subject until they met in some semblance of his true meaning. It was not what I expected from a former military man whose correspondence with me had been crisp and brief, nor from a man who I thought might be a suspect in Mr. Sanderson's murder.

Julia cut an enormous slice—the sound of the knife chinking against the cake stand seeming to add emphasis to its size—and slid it onto a plate. She handed it to the colonel with a warm smile. We had dismissed our footman, for discretion, and Julia was doing her charming best to make our visitor feel comfortable. The colonel, however, was still sitting ramrod straight on the sofa opposite us. He had clearly been, by breadth of shoulder and chest, a burly man in his prime, but the years since retirement had settled around his middle and now strained his well-cut navy waistcoat. He had also limped into the room upon a handsome mahogany walking stick, so perhaps he had been truly afflicted with the gout, after all.

We had finally gotten through the inquiries after his health—greatly improved, it seemed, although I did glaze over during his response, so maybe not—and his thoughts upon the cold weather—not unseasonable, mind you, but rather unusual for October, so, yes, quite unseasonable—and I was impatient to move on to the first purpose of the meeting: what he remembered of the duel.

I sat forward.

"Tea?" Julia asked him.

Damn. I sat back, waiting for his response to wend its way toward positive or negative.

Apparently, he was, indeed, thirsty.

Julia poured him a cup and said, "You must be wondering why we have asked you here, Colonel." She passed the tea across and shot a quelling glance at me, sensing my irritation. "My sister and I are hoping you will answer some questions about an event twenty years ago. The duel between Mr. Sanderson and Lord Evan Belford."

The colonel, in the middle of settling his cup and saucer, blinked blankly at my sister. "The duel?" he said, his astonishment moving him to utter two direct words.

"Yes," I said, sitting forward again. "By all reports you were with Mr. Sanderson at the moment of his passing. Is that correct?"

His slightly protuberant eyes swiveled to me. "Mr. Sanderson?"

"Indeed," I said, trying to keep the impatience from my voice. "Mr. Sanderson."

"Sanderson," he echoed. "I have not heard that name for many a year. Sanderson." He mused for a moment. "Sanderson."

"Yes, Sanderson," I agreed. "Would you be willing to relate your memories of that morning?"

"It was twenty years ago," he said. "I do not have a clear memory of it at all."

"Please, do try, Colonel," Julia urged gently. "We would be most grateful."

Few people can resist Julia's sweetness. With a sigh, he began a somewhat rambling and patchy account of the duel that did not diverge in any important way from the reports I had already read in the *Gentleman's Magazine*: Sanderson had accused Lord Evan of cheating at cards at White's club; a challenge was issued and accepted. At the dawn meeting, Sanderson was pinked by Lord Evan across the chest and upon that injury had retreated to the tree line with the colonel, Lord Cholton, who was Lord Evan's friend and acting as his second, and the doctor in attendance. The doctor had then begun to treat the superficial wound, but Sanderson died.

"Were you in attendance upon your friend the whole time?" I asked.

"As far as I can recall, but"—he paused—"Sanderson was not my friend, Lady Augusta. No, indeed, I would not have called him a friend at all."

I glanced at Julia, whose face wore the bemusement I felt. "But you were his second," she said.

We had both assumed that acting as Sanderson's second implied some sort of friendship—a second could be called upon to settle a matter of honor if the challenged, or indeed the challenger, did not appear. Surely, only a friend would put themselves in such danger.

"Yes, yes, I was his second. But not as his friend. It was a business arrangement, you see," the colonel said.

I did not see at all. "An arrangement?"

"Not sure I should say." He peered first at me and then at Julia, assessing our suitability to hear his clarification. Evidently, we passed inspection, for he continued. "Well, it all happened a long time ago. Sanderson held a fistful of my vowels—a few months of mischance at the bones—and I was in danger of falling foul, so when he requested me to step up as second with the offer of ripping up the letters, I saw a chance to clear the decks."

He nodded at this expansion and lifted his cup, taking a restorative sip of tea.

I worked my way through the masculine idioms: a fistful of vowels were IOUs, caused by a run of bad luck at playing dice. The colonel had been having trouble paying back his debt of honor and Sanderson had offered to discharge the debt if the colonel stood as his second.

Not a motive for murder in any way. In fact, more likely the opposite.

"So you did not know him well?" I asked.

He was mid-mouthful of a large bite of cake and swallowed hurriedly, dabbing at his mouth with the napkin.

"As well as I wanted to," he finally said. "Not one to talk ill of the dead—bad form, bad form indeed—but he wasn't up to snuff in any way." He pondered Sanderson's deficiencies for a second, then added, "Can't rightly say I recall anyone who would have called him their friend."

"What made him so objectionable?" Julia asked.

"He was genial enough on the surface, but his core"—the colonel tapped his chest—"nasty. Took pleasure in humiliating people. Saw him hit a maid once for no reason. When I asked him why, he said she wanted the attention." He shook his head. "Belonged to a club that—" He stopped. "Well, it was bad. Tried to get me to go, but no, not for me. Not interested in that kind of thing. He probably had friends there, but I could not rightly say."

So, not many people liked Sanderson, but did anyone dislike him enough to want him dead? I needed to talk to someone who knew more about his life. "What kind of club was it, Colonel? Does it still exist?" I asked.

We came under assessment again. He shook his head. "You do not wish to know about it, Lady Augusta. Not for the ears of ladies, or anyone decent, come to that." He shook his head. "Bad business."

Since the ears of this lady were not as delicate as he thought, I said, "You are not referring to the Hellfire Club, are you?"

Beside me, Julia stiffened. "Augusta!"

The Hellfire Club had been a gentlemen's club created by Sir Francis Dashwood that was notorious for its dark rituals and orgies. I had read about it in one of my father's journal subscriptions. Not a subject talked about in polite company, let alone the company of two spinster ladies. Nor one that my sister would want to hear about.

I glanced at Julia: *Sorry, my dear, I must ask more.*

Julia compressed her lips: *If you must.*

"As far as my knowledge goes, that club disbanded mid–last century," I ventured. "Although I hear that Lord Byron has tried to revive it."

"I do not refer to Dashwood's gatherings or Lord Byron's recent attempt," the colonel managed to say. He was clearly disturbed by my blithe knowledge of depraved clubs but had rallied. "No, the club that Sanderson belonged to was much worse. Much worse indeed. They called themselves the Exalted Brethren of Rack and Ruin but I do not know if it still continues today. I do not wish to know."

Rack and *ruin*—both slang words for cheap liquor. A juvenile name, but then there were many ridiculously named clubs in London: the Sublime Society of Beefsteaks and the Most Ancient and Most Puissant Order of the Beggar's Benison and Merryland to name two.

"What do you mean, worse than Dashwood's club?" my sister asked, beating me to the question. "What can be worse than black sacraments and group congress?"

The colonel and I stared at Julia. The colonel, I think, shocked by the idea that Lady Julia Colebrook had just uttered the words *group congress*, and I because I had not expected my sister to have any knowledge of the Hellfire Club's activities. Perhaps she had found the same article that I had in our father's library.

The colonel was moved to a one-word answer. *"Justine."*

I was blank for a moment, then realized he meant the Marquis de Sade's novel. My good friend Charlotte, Lady Davenport, had lent me her French copy when it made its way across the channel in the brief truce of 1802. It had been eye-opening to say the least, and I did not find it a wonder that Bonaparte had imprisoned its author. "Are you saying the club dealt in torture? In sexual torture?" I asked. At the periphery of my vision, I saw Julia turn to stare at me in return. I had never told her I had read the book—in her eyes, just reading it would put my soul in danger.

"I never attended," the colonel said hurriedly, "but it was what Sanderson implied. And I could readily believe such activities would suit his tastes."

Did this club have some sort of connection to Sanderson's death? If he had indeed dabbled in the darkest recesses of the human heart, then perhaps he had made dark enemies along the way.

"And you have no idea of its whereabouts or if it still continues?" I asked.

He shook his head.

"Please, search your memory, it may be important," I pressed. "Even a member's name from twenty years ago might help."

"I think it was near Covent Garden, behind St. Paul's, and I know of only one other member, but his name will not help you. He is probably dead by now."

"Even so," I said.

The colonel shrugged. "Lord Evan Belford."

I stared at him. "What?"

He eyed my shock. "Were you acquainted with him?"

"Only in passing," Julia interjected, for I could not make a sound.

"I have always thought that maybe he murdered Sanderson over something to do with that club," the colonel said, picking up his cake again. "Or maybe not. Whatever the case, justice was served. The story came to its rightful end: Belford was found guilty and transported, and I discharged my IOUs. *Si finis bonus est totum bonum erit.*" He paused, the cake halfway to his mouth. "That means all is well that ends well," he added kindly for the unlearned women before him.

"The actual translation is 'If the end is good, all will be good,'" I said through my teeth.

And if I had anything to say about it, we were far from reaching the end of this story.

*A*s soon as the drawing room door closed behind the colonel, I rose from my chair and paced to the window, staring down at the square's central garden. The trees were already bare of leaves, the gravel paths deserted in the cold morning.

"I do not believe it," I said, turning from the bleak view. "Lord Evan would not belong to such a club. Nor would he withhold vital information about his dealings with Sanderson."

Julia watched from her chair. "I agree, it does seem unlikely. Perhaps the colonel is mistaken about the club—he did say he does not recall a great deal. But even if it is true, Gus, it was twenty years ago. All of us have changed."

I pressed my hands together, perhaps to squeeze away the tiny seed of doubt that had been sown. "To be involved in a club that—" No, I would not voice such reprehensible activities. "The colonel did seem very certain." I turned to my twin. "Oh, Julia, what if it is true?"

She rose from her chair and joined me at the window, her hand finding mine. As ever, the warmth of her grasp brought some measure of calm. She looked me squarely in my eyes—a prelude, I knew, to an important pronouncement—but I could not help noting that the crisp autumn light accentuated the darkness under her eyes and the drawn hollows of her cheeks.

"Trust him and trust your knowledge of him," she said. "If you do not think he would belong to such a club, then do not torment yourself with useless imaginings."

Good advice; the man I knew would not take pleasure in causing pain. Yet even through my distress, another—somewhat more opportunistic—thought arrived. "Still, if Lord Evan does know something of the club, then he might also know more about its members. Someone who might have more information about Sanderson."

Julia drew back, her mouth twisting wryly. "I see where this is going."

I squeezed her hand, hoping for understanding. "We have to speak to him." Even under the dubious circumstances, the chance to see Evan again sang in my heart.

"It is too dangerous, my dear. You said yourself Mr. Kent's Runners may still be watching us. Besides, how do you propose to find him? We have no way of sending him a message."

True, in both cases. Someone was watching us, and since Lord

Evan was supposed to be on his way to Jamaica, we had not organized a method of contact other than by letter when he had settled
on the island. I had no idea where he might be. Certainly not
London, since it was too dangerous, but that left a great deal of
England to search.

"I could try the White Hart again, where he used to stay. Or
maybe try to track where he went from Mr. Solson's when he bought
back Leonardo." I was not, however, convinced by either option.

Neither was Julia. "Frankly, he would be mad to go back to the
White Hart, and it would be impossible to track him." She con-
sidered the problem for a moment, then a small smile appeared.
"What paper does he read?"

"*The Times*, of course." I caught up with my sister's cleverness.
"Ah, an advertisement."

"Something that only you and he would understand." She
compressed her lips for a moment but could not quite contain her
mirth. "Maybe a matrimonial advertisement: Lady of Quality
seeks highwayman of good character."

I snorted and, despite the seriousness of the situation, couldn't
resist adding, "Must be of a quiet and sympathetic nature, highly
principled, and an excellent shot."

Julia bent over, helpless with giggling, and clasped my arms for
support. "Must exceed a height of six foot, dance every dance, and
be accomplished in all the manly arts: fencing, riding, and stealing
horses."

"He did not steal Leonardo!" I protested.

"But he stole Sir Reginald's horse."

I had to concede the point. "For a good cause, though." I
gathered some mock severity. "We will come up with something
more appropriate than a matrimonial advertisement, thank you
very much."

My sister's face sobered, the laughter gone. "But would you marry him if nothing stood in your way?"

I had not expected the question. But then again, it was not the question she was asking. I took both her hands from my shoulders and held them tightly in my own. "I am not going anywhere, dearheart," I said.

"But you may, one day, if we can clear Lord Evan's name."

"You know I would never leave you alone." It was her biggest fear: to be left alone. To die, alone.

And yet, if we did somehow rehabilitate Lord Evan Belford in the eyes of society, would I truly be able to deny my love? I had done so once already—watching him ride away from me on his way to Jamaica—and I knew the cost to my heart.

4

It took an hour or so for us to settle on the advertisement for *The Times*.

> MR LENNOX of Cheltenham. Renegade and Leonardo send their regards. Suggest meet at noon on Thursday 22nd at the place where it all started. Urgent. Respond likewise.

"Renegade?" Julia asked.

My cheeks heated, but I could not help smiling. "It is what he calls me."

"I see," she said, at her most opaque.

We debated using the name Hargate instead of Lennox, but Julia remembered that Mr. Kent knew that it had been Evan's highwayman alias. Lennox, however, was a name Evan had used only a few times and so was not widely known. I hoped it would catch my love's attention when he read the paper. If he was, indeed, currently reading the paper.

"I think we should tell Lady Hester that we are attempting to contact her brother," Julia said. "She will, no doubt, wish to communicate with him too."

Something clenched within me. "I think we should wait until he answers," I said. "I do not want to raise her hopes if he does not. Besides, the fewer who know our plans, the better."

Julia surveyed me for a long moment. "As you wish."

Now, how best to get it to Printing House Square and the *Times* office? I glanced at the mantel clock.

"It is gone five o'clock," I said. Damn, by the time we got there, the paper would be closed to notices. "Too late to put it in now. I shall have to wait until tomorrow morning."

"Gone five?" Julia said. "Lud, we must dress for the Berrys'."

In all the focus upon the advertisement and Lord Evan, I had forgotten we were expected at the Berry sisters' soiree.

"I am not in the mood," I said.

"Nonsense," Julia said, leading the way to the door. "You love the debate. Besides, it will take your mind off Colonel Drysan's revelation."

I followed her from the room. I would go to the Berrys', of course, but nothing was going to take my mind off the possibility that Lord Evan might be associated with the Exalted Brethren of Rack and Ruin.

*T*he Misses Berry held their famed "circle" at their home in North Audley Street. A rather modest abode, but neat and pleasant, rather like its two celebrated tenants.

We were met at the door by a young maid who bobbed a curtsy and took our wraps. Julia cast her eyes around the small hallway, painted in fashionable green and decorated with a rather flattering marble bust of the elder sister, Mary Berry, set upon a plinth. Sculpted, I remembered, by her good friend Mrs. Anne Damer.

"They have a new sideboard since we were last here," Julia murmured. "Chesterfield. Very nice." She cocked her head, eyeing the oak bureau that stood alongside the staircase that led upstairs. I suspected my sister would be consulting the Chesterfield catalog when we returned home.

"Lady Augusta, how lovely! And Lady Julia, always a pleasure," Mary Berry said, arriving at the drawing room door, her dark eyes alight with welcome. Behind her, Agnes—a somewhat paler and shorter version of her sister—smiled her own greeting. They both curtsied.

Like us, Mary and Agnes were unmarried sisters in their forties, although they were not twins; Mary was one year older, and the more outgoing and famed of the two in the fashionable circles in which we all moved. Also like us, they were financially independent. However, where we had received our inheritance from our father, they had received an inheritance from Horace Walpole, the 4th Earl of Orford, although they were not related to him in any way. It was said Walpole had considered the Berry sisters some kind of family he had collected. An odd concept: a collected family. Mind you, such a family might be more congenial than one formed by the usual means, since it held more intent upon its membership.

"It is a larger circle tonight than usual," Mary said, a twirl of her hand indicating the gathering as we followed her and Agnes into the drawing room. "By staying in London, His Highness has done us a great favor."

She meant of course the number of politicians who sat or stood with drinks in hand among the poets and actors. Usually, Parliament would have retired and the lord politicians gone to their estates, but the war with America, alongside the war with Napoleon, had forced the Prince Regent to delay his usual sojourn to his beloved Brighton.

I spotted our new prime minister, Lord Liverpool, who already looked exhausted, and beside him a rather worried-looking Viscount

Sidmouth, secretary of the Home Office, who had only come to the position in June. They were in animated conversation with Lord Milroy. I was sure he had seen me enter the room with Julia—a telltale flick of his eyes and pursing of thin lips—but he did not do me the honor of acknowledging my arrival. I was not overly distressed; I did not wish to speak to him either.

I counted only six other women in the room; Mary did not like to have too many of our sex at one of her drawing rooms. I once asked her why this was so and she said she did not want any gathering of hers to be thought of as a bastion of the bluestocking. She was, I thought, in great fear of being labeled blue and thus ridiculed. Perhaps this was why we were friendly but not great friends; to my mind, nothing would change if the rules made by men were not challenged by women.

"You are no doubt aware that your brother is here tonight too," she added, leading us farther into the room. "We are very glad to welcome him. Perhaps he will also become a regular." She peered around until her gaze fell upon a very familiar set of shoulders and head of thick chestnut hair: Duffy, his back to us, standing near the fireplace. "Ah, there he is, with Mr. Brummell."

Good God, what was Duffy doing here?

I glanced at Julia: *I will not talk to him.*

Julia tilted her chin: *You cannot ignore him.*

"Ah yes," Julia said to Mary. "We shall make our presence known to him now."

Mary nodded her approval and bustled off to greet more new arrivals.

"I am not going to make my presence known to him," I said under my breath. "I do not want to see him and I am sure he does not wish to see me."

"We must at least greet him, or it will look odd," Julia said just as softly and vehemently. She took my hand. "Please, Gus. Let us get it over and done with and then you can avoid him all night. Please. For me."

I could not deny my twin. With a nod I allowed her to pull me along to where our brother and Mr. Brummell stood in conversation by the fireplace.

George, who was facing us, noted our approach and immediately made an elegant bow. "Lady Augusta, Lady Julia, good evening."

Duffy stiffened at our names, which, to my shame, gave me some satisfaction: I was not the only one appalled by this encounter. He turned to face us.

"Mr. Brummell, good evening," Julia said. "And, Duffy, how lovely to see you."

We both curtsied to Duffy's brusque bow.

"Sisters, I had not expected to see you at such a gathering," he said.

"I cannot conceive why," I said, as brusque as his bow. "Surely you are aware we come here often?"

He glared at me. "I was not."

"Is Harriet here too?" Julia asked brightly. "I would so much like to hear about your wedding trip."

"Of course not. She would not presume to attend such a gathering. Like me, she considers political discussion the purview of men. She does not interest herself in such matters."

"Yes, it does take a good knowledge of current affairs and a keen mind to keep up," I said smoothly.

Mr. Brummell, sensing familial discord, sent me a glinting, amused glance and made another bow. "Duffield, if you will excuse me. Lady Augusta, no doubt we will speak later."

Upon his departure, Duffy leaned closer to me, his face flushed. "I cannot believe you left Duffield House and missed our wedding over the sale of a stupid horse. What kind of welcome into our family did that give Harriet?"

Since I had absconded from his wedding to rescue Hester from the asylum and not due to his underhanded sale of my horse, I could not answer. He clearly took my silence as further insult.

"No defense? Nothing to say. Of course not. What you did is unforgivable!"

"Surely not unforgivable, brother," Julia said, placing a pleading hand upon his arm.

He eyed his favorite. "What are you doing here, anyway?" he demanded. "This is a place for serious discussion, not gossip and cards."

That I could at least answer. "Where we go and what we do is none of your business, brother."

"Please do not make a scene," Julia admonished us both softly.

Duffy turned to Julia. "No doubt she has dragged you along tonight, but really this is not the place I would wish to see you, Julia. You are both fast approaching the age where such pretensions will make you laughingstocks and the latest on-dit." He mimicked a gossip's voice. "*Oh, the Colebrook sisters, thinking they have anything of interest or relevance to say to the prime minister.* If you do not care on your own account, then you can at least think how this reflects upon me and Harriet."

I balled my hand into a fist. It was time to make my exit before I did something that would definitely become an on-dit.

"Good evening, Duffy," I ground out. "I do hope you manage to keep up with the discussion."

I turned and strode through the assembly of men, sensing Julia scrambling to keep up at my elbow.

"He is impossible," I said when we reached the other side of the room.

"Well, it is over now," Julia said, but I heard the hurt in her voice. She did not like us to quarrel, nor, I think, had she liked the idea that our brother would not forgive me. "Come, Gus, you cannot stand here boiling about Duffy. It is already obvious to everyone that there has been discord."

My sister was right. I looked around the room for an acquaintance whose conversation would help me regain some composure. Agnes Berry was standing alone and was an interesting conversationalist, since she, along with her sister, knew everybody.

Upon that idle thought, an interesting fact rose to mind.

"Julia, am I right in thinking that Agnes Berry is a particular friend of Lady Deele?"

My sister, who was famed for her prodigious knowledge of society and its interrelations, looked at me in surprise.

"Yes, they have been friends since before Lady Deele married." She raised her brow at such a salient feat of memory—not my forte, at all. "Well done."

"We should speak to her. See if she has any information about Deele," I said.

"Alas, we have missed our chance," Julia said as we watched a notorious old roué—wearing the powdered wig and rouge of his heyday—approach Agnes. "Mr. Saxby has cornered her."

Poor Agnes.

Julia looked around the gathering, her attention falling upon a man standing near the window. "Look, there is Charles Whitmore. We were introduced last year. Do you remember? At Lady Melbourne's rout. And we have exchanged pleasantries at other events. He is an undersecretary at the Alien Office. Maybe he has something of interest to say."

We both looked across at the gentleman in question, standing alone and watching Lord Liverpool and Viscount Sidmouth with keen intent. I had to admit, I had only a very vague memory of him, so they could not have been memorable meetings. He stood barely an inch above Julia, with close-set eyes and a jittery energy that kept one finger tapping his port glass. The Alien Office had been created in response to the war with France and Napoleon and was, perhaps, the opaquest of the government departments, designed to gather intelligence about foreigners on our shores. Their involvement with the Home Office and the Runners was not quite clear, nor were most of their activities.

"What do you hope to discover?" I asked. Was she aiming to find out about Mr. Kent? Surely a man as high up in the department as Mr. Whitmore would not know anything about a lowly Runner.

"No idea. But do come."

She grabbed my hand, and so I was towed once again, this time to Mr. Whitmore.

"How lovely to see you here, Mr. Whitmore," Julia said, with all her substantial charm aimed at him.

Mr. Whitmore, slightly horrified at being set upon by both of us, bowed. At close quarters, his appearance did not improve overmuch: his mouth was rather small and currently pressed into a forced smile, and his chin seemed to recede into his neck.

"There is something I wish to ask you," Julia continued. "Are you acquainted with a Bow Street agent by the name of Mr. Kent? Our paths have crossed and I wish to know more about him."

My sister, it transpired, had decided upon a direct attack.

Mr. Whitmore eyed her for a bemused moment. "I have met him as one agent among many, Lady Julia. I cannot say I know much about the man."

"Tell me what you know, then."

At the corner of my eye, I saw Agnes Berry extract herself from Mr. Saxby's leering presence. I knew I could safely leave Mr. Whitmore under my sister's capable interrogation, and so, with a murmured pardon and a smile of farewell, I made my way to Agnes's side.

"Well done on getting away," I said softly, nodding toward Mr. Saxby. He had latched on to Anne Damer near the windows, and I could see her leaning ever so slightly away from him.

Agnes bit her lip. "I told him I had to help Mary prepare for Lord Sidmouth's address. I should have stayed, but he is so . . ."

"Indeed, he is so," I said, and we shared a wry, female smile.

"I hope you will join in the debate again tonight, Lady Augusta," Agnes said. "Last circle was so invigorating."

I thought of Duffy's pronouncement that I was a laughing-stock for such oratory pretensions. "Indeed, I will. Do you know Lord Sidmouth's subject?"

"I believe he intends to raise the specter of the French Revolution, the current Luddite outrages, and how to quell the revolutionaries." She referred to the workers—called Luddites by the newspapers—who had rioted in protest at the introduction of machines that had rendered their skills obsolete. Agnes looked across at the home secretary, then leaned closer, lowering her voice. "The use of the militia to quell the violence, writs to intercept mail, and even placing spies among the lower orders." Her mouth pursed. "No doubt necessary, but there is something unsavory about a government spying upon its own people to root out dissent, do you not think?"

"Are you saying that such agents are in action now?" It was well-known that the French Directory had used spies, agents provocateurs, and informers to send thousands of people to *la guillotine*.

Surely the British government did not follow such a notorious precedent of espionage. Particularly agents provocateurs. A disturbing thought.

"It is what I have heard from those who would know," she said. Considering the circles in which she and Mary moved, her intelligence had some credence. "Although I know most governments must employ such creatures," she added, "I cannot help but feel such maneuverings are despicable. It offends every sense of fair play."

"You sound as if you are on the side of the revolutionaries," I said archly.

Agnes clutched my arm in mock alarm. "For heaven's sake, Lady Augusta, do not even whisper such a thing."

We both laughed, but underneath her funning was a dark truth. It was too easy to be suspected of revolution these days, such was the extreme alarm of the government. On top of that was the fervor of those patriots who informed upon their fellow citizens to save England from the same fate as France. One only had to think back to 1793 and 1794, when men were executed or transported for gathering under the banner of reform. Even now, anyone could be under suspicion of being a dissenter, especially if one did not live within the confines of society's expectations.

"I believe you are friends with Lady Deele, Miss Berry," I said. Not the most adroit change of subject, but I could see that her sister had approached Lord Sidmouth, no doubt to prepare him to call for order.

Agnes smiled warmly. "Indeed I am. Are you acquainted?"

"No, but my brother is a good friend of his lordship and I know that Lady Deele is imminent with her first. I hoped to hear good news. I thought Lord Deele might even be here to ask, since I've heard he was in London."

"Oh no, he is not in London. He is at Cordale, their estate. Only yesterday I received a letter from Lady Deele to report the happy news that she has been safely delivered with the heir and that Deele is so pleased he is staying awhile. It is most gratifying, is it not?"

"Very gratifying." My gratification, however, was for an entirely different reason: Deele had not yet traveled to London and would now be temporarily diverted from his search for Hester. A brief respite, but one that might allow the poor girl to recover some strength.

"Lords, ladies, and gentlemen," Mary called out above the conversational hum, "please take a seat for Lord Sidmouth, who will be speaking upon the latest outrages in the north."

With a nod, I parted from Agnes and claimed a chair near the doorway. Julia had found a seat beside Duffy; her conversation with Mr. Whitmore seemed to have ended rather quickly. Had she discovered anything of interest? I suspected she had another task now—to persuade our brother to forgive me. I caught a fulminating glance from Duffy, his eyes as narrowed as my own. Julia's quest was, I suspected, futile, considering my own lack of forgiveness and his enduring disdain.

I turned my attention, along with my fellow guests, to Lord Sidmouth. If Duffy thought it unsuitable for a lady to debate among men, he was about to be entirely affronted.

As it happened, the evening's debate did manage to distract me for a short while from my unease. Duffy departed soon after Lord Sidmouth's address, but I did manage to make some very pertinent points before he left. Perhaps I should not have enjoyed the dark look upon his face when my neat skewering of an argument was applauded by Lord Sidmouth himself, but Duffy did bring out the worst in me. And I, alas, in him.

In the carriage home, I told Julia about my conversation with
Agnes and the welcome news of Deele's current location. She in
turn reported the information she had managed to extract from
Mr. Whitmore.

"He is not very forthcoming," she said, "which I suppose is an
excellent quality considering his position. He did tell me that Mr.
Kent has the reputation of being overly dogged in his pursuit of the
truth. Apparently, he sometimes continues to investigate when a
case has been declared closed by his superiors. Twice he has been
censured for such activity, although in both cases the wrong man
had originally been arrested and then was released upon Mr. Kent's
evidence."

"Well, that is all in Mr. Kent's favor," I said.

"I thought so too," Julia said. "He is always gentlemanly in his
thoughts and behavior, do you not think?"

"He is most gentlemanly," I said, earning a tired but beaming
smile from my sister.

And yet, it could not be denied that Mr. Kent was far from the
rank of gentleman. And therein lay the problem.

5

*T*he *Times* office was near Bridewell hospital prison, just up from the wharves around Blackfriars Bridge—not an area usually frequented by women of the ton.

I peered out the rain-smeared window of our town carriage, seeing only the grimy gray brick frontage of a brush maker's shop and a man hurrying along the narrow footpath, head down and broad-brimmed hat sagging wet. The morning had turned very gloomy indeed.

We had come to a standstill on Union Street, one of the routes leading to Printing House Square. I let down the window with a clatter and poked my head out, ignoring the cold sweep of mizzle across my face. From the shouts and curses ahead, it appeared a cart blocked the way and the driver was nowhere to be found. We were two equipages back from the obstruction. I turned to look behind. Had anyone followed us from Grosvenor Square? This was the moment when such an intrusion might become apparent. I could not, however, see past the wagon at our rear. Samuel peered around from the back footman's step, inquiry upon his wet face. I shook my head and turned my attention to the front of the carriage again.

"Weatherly," I called. No response. I increased my volume. "Weatherly!"

"Yes, my lady. Coming."

The carriage rocked—Weatherly descending from his lookout next to John Driver. I drew back inside the carriage and closed the window, brushing the sprinkle of rain off my velvet cap. From the limp feel of the feathers and silk flowers, it had not fared well.

Weatherly opened the carriage door, his greatcoat collar up and his hat dripping from the brim.

"Did you see anyone following us?" I asked. I had entrusted the task to Weatherly, since Samuel was not the most observant of young men.

"Perhaps, my lady," he said. "Three back, there is a hackney that has kept up with us from Grosvenor Square."

My heart quickened. It could, of course, be a coincidence.

"Are you sure it is the same?"

He nodded, wiping an errant drip from his eye. "I recognize the horse's blaze. And the driver wears a red kerchief."

So, a good chance we were being followed. But by whom?

"Can you see who it is? Would it be Mr. Kent, by chance?" It stood to reason that it was my sister's swain or if not him, then one of his colleagues.

Weatherly shook his head, sending a spray of water from his hat. "I cannot make out the passenger."

"How far are we from the *Times* office?"

"Three turns and we will be there, my lady."

Should I go back? I did not want to lead a Runner to *The Times* and more or less hand him the information that I was placing an advertisement. But I had to submit the notice today so that it went into the next paper.

Or someone had to submit it and not be followed.

I frowned, orienting our position on the map of London I held in my mind.

We were, by my calculation, very close to Ludgate Hill and Hatton Garden, the center of the London jewelry trade. And thus near my favored jeweler, Rundell, Bridge and Rundell. I opened my reticule and drew out the notice I had written.

"Weatherly, I want you to place the advertisement." I gestured for him to lean farther into the cabin, away from any interested eyes, and handed him the folded piece of paper. "Keep it hidden. We cannot have the Runners knowing our plans. I will walk up to Ludgate Hill, with Samuel, to draw the Runner's attention. Hopefully he will follow me. If he does, then take the carriage and proceed to the *Times* office and place the notice. Or go by foot, if the cart takes too long to clear. Once you are done, pick me up at Rundell, Bridge and Rundell. It will be as if I was heading there all the time and did not wish to wait for this cart to be cleared. If he does not follow me, then go straight to Rundell's and we will try again later."

Weatherly took the note, but his face was troubled. "I do not like this plan, my lady. Even with Samuel, this is not the place for a lady to walk. And what if this Runner approaches you?"

"It is only a short distance," I said. "And I doubt he will approach me. Especially when I go into the jewelers."

"Allow me to accompany you instead of Samuel," Weatherly said.

I placed my hand upon his arm—a liberty I would not usually take, but he had to understand the importance of the notice being placed safely. "No, my friend. I entrust this to you. No one else."

His mouth quirked—he still did not like the plan—but he nodded and drew back out of the cabin with the slip of paper secreted under his greatcoat.

I collected my reticule and umbrella and took his offered hand, alighting from the carriage onto the wet road.

"Samuel," I called.

My footman swung down from the rear step, landing with the sure bounce of youth. "Yes, my lady."

"I will not wait any longer. I am going to walk to Rundell's," I said loudly.

It had finally ceased to rain, so I handed my umbrella to him. With a last pointed glance at Weatherly, I started along the muddy footpath. At the corner of my vision, I saw Weatherly halt Samuel for a moment to murmur something in his ear. Samuel nodded at the instruction and with a few long-legged strides caught up to walk behind me.

It took all my self-discipline to refrain from looking over my shoulder to see if the occupant of the hackney alighted too.

I walked sedately to the corner of Union Street and Water Lane. If I was correct, the lane would take me up into Ludgate Hill, very near Rundell, Bridge and Rundell. I surveyed my route. Water Lane was a collection of soot-dark buildings standing cheek by jowl that ended in a crooked intersection with two other streets. Would it actually take me to Ludgate Hill? I had thought it would be teeming with people, but only two soberly clad men, deep in conversation, were climbing the lane's incline.

My self-discipline, it seemed, was far more limited than I thought: I could not help turning as if to address Samuel to swiftly scan the road and footpath behind his large figure.

Someone had, indeed, alighted from the hackney. It was what I had wanted and yet the sight of the man brought a prickle of alarm across my skin. He was not well-dressed enough to be Mr. Kent, nor did he have the Runner's height. Even so, he had a broad build and an athletic way of moving that reminded me of a middle-weight prizefighter. Was that a flash of red whiskers? Hard to ascertain: his hat was pulled down low and he wore a muffler high around his face. He slouched, too, rather like the man at Hyde Park. Was this the infamous Mulholland?

"We will go up Water Lane," I said unnecessarily to Samuel.

The two soberly clad men were no longer in sight, the lane now empty. I picked up the hems of my pelisse and gown and started up the narrow pathway alongside the road, the prickle of alarm resolving into an itch of danger between my shoulder blades.

It took some concentration to pick my way along the pavement. The excess of rain—rather appropriate given the lane's name—had sent rivulets cascading down the flags, the water picking up clumps of foul excrement and dirt along the way. About halfway up, I stopped outside a hatmaker and feigned fatigue, taking a moment to survey my surroundings.

The man had followed us up the lane. Weatherly would now be able to place the notice without being watched, but I had not counted upon the sense of threat I felt.

The stranger stopped about fifty feet away, hands thrust in the pockets of his greatcoat, watching us. No pretense of going about his own business. His stare, above the folds of his muffler, was flat and cold, and his slouching posture did not appear to be one of hunched self-doubt but rather of insolent confidence.

Samuel had finally seen him too. "Is that man following us, my lady?" he asked under his breath.

"Perhaps."

Samuel squared up, his fair skin flushed with battle.

"No. Do not acknowledge him," I added quickly. "We will continue."

I started walking again. Samuel, in the periphery of my vision, clutched the umbrella like a weapon. We reached the crooked corner. I read the street signs: to our right, Pilgrim Street; to the left, Little Bridge. Both with a curve that obscured their end. Where now?

"He is still behind us, my lady," Samuel reported.

Either way was a blind choice. Pilgrim Street, then, but only because the Bunyan book was one of Julia's favorites. I quickened my pace, Samuel adjusting his own to stay a step behind. We continued past a furrier—the window full of pelts in shades of brown—and a wine merchant, arriving at some speed at the curve in the road.

Ah, ahead was Ludgate Hill. I looked over my shoulder. The man was less than thirty feet behind us now. Enough was enough: I would not be cowed by this ruffian. Besides, Weatherly would have either taken the coach past the cart by now or continued on foot.

I stopped and turned to face our shadow. Samuel took up a position at my side, glaring at the man.

"Are you following me?" I demanded.

The man stared belligerently at me.

The answer came from behind us. "I am, indeed, Lady Augusta."

I swung around to face another man. Where had he come from?

I took in sandy hair, red whiskers, and no slouch in sight, but rather the bearing of a man who knew his own power. If his comrade was a middleweight, then this man was a heavyweight with the imposing height to match. It seemed Mulholland had finally made his appearance.

The street behind him was empty of pedestrians, but up ahead another man blocked the way of a lady and gentleman attempting to enter the street from Ludgate Hill. Indistinguishable words were exchanged and the couple scurried away, alarm in every line of their bodies. Dear God, the man was stopping anyone from entering.

We were trapped.

The realization made me step back.

"I do not believe we are acquainted. Who are you?" I demanded. At least my voice did not quaver.

The man inclined his head, an ironic gesture of courtesy. "I am James Mulholland, but I think you know that."

"What do you want?"

"I think you know that too." It was said with a smile that showed yellowed teeth. His features held the heaviness of his body: large chin, broad cheekbones—oddly sprinkled with pale gold freckles like a child—and thick sandy brows.

"I have no idea what you mean," I said.

He jerked that heavy chin at his comrade, and I heard Samuel yelp. I whirled around. The other man had shoved my footman up against the wall, his hand around the boy's throat. Samuel thrashed in the brutal hold using the umbrella as a club. The larger man plucked it out of his hand and threw it to the ground, then drove a fist into his gut. Samuel gasped.

I lunged forward. "Stop that! Let him go!"

Mulholland stepped across my path, blocking my momentum. "Are you on your way to meet Lord Evan Belford?" he demanded.

I drew myself up, mustering as much frostiness as I could manage. "I have no idea what you mean. I am on the way to my jewelers." He stood far too close—I could smell the mustiness of his clothes and body—but I refused to step back. He must not see the fear beneath my rage.

Mulholland nodded to his underling. The man drove his fist into Samuel again. The boy wheezed, his tricorn dropping from his head into the mud. He struck out wildly and landed a blow on the side of his attacker's head, but it did not seem to even register with the heavier man.

"Where is your mistress going?" Mulholland called to Samuel. "Tell me, and Pritchard will let you go."

"The jewelers, I swear it!"

Brave boy.

"Sure about that?" Mulholland asked. Another nod sent Pritchard's fist even harder into my footman's side with a dull thud. Samuel moaned.

I glared at Mulholland. "He has told you the truth. Let him go."

"I know for sure it ain't the truth because our mutual friend Mr. Kent told me that you and Belford were hand in glove up round King's Lynn way. So Pritchard here will keep serving your man until you tell me where Belford is situated now."

Mulholland knew about King's Lynn. And if what he said was true, Mr. Kent had betrayed us. Could I blame Kent? He was a Runner, after all, and he had made it clear he had fulfilled his obligation to Lord Evan. But surely he must realize he had placed Julia and me in peril. Perhaps his regard was not as strong as Julia hoped.

Whatever the case, it was clear that I, and more to the point Samuel, could no longer afford the pretense of ignorance. It would have to be the truth now. Or at least a version of the truth. "I have not seen Lord Evan Belford in three weeks. As far as I know, he is on his way to Jamaica. That is all I know. Now, release my man and step out of my way."

Mulholland tilted his head, assessing me with keen eyes. "I think there is more."

"My lady does not have to answer to the likes of you," Samuel threw out valiantly, earning himself another blow. I winced at his pained grunt.

"There is no more," I said crisply.

Mulholland lunged, his hand closing around my forearm, the pain of it shooting through flesh and bone. I was suddenly off-balance, wrenched forward, my injured shoulder slamming into the hard muscle of Mulholland's chest. The old ache shuddered through me into new agony. Something torn? I gasped, my breath a staccato of panting pain.

"Like it rough, do you, my lady?" He held me tightly to the length of his body, his mouth close to my ear, his breath a fetid mix of bad teeth and beer. "Where is Belford, you old cat?" he whispered, the soft question more threatening than if he had shouted it.

I wrenched my arm in his grasp but could not shift his brutal hold. "Do not touch me!" I rammed my body weight against his chest, making no impact upon his immovable bulk. "You cannot touch me in this way!"

He laughed. "Seems I can." He grabbed my breast, pushing the bones of my stays hard against the soft flesh. I strained back as he dug in his fingers. "Is this what Belford does? Knead your saggy dugs for yer? Where is he, woman?"

For a second my mind roared, an icy vise of horror and disgust that held me frozen. A man had never touched me in this manner. Never!

"He is gone," I hissed and slammed my bootheel down onto the top of his foot. He flinched, enough for me to haul my arm from his grip and stumble back, out of reach. I crouched, ready to strike, scratch, even spit, but he did not follow, merely watching me with a curl of disdain upon his thin lips.

"I shall report you to Bow Street!" I said, pressing my hand against my abused chest. "You may be hired by them, but they will not stand for this violence against someone of rank."

Mulholland sniffed. "Go ahead. Report me. Nothin' will come

of it." He gave an elaborate bow. "Even for someone of your rank." He turned his attention to his man. "There's nothing here. Let's go."

Pritchard released Samuel, giving him one last vicious gut punch. My footman sagged against the wall, gulping for breath.

The two men strode toward their comrade at the top of Pilgrim Street. They did not look back. As they turned the corner out of sight, I realized I was still crouched. Still pressing my hand against my chest. I straightened, steadying my breath.

"Forgive me, my lady. I should have stopped him," Samuel said, using the wall to haul himself upright. "Mr. Weatherly will have my guts for garters."

"We were ambushed, Samuel. No fault of yours. Can you walk?" I was not entirely sure I could; my legs were trembling.

"Of course, my lady." He tugged his waistcoat into order and bent to pick up his sodden tricorn, wincing at the movement. A shake of the felt hat and it was back upon his head. He crossed the cobbles—the youthful bounce gone—and offered me his arm. "I've had worse from my brothers."

Clearly a lie, but I let it pass. I would send for Dr. McLeod when we got home, make sure the boy was in one piece.

I took his arm and together we limped up toward the busy thoroughfare of Ludgate Hill.

6

*M*r. Bridge was somewhat surprised to see me arrive without an appointment, but as ever welcomed me into his elegant showroom, offered refreshment, and brought out the new turquoise parures that I shakily requested to see. His calm and gently jovial presence, along with two glasses of excellent canary, helped steady the trembling in my legs and dissipate the ice in my innards.

I ordered a turquoise set for Julia for Christmas and chose two neat silver boot daggers set with ruby cabochons: one for Lord Evan with his initials to be engraved upon the cartouche—an elaborately flourished *E* and *B*—and one for myself with an *A* and *C* upon it. After this morning's events, a dagger of my own seemed a prudent idea.

By the time Mr. Bridge had engraved, boxed, and wrapped the daggers, the carriage had pulled up outside and Weatherly had swung down to open the carriage door. He gave a small nod through the jeweler's window: the notice had gone in. The tension in my body eased.

Before long, I was back in the carriage with Weatherly in the seat opposite.

"So, all went well? No one was watching you?" I asked as we pulled away, the momentum jerking me back against the seat.

"No one, my lady. The notice will be in tomorrow's paper and for the next week, saving Sunday, of course." He paused. "Samuel told me what happened. The boy is shaken and mortified that he did not protect you adequately. Are you . . . ?"

"Well enough," I said quickly, ignoring the new pain in my shoulder. "Samuel had the worst of it. He kept to the Rundells' story even under great duress."

"I told him no one was to know our real destination. He's a good lad," Weatherly said.

"Indeed. As soon as we are home, send Thomas around to bid Dr. McLeod come see the boy."

Weatherly nodded. He paused, his gaze gently assessing. "And perhaps for yourself, my lady," he ventured.

I waved away the suggestion, trying to control an absurd rise of tears. "I am well enough," I repeated and looked out the window, away from his concern. "It was an insult, but not much more. There is no need to speak of it again. To anyone."

Weatherly kept his gaze steady upon me.

"Mulholland—" I stopped and swallowed the sourness that accompanied his name. "Mulholland said Mr. Kent divulged our connection to Lord Evan."

"It may not be true," Weatherly said. "Or perhaps it was said under pressure. I cannot see him placing Lady Julia in danger."

"Perhaps. I hope not. The real worry is that Mulholland does not seem to fear any repercussions. In fact he challenged me to report his attack."

Weatherly considered that information with a frown. "That can only mean one of two things."

He was right: there were only two possibilities. His mind clearly worked along the same paths as my own.

He tapped one gloved forefinger against the other, counting

off the first. "Mulholland is an overconfident fool who cannot foresee consequences."

"He is no fool," I said flatly.

"No, I do not think so either." He tapped off the second. "He considers himself protected by someone of rank."

"I think it is even worse than that," I said.

"Indeed," Weatherly said softly. "He is not only protected by someone of rank but, considering his notoriety, he is protected by someone who may have ordered him to kill Lord Evan, not bring him in alive."

"Yes." I looked out the window at the passing shop fronts. The rain had started again, a few umbrellas opening above the well dressed, but most people hunching their shoulders and quickening their pace along the mud-tracked footpaths. "So who wants Lord Evan dead and why?" I looked back at Weatherly. "And more to the point, can we stop them?"

Weatherly eyed me with a wry smile. "I do not know, my lady, but I gather you are going to try."

*T*he carriage pulled up outside our house in Grosvenor Square. I rubbed my shoulder; the ache had not shifted during the ride home. Perhaps it would be prudent to see Dr. McLeod, after all.

As Weatherly alighted in readiness to hand me down, I gathered the Rundell box and glanced out the other window at the large fenced garden that stood at the center of our square. A black horse stood tethered to the iron railings. A familiar black horse, with an equally familiar Elliott saddle.

Caesar, Mr. Kent's mount.

So, how long had Mr. Kent been here? And what was I to say to him now that it was likely he had betrayed us to Mulholland?

"We have a caller," I said as I took Weatherly's hand and descended the carriage step.

"Yes, I saw." Weatherly closed the door. "Is there anything you wish me to do?"

I looked up at our drawing room window. "No, I will handle it."

Inside, Weatherly divested me of the box, then my gloves, cap, and pelisse. Mr. Kent's hat had been placed on the side table, but I did not see his coat. A short call, then. Perhaps even shorter than he expected.

"Tell me when Dr. McLeod arrives," I said. "I will see him, after all."

"Of course, my lady." I heard the relief in Weatherly's voice.

In all truth, etiquette and common sense demanded that I change my damp carriage gown and muddied boots and see to my shoulder, but this confrontation could not be delayed. I smoothed my side curls, shook out my damp hem, and focused beyond the pain.

Ready for battle.

I climbed the stairs at a sedate pace, for it was more than possible that I brought distress to my dear sister, and, for all the seriousness of the situation, I could not hurry toward that outcome.

No footman outside the drawing room door. Unusual.

I raised my closed hand to knock and stopped. Voices inside. And my sister's laugh. Bright and carefree. I had not heard it so full of delight for a long time. I stood a little longer listening through the closed door, ignoring the wagging finger of my conscience. The muffled voices held the quick rhythm of lively conversation—perhaps even coquetry—punctuated by both my sister's laugh again, and the lower register of Mr. Kent's amusement.

I did not want to end Julia's enjoyment, but I had to know if we had been betrayed.

I rapped upon the wood and opened the door.

"Augusta!" Julia said. She and Mr. Kent stood in front of the Lawrence portrait of us in our youth. My sister's eyes were alight and her mouth still held the shape of a laugh. Mr. Kent, whose arm was in a sling as a result of our last adventure, had been standing rather close. Julia took a nonchalant step away. "You are back."

Clearly.

"Mr. Kent and I were studying Mr. Lawrence's brushstrokes," she added as I entered the room.

"Lady Augusta, how good to see you again." Mr. Kent bowed.

As was his custom, he wore a very well-tailored ensemble: a blue wool jacket that made the most of his broad shoulders, a scarlet satin waistcoat—often worn by the Runners, which had earned them the nickname Robin Redbreasts—and extremely well-fitted pantaloons. Even his sling was well fashioned in crisp white muslin. His face, like my sister's, also held the remnants of laughter, hardly the expression of a man who harbored a secret betrayal.

"What is wrong?" Julia said, for she had finally set aside the moment I had interrupted and looked squarely at me. She crossed the floor, took my hands, and peered closely at my face. I could not hide much from my twin. "You are hurt!"

"Mulholland," I said, and looked across at Mr. Kent. "He attacked me and said you had informed him of our connection with Lord Evan."

"Attacked you?" he and my sister said in unison.

"We must send for Dr. McLeod," my sister said, clasping my hands more tightly. But her eyes were upon Mr. Kent again, this time in reproach.

Mr. Kent came forward. His concern seemed genuine, as did the stricken expression upon his face.

"Samuel was hurt. I was merely insulted," I said. "Dr. McLeod is on his way for both of us." I was certainly not going to detail the attack in front of a man. Julia eyed me, unconvinced. I hurriedly moved on, glaring at Mr. Kent. "Did you inform Mulholland? He knew that I had been with Lord Evan in King's Lynn!"

"I assure you I did not inform him." He half turned to Julia. "Upon my honor, I did not. I have not spoken to the man."

I had seen Mr. Kent's honor—staunchly upheld even when it did him no good service. It would seem he spoke the truth.

"I believe you," Julia said, laying her hand briefly upon his un-injured arm. I saw him note the intimacy. As I did. Julia glanced at me—an anxious check upon my thoughts. So be it. I inclined my head. "We believe you," she added firmly.

He bowed.

"But, that being the case, how does he know Lord Evan and I were in King's Lynn?" I demanded.

"I submitted my report about the asylum to Bow Street," Mr. Kent said. "It was a confidential report since it held information about members of noble families, and I assure you it did not mention Lord Evan or you by your real names."

"Then someone has discovered we were involved."

"Mulholland may have worked it out himself if he has seen the reports," Mr. Kent said. "He is a clever man and he has resources to go to King's Lynn and question people. Even so, confidential reports are for magistrates only. If it is the case that Mulholland has seen it, then someone within the upper sphere of the Magistrates' Court may be assisting him."

Or commanding him, I thought, but did not voice it. "A magistrate within Bow Street?" I asked. That could limit the possibilities.

"It could be any of the courts. And it could be any number of magistrates, or indeed any of those who may have access to them, officially or otherwise." He stared into the distance for a moment. "Or the Home Office or, indeed, the Alien Office."

"That is a lot of people," I said, deflated.

"I am shocked that Mulholland attacked you," Julia said. "Surely he knows there will be reprisals."

I hesitated. Did I wish to draw Mr. Kent into it all?

He eyed me narrowly. "He does not fear reprisal, does he?"

The Runner was far too astute. "He does not. Instead he invited a report."

"Ah." Mr. Kent rubbed his chin. "High indeed," he murmured.

Our eyes met in a moment of shared comprehension.

"Be wary when you leave the house," Mr. Kent added. "Mulholland has noses everywhere in London."

"Noses?" Julia echoed.

"My apologies, Lady Julia. It means informers in the thieves' tongue." Mr. Kent's weathered skin colored slightly at his use of such base cant. "He pays well or extracts loyalty through coercion."

Was that how he suddenly appeared in Pilgrim Street behind me? Noses keeping an eye upon our travel route?

"I assume Lord Evan is well gone, as was his plan?" Mr. Kent asked.

"Yes," I said quickly, to forestall any unfortunate candor from Julia. "I told Mulholland the same, although I think he chooses not to believe me." I glanced at my sister. Thankfully, she showed no inclination to tell Mr. Kent the truth.

"It may be that now Mulholland has confronted you, he will leave you alone," Mr. Kent said. "I will take my leave and endeavor to find out as much as I can about his plans and his intent toward you." He bowed, his eyes upon Julia.

"But surely that will put you and your position at risk," Julia said.

"An agent is always at risk, whether it be from inside the court or out," he said dryly. "But do not fear, I am not altogether dispensable."

"Thank you," Julia said, and smiled at him.

I murmured my own gratitude but I was plainly extraneous to the exchange.

The door closed behind him. It occurred to me that I did not know why he had called in the first place.

"Did he give you any particular reason for the visit?" I asked Julia.

"No." Then she smiled again. "Which of course is a particular reason in itself."

"Are you sure this friendship is wise?" I asked.

Julia lifted her brows. "I rather think you should look to your own friendships before you question mine," she said crisply.

Touché.

A loud knock startled us both. Was he back?

"Yes?" I called.

Weatherly opened the door. A young man stood behind him, dressed in sober black and wearing a wide-brimmed Clericus.

Dr. McLeod had arrived.

7

The doctor prescribed rest over the next few days for both Samuel and me. Samuel had a cracked rib and I had suffered no more than a wrench to my previously injured shoulder.

It had to be said that resting did not come easily to either of us. In the end Weatherly had to set Samuel—who was back to his ebullient self—the task of cleaning the smaller silver just to get him to sit down. Julia insisted I convalesce with Lady Hester and amuse her with games rather than pace the house waiting for *The Times* to arrive.

It transpired that Lady Hester particularly enjoyed piquet, and so for the next two afternoons we sat for as long as she could manage at the small table in her bedchamber and played hand after hand under the watchful eyes of Miss Grant. In the three weeks or so since we had rescued Hester from the asylum, she had gained some weight and strength on her tall frame. The ominous gray cast to her skin had receded and her high Belford cheekbones were no longer just stark bones. Even so, she remained weak and able to move around for only a short time before fatigue laid her low.

Occasionally she talked of her eldest brother, her voice still heartbreakingly hoarse from months of fugue silence. I admit I encouraged any stories of Lord Evan. It seemed he had always been generous to his little sister, or perhaps it was the glamouring of memory—or my own bias—that made him seem so kind. She did not mention Lord Deele at all, an understandable omission.

Every now and then as we played, I saw a glimpse of Evan in Hester's face and it clenched my heart: her smile, so like his, and the mischief in her blue eyes when she held a winning hand. At other times, the specters of the asylum would drain her features into a gaunt otherworldly mask. Then the sound of a door closed too heavily or the clatter of a dropped pan would shudder through her body and leave her shaking for minutes after. At those times, Miss Grant would hold her, murmuring soothing words and drawing Hester's head upon her shoulder. At those times, I would leave them, unnoticed, and carefully close the door behind me.

During one game, she paused before placing her card and asked, "Do you think my brother will communicate soon, Lady Augusta? I so wish to see him again."

"I do not know," I said, which was more or less true, since there was every possibility that Evan would not see the notice. Still, her words brought a pang of guilt.

"We must speak to him at the earliest opportunity," Miss Grant said from her own chair. She stood and walked across the room, her steps too purposeful for the space. I recognized the impulse to walk out a frustration—I did it myself, often enough. She looked out the window, then swung around to face me again. "I believe we must leave in the next week or so, and Lord Evan may know the best way to proceed."

I could not argue with her urgency. I even agreed with it. Yet I still did not tell them of my plan to meet him. Instead, I picked up a card, returning us to the game.

*O*f course, I could not expect an answer from Evan in the first few days. He would have to first read our notice, then write his return and deliver it to be published in the next day's edition. At least three days, or more with no paper on Sunday, or if he did not see it the first time it was published. The wait was torturous.

Finally, on the fourth morning, I opened the newspaper at the breakfast table and scanned the pages, my searching gaze catching upon the words *To RENEGADE*.

"Julia, it is here!" I could not contain my smile or the leap of my heart.

She rose from her chair to look over my shoulder. I pointed to the sliver of text and read it aloud. "To RENEGADE. Invitation accepted. LENNOX."

"Well, that is to the point," Julia said. She patted my shoulder. "Soon you will know about his association with that club." She returned to her chair. "And you must tell Lady Hester that you are meeting him. She will want to send a message, I am sure."

I made a noncommittal sound as I read his words again. Very to the point. A tiny part of me was disappointed, but what did I expect? A love letter at a halfpenny a word?

"Gus!"

I looked up at my sister. "Yes?"

"Why are you refusing to tell Lady Hester and Miss Grant about this meeting?"

I opened my mouth to deny the accusation but met Julia's stern look. I could not lie to her, or indeed to myself any longer.

The truth, then, to my shame.

"What if Lord Evan decides the only course of action is to take his sister far away from their brother? I do not want to stand in the way of Hester and Miss Grant's safety, but I do not want Evan to leave either."

"You thought he was leaving three weeks ago, and you had come to terms with it then," Julie pointed out.

I looked down at the notice again. *To RENEGADE.* "I was fooling myself."

"You are also assuming that will be the plan. Who knows what resources Lord Evan has at his disposal?" She rose from her chair. "Come, let us go upstairs and tell them now."

Grudgingly, I put down the newspaper and followed her from the room. I did wonder, however, whether she was accompanying me upstairs for moral support or to ensure I finally informed our guests of my imminent meeting with Lord Evan.

I wish to accompany you," Lady Hester said, propped up against her pillows in her bed. Miss Grant picked up the tray on which sat the remains of Hester's breakfast. The plate held an intact omelet. Cook would be most disappointed she had not tempted the invalid.

"No, you cannot come," I said flatly. "You are not up to it."

"I am up to it. I insist on accompanying you." She looked across at me, her mouth held in the same obstinate line as Lord Evan's when his mind was made up.

"I think my sister means that it is quite a distance and you are not well enough for such a journey," Julia said more diplomatically. "Let us carry a letter for you."

Us? I shot a look at my sister standing on the other side of the bed; did she think she was coming as well? I had imagined my reunion with Lord Evan a thousand times over, and every time it had been the two of us. Alone.

She met my frown with a tilt of her head: *Of course I am going—you cannot meet a man by yourself.*

Hester twisted the top of her sheet in her hands. "No. I must see him! You do not understand. It is imperative."

"Dearheart, Lady Julia is right. You are not yet strong enough. I will go to meet your brother and speak to him on our behalf,"

Miss Grant said, placing her hand over the frantic twisting of cloth. "You must not overexert yourself."

Miss Grant too? This was rapidly becoming a crowd. "No, I am going alone," I said. "It will be hard enough to leave this house without the Runners or Mulholland following me, let alone the entire household shifting itself."

"No need to exaggerate, Gus," Julia said. "I am sure you have a plan to hoodwink them all."

I did, in fact, have a plan. But that was not the point.

Miss Grant directed her attention to me. "It is time Hester and I planned our future, Lady Augusta, and Lord Evan is crucial to those plans. I must speak to him as a matter of urgency. A letter will only create a delay that is not necessary."

A good point. But I rallied. "What if you are seen?"

"There is going to be risk whatever we do. For me. For you. And especially for Lord Evan." She straightened. "I am beginning to think you are trying to obstruct us. First you did not tell us you were contacting Hester's brother and now you do not wish me to accompany you."

I looked at Julia for support, but her mouth pursed: *She is not altogether wrong.*

Damn. I gave a truculent sigh; farewell to a solitary reunion.

"There is no obstruction, Miss Grant." I smiled tightly. "Of course you may accompany us tomorrow. And my sister is correct—I do have a plan, so we must start making our preparations."

Miss Grant gave a curt nod. "Thank you."

Only one more day before I saw my love again. At least there was that.

꒷꒦꒷

8

*J*ulia, Tully, my maid, and I stood on the footpath opposite Mr. John Hatchard's bookshop waiting for a break in the line of carts, carriages, and horses that processed along Piccadilly.

Hatchards had recently moved from its original premises farther down the road—to make way for the newly completed Bullocks Museum—and the new shop was much larger than the original. A double frontage with two huge display windows that curved elegantly in toward the entrance to show the latest literary offerings.

"Do you think Miss Grant has arrived yet?" Julia asked.

"I hope so," I said. "If she has not, then something may have already gone wrong."

Julia shot me a worried glance. "Do not say that."

"What did you want me to say? That she is out the back in the carriage waiting for us as we have planned? It is impossible to know if she is or not." My tone was oversharp, but I did not fully trust Miss Grant to follow my instructions. Still, that was not my sister's fault. "The shop looks busy," I added, softening my tone. "That must be to our favor."

Indeed, the two benches set outside the shop for waiting servants were fully occupied by maids and footmen, and a number of carriages waited farther along the road.

"Tully, when we go in, see if you can find a seat on the bench," I said.

"Yes, my lady." Tully's face had pinked with the excitement of being part of the plan. I had asked her to wear her scarlet cloak—unmissable among the drab livery of the footmen—and to make sure she was visible outside at all times.

"Look, we can cross now," Julia said.

A gap had opened up between the vehicles. We picked up our hems and made our way across the wide road, evading the mounds of dung and churned mud. I refrained from looking over my shoulder, but I was sure the lanky, unkempt Runner was still trailing us. I knew him for one of the Bow Street agents who had stood outside our former home in Hanover Square a month ago. Was Mulholland watching us as well? Perhaps one of his "noses" was at this very minute darting back to inform him of our whereabouts.

We made the footpath outside Hatchards safely, our arrival prompting a wave of bobs and bows from the waiting servants.

I looked up at the dark green painted frontage. Our father had first taken us to Hatchards when we were ten. He had always bought his books there—as we did now—and from the first moment I stepped into its dim, book-lined quietude, I felt a particular kind of excitement. So much imagination and knowledge on the mahogany bookshelves waiting to be leafed open, that heady scent of glue and ink released from the pages. Although the shop of my memories no longer existed, I still felt that same thrill whenever I entered this new Hatchards.

"Wait for us here," I instructed Tully, loudly and unnecessarily. "We will be some time." An addition just in case one of the noses was among the waiting servants.

She curtsied. A footman immediately rose from the bench and offered her his seat.

"I hope this works," Julia murmured as we passed over the bookshop's threshold.

I did, too, for I was relying on the power of assumption and a little help from a friend. I knew my plan to leave London without detection was elaborate—perhaps overly so—but I could not bear the thought that we could inadvertently lead the Runners or Mulholland to Lord Evan. If the Runners caught him, it would be the gallows, and if Mulholland reached him first . . . No, I did not dare countenance such a possibility.

Inside, I drew a breath of warm air scented with book. Although most of the ton families had gone to their estates, the shop was abuzz, no doubt due to the arrival of the latest edition of Lord Byron's *Childe Harold's Pilgrimage*. It was still the talk of society, as was his blatant affair with Lady Caroline Lamb. Neat stacks of the new pressing had been placed upon a table near the entrance, and two young women in pastel pelisses—one of them wearing a Lord Byron miniature upon her bodice—were reading small snippets of the poem to each other. I had heard of this new rage to carry an image of Byron around, but this was the first time I had seen one displayed so proudly. It seemed almost religious in its devotion. But then, I could remember the fervors of my own youth and how at fourteen I had drawn very bad likenesses of a young curate who had once smiled at me. In truth, my own imaginings about Lord Evan were probably not so far removed from this girl's infatuation. If I had a miniature of Lord Evan, I would probably carry it too.

For a breathtaking second, our last moment together rushed through my body as if he still stood before me: outside the asylum, his mouth pressed upon my own, our farewell kiss running through every nerve in my body, locking us together forever. We had both thought it was the last time we would see each other for months, or perhaps even years.

"Lady Augusta?"

I blinked, wrenched back to the bookshop here and now.

Thomas Hatchard stood before me. He bowed elegantly, his sober garb a copy of his father's well-known uniform of black frock coat and plain waistcoat buttoned to the throat. "A pleasure to see you again, and Lady Julia," he said.

Thomas was John Hatchard's second son, and as much a vehement abolitionist as his father. We had formed our acquaintanceship at Mr. Wilberforce's meetings and, through mutual outrage and a similar wry sense of the world, had developed a friendship despite our age difference. It was, on occasion, a disquieting thought that I was old enough to be his mother.

"Did you receive my order, Mr. Hatchard?" I asked, lifting my brows. I had sent him a message to solicit his help, along with a package to aid our departure. But was he willing to help?

"I did, indeed, Lady Augusta, and I believe we can fulfill the entire order," he said, with a small smile. Although an earnest young man, he was, I think, enjoying the intrigue. Besides, Hatchards was famed for exerting the utmost effort to satisfy its customers, whatever the request. "Please, come this way."

"How delightful to see you, Lady Julia," an all-too-familiar voice called across the shop. We both swung around abruptly to face Mrs. Ellis-Brant, my friend Charlotte's cousin by marriage. She was already bustling toward us past the busy central counter, orange and blue feathers bobbing upon her neat cottage hat.

"Oh Lud, it is the Ermine," Julia murmured. I stifled a snort. I had once mentioned to Julia that I thought Mrs. Ellis-Brant looked like the sleek, dissatisfied ermine in the Da Vinci painting, and the name had taken hold.

"And Lady Augusta, as hale and hearty as ever," Mrs. Ellis-Brant said, approaching with her rodent smile. She curtsied, which we acknowledged with nods, then she leaned in and whispered, "Are you well again, Lady Julia? It was such a shock when you swooned at dear Charlotte's dinner party."

Julia's polite smile stiffened. A few months ago, she had mistaken the dosage of her blue mass pills and had fainted in Charlotte's drawing room. Although, in all truth, I feared it might have been more than that.

"As I said on the night, it was only the aftereffect of a migraine," Julia said. "But thank you for your concern."

"Of course, and I have not said a word to anyone about it, just as dear Charlotte asked," the Ermine said, which meant she had told her intimates and anyone else in earshot. She turned her attention upon me, collusion in her eyes. "I remember you asking about Lady Hester Belford that evening."

I had, indeed, shamefully exploited the woman's love of gossip to discover the story around Lord Evan's sister. And it seemed I was about to do so again. "Yes, you thought she had run off with a companion."

"It seems I was right," Mrs. Ellis-Brant said triumphantly. "Have you heard the latest?"

I glanced at Julia. This did not bode well. "No, we have not."

"Well, it is said they are hiding somewhere in London. She and her companion. Here, would you believe it?"

"Really?" Julia managed. "Who told you that?"

She flapped a noncommittal hand. "I cannot recall. However, it is said Lord Deele thought . . . did you know Lady Deele has delivered a much-longed-for heir and son?" We both nodded vigorously, hoping to curtail the tangent. "Ah, you have heard. Well then, it is said Deele thought his sister and her companion had fled to Scotland and had been searching in that direction, but now he is set to search London once he has done his duty by his wife and new son. Some intrigue for those of us still left in the city."

George Brummell had been right; Lord Deele was well on his way to finding Hester and Miss Grant, especially now that he had determined they were in London. And if he did, the law stood firmly on his side. As Hester's guardian he had the right to forcibly remove her and do with her as he wished.

The Ermine held up her copy of *Childe Harold*. "Are you here for this too? I daresay I shall have to read it now, since no one will talk of aught else."

"Actually, Mr. Hatchard has a special order for us," I said, finding a chance to escape. "If you will excuse us . . ."

Thomas took the hint and gestured elegantly toward the back of the shop. "This way, my ladies."

We nodded our good-byes to the Ermine and followed Thomas. I looked back through the huge front display window. Tully, in her red cloak, still sat upon the bench, chatting with another maid. To an onlooker—or a nose—a lady's maid outside a shop was a certain indicator that her mistress was still inside. It would give us at least twenty minutes or perhaps even half an hour to slip out the back to Miss Grant and our waiting carriage—with John Driver and his blunderbuss at the ready—and head toward our rendezvous with Lord Evan before anyone noticed. I would have preferred to have Weatherly with us, too, but I needed him back at the house to ensure Lady Hester's safety.

"If what she says is true, Deele will be in London soon," Julia whispered to me as we passed the shelves devoted to the travelogue and the picturesque. "We can no longer wait. We must find a safer place for them."

I nodded mutely. Clearly Hester and Miss Grant must escape London, but that meant Evan would most likely go too. It would hurt—oh, how it would hurt to have him so near, only to be gone again—but it was for the best, since everything pointed to the fact that Mulholland was trying to kill him.

*T*he back entrance to Hatchards led to a space that was packed with crates on either side, leaving a narrow path through to a gate painted in the Hatchard green. At the back doorway, Thomas retrieved the large package that had been delivered with my note and handed it to me. I ripped open the brown paper and pulled out the two cloaks I had sent in preparation for this moment.

"One for you," I said, offering the blue wool to Julia. I swirled the burgundy velvet over my shoulders. An easy way to change our apparel. I returned the packaging to Thomas. "Thank you, Mr. Hatchard."

Thomas bowed. "I wish you well. Jermyn Street is up through there."

His nod directed us to the laneway behind the shop. I drew the cloak close around my body—the crates had ragged edges just built for snagging cloth—and led the way through the gate and into the cobbled lane. So far, so good.

"I hope the Ermine does not note we have not returned. I would not put it past her to wait for us in the hope of an invitation," Julia said as we negotiated the flagstones slicked with mud.

Ahead, two middling women raised upon wooden pattens walked past the laneway entrance, the clack of their shoe coverings ringing upon the stone. A scruffy tan dog trailed behind them, stopping to sniff the corner before running off as we approached.

But no sign of our carriage. Damn, I had hoped it would be waiting for us.

"Even if she does, we will be well away," I said as we stepped over the water-filled rut that separated the laneway from Jermyn Street. "Besides, Mr. Hatchard will deflect any interest."

We both surveyed the street, searching for our transport. It was not overly busy: three delivery wagons making their slow way toward St. James's Street, a man driving a bullock in the opposite direction, and a gentleman on a rather fine bay mare conversing with a man outside a shop.

"It is not here," Julia said, stepping back as a beefy man barreled past, touching his cap. "Why is it not here?"

I searched the street again, as if the carriage would magically appear. "They are probably just held up. A turned cart or something."

"I hope they are not too long. We are rather conspicuous standing here so close to St. James's Street," Julia said.

My sister was right; we were dangerously close to the notorious gentlemen's clubs at the end of the street, but we could not go back.

"Perhaps we should start to walk toward Piccadilly," I said.

"Wait! Look!" Julia pointed toward Duke Street. A familiar carriage had turned the corner. "That is ours, is it not? Thank heavens."

I blew out a relieved breath. Yet something was not right. I narrowed my eyes, focusing upon the driving seat. Two sat upon it. Was that Weatherly beside John?

"Weatherly has come too," Julia said, echoing my surprise. "That was not part of the plan."

Indeed, it was not. Nor was it customary for Weatherly to disregard our instructions.

"Oh dear, this cannot be good," Julia said.

As our carriage approached us, the expression upon Weatherly's face became clearer. Our butler was perturbed. Good Lord, what had happened? It took a lot to perturb William Weatherly.

John Driver pulled up the horses and Weatherly swung down from the seat to stand at the carriage door, ready to open it. The curtains had been drawn across the windows to hide the occupant; at least Miss Grant had followed my instructions in that matter.

"What is wrong?" I asked Weatherly.

"I tried, my lady," he said, and opened the door.

Inside the dim cabin, two pale countenances peered out: Miss Grant, stony-faced, and beside her, Lady Hester, mutinous.

What on earth was Miss Grant thinking, allowing her to come?

Behind me, Julia gave a sigh.

I glared at Miss Grant. "Why is she here?" I demanded, my irritation making me abrupt.

Lady Hester leaned forward, eyes overbright and gloved hands clenched tightly around her reticule. "I will see my brother, Lady Augusta. I will not allow you to stop me." She glanced at her paramour with some reproach. "I will not allow anyone to stop me. It is imperative that I talk to him. He will listen to me!"

"You will make yourself even more ill; then where will we be?" Miss Grant muttered, folding her arms over the gold frogged trim upon her bodice. She met my glare with a worried frown: half apology, half defiance.

Weatherly leaned closer. "It is why we are late," he murmured. "There was a . . . debate. But after what Lady Hester has been through, and thinking upon our earlier conversation, I did not think you would want me to stop her with physical force or lock her in her room."

My turn to sigh. "Quite right, Weatherly."

Lady Hester already looked burned to the socket, but if we

took her back to the house—or even sent her back in a hackney, alone—the Runners might be tipped off and all my careful preparations ruined. Not to mention someone seeing her and reporting back to Deele.

"Get in, Gus," Julia urged behind me. "We cannot stand here making a scene."

Indeed, the last thing we needed was to garner attention. I took Weatherly's hand and stepped into the cabin, taking the seat opposite Miss Grant. Julia followed close behind and sat beside me.

"We will go on as planned," I said to Weatherly, who waited in the doorway.

He nodded and closed the carriage door.

Across the footwell, Lady Hester settled back into her seat.

"Do not think we will return if you faint," I said crisply. A horrible thing to say, but I resented this flouting of my plan.

"I have no intention of fainting," Lady Hester said, looking as if she would do so at any moment.

"The doctor said absolutely no unnecessary exertion, but, of course, you know better," Miss Grant said under her breath. Lady Hester turned a little in her seat, away from the remark. A surprising discord—I had only ever seen them show a united front.

Julia touched my arm. "It is no great change to the plan, my dear," she said softly, reading my expression. "We are still on schedule and your ruse seems to have worked perfectly."

My sister, as ever, was right. Nothing had changed. Only one extra person within the carriage. And yet, as I studied Lady Hester—the prominent bones of her pale face testimony to the maltreatment she had suffered at the asylum—I knew that if she asked her brother to flee to another country, he would do so. How could he not?

9

I carefully let down the carriage window, cushioning the usual clatter with the pads of my fingers. The intrusion of cold air brought a grunt of protest from Miss Grant, who cradled Lady Hester against her shoulder.

"We are almost there," I said, forestalling her complaint.

"Thank goodness." She glanced down at Lady Hester's drawn, sleeping face. "I hope we do not have long to wait." As we had all suspected, the journey—with all the infelicities of the road—had been hard upon Hester's fragile state.

If I recalled correctly, we were coming up to the sweep of road—currently bordered by russet hazels—where our coach had been stopped by two highwaymen, one of whom I had accidentally shot. My future love. The beginning of it all.

A stand of trees came into view, its pattern of trunks and branches reaching into my memory. Ah, this was it. Just as I raised my hand to rap on the cabin wall, I heard John Driver call to the horses and our momentum slowed. He must have recognized the place too. After all, he had faced the same highwaymen and shot at Evan's erstwhile partner.

"We are here," I announced.

Miss Grant gently shook Lady Hester's shoulder.

"Are you sure this is it?" Julia asked, evaluating the unkempt autumn woodlands on either side.

"I am certain." I lifted my fob watch upon its chain and checked the time. Nearly noon, the appointed hour of our meeting.

Was Evan here yet? Colonel Drysan had given me a possible clue to the truth about the duel: the Exalted Brethren of Rack and Ruin. Could that scrap of information offer some hope of finding who wished Evan dead and a way to clear his name and save his sister?

The carriage stopped. I rose and poked my head out the window, the same action I had done when we had first stopped here. Then, it had been dusty, hot, and chaotic. Now it was wet, cold, and quiet. No sound or sight of anyone else on the road; no nicker of another horse, no shadowy figure of a man waiting in the trees. Just the muddy road stretching behind us and ahead. I drew back into the cabin and shook my head at Julia's unspoken question.

"He will come," she said.

I heard the muffled sound of an exchange between Weatherly and John Driver and then the carriage rocked—Weatherly alighting from his position up front, for he appeared outside the open window.

"My lady, John Driver and I believe this is the section of road."

"Yes, I think so too," I said.

Lady Hester finally raised her head from Miss Grant's shoulder, eyes heavy with fatigue. "I wish to go outside," she said.

She did not look able to stand, let alone wait outside in the cold air. "You should stay here," I said. "We do not know how long Lord Evan will be."

Miss Grant nodded. "Lady Augusta is right, my dear. Stay inside. At least until your brother arrives."

Despite that plea, Lady Hester rose from her seat—albeit

unsteadily—and fumbled at the door latch. Weatherly, on seeing her attempt, opened the door.

And so we all descended the steps to the roadside. Julia and I stood together beside the carriage and watched Lady Hester, supported heavily under one arm by Miss Grant, walk a little way ahead, their hems dragging through the mud.

"Her body may be healing," Julia said softly, "but I fear the hurt to her spirit is irreparable. Did you know she refuses to pray?"

"One can live without prayer," I said. After all, I did so every day.

Julia placed her hand upon my arm. She still grieved my apostasy. "But one cannot live without forgiveness, Gus. How does one forgive such a deep betrayal? Her own brother—charged with her care—rejecting all that she is and incarcerating her in such a place. In a hell that nearly killed her!"

I had no answer to that, for I had yet to discover a way to forgive Duffy for his lesser crime of jealous high-handedness. Perhaps that was Julia's point. I knew she could not fathom how I could live without God. Indeed, how did one live without religious faith? It was, I suspected, the nature of humanity to place faith in something, whether it be a god or rationality or perhaps fate. But what now did I place my faith in? A question I was yet to resolve.

In silence we watched Lady Hester and Miss Grant stop where the bushes and trees were more densely packed. There was some discussion between them—or more accurately a protest from Miss Grant and a dismissal from Hester—then they tentatively forged a way through the foliage. Hester did seem to find some solace in the midst of nature. Or perhaps she was merely looking for a private place of relief. It had been a long journey.

As they disappeared from view, I heard the thud of hooves—walking, not galloping—and turned toward the sound, my heart quickening. About a hundred yards or so back along the road, a man leading a bay horse emerged from the woods, his lean silhouette as familiar to me now as my sister's form.

"Thank God," Julia said.

Behind us I heard Miss Grant call, "He is here, Hester! Let us return." I looked over my shoulder to see her step back into the undergrowth to retrieve her beloved.

Julia ushered me forward. "Go, while Hester is indisposed and you have the chance to be private."

Evan had tied his horse to one of the bushes and was striding toward us. Julia was right. Lady Hester would not wait politely while I spoke to her brother, and I had so much to say. I picked up my hems and walked swiftly to him.

What if he was not as eager to see me as I was to see him? It was quite possible I had placed too much upon one good-bye kiss. Perhaps he no longer felt as strongly as I did. Or maybe the force of emotion between us had just been within my own imagination. A chastening thought.

I drew a deep breath. My feelings, at least, had not changed.

The distance between us was almost closed, his expression as anxious as my own. And then he smiled and it was full of warm welcome and tender delight.

"Gus—I am so glad to see you."

Lud, the way he said my name; it was as if I could lean into that soft sibilance and feel the wrap of it around me like two strong arms.

"You are here." A stupid observation, but I could not contain my relief at his safe arrival and the sweetness of his greeting. He was alive and well, although somewhat bedraggled. Clearly, he had not shaved for some time—his dear face gaunt beneath thick stubble—and leaves and mud clung to his greatcoat.

"Of course. I will always come when you ask."

We both stood still, caught in the hesitation of where we had left each other three weeks ago. That had been a beginning, sealed with that good-bye kiss, but certainty was not ours to claim. Not yet. And so he reached for my hand and took it to his lips, the press of his warmth against my skin blazing through my body. Ah, there it was—the matching blaze within his eyes. We stood, fingers entwined tightly, the final step into each other's arms only a breath away.

"Evan!" Lady Hester shouted from the edge of the woods.

"Hester." He released my hand and raised his own in greeting, but I saw his jaw clench. "Why is my sister here?" he asked under his breath. "I thought her too fragile to travel. Is she the reason for our meeting?"

"She insisted on coming to see you despite our protests. Deele is aware she has left the asylum and is taking refuge in London."

"Well, that was inevitable."

He moved forward to meet Hester, but I grasped his arm and halted him.

"She is not the reason why I placed the notice. I need to ask you something."

He looked down at my tight hold. "Clearly something important. What is it?"

I released him, then took a deep breath, the words rushing out. "Did you belong to a club called the Exalted Brethren of Rack and Ruin? Sanderson was a member."

He squinted. "The what?"

"The Exalted Brethren of Rack and Ruin. Colonel Drysan said you were a member. It was—" I paused. How best to describe it? "Along the lines of the Hellfire Club. But worse."

"Worse?" His mouth quirked up. "You are a constant surprise, Augusta. But no, I have never belonged to such a club."

"Are you sure?"

I was relieved that he denied any dealings with such a place, yet a part of me was disappointed too. Was my only clue about to disappear into nothing?

"I think I would remember something worse than Dashwood's club." He frowned, eyes fixed for a moment upon the tree line. "Wait, was it in Bedford Street, behind St. Paul's in Covent Garden?"

"Yes. Colonel Drysan said it was near St. Paul's."

"I was taken to a strange club a few times by a friend from school. I was foxed a great deal in those days, so I can barely remember, but"—he grimaced—"well, it was not to my liking. Definitely along Hellfire lines. Why is it so important?"

"Colonel Drysan thought there was a link between you and Sanderson through the club. And through that link, a possible reason for Sanderson's death other than the challenge at White's."

Evan shook his head. "No, the duel came out of White's. Sanderson falsely accused me of marking the cards when he was the one who was cheating. The colonel's hypothesis sounds a bit far-fetched. Especially since I was not a member of this Rack and Ruin club."

"Even so, it is a link between you and Sanderson that was never considered during the trial. As far as I can tell, it has always been stated that you were strangers to each other before that card game."

He nodded. "We were strangers—we did not move in the same circles. Besides, wouldn't such a link consolidate my guilt rather than prove my innocence? I did catch him across the chest in the duel and he did die on the field before witnesses."

"Yes, but you only pinked him. You said so yourself. I think there is more to it." I hesitated—the next would infuriate him— but he needed to know. "Two days ago, I had an encounter with Mulholland. He is a violent man—"

"Good God, did he hurt you?"

"He grabbed me. I was not harmed, but his henchman beat my poor footman. He was looking for information about you and he did not fear any repercussions for the interrogation."

"How dare he lay hands upon you!" He drew himself up. "This is all becoming far too dangerous. You must distance yourself from me."

I looked at him in exasperation. Ridiculous, noble man. "Even if I wanted to distance myself—which I do not—we are well past that contingency. The link between us has been made."

"Still, I cannot have you or your sister in danger."

"Evan, you are missing the point. Mulholland does not fear any repercussion for attacking me. He expects to be protected. And he is known to kill his quarry."

As I expected, he quickly made the connection. "You think he has been hired by someone to kill me?"

"Someone of high rank."

"Why? I have not been in the country for twenty years. What could be the reason?"

"I think it has something to do with this club. As you say, you have been away for twenty years. You cannot have done anything to create such animosity while you were in a prison colony on the other side of the world. Therefore, it stands to reason that the motive for this attempt to kill you originates from back then too."

He cocked his head, clearly unconvinced.

"I know it may be clutching at straws," I conceded. "But we need to discover more and that is the only place I can think to start."

"How, though?"

"Go to the club."

"Does it still exist?"

"The colonel believes so."

"It has been twenty years, Gus. What do you hope to find?"

I took his hands, as if holding them would somehow convince him I was right. "I do not know. But if we fail to even try, then everything stays the same. Do you not see? You running from Mulholland and the gallows, Hester at the mercy of Deele, and me in Grosvenor Square unable to help—"

"Brother!"

I looked over my shoulder. Lady Hester and Miss Grant had finally reached us.

"My dear girl," Evan said as Hester shuffled forward. I was forced to let go of his hands and step aside. "How good it is to see you again." Although he smiled, his expression held a slight rictus of shock at her condition. She indeed looked ghastly: pale lips dry and cracked, skin ashen, with a blue cast under her eyes and around her mouth. He bowed slightly. "Miss Grant, I had not expected to see you and Hester here." His voice held a good deal of reproach.

Miss Grant was having none of it. "We have come to—" she started, but Hester leaned in close to his face.

"We must go, brother. Immediately. To the Continent or the West Indies or somewhere. Far away."

"The Continent? There is a war on, my dear." He took her outstretched hand. "I do not think we can travel, Hester; you are not well enough. To be frank, you look completely done in. We must wait until you are stronger."

It was not an idle comment. He'd been the physician's assistant at the colony prison for years and had learned a great deal of medicine. He glanced at me, the swift connection confirming what we all knew: Hester was still gravely ill.

She shook her head. "No, we must go now. Deele will come. He hates me and Lizzie, you know that. He hates us." She dragged upon his hand. "Please, Evan. Deele will put me back into one of those places. And I cannot go back . . . I cannot. I will die first."

"You will not go back, Hester," he said, trying to soothe the throbbing mania in her voice. "I will not allow it."

She stared at him for a second. "Not allow it," she repeated. Her cracked lips curled back. She wrenched her hand from his grasp. "Not allow it? This is all your fault. If you had not fought that stupid duel, you would have your rightful title. You would be Lord Deele, not our brother, and Lizzie and I would be safe. It is your fault!"

Evan flinched as if she had slashed a whip across his face.

"It is all your fault!" she screamed, the words climbing into a hellish shriek.

Upon the frenzy of her despair, she collapsed, her weight caught by Miss Grant.

"Hester!" Evan sprang across and took Hester's other arm, both of them holding her upright.

"Weatherly," I yelled, "bring a rug and the medicine chest."

"She is insensible," Evan said. He glared across at Miss Grant. "Why did you allow her to come?"

"She is a Belford," Miss Grant snapped back. "You try stopping her from doing what she wants."

Weatherly appeared with the rug, Julia close behind me with her medicine box already open. "What does she need? Smelling salts?"

Weatherly laid the rug upon the road, and Evan and Miss Grant carefully lowered her upon it, with Miss Grant cradling her head. Julia kneeled beside them and held the small bottle under Hester's nose. We all leaned in. No response. Hester remained unmoving, only her chest rising with each shallow breath.

"We must get her back into the carriage," Evan said to Weatherly.

Julia sat back upon her heels. "We need to get her to a bed and a doctor."

"Brighton is close, my lady," Weatherly said.

Julia shook her head. "If we go to Brighton, we will have no lodgings. We cannot take Hester and Miss Grant to any of our acquaintances or risk public exposure in a hotel. It will get back to Deele."

"We must return to London," I said.

It did not take long for Evan and Weatherly to settle Hester back into the carriage in Miss Grant's arms. Julia sat opposite, keeping a watchful eye upon Hester's breathing, smelling salts at the ready.

I foresaw an anxious journey back to Grosvenor Square.

I passed Julia the rug that had been used as a pillow on the roadside, then took the few steps to Evan, waiting with his horse. We had barely seen each other, our reunion far too brief and far too crowded. And yet here we were, another farewell at a carriage door.

"Do not worry. We will take care of her," I said.

Evan drew the reins over his horse's head, ready to mount. "I will follow."

"No! You cannot. You will only put yourself in danger. Mulholland has noses everywhere."

"My sister is right," he said, his voice low and full of self-reproach. "This is my fault and I must try to put it right."

"That is not true—" I began, but he shook his head.

"I see now that Hester is desperate to flee our brother, and if I thought I could do so safely, I would take her on the next ship. But I cannot see her surviving an extended sea journey, or even a land journey. You have started this search for the truth, and with it, a hope for my exoneration. We must continue as swiftly as possible. I must do everything I can to take my place in my family again and save her from another five years of my brother's rule."

It was heartening to see him so galvanized and so set on staying in England despite the ever-growing danger. Still, I had to voice the hard fact that lay before us. "Forgive me, but even if you are exonerated, there is no guarantee it will be enough for you to claim back your title and become her guardian. I doubt your brother would give up the title without a fight."

He gave a sober nod. "You are right, of course. But perhaps I can claim back a life within the law and offer Hester and Miss Grant some kind of haven. I am not without friends, Gus. Old friends with some influence who may be willing to assist if there is proof that may help my cause." He looked into the distance, clearly deciding upon a plan that might bring about that outcome. "Will you meet me in Bedford Street two days hence? At dusk—these types of clubs do not open until late in the evening. We will do as you suggest. We will find this place if it still exists, and see if there is any proof to be found."

"Of course, I will always come when you ask." A return of his own promise. Our new certainty.

He smiled—that wonderful, warm smile. "I know."

10

$\mathcal{W}$e arrived in London in the early evening, smuggled Hester and Miss Grant back inside the house via the mews, and sent Thomas for Dr. McLeod. The dear man came immediately, but the prognosis was not good.

"She has declined rapidly," he said to our anxious gathering in the corridor outside Hester's room. "Overexertion. I prescribe complete bed rest and sustaining broths. I will have a draft made and send it around. No exercise for a week or so, and then gently so that she can build stamina."

Miss Grant nodded and, with a curtsy, returned to watch over her beloved.

Dr. McLeod waited until the door had closed, then said to Julia and me, "Her body, including her heart, has been severely weakened by the treatment at the asylum. She must not exert herself, certainly no long-distance travel." The careful lack of reproof in his voice was reproof enough.

"We understand, Doctor," Julia said.

My sister, too, looked exhausted. I feared we were overlooking her health in the emergencies of Hester's situation.

"And how are you faring, Lady Augusta?" Dr. McLeod asked me, placing his black Clericus upon his head. "Is your shoulder still bothering you?"

"Not at all, thank you." I turned to my sister. "Julia, you said you wished to speak to Dr. McLeod privately."

I lifted my brows at her: *He is a good doctor; ask for a second opinion.*

Julia frowned: *I do not want a second opinion.*

The doctor removed his hat again. "How may I be of service, Lady Julia?"

"I will leave you to your conversation," I said. "Good evening."

I swiftly withdrew down the staircase, ducking Julia's glare. Perhaps it was presumptuous on my part, but Julia would not act on her own behalf, and her health was, in my view, deteriorating under Dr. Thorgood's ministrations.

A little while later, Julia joined me in the drawing room. I put down the absorbing novel I was reading, coincidentally about sisters—one sensible and one full of sensibility—and rose from my chair. "Weatherly reports that dinner will be another half hour," I said as she closed the door. I picked up the brandy decanter. "Would you like a glass?" A vain attempt to deflect the reproach coming my way.

"That was ill-done," she said, meaning, of course, Dr. McLeod. She cocked her head at the decanter. "Brandy? Before dinner?"

Indeed, it was unusual. Brandy was usually taken after a meal and generally by men. Nevertheless, I thought the situation called for something a bit stronger than ratafia or canary. Besides, it was a very good brandy, almost certainly smuggled from France. I did not question Weatherly's sources and he did not tell.

"Call it medicinal," I said.

She gave a weary nod and sat down on the sofa, looking into the fire burning in the hearth. I poured the brandy and handed it to her, the silence between us lengthening.

I sat in the chair opposite. "Did you speak to the doctor?" I asked.

She looked up at me, her expression unusually closed. "That is between me and Dr. McLeod."

Ah, so that was to be my punishment: to have the outcome of my intervention withheld. My sister certainly knew how to admonish me.

Another subject, then.

"I have arranged to meet Lord Evan in Bedford Street two nights hence," I said.

"For the club?"

I nodded. "The odds of discovering something are not in our favor, but I feel we must try."

Julia took a sip of brandy. "It is dangerously close to Covent Garden, my dear, and you really cannot be seen there. Not after the scandal."

She meant, of course, being seen in the low Covent Garden brothel where our father had died. I had gone to rescue his body from the gawking onlookers, and my presence—and interaction with the residents—had become a scandal. A number of people had turned their backs upon both of us until dear Charlotte and George Brummell had nipped that ostracism in the bud.

"I know. But it is on the far side of the Garden behind St. Paul's. Besides, I plan to be dressed in men's clothes on the night."

"I should protest at such a mad plan but I am too tired and I know you will take no notice of me."

I took a sip of my own drink and watched my sister over the brim. She did not often admit to fatigue nor in such an irritated manner. Had she truly spoken to Dr. McLeod? Maybe I could ask the good doctor if she had consulted him. No, he would not tell me. He was the very model of medical discretion, which, after all, was the very reason Evan had recommended him to us.

"I think it would be prudent to visit the street beforehand," I said. "To get the lay of the land."

"How do you propose to do that without being followed by Mulholland or becoming another on-dit?"

"By having a legitimate reason to be there," I said. "I thought we could see a play at the Lyceum. If you are feeling up to it. We could then drive through Bedford Street—very slowly—on the way home."

"So you need me for respectability?"

"Always, my dear," I said, raising my glass.

She looked at me, eyes narrowed. "I am not sure I want to be the respectable sister."

Now, that was a surprise; reputation had always been important to my twin. Ever since childhood, she and Duffy had been the most upright and virtuous members of our family. Was she beginning to enjoy our unsavory adventures? Or was it something or someone else exacting this change? A certain Runner, perhaps; a man who would be seen by the ton as barely one step up from the ruffians he brought to justice. A man who Lady Julia Colebrook should not know even existed.

"Do not worry, I know the truth," I said lightly, to cover my disquiet. "I've seen you storm a brothel brandishing a blunderbuss. You are barely respectable and totally disreputable."

Reluctantly, she smiled. "Very well, then, what is playing at the Lyceum? Heaven forbid it is Sheridan. I'm not sure I could sit through another one, even for Lord Evan's sake."

*F*ortunately the play was not a Sheridan, but a rather clumsily abridged *Hamlet*. At the final curtain, Julia and I slipped out the little-used side entrance and made our way to the end of Exeter Street, where John Driver waited with the carriage. The hope was that our exit would be obscured by the surge of departing theater patrons and their carriages at the front entrance. As it was, I saw no one watching us with any particular interest as I ascended the carriage steps behind Julia.

"I thought the Ophelia was rather good," Julia said as I took my seat opposite her and rapped upon the wall for John Driver to walk on. "A pretty girl with some skill."

I did not answer immediately, for my attention was upon the road as we jerked into motion. Still no watchful eyes upon us.

I sat back against the silk cushioning. "A bit too whispery for my liking," I finally said. The genuine madness I had encountered at the Bothwell House asylum had been heartbreakingly loud and in no part pretty.

I had instructed John Driver to take the long way around Covent Garden, and before long we were progressing up Bow Street. As we waited to turn into Hart Street, Julia leaned forward in her seat to look at the street behind us, her gaze intense. I twisted back to see what had caught her attention. Ah, the Bow Street Magistrates' Court, its colonnaded portico abuzz with all types entering and exiting. Bow Street was always open.

"I wonder if he is in there," I said blandly.

"I am sure I do not know what you mean," she returned primly.

I did not follow up on my comment. It seemed Julia was not open to discussing either her health or Mr. Kent.

Before long we turned into King Street. The dwellings and shop fronts were small and the pavements busy with gentlemen on their way, no doubt, to the nearby pleasures of Covent Garden and the ladies from *Harris's List* who worked there. On one corner, a balladeer sang for pennies, a small group clustered around him, and the patrons of a gin shop had spilled out onto the road, yelling their own raucous songs. We turned into the wider part of Bedford Street and I rapped upon the wall for John Driver to slow our momentum.

"What are we looking for?" Julia asked, peering out her window at the passing frontages.

A good question. The street was ill-lit and I did not want to draw attention by ordering Samuel to walk alongside with a lamp. "I'm not sure. Something that looks like a gentlemen's club."

Julia looked back at me with eyebrows raised. "And what exactly would that look like?"

I had no answer, of course—neither of us had ever been near St. James's Street to view the elite gentlemen's clubs. To do so would have been social death.

John Driver kept the horses at walking pace as we progressed down the street. On my side of the carriage, some establishments had light in the windows, some did not, but none of them gave any clue as to whether they housed a club of dubious activities.

"Anything on your side?" I asked Julia.

"I have no idea," Julia said.

I rapped on the wall and called out, "Stop!" The carriage drew to a halt near the corner of Maiden Lane.

"Perhaps it is up ahead," I said, peering into the final section of the street, which looked too narrow for our town carriage to pass.

Julia huffed an irritated breath. "Frankly, if we walked up and down the whole length of Bedford Street, we would have no way of knowing." She leaned across and opened the door. The carriage rocked as Samuel immediately descended from his position at the back and appeared alongside, ready to help us down. "We need local knowledge," she said over her shoulder as she took his hand and alighted.

"From whom?" I asked as I arrived behind her on the cobbled pavement.

I shivered, my silk evening cloak and gown not adequate for gallivanting on a cold night. Was Julia thinking of knocking on the door of one of the houses? How on earth would we explain a request for information about a gentlemen's club?

"From her," Julia said, nodding toward a hunched shape sitting beside a basket on the corner of Maiden Lane.

An old flower seller.

I had not even seen her there. One of the truly invisible.

"I would lay odds that she has sat in the same spot for years selling her flowers, just like Peggy in our square," Julia said. Peggy? But of course my sister knew the name of the flower seller near us. "She will have sat there unregarded, watching the world walk by. That is the local knowledge we need," Julia added.

"Brilliant," I said.

Julia acknowledged the accolade with a nod, then turned to our footman. "Samuel, bring the lamp."

Samuel unhooked the carriage lamp and followed us across the road. He still walked a little stiffly from his beating from Mulholland's man but otherwise seemed to have recovered from the ordeal.

The old woman looked up as we approached, immediately holding out a raggedy bunch of snowdrops. The tiny white bell blooms trembled in her hold. "Flowers, milady? Flowers? Penny a posy."

In the light of the lamp, I could make out a deeply lined face with inflamed, crusted eyes and a sunken mouth. She wore an old knitted shawl tied over a threadbare coat, and a straw bonnet sporting a large hole and a frayed ribbon around the crown.

"I will take all that you have left," Julia said, peering into the basket. She worked open the drawstrings of her reticule and dug her fingers inside.

"All?" the old woman echoed. She peered into her basket too. "I got this many." She held up her other hand—wrapped in rags for warmth—and splayed her fingers. Four posies.

Julia withdrew a shilling and crouched beside her, holding out the coin. The old woman stared at it. "That's a shillin', that is. I ain't got the wherewithal to give back the difference, my lady."

Julia dropped the coin into her hand. "The shilling is yours. What is your name?"

"They call me Weepy Iris," she said, inflamed eyes fixed upon the coin cupped in her palm.

"What is your real name?" Julia asked gently.

The woman looked up and blinked in the lamplight. "Dorothy, my lady. Dorothy Martindale." Her voice rasped on the *n*, as if she had not spoken the name in a long while.

"How long have you sold your flowers on this corner, Dorothy?" Julia asked.

The woman closed her hand around the coin. "Nigh on twenty years, my lady."

"Am I right in thinking you see everything that happens in Bedford Street?"

She considered Julia for a second, a lightning-fast reckoning of an unusual situation. A lady did not often crouch on the pavement beside a flower woman for a chat. "That I do, my lady," she finally said.

Julia held up another shilling. "Can you tell us something?" She gathered me into the conversation with a glance. "I am Lady Julia and this is my sister, Lady Augusta. We wish to know if there is a gentlemen's club somewhere along here. A club called—"

"The Exalted Brethren of Rack and Ruin," Dorothy whispered.

She glanced across the corner and gave a small nod. "Number 2, down there."

Julia handed over the coin, quickly closed in the filthy hand.

"But you don't want to go nowhere near it, my ladies," Dorothy added. "It's a bad place, full o' bad men."

"In what way?" I asked, although I already knew from the colonel's report.

Dorothy drew in a portentous breath. "Sometimes girls go in there and I ain't seen 'em come out." She looked at us defiantly. "It's true."

"We believe you," I said. "When does the club open? Is it every night?"

"Most, my lady. After the Evensong bells." She leaned forward, her voice dropping into a whisper again. "Sometimes even on Sundays. Most of the coves come out 'bout a few hours before dawn. All of 'em foxed. They wear masks too."

"Masks?" Julia asked. "You mean like loo masks for a masquerade ball?"

"No, like the old mummers."

So, they kept their faces completely hidden.

Julia looked at me: *Anything else we should ask?*

"What do you think happens to the girls that do not come out?" I asked. "Have you heard any rumors?"

Dorothy shrugged, wariness shrinking her sunken mouth even more. "Maybe I'm wrong and they go out another way. There's a yard out the back of them row of houses. Could be they go out there."

She huddled back into her ragged clothes, ducking out of the light of the lamp. Our shilling, it seemed, had run out.

"Thank you, Dorothy," Julia said, rising from her crouch. "We appreciate your help."

"Don't forget your flowers, my lady," Dorothy said, and gathered up the small posies. She held up the bobbing blooms, her faded eyes darting from Julia to me, then back again. A decision made. "Don't know if this 'elps," she said slowly, "but I 'ave seen somethin' time to time that struck me as another kind of odd: a handcart pushed by two men comin' and goin' from that yard. In the wee hours. Only stays for a short while. Looks like a delivery cart, but it goes in empty."

"Do they bring something out?" Julia asked, taking the flowers.

I glanced at my sister: *Like, for instance, a brutalized girl?*

Julia quirked her mouth: *Exactly.*

Dorothy shook her head. "Never seen nothin' in it. Goin' in or out." She shrugged. "Always empty. Thought it was odd, ay?"

An empty cart. Odd, indeed.

11

The following afternoon, I viewed myself in my dressing room mirror with a critical eye. I had worn men's clothes before, but they had been my father's and of excellent cut and cloth. This ensemble was baggy in unusual places, and the cloth was only a step or two away from threadbare. Still, the excessive wear had made them unusually soft, and once again, I reveled in the ease of breeches.

"What do you think?" I asked Julia and Tully, my maid.

"Rather good," Julia said from her seat upon the chaise. "But you must not forget to glue on your side-whiskers."

I nodded at the reminder as my maid walked around me to view the whole of the ensemble. She was now practiced in voicing her opinion about my disguises and had, in fact, bought the secondhand men's clothes we were now appraising.

"The shirt and breeches are probably cleaner than what would be worn by one of the lower ranks, my lady, but I figured you didn't want me to buy any that were infested with lice or fleas."

I wrinkled my nose. "Absolutely not. We do not have to strive for that much authenticity."

"Perhaps I could take the neckerchief and dirty it up a little," Tully said. "The coat hides the cleanliness of the breeches, I think, since it is patched and of a drab color." She narrowed her eyes in further evaluation. "The hat is an excellent shambles, but we must oil your hair and make it less . . . done."

"Then, let's to it," I said, untying the neckerchief and passing it to my maid. "I must be away before sundown."

Tully curtsied and left the room on her errand.

"Miss Grant is pressing me to find a solution to their situation," Julia said.

I looked up from smoothing my jacket collar. "She has said nothing to me."

Julia did not comment, which was comment enough. How had I been cast as the villain in this piece? After all, I had been right about Hester accompanying us to see Evan. Besides, Dr. McLeod's latest examination had concluded that she had rallied a little but not enough to be moved. Not yet.

"If she had spoken to me, I could have told her that I have written to Charlotte on their behalf," I said. "If Lord Davenport is not in residence at their estate, she might be able to offer them refuge under the guise of an extended visit from us. What do you think? It is the best I can come up with at present."

Julia considered the option. "It places a great deal upon Charlotte, and we have already asked so much of her." She bit her lip—a prelude to something preying upon her mind. "My dear, you may want to consider including Lady Hester and Miss Grant in these decisions. They may think it unsuitable."

I frowned. "Unsuitable? They do not have that many options, do they?"

"Even so, one does like to have control over one's own life. Especially after having so little."

I did not know why my sister was being so particular. "Certainly, but at the moment, that control is somewhat hampered by

Hester's condition. Charlotte is the best option and you know she will do it gladly. Anyway, I have sent the letter so we should hear back soon, either way." I pointed my foot and studied my secondhand boots. "Do you think they look too new?" I asked my sister.

"Hardly," she said. "They are appalling."

"Well, I shall find some mud in the stables and walk through it," I said. "To be safe."

"Safe?" My sister snorted. "You do realize that our ruse at Hatchards has more or less confirmed to the Runners and Mulholland that we are trying to move without their surveillance, and thus are likely to be meeting with Lord Evan."

"I know," I said soberly.

"Then how do you propose to get out of the house without being followed?"

"I will exit the mews with Thomas and Samuel. We are to be fellows slipping out for some fun."

Julia's mouth pursed. Unconvinced.

I picked up a collection of coins—a few half crowns, shillings, farthings, pennies, and sixpences—and shoved them into my jacket pocket. I had learned to be armed with money, for it could oil a situation better than wits or weapons. "They are not going to be looking for me dressed in men's clothes, are they?" I added. "Especially the clothes of a workingman."

"I suppose not," she conceded. "Do you propose to enter the club?"

"I do not know. Lord Evan and I will figure it out when we are there."

I contemplated my reflection again. Neither Lord Evan nor I would be able to enter as gentlemen since neither of us would be clothed in the appropriate evening wear. How, then, would we get in? As ever, we would make it up as we went along. I smiled at the thought, eyeing my grinning reflection. There was a good chance I was enjoying this too much.

"I received a note from Mr. Kent a half hour ago," Julia said into the silence.

I turned to face my sister. I had not heard a messenger arrive. And a note, only to Julia? By all rights, he should have written to me—I was the elder sister and head of the household—or at least to both of the Colebrook sisters, to keep it within the bounds of business . . . and propriety.

"Is that so?" It came out rather more sharply than I had anticipated. "When did he start writing to you and not us?"

"You receive notes from Lord Evan," Julia countered.

We stared at each other. She was equating Mr. Kent with Lord Evan? Julia's fair skin flushed; she had more or less admitted she felt an attachment to the Runner. She busied herself adjusting the lace upon her sleeve. "He has been investigating on our behalf."

"May I read the note?"

She eyed me. "No," she said, drawing the soft refusal out, "but I can give you the meat of his news."

What on earth had Mr. Kent written to my sister that she would not allow me to see?

"Are you really not going to let me read it? I let you read my notes from Lord Evan."

She gave a slight lift of her shoulders. "I am allowed to have my own letters, Gus."

"Of course you are," I said, but her refusal still stung. "What is his news, then?"

"He says that Mulholland thinks Lord Evan is still in England. I think, too, that Mr. Kent is aware you lied to him about Lord Evan's departure."

"Well, it was bound to happen. The man is not stupid," I said. "Thank you for keeping quiet on that score."

"Of course," Julia said. "Although I do not like lying."

Especially to Mr. Kent, I thought.

"Mr. Kent also says Mulholland is not officially attached to the Runners in regard to pursuing Lord Evan," Julia continued. "In other words, he is not under the Bow Street aegis, although Mr. Kent has seen him in the vicinity of the court. Interestingly, upon Mr. Kent's discreet inquiries, he was warned off asking any questions about Mulholland, and his informant suggested that such interest could jeopardize his position."

I chewed on my lip. "A subject not to be discussed. Mulholland is, most probably, using the resources of Bow Street but not subject to their oversight."

"Mr. Kent suggests the same. If Mulholland does anything egregiously outside the law, it will not be associated with Bow Street or the Home Office."

"Innocence through denial," I murmured. "And an obscured path to the top."

So Mulholland knew Lord Evan was in England and had not fled the country as I had tried to convince him. Not only that; our supposition that Mulholland was working for someone of high rank who, for whatever reason, wanted Lord Evan dead appeared to be confirmed. Bad news, all round. And that included, I could not help thinking, my sister's refusal to share Mr. Kent's letter with me. I could see only heartbreak for her in that connection—the difference of rank and society between them was too great. And surely my sister had already suffered enough heartbreak in her life.

The old hackney carriage smelled of wet straw, sour sweat, and the faint, ever-present perfume of dung. I shifted on the bare wooden seat—the upholstery had for some reason been ripped out—and looked out the window at the passing view of Bow Street.

The sky was darkening toward dusk, my appointed time to meet Lord Evan, and the encroaching evening had already brought out the pleasure-seekers. A pie seller did a brisk trade on a corner to a group of young men, and a well-lit tavern full of patrons flashed by, the scraping lilt of folk fiddlers within following us along the street. If I recollected correctly, one of the entrances to Covent Garden was coming up on our left. I knocked sharply on the cabin wall.

"'Ere will do," I yelled. Better to walk the last few streets, especially in this guise. Not many men of my "rank" would spend the coin to hire a hackney, even one as shabby as this piece.

The carriage pulled up. I opened the door, took the step down to the footpath, and lifted my hand in thanks to the driver. Since I had already paid, he tipped his hat and drove on, looking for another fare.

I stood for a moment to get my bearings, earning the muttered curses and irritated glances of those hurrying along the footpath. Ahead was the corner of Russell and Bow Streets. I could walk the long way around to Bedford Street or cut across Covent Garden, a much shorter route. One I would never take on foot as Lady Augusta Colebrook.

I smiled.

Covent Garden, then. And finally, some time alone with Evan. It still felt strangely forward to think of addressing him without a title, even with his invitation. It was an intimacy that I had not had with any man before. Even my brother was Duffy, or Duffield, never James.

"Evan," I said aloud. Practice made perfect, or at least not so awkward. "Are you well, Evan?" A passing woman glanced warily at the shabby man talking to himself and gave me a wide berth. Quite right. I ducked my head and lengthened my gait into a manly stride toward the market.

The Russell Street entrance into Covent Garden was little more than a narrow laneway between Carpenter's Coffee House— one of the ramshackle permanent buildings that bordered the square—and a higgledy-piggledy collection of stalls, lean-tos, baskets, and carts. Some of the vendors were packing up their wares for the day, but a good number were still selling in the last of the light.

Through the rumble of carts, shouted instructions, and hum of chatter, I warded off calls to buy the last bushel of potatoes— patently not the last bushel—a pound of nuts, and a rabbit ready to be skinned for the pot. One of the basket women, a broad-shouldered amazon even taller than me, stepped into my path, offering to carry my goods for "penny o' mile" in a broad Irish brogue. I shook my head with a smile and received a gap-toothed grin in return as I headed alongside Carpenter's into the market proper.

If the entrance was a shambles, then the market itself was complete mayhem. I paused, looking for a way into the crowd, the noise and colors and clashing smells like a chaotic opera surging across every sense. Here was a world Lady Augusta would never experience, and the exhilaration of it sang through my blood.

"Get on, man." An impatient voice from behind chivvied me into action.

I waded in, threading my way past a secondhand shoe seller, half-empty baskets of glassy-eyed fish, and a collection of pungent oyster barrels surrounded by diners tipping their heads back to eat from the shell. A rug seller, stacking his intricate wares back into his cart, stepped back into me and touched his forehead in hurried apology. I showed him my palms—no harm done—and continued on past eels being fried over coals, the rich, meaty fish smell striking my innards. Ahead, four women called to a raucous group of young men. One of their number, a tall redhead in a grubby green gown that showed bony shoulders and a good deal of meager breast, mimed an offering with her mouth and hand, then laughed at the appreciative hoots from the men. As I approached, her attention swung to me.

"Fancy a fumble, love?" she called, flashing a surprisingly intact smile. "How about a tug for a penny?"

My face heated: I was not sure what she meant, but it was clearly obscene. I quickened my step, but amid my alarm, a thought occurred. We knew the whereabouts of the club, but maybe one of these women had actually been inside it or at least heard more about its activities. Indeed, maybe this woman. Surely she would prefer to take a coin for information than . . . whatever she was offering.

"Where?" I called back.

She jerked her head to one of the alleys between the permanent buildings.

Did I dare?

I gave a nod; apparently, I did.

She beckoned. "Let's see your coin, then."

I fished a penny out of my pocket and held it up. With a nod she turned, and I followed her past the three women who were still trying to entice the group of young bucks.

The alley was strewn with old cabbage, discarded pieces of wood, broken gin flagons, and a dismembered rat carcass. The stink of urine and rotting vegetation caught in my throat, making me cough. Lifting her filthy hem, my hostess picked a way to the far corner where the ground had been cleared of refuse but was still damp from use as a privy. She stood at least an inch taller than my own five foot nine and was perhaps ten years younger. Life had whittled her face into gaunt hollows, but behind the grime, her smile was friendly and a pair of rather pretty blue eyes evaluated me.

"Well now," she said, reaching for my groin. "Let's see what we have here."

I pressed myself against the wall of the building, rapidly realizing what a "tug" meant. "Wait!"

She withdrew her hand, squinting at me. "You don't need to be afeard of Long Sal, my love. I done this afore. I ain't gonna pull it off."

"How about a shilling, instead?"

She stepped back and placed her hands on her hips. "How would the likes of you have a shillin'?"

I dug my hand into my pocket and withdrew the larger coin. She eyed it, her mouth pursing. "And what would you want for that?"

"Long Sal, is it?" I asked.

"That's what they call me." She nodded to the building. "We can go inside, if you want. We got a straw mattress in there."

I shook my head. "I don't want that. I want to talk."

"Ha! You be funnin' me."

"No. I am serious."

She rubbed her mouth, considering this unusual turn of events. "A shillin', just for talk? About what?"

"There is a club in Bedford Street. In number 2. Do you know of it?"

"Aye," she said, puzzled. "It's for the quality. They get girls from here sometimes, but I ain't never been."

"Have you heard anything about their activities?"

She crossed her arms. "You talk a lot better than them clothes say you oughta. What's your game?"

"I am just trying to find out about the club. And you will get a shilling out of it."

Her eyes found the coin again. Would she talk or not? A shilling was a substantial lure, but maybe her natural distrust would overcome it.

"You are a queer one," she finally said. "From what I heard they got a taste for the floggin' and other specials like that. Most times not too bad and the coin is good. Enough to pay for any hurt. I knowed one girl got nearly enough for a year."

I leaned forward. "So girls come out hurt?"

"Sometimes, but a whole year of food and roof is worth it, 'ey?"

I nodded, more to hide my horror at such exigencies than in accord. "Have you heard about anyone who has gone missing from the club or died from their injuries?"

She narrowed her eyes. "You lost someone? Is that why you askin'?"

"No."

She considered me again. "I've heard that sometimes there be a girl inside the club who ain't from the Garden or in the game. A cit from the middlin's, or even genteel."

"Genteel girls, are you sure?"

She shrugged. "Just heard it. Might be runaways, 'ey? They oftentimes end up on their backs. But I ain't heard of anyone goin' missin' or slippin' the mort direct from that club."

That did not quite tally with what Dorothy the flower seller had told us: girls going in but not coming out.

Long Sal lifted a bony shoulder. "Mind you, there be a lot of us, and not just 'ere in the Garden. It could've happened. Lots of things happen to the likes of us and not a soul knows about it. Sometimes we're lucky and sometimes we're not. It's just how it is."

Her measurement of luck was very different from mine.

"One last question. Do you know the names of any of the men who go to the club?"

She laughed. "Aye, we meet up for a gin and chop every week." She held out her cupped hand. "They got no names, just like we don't for them."

I dropped the shilling into her palm. "Thank you." I paused, then smiled. "Long Sal."

She gave a wry huff of appreciation and bobbed a curtsy. "Thank you, sir, for the shillin'." She turned to go, then swung around again, her head tilted in a motherly fashion. "This much coin gives you a mod of advice too. You may be dressed like us, but I know you be a gentleman and . . . maybe not on the straight course." I opened my mouth to deny my gentle status, but she held up her hand. "Don't fret, I'll say nothin'. But it ain't good for the likes of you to be asking questions round 'ere. Alone. Go back to where you come from. And don't mess with them at that club. They got the world sewn up and no one's going to change it. Nothing changes, mister. We all stay where God puts us."

I gave a bow, for the advice and her discretion. She held up the coin with a grin—a triumphant celebration of her sudden wealth—then tucked it into the folds of her gown and together we made our way back to the main market.

Ahead, the Covent Garden St. Paul's Church rose above the stall and tent rooftops, my landmark in this sea of busy, noisy industry. Beyond it was Bedford Street and Lord Evan. With one last wave at Long Sal, I skirted a stack of baskets full of hazelnuts and headed for the church.

St. Paul's portico was littered with empty baskets and discarded crates, guarded by two threadbare little girls and an indignant brown terrier. The little girls each held up a hand as I approached but had no hope in their eyes. Long Sal's resignation still rang in my ears: *We all stay where God puts us.* I dug my hand into my pocket, found two farthings, and dropped one into each palm as I passed, then took the steps down to the yard behind the church. A sudden oasis of quiet amid the chaos. I nodded to an old man who sat upon a bench and crossed the cobbles to the narrow laneway that led to Bedford Street.

The lane smelled of cooked onions and cat piss. Ahead, a couple leaned up against the laneway wall, locked in what looked to be far more than an embrace. Should I retreat? I looked back at the church, but this was the quickest way through and I did not fancy trying to fight my way back across the market. I tucked in my chin and strode past the entangled pair, catching a shocking glimpse of grinding hips, pale thighs, and thrusting buttocks. I quickened my stride, trying to outpace the sound of skin slapping skin and gasping rhythmic cries.

I emerged onto Bedford Street, breathless, my skin hot with an odd shame. Good God, was that the Act? My friend Charlotte, Countess Davenport, had on my request described the mechanics of it, but I had never thought it to be so naked, so vigorous, so . . . loud. Part of me wanted to look back. No, such an urge offended all decency.

Eyes forward, I forged on, legs trembling, across Henrietta Street and toward Dorothy's corner, the old flower seller crouched as usual upon the pavement.

Across the road, at the junction of Maiden Lane, a figure rose from a doorway, holding a flagon. I recognized the broad shoulders and laconic tilt of the head, and my heart quickened in an entirely new way.

Evan.

12

took a steadying breath and raised my hand. He lifted his in quick response and I crossed the road to join him.

"How is my sister?" he asked in greeting, his anxiety plain upon his face. He had still not shaved—the stubble thicker than when I had last seen him—and had donned an old, patched greatcoat and a frayed hat. Even with such a shabby appearance, the very fact of his presence intensified the disquiet still surging through me.

"She has rallied a little," I said, forcing myself to focus. "Dr. McLeod is taking good care of her, as is Miss Grant."

"We must find them a safe haven," he said.

"I have written to Lady Davenport," I said, and told him my plan to take them to Charlotte's estate. "It is, I think, the best way forward for the moment, and she is the model of discretion."

"Thank you for taking so much care of Hester and hiding her from our brother. I cannot tell you . . ." He ducked his head, the relief, I think, overcoming him for a moment. When he looked up, he was smiling again. "Well, I can tell you it is greatly appreciated." He took in my disguise. "So, I take it you are not Mr. Anderson this time."

I had been Mr. Anderson on one of our other adventures, but

he had been a man of means, unlike my current pretense. "Jessup, at your service," I said, bowing. "And you?"

"I like to stay with the classics—Lennox."

I touched the side-whiskers I had glued upon my face. Still intact. We were a suitably scruffy pair for the task ahead.

He cocked his head. "You seem a little perturbed."

"Just the excitement of it." I was not about to explain what I had just seen, or the unseemly agitation it had prompted. "What is the plan?"

"We are to be foxed fellows tonight, sharing a quart," he said, giving the cheap earthenware flagon a shake. "I hope you do not mind sharing?"

"Not at all," I said, although the only shared vessel I ever drank from was the Holy Communion chalice. An experience that, for me, no longer held any intimacy with community or God. This sharing, however, already felt intimate: to be drinking from the same vessel, my lips touching the place where his had been. My lips pressed upon his: I blinked at the sudden memory of our kiss outside the asylum after we had rescued his sister.

"Here." He offered the flagon.

I grasped the handle. Our fingertips touched, the connection jolting through me as if electrified. He must have experienced the same, for he snatched back his hand with a low, surprised laugh that made me want to take a step closer.

Dear God. Was this going to happen every time we touched?

He clenched the offending hand as if trying to stop the sensation. We both stood, motionless, still caught in that heart-stopping moment.

Finally he drew in a breath and said softly, "I would very much like to kiss you now."

I swayed closer, my eyes upon his lips. But no. I pulled back.

"Probably not the best time for Mr. Jessup and Mr. Lennox to be kissing," I said. "In the street."

"No." Our eyes met in regret, the kiss still within them.

He cleared his throat. "My thought is to blend in with the gin shop across the road." He lifted his chin in the direction of Maiden Lane. The shop indicated was packed with patrons, some of whom staggered in a drunken dance or lolled upon the pavement drinking from flagons like the one I held. A few men and women were even locked in louche embraces.

"We will be just another couple of loose fish out to get foxed," he added.

"I have never tried gin," I said, and lifted the heavy flagon, glad to have something to focus on other than his lips and the strong traceable line of his stubbled jaw. "I have heard it is quite rough."

"They call it blue ruin for a reason," Evan said. "But do not worry. I filled that with lemonade. We need all our faculties and focus."

Indeed.

He gestured to the recessed doorway of a bookseller, dried brown leaves banked up against the entrance and the display windows on either side shuttered. "Our lookout for the night."

I sat down on the tiled entrance—the blue and terra-cotta design cracked and worn by decades of foot traffic—and leaned my back against the locked door. Evan sat beside me, our long legs crooked at the same angle.

So close together.

Part of me wanted to press my thigh against his and feel the warmth and solid muscle of his body. A question—an invitation, in truth—I never thought I would ask a man. Yet in my mind I saw the stark image of that couple against the wall. So naked, so primal. Could I ever expose myself in such a way? This forty-two-year-old body with its ungainly limbs, and flesh no longer plump and firm with youth. What if it was too old, too ungainly? What if it was too late? I slid my leg down, stretching it out straight. No, I could not ask the question. Not yet, anyway. Besides, we were not Gus and Evan, but two fellows sharing a quart of gin.

We had a good view of number 2 Bedford Street. It was at the start of the narrower end of the street, which a town carriage could not fit through; anyone arriving would either do so on foot or be dropped at the corner of Maiden Lane, or Chandos Street at the other end.

I lifted the flagon and took a swig of lemonade. Surprisingly good: tart and sweet at the same time.

"Has anyone entered the house yet?" I asked, passing the flagon to Evan.

"Not so far." He took a mouthful, wincing at the sour aftertaste.

And so began our watch.

As time and people passed by, we talked. I spoke about our mother's death when Julia and I were thirteen, my fear about my sister's illness—so like our mother's—and my intention, my hope, to take her on a grand tour when the Continent was no longer locked down by war. He told me how he had worked his way back to England on cargo ships and the wonders he had seen: gigantic whales jumping from the sea, squid as big as men, and majestic sea turtles. And also, a little bit about his time in the prison colony in New South Wales assisting the prison surgeon: a Dr. William McLeod.

Now, there was a familiar name.

"Is he, by chance, any relation to our own Dr. Robert McLeod?" I asked.

Evan nodded. "His uncle. William McLeod gave me a letter to carry to his nephew in the event of my return to England—an introduction, if you like. I believe he wrote about a time I saved his life from an attack by a demented prisoner. That is why, I think, the young Dr. McLeod is helping us so discreetly."

"It sounds as if you have completed an entire medical apprenticeship under the instruction of the elder McLeod."

An unusual accomplishment for the son of a marquess.

"No, far from it. As you can imagine, I have not had much experience with women's ailments." He gave a wry smile. "Your sister's illness, alas, is not within my knowledge, so I cannot offer much in the way of advice." He looked down at the flagon in his hands, his thumb tracing the stamped letters of the maker, Cunningham and Co. "I would say my specialties are flogging wounds, stabbings, dislocations, strangulations, and broken bones. Not really a full medical education."

There was something in his eyes—an inward, endless quality—that spoke of unimaginable suffering. There would always be so much I could never truly understand. Even, I think, if he wished to tell me.

"Well, I am heartily glad of your stabbing specialty." I touched my shoulder where the stiletto knife had done its damage a few months earlier. "Without you, my wound would have been a great deal more dangerous."

He looked up at me again, the abyss gone from his eyes. At least for now. "Is it still healing? Do you have pain?"

"It is little more than a scar now, thank you, Dr. Belford," I said, and bumped his shoulder with mine, to prove the point.

He swayed theatrically under the soft blow, then said rather more seriously, "Still, you must take care of it. Stiletto wounds are narrow but notoriously deep." His mock-stern expression shifted into sudden focus beyond me. "Look. The door is open."

Number 2 Bedford Street had come alive.

The two windows on the ground floor of the club showed cracks of light between the curtains, and the barred outer door stood ajar, the lamp above it lit. I pulled out my watch, hidden on its chain under my shirt, and squinted at the face in the dim light. Half past eleven.

"I believe the members are arriving," Evan said.

Two men in evening breeches and jackets had entered Bedford Street at the far end, from Chandos Street: one compact, with a smooth, athletic gait, the other built more on the stocky side. As they passed by a residence, the light from the windows momentarily caught their faces. Or what should have been their faces; they wore old-style mummer's masks. The devil. And the king.

Of course, Dorothy had mentioned they wore masks.

"They are keen to keep their identities hidden," I said.

"Indeed, and wearing them on the street before they even go inside," Evan said. "Although that fellow is still putting his on."

I peered at a third man, hurrying to catch up to the other two, trying to untangle the ribbons of his mask. Small and wiry. He seemed familiar. As he passed the glow of the house light, that familiarity hardened into recognition.

"Good God, that is George Whitmore. He is an undersecretary at the Alien Office."

"You know him?"

"I have met him at routs and salons before, but we are not really acquainted. More importantly, do you know him?"

Evan shook his head. "He's a good ten years younger than me. He'd have been a child when I was sent to Botany Bay."

True, there could be no direct association there. Yet our meeting at the Berry sisters' salon and his arrival at the Exalted Brethren of Rack and Ruin felt somehow connected.

Perhaps it was coincidence.

Then again, we were seeking a man of high rank affiliated with the Magistrates' Court or Home Office, and here was one before us. But if he was somehow involved, surely he would have known our connection to Lord Evan when we met him at the Berrys' circle. I had certainly seen no evidence of that knowledge, although, admittedly, I had not been searching for it—my run-in with Mulholland had been after the circle. Still, if he had known of our connection, he must be highly skilled in deception. An entirely possible proposition: he was, after all, serving in the Alien Office, and deceit was their business.

"What about the other two, anything about them that you recognize?" I asked.

Evan watched the three men climb the steps up to the front door. "No. Although I would say that the other two are noblemen by the quality of their clothes and the way they walk."

"The way they walk?"

"Do you not see? They own the world, Gus."

Another echo of Long Sal's wisdom.

"They expect everyone and everything to shift around them," he continued. "They always get what they want—no thought to the cost to those around them. You have a little of it yourself." He glanced at me, softening the statement with a small smile. "I used to walk like that too—a long time ago—until the other prisoners reminded me I owned nothing. I was nothing."

Although I wanted to know what had happened to him—I wanted to know everything about him—I did not ask how he had been "reminded." Painfully, I suspected.

And I? As an earl's daughter, I did expect the world to bend my way, although of course on many occasions it did not because of my sex. Now that I thought about it, I certainly held an expectation that my wishes and wants held intrinsic importance. Yet here sat

Evan, living proof that it was all arbitrary. He had held such a belief, too, and lived that belief, until he had been forcibly reminded that it was built from hierarchies, traditions and laws that were designed to keep people in their place. A place in life that was believed to be God-given and therefore immutable: Long Sal had certainly believed that. And yet it was another pillar of society that my new-found apostasy could not help but question. If there was no God, then rank could not be God-given. It was not immutable.

Lud, if I was not careful, I would be joining a Thomas Paine society soon and risking life and limb for reform.

I looked back at the three men as they entered the club, the athletic man first, then the stout one, and finally Whitmore behind them. No doubt that order was also governed by status. England was, if anything, an island of rank. So who were the athletic devil and the mid-rank king?

It transpired that half past eleven was the arrival time for the club. More masked men arrived in evening clothes, with one group escorting five women. They were, it seemed, of Harris's higher order of demimonde, for they all wore clean gowns, prettily styled hair, and reasonable slippers. One even had the trappings of gentility—she wore a plainer, respectable gown with her hair arranged in a neat middling braided style and no rouge or lip color.

"She does not look like a Covent Garden girl," I said. Was this one of Long Sal's cits or genteel girls? "She looks as if she belongs in a drawing room."

"She is probably just dressed up to look genteel. There are men who like to pretend to rape respectable girls. A specialty."

"Really?" I shook my head; I could not fathom such a debased predilection.

All five women were clearly inebriated, for they were stumbling and lurching upon the arms of their masked escorts. One was also singing a rather bawdy shanty in a tuneless voice, which the others were trying, unsuccessfully, to hush.

They all climbed the steps, amid some missteps and laughter, and entered the building.

"The evening's entertainment," Evan murmured.

"I wonder if they know how they are about to earn their coin," I said, unease settling in the pit of my innards.

Evan passed me the flagon. "I know a few of the Covent Garden girls—"

I stiffened at this casual admission—I could not help it. He eyed my reaction, then gave a crooked smile: *You must remember, I am living in the criminal world.*

I sent my own crooked smile back: *I know.*

Even so, had he lain with any of them? The unbidden thought brought a stab of wild jealousy. Ridiculous. I had to remember he was a man, untethered by marital bonds or family, and, unlike a woman, he did not need to contend with the possibility of bearing an illegitimate child or being cast out of society. Besides, to be jealous of his past was to walk a road to madness.

"From what the girls have told me, every encounter is a gamble," he said. "Will they get paid? Will they get hurt? Will they get the pox? Will they get with child? And sometimes all for just a few pennies."

I looked back at the club door, now closed, and took a swig of lemonade in an attempt to wash the unease from my mouth. Five women had gone in and, if Dorothy was telling the truth, five were not guaranteed to come out. A gamble, indeed.

Although I no longer believed in the grace of God, I sent a prayer up into the heavens. Or perhaps it was more a plea to the criminal world of good and bad fortune: let all of these five women be lucky.

13

~~~~~

*S*omeone was shaking my shoulder, insistent but gentle. I opened my eyes. Still dark. My cheek was pressed against Evan's broad shoulder, every breath drawing in the comforting smell of woolen cloth, soap, and warm male skin. I had, it appeared, fallen asleep and used him as a pillow.

"Sorry," I muttered, and sat up, my neck tight from the crooked position. I dug my cold fingertips into the stiff muscle and yawned, still somewhat bleary. "You should have woken me."

"Nothing has happened for the past few hours, so I figured you may as well sleep." He smiled. "I can report you do not snore."

I squinted at him. "I am glad to know it."

"But look." He nodded toward the club. "The meeting is over."

Men were exiting the building, still wearing their masks and clearly the worse for wear. Some of them staggered down the front steps or clung to the railing as they descended; others had cravats untied or waistcoats undone. They were eerily silent, none of the songs or laughter of their entrance, not even any conversation among them. I counted twenty-two members departing, ten making their way to Maiden Lane and twelve to Chandos. Our devil and king left together, while Mr. Whitmore hurried along Maiden Lane by himself.

After them, three women came down the steps. They moved

wearily, but from this distance, they did not seem injured. Two had their arms around each other, and the other walked alone, all of them heading up Maiden Lane toward the Garden.

"Where are the others?" I asked. All sleep bleariness had disappeared, chased away by the realization that two women had not departed.

"Perhaps we missed them coming out. Or maybe they went out the back way," Evan said.

"I did not see them come out." We watched the front door for another minute, but no one else emerged. "I think it is time to take a look inside the club," I said. And not only for the sake of our own investigation.

Evan gave a nod—my own unease reflected in his face—and pushed himself upright, making a low sound of discomfort as he stretched the cold-induced kinks from his long body. I followed suit, my own stretch propelling me into a limp-hop on cramped legs across the veranda tiles. Very elegant.

Evan picked up the flagon from the ground, swinging it to test the weight. "Not ideal, but it might stop someone in their tracks."

Another household item as weapon. Not that I scorned the idea. Lately I'd used a Wedgwood vase, a full chamber pot, and a large painting to good effect. Although the last had ultimately not protected me from the stab of a stiletto blade.

"A one-shot pot," I quipped.

His smile gleamed in the dim light. "I recall that is your specialty."

"I prefer Wedgwood," I said.

Evan gave a small bow. "Only the best." He lifted the flagon. "Mind you, this is a bit tougher than fine porcelain, with the added benefit that anyone seeing us carrying it will probably dismiss us as drunkards."

And so Mr. Lennox and Mr. Jessup, arm in arm and waving a gin flagon, lurched drunkenly across Maiden Lane toward the stretch of terraces that housed the Exalted Brethren of Rack and Ruin. From the corner of my eye, I saw Dorothy watching with some interest. I wondered what she made of us.

By the time we reached number 2, the front door was closed, although there was still some light within.

"The old flower seller said there was a yard behind these terraces," I said. "Perhaps we can get in through there."

We weaved along the pavement, finding a roughly cobbled laneway between the first set of terraced houses and the second. With a nod to Evan and all pretense of drunkenness gone, I led the way along the rough stones, keeping close to the brick wall of the house that bordered the lane. We both ducked beneath a barred window—it was dark and curtained, but better to be safe—and continued to creep alongside the wall to the corner of the house and the mouth of the rear yard.

I stopped just as Evan caught my arm: we had heard the same sounds ahead. Female voices, the slosh of water, and the hollow clank of iron.

I glanced at Evan: *Our Covent Garden girls?*

He lifted a shoulder: *Maybe.* Then he jerked his chin: *Take a look.*

I slid my back along the cold bricks and carefully peered around the edge of the wall.

Not our two missing women but two young maids, one drawing water from a central well in an iron bucket, the other scraping a brush while fervently explaining something to her companion about beans—dried haricots, from the little I caught. It seemed rather early for such morning preparations. Then again, dawn was only an hour or so away and some households rose with the light. Were they from the club or one of the other houses?

I drew back and leaned close to Evan's ear.

"Two maids," I breathed.

He lifted his hand, palm out: *Wait, see if they go inside.*

A reasonable plan since we could not bluff our way into a private club in our current workmen's clothes.

We both settled back against the wall. The length of our arms touched, hands finding each other upon the rough bricks, our morning-chilled fingers entwining into a warm embrace. Perhaps it was not too late, after all. To be seen by this man in all my naked truth. And to see him. I smiled and, in the darkness, sensed the answering upcurl of his mouth.

It was not long before the voices and the clanking shifted, the sounds receding, then muffled, then no longer audible at all.

"Gone?" Evan murmured.

We released hands with a mutual press of our fingers: neither of us wished to let go.

I peered around the corner again.

"It is clear," I whispered.

I trod as silently as possible into the rear yard, Evan close behind. The cobbled area was shared by the four houses: each had three steps up to a back door that led into a kitchen or scullery, and a set of steps downward, enclosed by a railing and gate, that presumably led to the basement entrance.

We made our way past the closed doorways of numbers 4 and 3, shut fast against the chilly morning with no light or signs of life yet within. It was the same for the club: kitchen door closed, no light, no signs of movement. The one difference was that its basement gate had been left half-open.

The maids must have gone into the first house, for its kitchen door stood ajar, a glow from candles and a lit hearth showing the edge of a table and the glint of pans.

Keeping a wary eye upon that door, we climbed the club's back steps. I peered into the small side window, poised to run if someone was within the gloom. No one inside, but I made out the shapes of an unlit hearth, bare shelves, and unused hooks for hanging pots and pans. More or less empty, although a number of sacks were propped against the far wall, packed full of something that could not be recognized in the dim light. A lumpy something. What would merit so many sacks?

"It is clear," I whispered.

I drew back to let Evan peer in, a slight huff telling me that he, too, was puzzled by the unused kitchen. Would not a club serve food?

I tried the door handle, expecting it to be locked.

It turned, the door opening a small way under my tentative weight. I looked at Evan. He raised his brows.

Indeed.

Onward, then.

I pushed the door open and we stepped into the dark, deserted kitchen of the Exalted Brethren of Rack and Ruin.

I crossed the empty floor to the line of hessian sacks against the wall, listening for any kind of sound in the house. All was quiet, although I could not ignore the feeling that someone else was still inside the building, that preternatural awareness of another living presence.

Evan carefully closed the back door and just as silently crossed the room to join me at the line of sacks. Suddenly nervous, I glanced at him: *Ready?* On his nod, I tentatively pulled open the first sack in the line, ready to snatch back my hand. We both leaned in.

A gleam of green glass.

Empty wine bottles.

I breathed out, feeling a little absurd. What had I expected: body parts? I flipped the top of the sack back into place. As it happened, a little too forcefully: the slight tug of hessian dislodged the top bottle. The clink of glass against glass rang out in the silence. We both froze, listening.

No footsteps. No voices. No movement.

Even so, I whispered, "I do not think we are alone."

Evan nodded and lifted the flagon. "We should proceed with caution."

And with a blunt weapon, I thought but did not voice.

He led the way to the kitchen door—with no actual door attached—and peered around the jamb. Over his shoulder, I could see the wall of a hallway and the gold glint of a picture frame, the painting within too dark to make out in the gloom.

"No one," Evan whispered, then crept out into the hall.

I followed, immediately seeing the glow of candlelight emanating from the two front rooms. Close to the painting now, I could make out its subject: a depiction of a man and woman in congress, the woman clearly not consenting to such activity. It seemed tonight I was to be confronted by the Act from all angles. I averted my eyes and quickened my pace behind Evan, who was making his way silently toward the front rooms.

We passed a doorway—closed—and came to the staircase, its steps leading both down to the basement and service rooms and up to what would have been the living areas, if this were just a normal house.

Evan paused at the basement steps for a moment and looked back, eyebrow raised: *Want to go down or keep going?*

I pointed ahead: the front rooms would have been where the men had gathered.

We passed the stairs and made our way to the front of the house and the two doorways opposite each other. We stopped short of them; the doors stood open. Evan pointed to the left one and I nodded—I would check it. He crossed over to the right side of the wall, flagon raised. We both edged closer to our doorways. I tilted my head to peer around the jamb, rapidly scanned inside the room, then drew back.

Bookshelves, card tables, chairs, more bottles. But otherwise, empty. It looked like any other card gambling room. Across the hallway, Evan's shoulders had relaxed a little, the flagon once more at his side. His room must be empty too.

He joined me on my side of the hallway.

"It's just like a normal club," he whispered. "Armchairs, sofas. It's a mess, but that is typical after a night's revelries."

I nodded. Not the scenes of sexual debauchery I had dreaded. Perhaps they were upstairs, in the bedrooms. "I'm going to take a closer look in here, then maybe we should go upstairs."

"I'll take the other."

We parted ways.

I entered the card room. It was a mess too—bottles left on the tables or strewn across the carpeted floor, used wineglasses and whiskey tumblers, the ends of cigarillos, playing cards left in disarray, and the remains of a roasted haunch on a sideboard. So food was served after all, most likely brought in from one of the Covent Garden inns. I screwed up my nose: the air stank of cheap perfume, cooked beef, piss, and vomit. A stomach-churning mix. I spotted two chamber pots in the corner, filled to the brim. That explained the piss and vomit. The perfume had no doubt belonged to one of the women. I weaved around the eight tables, not sure what I was looking for—evidence of malfeasance, perhaps—but saw only the remains of a night of hard gambling. I had experienced it often enough myself at routs and assemblies, although not so robustly foul.

I turned my attention to the bookshelves. Annual bindings of the *Gentleman's Magazine*, a well-used collection of the de Sade novels, and a great number of illustrated books and folios. I pulled one of the books from the shelf and opened it, only to be confronted by a drawing of a man behind a donkey, mid-congress. A little too meticulously drawn. Good God. I snapped it shut and pushed it back into its place on the shelf.

"Gus." I turned around at the hiss of my name. Evan stood at the doorway, gesturing urgently for me to follow.

Had he found something?

14

I followed Evan into the room opposite.

It was a salon, if you could call it that, for its red velvet uphol-stered armchairs and sofas had been arranged to view two chaise longues rather than in the usual conversation groups. For a moment I could not conceive why the chairs and sofas would be arranged in such a way. And then I could. I clamped down upon the lurid imagining.

Like the card room, it had been left in a foul state—bottles and glasses and a woman's stocking wet upon the floor—but at least it did not stink as much as the card room.

Evan had picked up one of the candles and waved me over to a carved lectern that stood facing a wall tapestry that depicted Bacchus and his acolytes in grape-laden revelry. A large leather-bound ledger sat open upon the wooden stand.

"It is the wager book," he whispered. He held up the candle for me to read.

The entries were in different hands, each page divided into five columns: *Date. Names. Wager & Stake. Result. Winner.*

I ran my finger down the names, but they were all in code: the names of Greek gods. Rather grandiloquent. The wagers and the results, however, were in plain English.

I read the last entry.

Date	Names	Wager & Stake	Result	Winner
Oct 1812	Zeus vs Erebus	Miss Catherine Hollis	2,10	Erebus
				2,17 for £2000

I looked up at Evan, my neck prickling oddly, as if I were in danger. "Who is Miss Catherine Hollis? What does it mean?"

Was she one of the women who had not emerged?

Evan shook his head. "I do not know."

I turned the pages back in large chunks, watching the dates shift backward: 1810, 1807, 1805. The word *cat* caught my attention. I stopped turning.

Wager & Stake: Find a man to eat a cat alive. £5,000.

Good God, that horrid story was true? Nausea rose through me at the thought. I traced my finger across the page to the names: Kratos and Dionysus. One of those names must be Lord Milroy, if the rumor was accurate. So he was a member, but was he Kratos or Dionysus? I hurriedly turned the page away from the sickening wager.

1802, 1798, 1792.

"I think we should search the house for the missing women," Evan whispered.

"Evan, look! This goes back more than twenty years." I pointed to the year of his duel.

He looked over my shoulder at the faded scrawl. "What does it say? Is there anything odd?"

I gave a dry laugh. "Odd? It is all odd. And heinous."

He reached down, pointing to an entry. "Look at that name, in May, the month before the duel."

I leaned closer, making out the elaborate hand: Miss Sally Lawrence.

Lawrence? I knew that name. I gasped, the sudden recognition halting my breath. "It is the same name as the doctor who attended the duel."

"Indeed it is," Evan said, frowning.

I read the rest of the entry. It, too, had a wager, stake, and result: 2,35, £1000, 2,30. The winner was Chronos.

"Could it be a coincidence?" I asked.

"It could be. This lady might not even be connected to the doctor. Lawrence is a common enough name," Evan said. "Even so, I think it is worth following up."

"I think so too." I eyed the page. It was near the start of the book. Before I could change my mind, I grabbed the top of the page and wrenched it out. A clean rip at the stitching.

Evan stared at me. "What are you doing?"

"Evidence." I folded it and shoved it into my jacket pocket. "It will not show. Look."

I turned the bulk of the book pages back to the current date. We both bent to study the spine. "See, you cannot even tell."

At the corner of my eye, I saw something move at the door.

"Oi," a thick voice called. "What are you doin' 'ere?"

Evan and I whirled around.

With heart hammering, I stared at the old man, who stood inside the doorway watching us with a frown. He folded his arms across his leather apron, a limp hessian sack dangling from one hand.

"You shouldn't be in 'ere." His diction was oddly drawn out, his voice without intonation. "Where's Reed and Gibbon?"

"Sick," Evan said promptly and lifted the flagon to suggest

exactly what kind of sickness they suffered. It seemed we had been mistaken for someone who was expected, and Evan—quick as ever—was already improvising. I, on the other hand, was still hunched in alarm. I straightened, trying to conjure a manly stance.

The old man eyed Evan for a moment—as if registering his answer—then said, "Didna they tell you to go straight down, through basement? House ain't for the likes of you." He was obviously some kind of caretaker. His gaze fell upon the flagon, raised in Evan's hand. "Any left?"

Evan shook his head and lowered the flagon with a shrug of apology. "They didn't tell us about the basement," he said.

The old caretaker pointed to his ear. "Can't hear you, man. Deaf as a post. It don't matter. Just go outside and back down basement steps. The other set is inside, to right." He lifted the hessian bag. "You'll find sacks waitin'." He frowned, squinting at the crack in the heavy curtains. "Best be quick about it. Not much time."

Evan turned slightly toward me. "He thinks we are dustmen," he murmured.

It stood to reason: the place was a mess and we were dressed raggedly enough to be the men who collected and scavenged the waste from London houses.

"We should do what he says," he added. "We can make our way up through the house from the basement."

Still set upon searching the house. Yet, if this man was expecting dustmen, then the real scavengers would turn up before long and our ruse would be uncovered. Perhaps we should take the opportunity to make our escape. A tempting thought, but could we in all conscience leave without making sure the two missing women had left the house too?

"Come on, then," the old man said, gesturing for us to follow.

He silently led the way back along the dark hallway, his pace as measured as his words. We passed the interior staircase that led down to the basement, but that was patently not for the use of dustmen like us. Back in the kitchen, he opened the door and stood aside as we descended the steps into the yard, his mind patently on other matters. I looked over my shoulder as we made our way to the basement gate, but he had already shut the door behind us. Not a man for society.

Beyond, the kitchen door of the first house was also shut. The maids had, it seemed, moved on to other tasks inside.

"Now we know why this was left unlocked," Evan said, pushing the iron gate fully back upon its hinges with a rusty squawk.

"Wait." I patted my pocket. "We have what we came for. Perhaps we should leave before the real dustmen come."

Evan stood with his hand on the railing, his body still turned to the steps. "If that is what you wish," he finally said.

Clearly it was not what he wished.

"Are you convinced the women are still inside?"

"Not convinced," he said, "but if they are, they may need medical attention."

He was more of a doctor than he allowed. I could not deny that compassion within him—it was an essential part of the man I loved. Besides, with some caution, we should be able to search the house in fifteen minutes or so. Hopefully enough time to get out before trouble arrived. "Then if they are in there, let us find them."

Brave words, but in truth I was feeling far from brave as I followed him down the rough stone steps to the small basement yard. I had been pursued through a basement and house before, and that escape had not gone entirely as planned. I had the knife scar and bad dreams to prove it.

A candle had been left in the small window next to the basement door. Its light showed a bucket against the wall with a mop inside, and a pile of sacks with a heavy brick on top to weigh them down.

Evan opened the door.

I peered over his shoulder. To all intents and purposes, the basement looked like every other basement I had ventured into—a corridor with service rooms on either side—yet something was not quite right. While I did not ascribe to the gothic authors' conjuring of all things ghostly in dark, deserted places, I shivered as I followed Evan inside. Maybe it was just the cold air. The rooms usually set aside for the housekeeper and butler were empty, without hearth fires to temper the underground chill, and no candle sconces lit the way along the corridor.

Evan passed me the flagon and picked up the candle in its tin holder, holding it up. Ahead, another staircase alongside the right wall led down to a deeper level, a faint glow from below picking out the wooden steps. Probably a cellar for wine and cool storage.

"The caretaker told us to go down the other set of steps. I think he meant these," Evan said, crossing the stone floor to the staircase.

I studied the descent in the dim light: worn treads, stone walls, and a small landing that turned the stairs and kept the ultimate destination from sight. An odd, sweet smell too. My sense of unease hardened into trepidation.

"What would dustmen be cleaning up down there? It is a cellar."

"It could be a faro house. A place like this would have a game set up."

A reasonable supposition: this place was a gambling club, and since it was illegal to keep a faro bank, hiding it in a cellar would be more than possible. Yet my clenched innards were telling me to walk away from those stairs. Too closed in, only one way out.

"I vaguely remember being down here," Evan said.

"You were here? You remember it?" I tried to contain my anticipation. If he could recollect something, it might help us in our search for the truth about the duel, but I did not want my excitement to overwhelm any gossamer thread of memory.

He squinted in the effort to recall. "Not really. It is just a sense that I have been here before." He shook his head. "No, too long ago, and no doubt I was in my cups at the time. Or I might even have been chasing the dragon." He saw the question on my face. "Opium."

Ah. Something I had never tried, although Charlotte smoked it on occasion. She had reported that it brought a feeling of great sensuous delight, although it could also plunge one into rather disturbing hallucinations.

"I say we do a quick search of every floor starting down here," he said. "We should be able to keep out of the caretaker's way."

I put aside my disappointment at the stalled memory and, since that had been my own search plan, nodded my agreement.

We started down the steps, the treads creaking loudly under our feet. Evan glanced back at me with a resigned grimace; not much we could do about old wood. If anyone was still down there, they would definitely know we were on our way.

15

So, it is not a faro bank," Evan said dryly.

We both stood on the bottom step of the staircase, the large room before us an assault upon the soul. A number of silver candelabra supplied enough light to see the lurid wall frescoes that depicted life-sized people and animals in acts that I had not considered possible. Strange contraptions made of wood and metal and leather stood at various intervals around the room. At first, I could not quite make sense of them, but that primal part of me that recognized threat certainly understood. I grasped the banister for support, my sight too full of straps, buckles, spikes, and a leather helmet that enclosed the whole head.

"Good God," I managed. How would someone breathe in it?

One machine I recognized from my history studies—a medieval-type rack—and another from the abolitionist pamphlets—a flogging frame.

"Go upstairs, Gus. Wait for me in the basement," Evan said, his eyes fixed upon the flogging frame. There was a new hollowness—a bleakness—to his voice that I had never heard before. Was he remembering the men he had doctored, or had he been upon such a frame himself? A ghastly thought. "Go upstairs, Gus," he repeated. "Please. You should not be tainted by this devilry."

I placed my hand on his shoulder, his broad muscles tense

under my fingers. "I am not a child, Evan. I can look after myself. You are not the protector of my soul."

He looked back at me, his expression holding a strange kind of fierceness. "But I am, if you will let me. I am, as you are of mine."

I stared at him, a sudden ache in my throat. He was right; we were, indeed, the guardians of each other's souls.

"Then we go together," I said, meeting his fierceness. Our eyes locked in that promise. Or perhaps it was a vow.

He gave a nod. "Together."

We took the last step into the chamber, our hands clasped.

I had, to some degree, become accustomed to the sight of the obscene furniture and frescoes and could focus beyond them on the room at large. The roof was higher than usual in a cellar, and an antechamber, separated by a half-drawn red velvet curtain, was visible to our right. To our left, a side table had been set against the wall with three matching silver candlesticks upon it, the wax candles burned to nubs. An ornately painted blue wardrobe stood against the wall, and a little farther along, a rather handsome longcase clock.

"There is blood on those," Evan said, holding up a candle to illuminate a bunch of birch rods upright in a stand next to the flogging frame. He studied the floor around the contraption. "Here too. Probably not a flogging for pleasure," he added grimly.

Flogging of any sort was not my idea of pleasure, but then, I had heard a great number of men and women enjoyed the practice. So much so that it was called "the English perversion" on the Continent.

I released his hand and walked over to the wardrobe. It was large and in the Italian style, the wood painted bright blue with flowers and vines decorating the two doors and the top edge. Very pretty, if you liked that sort of thing. I opened the doors. One half was shelves—stacked with cloths—the other a wider space that held no shelves, but tall birch rods propped in the corner.

"I am glad to report they are not going to run out of birch," I said. Dark humor for a dark place.

Evan, who was studying the rack contraption, gave a grim huff of laughter.

I closed the doors and turned my attention to the clock. The mahogany case was inlaid with gold, and its maker's name— J. Barwise of London—was written upon the face. A very good maker and a rather incongruous addition to such a chamber. "It would seem one needs to know the time when one is being flogged," I said. This time I got no answering laugh. I turned to see if he had heard me.

He stood inside the antechamber doorway, the curtain drawn all the way back to reveal little more than a storage space.

Seeing me turn, he said in a low, tight voice, "Do not come here."

Surely he knew I was not going to obey. I crossed the room. "What is it?"

He sighed and motioned inside the antechamber. I leaned in to see two large, full sacks heaped upon the floor—both tied at the top with rope, one with an ominous dark patch staining the hessian.

"I hope they are full of bottles too," I said, without hope.

He looked at me, mouth pressed into resignation. "You are going to do this with me, come what may, aren't you?"

"Yes."

"Hold the candle, then. I'll open the sacks," he said.

Since I did not wish to be the one to open them, that seemed like a good plan.

We crouched on either side of the closest sack. I placed the flagon on the stone floor and Evan passed me the candle, or what was left of it, since it was almost burned out. Still, it had enough wick to show us whether a woman lay inside. There was no mistaking the metallic smell of blood or the glossy smear of it across the gray slate. Evan dug his finger into the clumsily tied rope and released the knot. Gently, he pulled down the hessian.

Her hair was still in its braided bun, her pale face unmarked but for a split lip. A bare shoulder showed the sweep of collarbone beneath pearly skin, then the sudden red pulp of flogged flesh. Someone had closed her eyes, or perhaps she had died with them shut. Her gown and reticule had been stuffed into the bag beside her body, her own blood staining the little blue knitted purse.

Evan leaned closer and pressed his fingertips to her poor bruised throat. I loved him for his hope, but we both knew what he would find.

He sighed. "Yes, she is dead." He gently pulled out the reticule and passed it to me. "Maybe it will have some clue to where she belonged."

I stared down at the pretty purse. "They killed her." I blinked, my sight blearing with tears: pity and horror, but mostly fury. I rubbed them away with the back of my hand. "They killed her for pleasure."

"And most likely a wager," Evan said. "I would hazard this is Catherine Hollis from the wager book."

I drew in a sharp breath. "I think I know what the numbers meant beside her name." My scalp crept at the heinous realization. "It is time. The numbers are time." I looked across the room at the handsome longcase clock. "That is why they have a clock in here."

Evan frowned; then his face, too, twisted into fury. "You mean they wagered on how long it would take her to die? Jesus Holy

Christ." He stared at the floor for a moment, fists clenched. His desire to punch something was palpable.

Then it dawned on me. I touched the paper in my pocket. "Sally Lawrence had the same time wager against her name. They killed her too."

"And you think there is a link between Sally Lawrence and the doctor at the duel?" Evan said.

"I do. If she died in the same manner as this poor girl, then perhaps that is a motive." I looked at the second sack. "How many girls have died down here?" I whispered.

He followed my gaze. "At least one more." He reached across and untied the rope, pulling the hessian down.

The other missing woman. A grubby silk stocking was still tied around her throat, and the pallor of her skin showed a stark flush of tiny red dots across her cheeks. She looked to be still clothed in her chemise. I shuddered, remembering the other silk stocking in the wager book room upstairs. Had this strangulation been some kind of spectacle?

Evan sighed and pressed his fingertips on her throat above the ligature.

I pushed the knitted purse into my pocket—not quite up to opening it yet—then sat back on my heels. "Do you think—"

"Wait." Evan frowned and slid searching fingers up under her jawline. "Gus . . . I think she is still alive."

"What?" I stared at the woman's slack face as Evan held his hand under her nose. Did I just see the flicker of a swollen red eyelid?

"Yes, she breathes." He snatched back his hand and pulled the hessian down, past her chest. "Help me get her out of the sack."

He gathered her up under her arms and lifted as I dragged the sack down her body, disentangling her bare feet from its folds. Her skin was so cold to the touch.

"Chafe her hands and her feet while I get this stocking off. We must get her blood moving."

I grabbed her freezing hands and rubbed them between my own, then switched to her bony feet. Evan had taken a small knife from his boot and was sawing through the silk ligature.

"There," he said triumphantly as it fell from her throat, revealing the hideous red mark of strangulation. "They must not have checked she was dead. Thank God."

He started to feel around her head, fixed upon his work. "She does not have any lumps or swelling."

Her eyelids flickered again. "I think she is coming to her senses," I said.

A soft moan. And then her eyes opened wide, terror in their bloodshot depths. She thrashed weakly against Evan's hold.

"No, stop!" I said. "You are safe. We are friends. Friends!" I caught her hands again, holding them. "They are all gone. You are safe now."

She eyed me, still terrified. "Out." She swallowed, a grimace of pain accompanying it. "Get out." She struggled to sit up, managing it with Evan's help.

"Yes, we will get you out," I promised. "My friend here is a physician. He will help you."

She looked back at Evan. He smiled: the reassuring doctor. It seemed to have some effect, for she took a deeper, shuddering breath.

"Can you tell me your name?" he asked.

"Jenny." Her voice was so hoarse, the utterance painfully found.

"Do you know where you are? Can you tell me what street we are on?"

"Bedford Street."

"Good. Can you swallow, Jenny?"

She did so, then nodded. "Hurts."

He nodded sympathetically. "It will. Do you have a bad ache in your head? So bad it feels as if your skull will split?"

"No." She lifted her hand, spreading forefinger and thumb.

"A small ache?" I asked.

She gave a tiny nod, wincing at the movement.

Evan smiled. "That's very good. Are you dizzy? Does the room spin?"

Jenny looked over at the other sack and gasped, pushing her feet weakly into the floor to shift away. "Cathy?"

"You know her? Is she Catherine Hollis?" I asked.

Jenny gave another pained nod.

So we were right. "They killed her," I said softly. "Do you know who any of them were?"

She shook her head and rasped, "Masks."

"Do you think you can stand?" Evan asked. "We do need to get out of here."

She nodded and slowly drew her legs underneath herself, levering her body up onto all fours. I stood and offered my hands. She gave a slight shake of her head and, drawing in a deep breath of effort, clambered to her feet, pressing her hands on the wall for support.

We all heard the noise above at the same time. Footsteps and voices.

"They've left 'em down below again," a man's voice called. "We'll have to haul them up the steps."

Good God, the real dustmen.

16

*E*van was already moving. He pulled the hessian back up over Miss Hollis's head.

"We'll have to hide." He grabbed the empty hessian bag and the flagon and rose from his crouch.

Jenny stood frozen against the wall. "Who?" she rasped.

"Dustmen," I whispered. "To pick up the . . . bodies."

That galvanized her into action. She took my offered support, leaning heavily upon my arm. I blew out the last of the candle and we followed Evan into the main chamber.

"We could confront them," I whispered to him. "We should confront them!"

"No, they might be armed"—he paused to twitch the curtain closed—"or there could be more than two of them. We need to know what they are doing with the girls if it is to be stopped."

I looked at Jenny's bruised throat and dazed eyes. Yes. It had to be stopped.

There was only one place to hide. We crossed the room just as a creak sounded above. Feet upon the old wooden steps.

Evan pulled open the wardrobe doors. I shoved the spent candlestick onto an adjacent shelf, then crammed myself into the other compartment, shuffling to one side as Evan firmly guided Jenny into the cramped space. He deposited the flagon and pressed himself in beside me. It was so tight I shuffled straight into the birch rods, gasping as a sharp tip dug into my hip.

"I'll go to the back," Evan whispered, and with some difficulty maneuvered himself behind me, taking the brunt of the stored rods. The smell from Jenny beside me was almost overpowering: fear and sweat and the pungent odor of old urine. I braced her arm to keep her upright, but my touch made her jump and gasp. Underneath my grip her whole body trembled. Dear God, we would be lost if she could not stay still and quiet.

I felt Evan's hands rest on either side of my waist, and then I was drawn back against his solid chest, our legs positioned in an entirely improper manner. But we had enough room now to close the door. I grabbed the wooden frame, dug my nails into the wood, and pulled the door almost shut, leaving barely a half-inch gap. The sliver afforded me a view of the antechamber but little else. I found a better grip on the wood—the last thing we needed was the door to move or swing open. My heart thudded, hard and fast. Surely Evan could feel it pounding, too, for his body cocooned mine. I certainly felt his warm breath against my ear.

"Can you hold it?" he whispered.

I turned my head slightly and nodded, my cheek brushing against his in confirmation. The unbidden caress was rather hairy— I had forgotten my false whiskers. The surprise of it brought an unseemly rise of mirth, even in the gravity of the situation. I felt his own quick smile against my cheek; then his embrace tightened at the sound of approaching footsteps. All amusement within me vanished.

I peered through the gap.

Two men walked into view. The first was shorter than his companion and wore a new black John Bull hat, its smartness in sharp contrast to his shabby coat and dirty breeches. The second man wore a jaunty blue neckerchief and walked with one shoulder hitched higher than the other.

"This place gives me the collywobbles," Blue Neckerchief said. "I feel like someone is watching us." He turned, surveying the room, his gaze passing over the wardrobe.

I held my breath, feeling Evan tense behind me. What if Blue Neckerchief noticed the gap?

"For chrissakes, stop whining," John Bull said. "You're givin' me the collywobbles." He pushed back his hat. "They always put 'em in there." He pointed to the antechamber. "Out of the way, like."

Through the gap, I watched them walk to the curtain and pull it back.

"There's only one. I thought he said there was goin' to be two this time," Blue Neckerchief said.

John Bull turned and scanned the room again, frowning. "There ain't another."

Beside me, Jenny shifted in alarm, her breath quickening. I leaned against her slightly, willing her to stay still.

Finally, John Bull shrugged. "Never been two before. Deaf fool must have got it wrong."

"At least they already bagged it," Blue Neckerchief said. "Coulda tied the top proper, though."

"You get the head, Gib, I'll get the feet."

Ah, so Blue Neckerchief was the expected dustman called Gibbon. That made the other man Reed. And Gib and Reed knew what they carried.

"Not on yer life," Gib said. "I'll take the feet."

With some muttering, Reed switched places and, with little ceremony and less care, they hoisted the sack up between them. In that moment, I hated them almost as much as I hated the men who had murdered Miss Hollis and tried to strangle Jenny. They shuffled their burden to the steps, moving out of sight. We heard the slow creaking ascent amid gruff instructions and muttered curses, and then the footsteps receded, became muffled thumps and scrapes, until all was silent again.

"I think they are gone," I whispered.

Cautiously, I pushed open the wardrobe door. As expected, the chamber was empty.

With some inelegance, we extracted ourselves from the wardrobe. The rush of fear had, it seemed, restored some of Jenny's strength, for she stood without assistance and her eyes were no longer dazed.

I crossed to the staircase. Empty, too, and no more sounds of obscene haulage. I did, however, hear a faint, familiar squawk of metal. The gate. "I think they are out of the house. In the yard."

On that report of comparative safety, Jenny walked—almost steadily—to the side table and grabbed one of the silver candlesticks. "I'm takin' this," she said with a challenge in her bloodied eyes.

"You should take them all," Evan said. He returned to the wardrobe and pulled out the hessian sack. "Here, use this."

Jenny cocked her head at such unexpected amiability, then took the offered bag with a nod of agreement. All three candlesticks were quickly shoved into its depths, their clank and clash loud in the room.

"Not so loud," I said, holding up my palms as if I could muffle the noise. "We do not want them to hear us and come back."

"What you two gents doin' here, anyway?" Jenny asked, lowering her voice to a whisper. "I'm grateful an' all that, but you ain't bad coves like them two up there."

I looked at Evan. "We are trying to find out what happens to the girls who do not come out."

"Well, now you know," she said dryly, pointing to the heavens.

"But you survived," I said slowly, an opportunity dawning through the horror of the last hour. "If we can find out who is behind this, would you stand witness?"

"Against them who did this?" She touched her bruised throat. "Stand against the quality? You're off yer nut."

"But there will be other girls—"

"No one'll listen to the likes of me," she said. "And I don't stick my neck out for no one." She gave a yellow-toothed smile, dropping her hand from her throat. "Especially now, hey?"

A woman of macabre humor.

Through the hessian sack, she collected the silver into her hand to muffle its clank, then swung her bounty over her shoulder. "I ain't stayin' no longer." She looked up the staircase. "Anyone left in the house?"

"A deaf caretaker," I said. "You should go out the front. The dustmen may still be out the back."

"Aye, I'm not stupid," she said.

Evan stepped forward. "When you get to safety, promise me you'll put cold rags on your neck. Ice if you can find it. It will stop the swelling and the pain. And take some willow bark. Every day for a week. You know it?"

She gave a nod—a thank-you and farewell in one—and started up the staircase, her steps still a little unsteady. Although it was a lost chance, I could not blame her for refusing to stand witness. She was right: not many would listen to a Covent Garden prostitute. Besides, it was a safe bet that the Exalted Brethren of Rack and Ruin had a good number of magistrates and judges in its membership.

We both watched her reach the top, pause to listen, then disappear from view as she turned to climb the next set of steps. The creak of the old staircase tracked her progress to the ground floor of the house. And then all was quiet.

"Will she recover?" I asked.

"She has every chance—no signs of permanent damage," Evan said, his expression somber. "Still, a strangulation that does not kill is difficult to treat. It can have effects that linger."

One of his specialties, but I did not say it. He had been reminded enough of his prison days.

I looked up the steps again. "Shall we go and follow our two bad coves? Do you think they will dump poor Miss Hollis in the Thames?"

"No, she would wash up. If I was getting rid of a body, I would take it to a cemetery. Bury it in a new grave."

"You sound as if you have thought about this in some detail."

"I have had a lot of time to think about a lot of things," Evan said.

He led the way up the staircase, the wood creaking under our weight. On the fourth step from the top, he paused to peer through the banister, checking the basement corridor.

A nod over his shoulder: no one in sight. He proceeded up the last few steps, his body crouched, his steps careful. I followed suit, keeping my progress as silent as possible.

We made our way to the basement door. It was still dark outside, but dawn could not be far away. A half hour, perhaps. If they were going to move a body under the cover of night, they would have to work fast.

With care, Evan opened the basement door.

"For chrissakes, get it flatter or it won't fit in," the voice of Reed said.

They were in the yard, above our basement-level sight. Which meant we were beyond theirs. I tapped Evan's arm and pointed to the arched coal store across the small basement courtyard. He nodded and we slipped through the doorway, a few steps taking us across the cobbles. I pressed my back against the brick archway, Evan beside me.

I pointed my finger upward: *I'm taking a look.*

He shook his head vigorously: *Too risky.*

Perhaps, but I was still going. I crept along the wall and climbed the first few of the rough steps, crouching so that I would not be visible as I ascended toward ground level. Halfway up I stopped and, holding my breath, peeped over the edge. Reed and Gibbon stood at the end of a large wooden wheelbarrow, man-handling the sack into what looked like a false bottom beneath the tray. I ducked back down. So that was why Dorothy the flower seller had only ever seen an empty cart. The body of the girl was underneath, in a hidden compartment.

Clever. And despicable.

17

I crept back down the steps to where Evan stood.

He raised his brows: *See anything?*

I nodded and mimed pushing a cart, my charade interrupted by a clank and thud above—my guess, the hidden compartment being slammed shut.

"Finally," Reed's voice said. "You sure know how to make a simple job damn hard."

"Screw you," Gib said, without heat.

Then one of them made a huff of effort and the yard was full of the sound of heavy footsteps and barrow wheels grinding across the cobbles toward the lane. We both stood motionless, listening as the sound of the men and the cart's progress slowly receded.

When they had, by my reckoning, turned into the side lane, I told Evan what I had seen.

"So, they can move through London without anyone knowing, even when it is daylight," I concluded.

"Even so, I still think they'll want to get rid of her before dawn," Evan said. "Let's follow them."

I was all for discovering the truth, but it was going to be a dangerous enterprise. These brutes could realize we were tracking them and confront us. Not to mention the ever-present threat of Mr. Mulholland and his noses. Our search had stumbled across something far more perilous than just a clue: a woman had died in hideous circumstances; another was sorely injured. Perhaps not by the hands of these two dustmen, but they were a part of it. This was no longer something we could handle alone.

By the time we peered around the edge of the wall into the laneway, Gib and Reed were turning the cart into Bedford Street and I had come to a realization that was not going to sit well with Evan. I touched his arm, drawing his attention from Bedford Street and our quarry.

"I think we must speak to Mr. Kent about the girls and the wager book," I said. "As soon as possible."

He stared at me, perplexed. "Why would we do that? The man is trying to hang me."

Admittedly, that was true. "But we have new evidence and Mr. Kent is a reasonable man. Once he has seen it, I am sure—" I stopped. Was I sure? "I believe he will rethink your guilt and investigate with us. He is known for such attention to the facts and he has helped us before."

Evan crossed his arms. "The last time we offered him facts, he said he did not care and tried to shoot me."

True again. But another glaring truth cut through all else. "There is no one else official we can trust in the Runners or the Home Office, is there?"

It was Evan's turn to concede the point. "What do you propose, then?"

A plan had started to form. "We meet Mr. Kent at my house as soon as we know the full story here. Then we can present our case about the club—tell him where the body of poor Miss Hollis ends up—and show him the wager page." I clicked my tongue in irritation. "I should have taken the most recent page, too, with Miss Hollis in it." I shook my head. "No, someone would have noticed.

Perhaps it is better that it stays where it is." He still looked unconvinced. "Mr. Kent will help us, Evan. Besides, you will be able to see Hester too. A visit from you will help her recovery. I am sure of it," I added, trying to seal the deal.

Evan sighed. "I must see Hester. I owe it to her and so much more." He looked down the laneway again. "If we are to involve Mr. Kent, we need to give him incontrovertible proof of a body. Come on, we must not lose sight of the cart."

He was right. Evidence was everything.

We made our way swiftly down the laneway and peered around the Bedford Street corner. The quiet, emptier streets of the early hours were giving way to a trickle of barrowmen, cooks, and maids heading toward their morning business in Covent Garden. It would not be hard to slide in among the foot traffic and follow our quarry. I spied Gib and Reed and the cart as they trundled past Dorothy the flower seller.

Dorothy. Now, there was an interesting thought.

"We'll slip in after these two," Evan said, tilting his head at a pair of market women who were walking past in loud, animated conversation.

We stepped in behind them, keeping our quarry in sight about twenty yards ahead. As we crossed the corner of Maiden Lane, that interesting thought blossomed into part of the plan.

I stopped beside Dorothy. "Go on ahead, I will be right behind you," I said to Evan.

"What?" He stopped, caught between staying with me and staying with Gib and Reed as they headed toward King Street.

"Trust me."

He looked down at the old flower seller and gave a nod. "I'll wait on the corner for you," he said, and continued behind the two market women.

I crouched beside Dorothy.

"What you want?" she said, clutching her patched purse. "I'll scream bloody murder if you touch me coin."

"No, Dorothy, I do not want your coin. Do you remember two ladies talking to you a few nights back?"

"You know my name?" She watched me warily. "You talkin' about the ladies who gave me two shillin's?"

"Yes, that is right. I'm one of them—Lady Augusta—but I'm disguised as a man." I peeled off part of my whiskers. "See, it is false hair."

She studied me through narrowed, rheumy eyes. "Well, glory be!" she finally said, wheezing a laugh. "What you doin' dressed like that?" Then she frowned and looked over at the club. "Ah, to do with that place, ain't it? I just saw a girl come out in her chemise with a sack on her shoulder. Never seen a mort move so fast. Her in bare feet and half-strangled too."

Nothing got past Dorothy.

"She was one of the lucky ones," I said. "She got out. But I think I know what happens to the girls who do not." I glanced up the road. The cart and Evan were both approaching King Street. Time was of the essence. "I need your help, Dorothy. Will you deliver a message for me? To my sister, the one who gave you the shillings?" I took out a handful of coins and offered them. "This will get you to her—take a hackney—and when you get there, she'll give you more shillings for the message and your trouble."

Dorothy considered the proposition. "Your sister is a good 'un—I'll say that. You know what's happened to them other girls?"

"I do."

She pursed her cracked lips. "What's the message, then?"

It did not take long to finalize the transaction. As I prepared to go, Dorothy stopped me with a grimy hand on my arm.

"They're dead, ain't they? The girls who don't come out?"

I placed my hand over hers for a moment. "They are. And we are trying to stop it."

She nodded grimly as I took to the pavement again.

*E*van stood on the corner, alternately watching for me and looking up King Street, where, presumably, Gib and Reed were traveling.

"They are not too far ahead," he said in welcome. "My guess is we are heading for either St. Andrew's or Bunhill Fields burial ground."

St. Andrew's was closer, but both cemeteries were quite a way by foot if he was right. We started walking. I caught sight of our quarry up ahead, parting the foot traffic on the pavement with the cart. To think, all those people passing by, not knowing what was hidden beneath that wooden tray.

"What did you do back there?" Evan asked.

I told him the message I had sent to Julia via Dorothy: summon Mr. Kent and wait for us to return with evidence. "I know you do not trust Mr. Kent, but I believe he will help us."

"It is a good plan." For a second, Evan's palm lightly touched my back. I wanted to take his hand—feel the solid warmth of his decency and honor—but of course I could not.

We followed Gib and Reed along High Holborn, the sky shifting into the lighter blue-gray of impending dawn. We passed the green expanse of Lincoln's Inn Fields, then veered slightly right, along Skinner Street rather than left onto Snow Hill, which meant we were not, in fact, headed for St. Andrew's or for Bunhill Fields.

Where, then, were we going?

It was not long before St. Sepulchre's Church and the Old Bailey came into view, the somber gray courthouse looming over the street. Streaks of dawn pink brightened the cloudy gray sky, and the air was smoky with the smell of freshly lit hearths amid the faint foulness of the nearby meat market. London was awakening.

"What are they doing this far east?" Evan said. He craned to one side to see past the couple in front, trying to keep Gib and Reed in sight. Even with the cart and the weight of its grisly cargo, they had kept up a quick pace for the whole journey and had drawn away from us. "Wait, they are turning, into Giltspur Street."

"What is up there?" I asked.

Evan frowned. "Smithfield meat market? You don't think they are going to take her there, do you?"

I grimaced. I would not put anything past Gib and Reed.

I caught sight of the two men as they took the Giltspur Street corner, wheeling the cart wide, then disappearing from sight. Evan increased his pace, forcing me to skip a step to keep up. A woman humped out a huge basket of washing from a laundry, blocking our way. We skirted around her and her load and finally turned the corner.

I shoved my sleeve up against my nose: the dung and rancid fat smell of the meat market was already overpowering. The street ahead was busy—cattle driven by yipping farmers, delivery wagons, dogs fighting over scraps, hackneys stopping for passengers, barrel men carrying their goods, and the infirm lining up outside the main gate of Bart's Hospital—but I could not see Gib and Reed amid the chaos.

I stood on my toes, searching the traffic again. They were gone. "We have lost them," I said over the clamor of hooves and voices.

"No, they must be down one of the lanes."

We started to jog along the path, drawing some censorious glances from those coming the other way. First, Green Dragon Yard: a blind alley with no one in it. Next, Bull Court: empty too.

Finally, Windmill Court, which curved away from the road, no clear view of the whole. I followed Evan down it at a run, our hurtling panic startling a yelp from a woman stepping from her residence. Another blind alley and no sign of Gib and Reed.

Panting, I followed Evan back to Giltspur Street. "The other side of the road?" I suggested, bending with my hands on my knees to help me draw breath.

Evan stared hard at the only other option across the way: Cock Lane. He shook his head. "They would have taken Snow Hill. It is quicker."

I straightened to see a small group of men ahead, dressed in black and wearing Clericus hats, entering a gate. Doctors. Where were they going?

Ah, of course.

"Up there. That is where they are." I pointed to the gray stone pillars and iron gate. "It is a side entrance to Bart's."

If there was one place in London where one could hide a dead body, it would be St. Bartholomew's Hospital.

18

We jogged up the footpath to the entrance. The iron gate stood open, leading to the large central quadrangle enclosed by the hospital buildings. I had never been inside Bart's before, although Julia and I had contributed funds to its expansion. I had to say the four buildings were rather handsome: frontages in the classic style with large windows and arched doorways and walk-throughs that were all reassuringly solid in their symmetry. Hospital attendants in smocks, nurses, and patients were already airing themselves or crossing the cobbled expanse of the quadrangle, and the doctors we had followed were entering the building to our right, conversing with some vigor. I caught the words *pneumonia* and *sputum* before a delivery wagon stacked with barrels came through the main gateway, the sound of its wheels and horses' hooves upon the flags overwhelming any other sound. "Look, over there," Evan said through the noise. He pointed to Gib and Reed pushing the cart toward a lane between the north and east buildings. "You have found them."

Still, we had no time to waste—they would be gone from view in a moment or two. We half walked, half ran across the quadrangle, using the horse and wagon as cover until Gib and Reed had disappeared into the lane. Evan increased his speed, his longer legs covering the ground in an athletic stride. I was not too far behind, but gulping for air, my lungs aching.

We rounded the corner just in time to see the back of Reed as he entered a side door halfway along the building, Gib and the cart no doubt already inside.

Evan drew to a panting stop. Thank God. I came to a halt beside him and leaned a steadying hand against the building, struggling for a deep lungful of air.

"So, we know what happens to the girls now," he said between breaths. I followed his upward gaze. A sign above the door declared THROUGH TO DISSECTION ROOM. "Mr. Reed and Mr. Gibbon are resurrectionists."

Good God. I had read about such resurrection men. Body snatchers who pried loved ones from their resting place and sold the corpses to anatomists and doctors for dissection. Indeed, I knew one family, the Purdams, who had been forced to mount a guard upon their father's grave until his corpse had decomposed to the point that it would no longer be attractive to the grave robbers. It was a foul profession that, to my surprise, was not entirely illegal. Interfering with a grave was only a misdemeanor, and punished by fine, if at all. If items were stolen from the corpse, however, then that could mean prison or transportation. How odd it was that theft of a few grave items was considered worse than dragging the body from a grave and selling it for further desecration. But then the law was not justice, was it?

And how wickedly clever of the men in the Exalted Brethren of Rack and Ruin to employ resurrectionists to sell their victims to hospitals or anatomy schools. Lost among the abandoned suicides and the criminals and the unclaimed poor.

"Should we catch them in the act?" I asked. "We can arrest them by law."

"And then what?" Evan said. "We cannot take them to Bow Street. We have just seen one of the undersecretaries of the Alien Department attend the very club where the murder took place. I do not think our report would go very far, do you? Besides, I cannot walk into Bow Street—I might as well string myself up now—and nor can you, in your current guise."

All true. Yet it did not sit well to allow Gib and Reed to profit from Miss Hollis's death.

Sometimes, however, inaction was the most intelligent course, even if it did feel morally wrong. We walked back to the corner of the lane and leaned against the wall: just two laborers loitering in Bart's quadrangle, or perhaps waiting for the open surgery to start.

I dug my hands into my jacket pockets, my left fingers closing around the knitted bulk of Miss Hollis's purse—I had forgotten I had shoved it in there. I pulled it out, nudging Evan for his attention. There was something so pitifully innocent about its homemade shape; a gift, perhaps, from a loving mother, or maybe knitted by her own hands to go with a new gown. Now it was stained with her blood and in my hands, a stranger who had followed her body to a dissection room.

Evan eyed it somberly. "All her worldly possessions?"

I worked two fingers into the opening and spread the tightly bunched drawstring apart. Inside, a handkerchief embroidered with flowers, a sixpence, and a folded letter. I returned the handkerchief and sixpence to the bag and unfolded the letter. The direction on the front of the packet was to Miss Catherine Hollis, Chapel Street, Cheapside.

"Her home?" Evan asked, looking over my shoulder.

"Probably." The sealing wafer had dropped off long ago, its gum discoloring the paper in a neat oval. I spread the page.

Tuesday, 18th June 1811
The Vicarage,
Whixley

My dearest Cathy,

I know you will probably not write back to me, you said as much in your last letter, but I want you to know that Mother and I are still here and still hoping you will return home.

Mother has been ill again. The doctor says her chest is weak and she needs sea air. Father is hoping to take her to Lyme Regis in the spring. After a bleak time of it after you left, he has been able to take up the ministering of two new parishes, so it is more than possible we will have enough for Mother and me to make an extended visit for her health.

I am happy to report, dear sister, that Father has mentioned you in kinder terms during the past few months. It is, I think, the relief of new income and some distance from that terrible day when you told him the truth and then lost the little life that you carried. Perhaps it is a sign that he will allow you to come back to us.

Please, if you can, write a note to let myself and Mother know you are well. And if you wish to return anytime, I will try my hardest to send you the fare and we will find a way together for Father to forgive you. And you him.

Your loving sister, always,
Rosalie

What had happened in that genteel vicarage? Clearly, something tragic that had seen one tiny life lost in the past, and another life lost now.

"They should know what has happened," Evan said.

Indeed. To never know the fate of a missing loved one would be purgatory on earth.

"We have an address," I said, refolding the letter. "I will write to them and tell them the terrible news."

How did Miss Hollis—the daughter of a vicar—end up in the basement of the Exalted Brethren of Rack and Ruin? Was it just by chance—one of Long Sal's runaways who ran out of luck? Yet Long Sal said other genteel girls had been seen inside the club, so Miss Hollis was not an anomaly. A nasty possibility sprang to mind: was that part of the wager too? To seduce respectable girls and take them into the bowels of hell? I would not put such degradation past the Exalted Brethren.

It was at that moment that the side door opened again. I thrust the purse and letter back into my pocket as Gib and Reed came out with the cart, their expressions smugly satisfied.

On seeing us lounging against the wall, both men stared for a belligerent moment but clearly saw no threat. It was lucky they could not see into my heart and the rage that roiled within me. By the way Gib pushed the cart across the quadrangle, I knew it no longer held Miss Hollis. In that moment, every part of me wanted to make Reed and Gib suffer for so blithely delivering her to this final desecration. But then again, they were not the true villains. Merely foul adjuncts to the brutal killers at the club.

"Let's go in," I said, heading back to the door. "I want to find out what the anatomists have to say about buying a body that has so plainly been murdered."

*T*he door led into a dingy corridor with scuffed pale walls and a parquetry floor that crunched underfoot with tracked-in gravel and dried leaves. A number of the wall lamps were guttering or already spent, any light left drawing the flutter and buzz of moths and flies. At the other end of the corridor, a man pushed a basket upon a cart, the sound of his squeaky-wheeled progress receding into the distance. A rancid fatty blood smell, not unlike that from the meat market outside, hung in the air, mixed with the stink of alcohol and feces. I closed my eyes for a second, trying to suppress the desire to gag.

"Over there," Evan said. I heard the same reflex in his voice. "That might be where they went."

I opened my eyes. A doorway farther along bore the legend DISSECTION PREP.

We approached, the dead-flesh stink intensifying. I peered around the doorway. A young man in a smock sat at a desk writing in a ledger, a single candle providing light. Behind him, two wooden trestle tables stood with a body upon each, draped in a grubby, stained sheet. Or that is what I presumed was under the cloth by the shapes of what lay beneath. Was one of them Miss Hollis? A number of flies crawled upon the dark stains, occasionally rising into buzzing flight and landing upon another damp patch. A glint of metal upon one set of shelves marked a jumble of instruments—saws, knives, forceps—some rusted, some new, some still coated in dark matter. Another shelf held dozens of ledgers.

The young man, sensing our presence, looked up, quill poised over his entry. "What is it?"

He looked to be about twenty and not in the best of health— no wonder since he sat among death and decay. His movements were nervy quick and his complexion a sickly yellow, with blemishes that stretched his skin in large red lumps upon cheeks and chin.

"Have you brought a body?" he asked as we entered.

"No," I said, making my voice as gruff and manly as possible.

Behind me, Evan closed the door and lounged against it, the pose both relaxed and threatening at the same time.

The young man frowned. "What are you doing?"

"We are asking you why you just accepted the body of a young woman for dissection when she has clearly been murdered," Evan said pleasantly. "What is your name?"

"I am not going to tell you my name," the young man said, puffing a little at the outrage of our intrusion.

"Everyone needs a name," I said. "Like the young woman those two coves just brought in." I glanced at Evan. "Let's call him Napoleon."

Evan considered my suggestion. "It suits him."

"My name is not Napoleon," the young man said, outraged. A true patriot. "I am Reginald Drake and I have no recollection of a young woman."

I walked over to his table. He pushed his chair back, scooting it across the floor in a dull screech of wood upon wood and revealing a pair of reasonably clean stockings and good shoes with silver buckles. A young man of reasonable means. Perhaps a medical student working his way through his studies.

I leaned over to view the ledger. "Ah, this unfinished entry you are writing: unidentified woman, approximate age twenty-five. Marked upon back and neck."

He eyed me. "You can read?"

"It would seem so," I said. "Allow me to ask again: why are you taking the body of a woman who has so plainly been murdered? Is that her under one of those sheets?"

"Yes," Reginald muttered, his eyes darting to the left table. "I don't know what you want from me. I just do what I am told. The doctors say take whatever bodies come in. It does not matter where they are from."

"It does to their people," I said as mildly as I could. I glanced at the patently female figure beneath the stained cloth, struggling for a moment to contain my fury. I would write to her family as I had vowed, but could I tell them what had truly happened to their daughter and sister? How she had died and what was about to happen to her body in this terrible place? Surely it would just compound their grief and add the ongoing misery of imagined torture and lonely death. A decision to face when I had pen and paper.

I resolutely turned back a page of the ledger. It detailed the bodies and dissections from the previous week. Another page, another week. Rather like the hideous wager book . . . which presented a rather interesting idea. "How far back do these ledgers go, Reginald?"

He glanced at the shelf of ledgers beside us. "Fifty years or so."

I looked across at Evan, eyebrows raised.

He nodded: *Interesting.*

With menacing grace he levered himself away from the door and walked over to the shelves, running his finger along the spines of the bound ledgers. "Here we are, 1792."

"I wasn't here then," Reginald said quickly.

"We rather gathered that," Evan said dryly. He started to flip through the pages.

"You should get more fresh air," I said to Reginald.

He gave me a sour look. "I would if I could."

At the corner of my eye, Evan stopped flipping through the ledger, his attention fixed upon a page. "May 1792," he said, looking up at me.

"Anything?"

"Not many listed. But there is one unidentified female about the right age and around the right time." He frowned and brought the ledger over to Reginald, pointing to an entry on the page. "What does that mark mean?"

Reginald leaned over. "It's a *P*. It means the female was with child. She would have been dissected whole. Females are usually only dissected whole if they are . . ."

"Pregnant?" I supplied through my teeth. Did the Exalted Brethren kill not only a woman but a child too? Their depravity was beyond comprehension.

"Yes," Reginald muttered. "Did you know her?"

"I don't know," Evan said slowly, but it was said more to me than to our jaundiced friend.

"You remember something?" I asked.

He shook his head, not in denial, but more as if he was trying to shake free a memory. "Something is there but I cannot grab hold of it."

"At least we know now what happens to the women." I considered the ledger entry. Another piece of evidence. Well, in for a penny, in for a pound. I took hold of the page and ripped it out of the ledger.

Reginald sprang to his feet. "You cannot do that!"

"It seems I can and I have," I said. "But if you keep quiet about it, I am sure no one will be any the wiser."

He glared at me.

I dug into my pocket. "Here, something to help your silence." I placed a half crown on the table. Even as I did so, another possibility presented itself. A way, perhaps, to bring some peace to the family of Miss Hollis. And a way for her to have some dignity in her death. I placed another half crown next to the one already on the table and nodded to her nearby shrouded body. "Guard that woman and hand her over to some undertakers who will come to collect her this afternoon. If you do this, both coins are yours and the undertakers will give you a guinea on top for your trouble."

He stared at the two half crowns: it was a sizable amount for someone who had clearly accepted an unsavory position to survive. A guinea on top of that would be largesse, indeed. "I will not take stolen money," he said stiffly, although he could not take his eyes off the coins.

"Then you are in luck. It is not stolen," I said, rather liking his stand upon the matter. "Do we have a deal, Reginald?"

He hesitated. Rubbed his mouth. It was, after all, a lot of money. Finally, he sighed. "Tell the undertakers they must come up the back way by Little Britain into Well Yard to collect her. By six tonight."

"I will." I picked up his pen and drew a thick line through the half-finished entry in his ledger, obliterating the words. "She was never here. Is that clear?" Reginald nodded as I returned his pen to its rest.

Evan opened the door, the arrival of some slightly less fetid air from the corridor a welcome reprieve from the stink.

"We were not here either," he said, every distinct word holding a warning. "You never saw us."

Reginald picked up the coins and returned to his chair. "Of course not. It is just me and the dead here." He pocketed the money. "Always just me and the dead."

19

The hackney I hailed outside the meat market had, unlike the one I had taken to Covent Garden, retained its stained upholstery but still reeked of the sweaty humanity that had passed through it. Perhaps it was a characteristic of such travel in London—I did not know since I usually took my own carriage.

Evan took the bodkin seat, opposite me, and shut the carriage door, muffling the morning cacophony of Giltspur Street and the free surgery queue outside Bart's. I thumped my fist on the wall to let the driver—who, on seeing our shabbiness, had insisted on being paid in advance—know that he could leave. We jolted forward, finally on our way back to Grosvenor Square.

Evan took off his hat and ran his hand through his hair. "You are sending undertakers?"

"The same who dealt with my father. They are discreet. I will instruct them to take Miss Hollis back to her family in Whixley once Mr. Kent has viewed her body as evidence. I thought it prudent not to scare Reginald by announcing an imminent visit from a Bow Street Runner."

"Indeed, he is a skittish one." Evan scrubbed at his eyes, then replaced his hat. "Sending her back to her family is a great kindness and one that will hopefully give them some solace. Even so, I think

it must be done anonymously. They may wish to find their bene-
factor and demand more answers than we can afford to supply."

I had planned to do so anyway but gave a nod. We both looked
out the window, a few silent seconds of memorial for Miss Hollis.

"So, Sally Lawrence may have been pregnant," Evan said,
drawing us back to the situation at hand.

"If the dissection entry is actually Sally Lawrence—we have no
way of knowing if that is the case," I said. And as the reality of that
sank in, I added more gloomily, "Or proving it. Or even if she was
related to the doctor who attended the duel."

"Speaking of proof, what if Mr. Kent is not waiting with your
sister? What if she did not get the message from the flower seller or
he refused her summons?"

"If Dorothy delivered my message, then Julia will have done
everything to bring Mr. Kent to her side. He will be there." Of
course, I could not be certain of him, but nor could I allow the possibility that he would not answer my sister's call for help. But would
he listen to our evidence with an open mind? Mr. Kent was a man
of duty, but was that duty to the Runners or to the truth? And if he
refused to help, then I was not sure where next to turn.

"If he tries to arrest me, I must warn you I will not allow it. I
know your sister holds him in some regard, but I will fight my way
out and I will not hold back. I cannot leave Hester to Deele's piety
again, and I certainly do not wish to hang."

"If he does try, I will fight beside you," I said. "And so will
Julia."

"Well, let's hope she has her blunderbuss ready," he said with a
glimmer of his droll humor, but I could see the prospect of relying
upon Mr. Kent did not sit easily. And I had to admit, now that the
moment was almost upon us, I did not feel particularly confident
either.

"Perhaps I should go in alone and speak to him," I suggested.

"I am not afraid of him," Evan said stiffly. "Besides, I need to see Hester. Things are not right between us. I need to remedy that."

Clearly, this peacemaking visit was important to him, but I feared the only way he could appease his sister's anger would be to spirit her away to another country or take back his title and become her guardian. And neither of those remedies was currently possible. Still, I did not voice my pessimism. Instead, I said, "I expect to hear back from Lady Davenport soon, and if she agrees to our visit—which I believe she will—we will travel to her estate once Hester is able."

We subsided into silence again as the hackney crossed morning London, both of us lost in our thoughts and the anticipation of what lay ahead. Finally we pulled up in Mount Street, outside St. George's workhouse, as I had requested.

"I figured we would not stand out here as much as we would in the middle of Grosvenor Square," I said, opening the door. We would also be able to creep up Charles Street and enter the house the back way, via the mews.

We alighted, the hackney clattering away as soon as we both made the footpath. Some of the inmates of the workhouse were already outside chopping wood, the thud of the axes a counterpoint to the sound of children chanting their catechism in the airing grounds beyond. The gates were open, ready for visitors, for it was not a prison, or so the authorities insisted. Still, it was possible I had made a mistake fetching up outside a workhouse where so many had links to the criminal world. Any one of the people milling around the entrance could be in the pay of Mulholland or the Runners.

"Come on," I said to Evan.

We crossed the road and made our way up Charles Street to the mews.

"Wait here," I said, and jogged along to the entrance to Grosvenor Square. A quick look around the corner of the last terrace confirmed what I half hoped and half feared to see: a black horse tied to the rails of the central garden opposite our house.

I returned to Evan.

"Kent is here," I said.

I ripped off my side whiskers—a somewhat painful process—and took off my hat as we entered the house via the kitchen yard. I did not want Cook and her scullery maids to think they were being invaded by ruffians. Although to be honest, I would pity any ruffian who tried to enter Cook's domain without a pass.

"Good morning, my lady. Good morning, sir," that formidable individual said, curtsying alongside her girls as we entered the steamy kitchen. "Lady Julia has ordered a full breakfast to be served at eight o'clock, but would you like me to send up something beforehand?"

A full breakfast so early? Unusual, but the smell of frying bacon, fragrant kedgeree, and freshly baked bread was welcome. Lord, I was hungry.

"Yes, excellent," I said. "As soon as possible."

We made our way along the hallway, its warmth, the smell of wax polish and newly lit hearths, and Julia's huge vases of flowers a welcoming order that I had not realized I needed. Weatherly met us in the hallway at the foot of the stairs, our arrival heralded, no doubt, by one of the maids who had heard us enter the kitchen. He bowed, patently relieved to see me safe, for his mouth was almost curled into a smile.

"Good morning, my lady, good morning, Lord Evan," he said. "Lady Julia is in the drawing room with Mr. Kent."

"Good," I said. I handed him my hat and my side-whiskers,

which he took with equanimity. "Lord Evan will need a loaded firearm and may require a quick exit. Can you organize that, please?"

"Of course, my lady."

"I wish to see my sister first," Evan said, handing over his own battered hat. "In case Mr. Kent does not look favorably upon our proof and I need to make that quick exit."

"I am sorry, my lord, Lady Hester is not yet awake," Weatherly said. "From the report of Miss Grant, her ladyship had a very bad night and was given some laudanum only an hour past."

The look upon Evan's face clutched at my heart.

"We could try to wake her if you wish," I said.

He shook his head. "No, she needs to rest. We will see Mr. Kent first."

Weatherly cleared his throat. "Lady Julia also wished you to know that she received a note from Lord Duffield last night. He intends to call this morning for breakfast."

Duffy? What on earth did he want at such an early hour? Certainly nothing good. But that explained the full breakfast. It also meant I must go upstairs and change into a gown before he arrived. Although, I had to admit, it would have been entertaining to see his reaction to my masculine attire.

"If Lord Duffield arrives before we come down, show him to the dining room, not the drawing room." It would be irregular, but I did not want Duffy meeting Evan in such a manner. Or, indeed, Mr. Kent. I glanced at Evan. "Go with Weatherly; he will provide you with a weapon. I must change and then we will go into the drawing room unannounced."

Unannounced, but not unprepared.

With Tully's help, I changed into a gown in ten minutes, all the while giving her a brief update of the night, her gasps of shock not interrupting her deft buttoning of my sleeves. I then instructed her to choose one of my plain white gowns as a shroud for Miss Hollis while I took a few minutes to write a note to Messrs. France and Banting, Undertakers, to retrieve Miss Hollis at six o'clock and await further instructions. I closed it with my wax seal and handed it to Tully, along with the additional guinea for Reginald.

"Deliver these and the gown into the hands of Mr. France and make sure he understands that this is to be strictly confidential. Tell him he and his partner will be amply compensated for their discretion."

"You said you found Miss Hollis without any clothes, my lady," Tully said, her face uncharacteristically grim. "Should I choose a chemise and hose too? For her family."

I smiled at such thoughtfulness. "Take whatever you think would be suitable. I trust you to choose well."

With Tully set on her task, I drew a steadying breath and made my way down the staircase with the Rundell box in hand.

Evan stood waiting in the hallway, holding the gun that Weatherly had given him.

"I have something else for you," I said, offering him the box.

"A gift?" I nodded as he carefully placed the gun upon the sideboard and took the box. He opened it, a smile announcing his pleasure. "Ah, now, that is beautiful." He picked up the dagger and rested the blade across two fingers, the ruby set in the handle gleaming in the morning light. "And you have had my initials engraved upon the cartouche." He traced his fingertip around the *EB* etched into the silver.

"It is only a knife," I said, and added a little self-consciously, "I have the same with my own initials. A pair." I patted my sleeve, where I had hidden my sheathed dagger.

"It is far more than just a knife. The balance is superb." He looked up from admiring the blade. "It is a long time since I have owned such a beautiful thing. The one I have is little more than an eating knife."

"I meant to keep it for a Twelfth Night gift, but I think, under the circumstances, it would be more useful now," I said.

"Quite." He set down the box and slid the knife into its accompanying leather sheath. In one swift, practiced movement, he removed the blade already secreted in his boot and replaced it with my gift. "There, I am armed and ready." He placed the old knife in the box and picked up the gun again. "Gus, if this does not go our way . . ."

I took his hand. The one that was not holding the loaded gun. "I know. Whatever happens, we will rally."

"And you must tell Hester I am sorry."

"I will."

He bent and kissed me upon the lips—a swift token, for Julia and Mr. Kent awaited us upstairs.

"Thank you," he said, and I knew he meant it for far more than the knife.

20

{decorative flourish}

Samuel bowed as we approached the drawing room doors, his gaze dropping to the gun clasped in Evan's hand. His expression, however, did not change. Good lad.

I glanced at Evan: *Ready?*

His mouth firmed, as did his grip upon the gun: *Ready.*

I nodded to Samuel, who promptly opened the drawing room doors.

We walked in.

"Ah, you are here," Julia said brightly from her seat upon the sofa, beside Mr. Kent. Very close beside Mr. Kent.

The Runner stood—his arm no longer in a sling and his stance wary. Beneath his well-fitted jacket, he wore the smart scarlet waistcoat of his vocation. Was that a sign of intention?

"I thought this was going to be a peaceful meeting," he said, his eyes upon the gun in Evan's hand. He made a bow. "Good morning, Lady Augusta. Good morning, Lord Evan."

"It will be peaceful if you do not do anything stupid," Evan said pleasantly.

"And by stupid you mean arresting you for the crimes you have committed?" Kent countered.

Well, this was not starting as well as I had hoped.

It had not occurred to me before, but the two men were evenly matched should it come to a physical fight. Both above six foot, similar muscular builds, although Mr. Kent had a small advantage of weight. And each as stubborn as the other.

Julia rose to her feet beside the Runner and placed a hand upon his arm. "Please, Michael, give them a chance to present their proof."

Michael? That was a development. My sister, however, did not acknowledge my raised brow.

"I do not have much choice, with a gun pointed at me," Kent said.

I glanced at Evan.

He quirked the side of his mouth: *Really?*

I gave a nod.

With a sigh, Evan lowered the gun and placed it on the sideboard next to him.

Mr. Kent considered us, doubt clear upon his face. "Lady Julia's note said you have evidence to give me. What kind of evidence?"

"I think we need to start at the beginning," I said.

And so I told the story of twenty years ago: of Sanderson, and the Exalted Brethren of Rack and Ruin, and of Evan's memory of visiting the club. Of the duel forced upon him at White's, and the death of Sanderson, for which he had been transported. And the story now: of discovering the heinous wager book and Miss Hollis's body, dumped at Bart's, and the wager entry made twenty years ago—one month before the duel—over Sally Lawrence, possibly with child, who had the same surname as the doctor who had attended the affair of honor.

"That is despicable," Julia said, shaking her head. "To wager upon another's suffering and death. Are you sure? I cannot believe there is such wickedness. And by men who claim to be gentlemen."

"I ripped the entry out of the wager book," I said, and dug into my pocket, bringing out the two folded pages. "See, the names of the club members are in code, but their victims are not. And the other page is from the dissection ledger at Bart's. A nameless pregnant woman dumped there at the right time."

I passed Kent the pages. He unfolded them and studied the entries, Julia looking over his shoulder. I could see my sister's horror growing.

Kent refolded the papers but did not look as impressed as I had hoped. "So, you think this Sally Lawrence is connected to the doctor at the duel?"

Evan and I both nodded.

"And you think that if he knew how she had died, he might have had motive for killing Sanderson, if Sanderson was indeed the man who had killed her?" Kent held up the pages. "This is not proof at all, Lady Augusta. We have no way of knowing who the club members are; you have not established any connection between the Sally Lawrence on this page and the doctor who attended the duel or, indeed, Sanderson's culpability. Not to mention the fact that you illegally broke into the club—members of which you claim number among the Alien Office and House of Lords—and stole the page from the book and ripped another from a hospital ledger. Those are transportable offenses."

Ah, I had not thought of it in that way. Even so, it did not negate what we had found.

"But do you not see the connections?" I demanded. "You yourself posited that someone of high rank in the Magistrates' Court or Home Office has ordered Mulholland to kill Lord Evan, and now we have found a nefarious club, of which Sanderson was a member, which Lord Evan visited, and whose membership includes people of high rank in the Alien Office and probably the

Home Office. It all adds up. We saw Miss Hollis's body, Mr. Kent. They are killing women! For their amusement! You can go to Bart's now and see her corpse. See what they have done to her!" I turned to Evan. "Perhaps you saw a murder twenty years ago. Perhaps that is why someone is trying to kill you."

"I cannot remember seeing anything," Evan said. "I am sorry, but I cannot."

"I think that what you say is plausible, Lady Augusta, but it is not anything I can act upon. Especially since you were involved in the theft of this page. I cannot even act upon the death of Miss Hollis—you have not established that connection either. I have no way of proving anything about her demise that would not draw you into scandal and prosecution." Kent passed the pages back to me. "If I were to bring that evidence forward, it would not clear Lord Evan's name, but it would incriminate you."

"I told you he would not listen to reason," Evan said.

"I listen to reason and proof," Mr. Kent snapped, "just not wild supposition or evidence obtained by theft."

"What do you need, then?" I asked. "Tell me what you need and we will find it."

"Frankly, you would have to find someone else to confess to the crime," Kent said. "Even then—"

"But how—"

A knock upon the door silenced us both.

"Who is it?" Julia finally called.

The door opened.

Miss Grant peered in and, upon seeing Lord Evan, exclaimed, "So you are here—I thought I heard your voice." She walked in, her stride full of purpose. "I wish to speak to you urgently, and this time you must listen. We cannot stay—" Belatedly she noted

Mr. Kent. "Ah, I beg your pardon." She managed a credible curtsy, although her body still held the stiff intent of unspoken demands.

Damn, I had not anticipated this meeting. Nevertheless, Miss Grant and Mr. Kent were connected even if they did not know it yet. Perhaps that could be useful.

"Miss Grant, may I introduce Mr. Kent, from the Bow Street Magistrates' Court. You did not meet him at the time, but he is the agent who helped rescue Lady Hester from the asylum and kept us all safe afterward. He is a great friend to us. And continues to be so."

Mr. Kent made a small sound of denial, but I had cornered him in his own service and he knew it.

"Mr. Kent, this is Miss Grant, Lady Hester's companion."

He bowed.

Miss Grant—momentarily taken aback by the introduction—scrabbled for her manners and, thankfully, found them. "Mr. Kent, Hester and I owe you a great debt of gratitude. Thank you so much for your assistance in rescuing Hester," Miss Grant said, smiling. She could be rather charming when she tried.

"Not at all," Mr. Kent said, bowing again. "I do hope Lady Hester's health has improved."

"It is why I am here. Hester had a bad night but overall she has improved some and is now adamant—"

The sounds of commotion downstairs interrupted Miss Grant. We all looked down, as if we could see through the floor. Then Weatherly's voice shouted, "You shall not enter!" A huge slam reverberated through the house, like the front door being kicked back, and then the sound of feet, running. Up the stairs. Toward us.

Evan grabbed the gun from the sideboard and aimed it at Kent. "Did you lie? Are these your men?"

"I swear it is not," Kent said, but he had pulled his own gun—from his boot, I think—and aimed it at Evan. Of course he had a gun too.

I grabbed Miss Grant's arm and wrenched her back from the doorway, maneuvering her behind me. She gaped at the firearms but at least remained upright.

"Perhaps you should both aim at whatever is coming through that door," I said, pulling the sheathed dagger from my sleeve. "Julia, my dear, move behind Mr. Kent."

"Do as your sister says, Julia," Kent said.

Julia stepped behind the Runner.

Miss Grant clutched my arm. "What is happening?"

"Kent?" Evan said.

The Runner stared hard at him for a moment, then gave a nod. Both men shifted their guns to aim at the door.

We all stood silently, braced, as the sounds of yelled commands and feet upon the staircase—multiple pairs of feet—approached.

Good God, how many were there?

There was a cry—Samuel, I think—and the door slammed open.

In hurtled Mulholland, gun raised, Pritchard close behind.

21

With startling speed, Mulholland took in the armed situation and stopped abruptly, aiming his pistol at Evan.

"Cover Kent," he barked at Pritchard, who swung his gun toward the Runner.

"My lady, they have forced their way in," Weatherly reported, coming to a halt just inside the door with Samuel at his back— blood upon his face—brandishing a vase from the hall table. "Two others downstairs."

"Is anyone injured?" I was glad my voice did not waver.

"Samuel received a facer, my lady, but no other injury."

"Keep back, then!" I eyed Samuel sternly. He clearly wanted to avenge himself, but Mulholland was capable of anything to capture his quarry. Or kill his quarry. The thought brought a swamping wave of terror. I drew a breath and forced it back. This was not the time to show fear; not in front of Mulholland.

Miss Grant had come to terms with the situation and backed up against the wall. Sensible. My sister still stood behind Mr. Kent. For the moment, it was a stand-off: Mr. Kent would not shoot because Julia stood behind him, Evan would not shoot because I stood beside him, and Mulholland would not shoot—I guessed— in case he shot me or Julia. Quite the hanging offense. Not to mention the fact that once a shot was made, there would be no time to prime another.

And so I asked, "Why have you forced your way into our home, Mr. Mulholland?"

Mulholland eyed me over the barrel of his pistol. "We're not playing that game anymore, Lady Augusta." He glanced at Mr. Kent. "I saw you were here. But this is my tap. Get on your horse."

Kent kept his gun trained upon Mulholland. "No, this is my tap. I got here first."

Tap? It must mean arrest. At least I hoped it meant arrest and not kill. Had Kent meant to arrest Evan all along?

Mulholland sighed. "Don't make me throw you out, Kent. I've been given the word and you don't want to be around for the end."

"What do you mean?" Kent asked.

"He means he has been given the order to kill me, not arrest me," Evan said, his voice and aim still steady.

"Who gave that order?" Kent demanded.

Mulholland sniffed. "Don't matter. This is way beyond you."

"Have you got a writ to that effect?" Kent asked.

"I don't need a writ," Mulholland said. "And if you know what's good for you, you'll cut out and leave me to it."

"Michael?" Julia said.

"Stay behind me, Julia," Mr. Kent said, the familiarity bringing a raised brow from Mulholland.

I did not like how much this man observed—too sharp by half.

"I am not going anywhere," Mr. Kent said to the thieftaker. "You should, however, let the ladies leave the room."

"I am not leaving," I protested.

"Nor am I," Julia said.

"I would like to leave," Miss Grant said. "Please, let me leave."

"Who are you?" Mulholland demanded.

"I am Elizabeth Grant. I do not have anything to do with this—" She stopped, realizing the mistake she had just made, and cast me an agonized glance.

Would Mulholland recognize her name? It seemed unlikely. As far as we knew, Lord Deele had not hired the Runners to find his sister.

"Let her leave," Mr. Kent said quickly, covering the slip.

"No one is leaving," Mulholland snapped. "For chrissakes, Kent, this is simple. Lower your gun. I'll take Belford and you'll keep your position."

"Keep my position?" Kent repeated through his teeth. "Are you so sure you have the support you think you have? Soldiers like us are expendable, Mulholland. You should know that by now."

"I say, what is going on here?"

Good God, was that Duffy coming up the stairs?

At the doorway, Samuel abruptly stood to attention.

Weatherly stepped aside. "Lord Duffield, my ladies," he announced as if Duffy were joining us for tea.

"There was no one downstairs to greet me," Duffy complained, walking into the room. "The door was wide open and I—" He looked around the room.

"Who the hell is this?" Mulholland demanded.

"Mr. Mulholland, this is our brother, Lord Duffield, who is also a magistrate," I said, for once glad to see Duffy. "Lord Duffield, allow me to introduce Mr. Mulholland, a thieftaker, Mr. Kent, a Bow Street agent who is assisting us, and"—I paused—"and Peter, my groom. Mr. Mulholland has mistaken Peter for a desperate highwayman and has come to make an arrest."

Mulholland glared at me. "He is not your groom."

"Do not speak until you are given leave!" Duffy ordered

Mulholland. "And put your gun down, man. You are in the presence of ladies."

Reluctantly, Mulholland lowered his pistol and gave a nod to Pritchard, who followed suit. With a release of pent-up breath, Mr. Kent lowered his gun too. I nudged Evan. He glanced at me unhappily but brought his gun to his side.

"Augusta, are you saying these men have forced their way into your home?"

"They have," I said.

"Without a warrant, my lord," Mr. Kent added helpfully.

Julia stepped out from behind him. "They have scared us quite horribly, Duffy, but we are unharmed. Thank goodness for Mr. Kent here, and . . . ah"—she stumbled for a moment—"Peter, who have both defended us most admirably."

"No warrant?" Duffy echoed. "No warrant? Mulholland, is it?"

"Aye," Mulholland said, then recollected himself and added, "My lord. But she is lying. This man is not her groom. He is—"

"Lying? Do you call my sister a liar, Mulholland?" Duffy demanded, thunder building in his voice. "Lady Augusta is many things, but she is not a liar, and I'll not have the likes of you calling her such."

Not the most glowing of endorsements, but the kindest thing Duffy had said about me in a while. And, in this instance, spectacularly wrong. Moreover, he seemed to be just getting started.

"Look at yourself, man. You are standing in the drawing room of two spinster noblewomen looking for a highwayman without a warrant. Are you a fool or just wildly incompetent?"

Mulholland, no fool and dangerously competent, remained silent, glaring at me.

"Is this your man, Augusta?" Duffy asked, nodding at Evan.

"He is, Duffy. He is not a highwayman."

"Patently," Duffy said. "This is clearly a case of mistaken identity, Mulholland. You and your men, get out. Now, I say! You have left yourself open to charges of breaking and entering. A hanging offense, if I am not mistaken. I do not want to see you in Grosvenor Square again. Anywhere near my sisters. Do I make myself clear?"

Mulholland's mouth bunched in suppressed fury, but he nodded. "Aye, my lord."

"And mark my words, I will be speaking to the Magistrates' Court about this travesty."

Not that it would do much good, I thought.

Mulholland made a bow to Duffy—the courtesy a hairsbreadth away from insolence—then nodded to Pritchard to follow him from the room. I stepped back as he approached the door.

"You'll regret this, my lady," he said softly as he passed.

I gripped the silver knife more tightly. "I do not fear you, Mr. Mulholland," I returned just as softly.

He looked down at my hand clenched around the weapon and flashed a wolf smile. "You seem to be lying again, my lady."

I swallowed, my mouth suddenly dry.

With one last malevolent stare at Evan, he strode from the room, his henchman close behind.

I signaled to Weatherly to shut the drawing room doors, then slumped back against the sideboard. I longed to catch hold of Evan's hand but instead placed the silver knife on the wooden top, the shape of its ruby cabochon impressed upon the skin of my palm.

"Astonishing," Duffy said into the silence. "And there are those who think we should have an actual police force like the French. Can you imagine? Clodhoppers like that with actual power?"

Mr. Kent, as close as we came to such a police officer, seemed unruffled by Duffy's denigration of his profession. Julia, on the other hand, was appalled.

"Mr. Kent is a Bow Street agent, Duffy," she said. "He has helped us greatly. We owe him much."

Duffy eyed the Runner. "A good thing you were here." He paused. "Why are you here?"

"On another, trifling matter, my lord."

"I see." Duffy dug a hand into his pocket and pulled out some coins, holding them out to Kent. "Here."

Mr. Kent stared down at the offering, then shook his head. "No, thank you, Lord Duffield. I am paid for my services."

"Certainly, but even the lowliest of servants receive vails. Take it. You seem to have done good service here."

"Mr. Kent is not a servant, Duffy," Julia said.

"No, thank you, my lord," Mr. Kent said firmly.

"As you wish." Duffy pocketed the coins again.

"I shall take my leave, my lord, my ladies," Mr. Kent said, bowing. "Peter, come with me."

"Yes, Mr. Kent," Evan said, making his own bow.

It was said with an admirable pretense of humility, but I knew it stuck in Evan's throat. He followed Kent to the door. Evan looked back at me, but for once I could not read his expression. He still had his gun, as did Kent. Good God, would the Runner try to arrest Evan now?

This was not even close to finished.

As Weatherly closed the door behind them, I made to follow. "Excuse me, Duffy, I must see if—"

"Augusta, who is this lady?" our brother demanded, finally noticing Miss Grant. "We have not been introduced in all the excitement."

Good God. I looked wildly across at Julia. He could not know her real name. Julia, however, was still fixed upon Mr. Kent's departure, an expression of distress upon her face. The first meeting between her Runner and Duffy could not have gone worse; it had been inevitable, but that did not make it any easier for my dear sister.

Miss Grant's safety was up to me, then. I scrabbled for a pseudonym. Smith too obvious, but nothing else came to mind. My frantic gaze fell upon the novel I had left upon the side table. Ah yes, that would do. "Lord Duffield, allow me to introduce Miss Dashwood. She is staying with us for a short while."

Miss Grant stared at me for a hard moment, then smiled at Duffy and curtsied. "How do you do, Lord Duffield?"

"Miss Dashwood." He bowed. "Unfortunate circumstance, but here we are. I hope you are not too discomposed."

"Not at all, Lord Duffield."

Weatherly entered. "Breakfast is served, my lady."

"Ah, excellent," Duffy said. "Miss Dashwood, allow me to escort you to the dining room." He offered his arm. To her credit, Miss Grant hesitated for only a second before taking it. "I say," he added as they made their way out of the room, "are you related to the Dashwood-Kings, by chance?"

It was testimony to Weatherly's management of our household that everything was already back in order. Duffy and Miss Grant led the way down the stairs to the dining room, Julia reaching for my hand as we followed.

She bit her lip: *What are we going to do now?*

I gave a reassuring smile: *I will handle it, do not worry.*

In all truth, I had no idea how to handle what had just happened, but I had faith that an idea would come along at some point. Hopefully sooner rather than later.

At the bottom of the steps, I released her hand and said to

Duffy, "If you will excuse me, I must see to something. Do start breakfast, I will not be long."

"If you must, Augusta, but do return swiftly," Duffy said. "I came here for a reason and I cannot stay long. Harriet wishes to go to morning service as well as the evening."

Of course she did—she would not wish to miss the fashionable gossip at the main services of the week. And of course Duffy had come for a reason. He only ever visited "for a reason." And I had, in all my days, never liked any of his reasons.

Still, I had other problems to deal with first. Two problems, in fact, who were at this moment more than likely at each other's throat.

22

I found Evan and Mr. Kent in the small library I had established at the back of the house. A private space with three walls of bookshelves full of my books, a desk, and a wingback chair set near the small hearth, like the one my father had in his study. The two men stood on opposite sides of the room, some heated conversation having—it would seem—just ended. Mirror images of their dislike for each other.

Now, there was a thought worth exploring.

"So now do you see, Mr. Kent?" I said, closing the door behind me.

"See what?" he asked truculently.

"That Mulholland is going to kill Lord Evan as soon as he finds him again." I glanced at Evan, seeing him square up to that fact. "It is set to be a straight execution, Mr. Kent. I think we can all agree that my brother's warning will have no effect and Mulholland will stay nearby. He will wait to complete his mission now that he knows Lord Evan is trapped here."

Kent nodded, conceding the truth of it.

I crossed my arms. "As I see it, we must find a way for Lord Evan to leave this house safely."

"We?" Kent said.

"You have just lied to a magistrate and abetted a criminal, so I think you are part of 'we.' Besides, I do not think you are willing to stand aside and see a man killed without due justice. Your honor would not allow it."

Kent closed his eyes for a second. "You and your sister will be the death of me."

"I sincerely hope not," I said.

Kent paced across the room, clearly weighing up the situation. He knew if he agreed he was stepping over a line that could mean the end of his career, not to mention his life.

He released a long breath. "And so, it seems I becomes we."

"Thank you," I said.

Across the room, Evan bowed. "You have my thanks as well."

"I am not doing it for you," Kent said.

I considered the two bristling men in front of me. Would it work? Was it too risky?

"I have an idea," I said.

Evan smiled. "I never doubted it."

"Totally insane, I presume," Mr. Kent added.

"Totally." I looked across at Evan. "Do you agree you must go? This will be highly dangerous. You know you can hide here as long as you wish."

"However much I would like to stay here, you are right. I put you all at risk this morning, and my presence here will continue to do so."

I waved the men forward. "Here, then, is my idea."

*D*uffy looked up from carving a slice of roast beef from the cold haunch before him. He sat at the head of the table, of course.

"Ah, good, you are back." He laid a slice of the meat on a plate and passed it to Miss Grant. "Julia, will you partake too? You do not eat enough."

"No, thank you, Duffy," she said, seated at his left. "I am content with tea and a roll."

She shot an anxious glance at me.

I gave a slight nod: *All in hand.*

Well, as in hand as it could be, considering my plan and the stakes.

I took a seat beside Julia, where I had a view through the window at the square outside.

Samuel brought over the coffeepot and poured me a cup; Weatherly was otherwise engaged, procuring the necessary props for our plan. Before me was spread one of Cook's feasts: the cold beef Duffy was carving and a haunch of ham, crisp bacon, fresh rolls, baked eggs, caraway seed cake, toast, a wheel of cheese, and a tureen of the kedgeree. I reached for a bread roll and placed it on my plate, then speared a good slice of ham.

"I came by this morning because Harriet and I are returning to Duffield House today," Duffy said, cutting a slice of beef. He forked it into his mouth and chewed reflectively.

"Are you going for the assizes?" Julia asked politely.

"Mm, that and other matters," he said. "But I am here because I received a letter from Lord Deele that was somewhat surprising."

Opposite me, Miss Grant stiffened slightly but, admirably, continued to eat her slice of seed cake.

"What did he write?" I asked, taking a nonchalant bite of bread and ham.

"He asks me to inquire whether or not you are hiding his sister, Lady Hester, and her companion, Miss Grant, in your house. Apparently Lady Hester is unwell but has absconded from an insane asylum with this woman—a bad influence, he says—and Lord Deele is worried for her safety and health."

"How extraordinary," Julia said, focusing upon buttering her bread. Her hand shook slightly. "Why would he think we were hiding them? We have never met Lady Hester, have we, Gus?"

I took a moment to swallow my suddenly dry mouthful. "Not that I can recall."

"It seems someone wrote to him with a rumor and he feels obliged to follow all intelligence upon the matter," Duffy added.

"Well, as you see, we do have a guest, Miss Dashwood, but she is hardly hiding," I said, smiling across at Miss Grant, who managed to rally her own smile. "Perhaps that is where the mistake has been made."

"No doubt," Duffy said, nodding to Miss Grant. "I only check up on the matter because Deele and I are old friends. You know, Eton and Four-in-Hand club and so forth."

"Yes, of course," Julia murmured.

"My other purpose is to invite you to Duffield House. As you are no doubt aware, Augusta, Julia has begged me to forgive you, and, indeed, Harriet is of the opinion that it is the Christian thing to do. So I invite you both to Duffield House for Christmas and an extended stay. Miss Dashwood, as a guest of my sisters, you are most welcome, too, of course."

Miss Dashwood gave a small bow in her chair and murmured her gratitude, but I could see the panic in Miss Grant's eyes.

An invitation to return to Duffield House was a huge concession on Duffy's part. Even so, it was not I who needed to be forgiven, and I did not believe for a minute that Harriet's opinion came from any Christian impulse. By the hopeful expression on Julia's face, I knew she desperately wanted me to accept, and usually I would do as she wished in these matters. Her happiness was my happiness. However, this was not the time to heal the breach. Quite the opposite. We needed to put as much distance as we could between us, London, and Lord Deele's spies, one of whom, it seemed, was now our own brother.

Through the closed dining room door, I heard the muffled sound of voices in the hallway.

At last.

I looked past Duffy and his sourly expectant face to the view outside the window, but my vista of the square was too limited. I pushed back my chair and stood, crossing to the window.

"What is it, Augusta?" Duffy demanded. "Why do you go to the window?"

I ignored him.

"Augusta can go to the window if she wishes, Duffy," Julia admonished gently.

I peered through the pane into our square. Was anyone waiting out there?

Peggy the flower seller crouched at the garden gates as usual. Farther along a well-dressed couple walked arm in arm, and a nursemaid pushed a child in a perambulator along the pavement. And a man—dun greatcoat, big build—leaned against the wall at the diagonal. Not Mulholland, but Pritchard by the heavyset shoulders and slouch.

I had hoped—gambled—that Mulholland would assume a desperate criminal would make his escape through the back of the house, not the front door, and so he and his posse would wait for their quarry in the mews. Pritchard was, in a strange way, a welcome sight: the lone sentinel stationed to ensure Mulholland was right. Still, the man was not blind nor particularly stupid. And luck, as we had grimly learned that morning, was notoriously fickle.

From my angle, I saw Weatherly open the front door and nod to Mr. Kent. The Runner returned the nod and limped down our front steps, making his way across the road at an easy pace to where Caesar stood, tied to the garden rails. His fashionable high collar and the brim of his hat obscured his chin and half his face, but there could be no mistaking the uneven but confident gait of the Runner. Would Pritchard notice that his jacket did not sit quite as well as usual over his broad shoulders, or that his Bow Street scarlet waistcoat seemed a little loose across the chest? Or, indeed, that he wore black hussars and not black riding boots?

Across the square, Pritchard straightened from his slouch and watched the Runner untie his horse. Had I misjudged his powers of observation?

I held my breath as the Runner stroked Caesar's neck, then stepped into the stirrup and mounted with athletic ease. With a pull upon the reins, he turned the big black horse and rode, at a sedate walk, away from Pritchard's scrutiny and toward our house. As he passed by my window, he glanced inside, and for a second I met my love's gaze.

Farewell for now, Renegade.

I smiled: *Farewell, my heart.*

Then he rode beyond my sight.

Across the square, Pritchard leaned back against the wall, arms crossed, and continued to watch the house. I released my breath.

"Well, Augusta?" Duffy prompted. I could hear the irritation in his voice. "Why do you stay silent? Harriet and I are willing to overlook your appalling behavior and allow you back to Duffield. Surely that demands the courtesy of a reply. And, I would add, sincere thanks."

A knock upon the door forestalled any answer.

"Come," I said.

Weatherly entered carrying the silver mail salver. He presented the note upon it with a bow. "My lady."

"Thank you." I took the note and opened it. The writing was as neat as the man.

> *He has departed safely. Mulholland is still out in the mews. I await the final part of the plan. Thank you for your father's jacket and breeches; the tailoring is excellent. K.*

I smiled—I knew Mr. Kent would appreciate the cut of my father's clothes. I folded the note and reclaimed my chair.

"We cannot visit you and Harriet, Duffy," I said. "We are promised to Lord Cholton for a house party. We leave tomorrow and expect to stay over Christmas."

We were, of course, not invited to a house party at Bertie's, but his seat was in the opposite direction from the Davenport estate where, I hoped, Charlotte would be able to hide Hester and Miss Grant. And if that was not possible, then we must find somewhere suitable along the road. Whatever the case, we had to leave London as soon as we could. I reached under the table and caught Julia's hand, giving it a squeeze.

She glanced at me: *Is he safe?*

I gave a small nod: *Safe.*

A knit of her brow: *And Mr. Kent?*

I lifted my brows: *You'll see.*

Duffy sat back in his chair. "Cholton?" He looked across at Julia. "Surely you would come to us rather than go to Bertie Cholton."

"It is a kind invitation, Duffy, but we cannot disappoint Bertie," Julia said. I knew it pained her to refuse our brother and the possibility of our renewed family harmony. I squeezed her hand again—this time in thanks. And in preparation.

"Frankly, Duffy," I said, "I would rather spend Christmas in a workhouse than with you and Harriet."

"What?" He stared at me for a second, unable to comprehend my words, then collected himself into righteous indignation. "Am I to be refused with so little civility from my own sister?" He turned to Julia. "You asked me to forgive her, and here I am—as you asked, as you begged—offering the olive branch. But she is bent upon maintaining a grudge. You must see it now. And she is dragging you into her old-woman venom. Do not think this invitation will be repeated."

He stood, making a jerky bow to Miss Grant and Julia. "I will take my leave, Julia, and of you, Miss Dashwood." He glared at me. "I do not take my leave of you, Augusta. You will not receive my courtesy until you behave in the manner of a gentlewoman and a sister."

On that, he walked from the room, Samuel scrambling to open the door for him.

"Oh dear," Julia said softly as our footman followed our brother from the room and closed the door behind their departure. "I suppose that was necessary."

I squeezed her hand again. "I am afraid so. He is too close to Deele."

"Are we really to go to Lord Cholton?" Miss Grant asked, frowning. "If Lord Duffield mentions it to Lord Deele—"

"No, we do not go to Lord Cholton. We go to the Countess Davenport." I held up my hand, forestalling any further discussion to listen to the sound of Duffy in the hallway, demanding his cane and hat from Weatherly, then the front door opening as Samuel ducked out to call our brother's coach waiting farther down the square.

I gestured to Julia to accompany me to the window. She followed with alacrity and we both looked out at the square. In a clatter of quick hooves, Duffy's coach pulled up at our doorstep, his footman springing down from his rear seat to open the door.

Our brother stalked down our front steps and into his equipage. Behind him, another man exited our door and descended our steps: tall, dark-haired, smartly dressed, leaning slightly more than usual upon a silver-tipped cane. He glanced up at our window as he crossed to our next-door neighbor's house—a quick roguish smile directed at my sister—then quickly ascended the steps to their doorway, behind the cover of the coach.

"You persuaded him to do this for Lord Evan?" Julia asked.

"He did not do it for Lord Evan, my dear."

As our brother's carriage set off in a clatter of hooves, Mr. Kent descended our neighbors' steps as if newly emerged from their front door. He turned in the opposite direction of the slouching, uninterested Pritchard and strolled across the square, a brief, jaunty lift of his cane bringing a radiant smile to Julia's face.

For better or worse, my sister had found her heart too.

We watched Mr. Kent disappear around the corner to safety. When Mulholland worked out what had happened, he would take such a humiliating defeat personally. Evan was in more danger than ever, as was Mr Kent, and we could not hide Hester forever.

Mr. Kent had demanded evidence that proved Evan had not murdered Sanderson, and so would the courts. We had one possible pathway to that evidence—Dr. Lawrence—and Evan was now set upon finding him. I hoped the search took my love far from London, for it was not safe for him, or indeed Hester, to stay in the city.

As the Bible says, there is no rest for the wicked. I opened the dining room door and found my butler and footman in the hallway watching the escape unfold through the sliver of window at the side of the closed front door.

"Weatherly," I called.

He turned, ready as ever. "Yes, my lady."

"Prepare the household. We are traveling tomorrow."

Bad Medicine

23

About ten miles from the Davenport estate, our carriage slowed and Miss Grant turned in her seat beside me to peer out the rain-spattered window.

"Soldiers," she said.

Her surprised voice seemed unnaturally loud in the cabin. Lady Hester and Julia had fallen asleep somewhere outside Manchester, and Miss Grant and I had not spoken since then in case we woke our exhausted companions.

We both looked across at them, propped in their respective corners among cushions and rugs, but they still slumbered.

I leaned over to look out of Miss Grant's window. No wonder she had felt the need to comment. At least forty red-coated soldiers carrying bayonets had moved to the side of the road to make way for our carriage.

"They must be here for the Luddites," I whispered, watching the soldiers' mud-spattered faces watch us as we drove by.

A few hours ago, we had driven past an eerie blackened mill in Manchester that had, according to the post innkeeper where we changed horses, been burned down by the Luddites in March. He had implied the troubles had come to an end. Perhaps they had only come to an end in Manchester.

Miss Grant sat back, our moment of unity gone. She had, I

suspected, stayed silent not only out of consideration for Hester and Julia, but also in protest. We had been on the road for three days, staying in two reasonable inns along the way, but in truth I had pushed us hard to reach Charlotte's estate. We were all exhausted and Miss Grant held me singly responsible for Hester's increasingly fragile state.

She had a point. Still, it was imperative that we reach Charlotte as soon as possible. Miss Grant herself had seen Mulholland's deadly agenda in our drawing room. His invasion had finally brought home just how precarious Evan's freedom, and indeed his life, stood, as well as their own. Although there had been some resistance from Hester, who had clung to the idea of fleeing the country, they had eventually conceded that refuge with Charlotte was the best path we could take.

Charlotte had written back to my request for refuge with a generous invitation to stay as long as we wished and an assurance that we would be her only guests for some time. Traveling to her home in Lancashire would perhaps fox Lord Deele's search for a while, but not Mulholland's. Although I had not seen anyone following us, I had no doubt the thieftaker would be seeking our whereabouts. We were his only link to Lord Evan, and he would not give that up easily. Thankfully, Evan was safely away, looking for a way to find Dr. Lawrence. Well, as safe as he could be with a thieftaker intent on killing him.

I thought back to my visit to Messrs. France and Banting before we left London. Since Mr. Kent had declared he could not pursue Miss Hollis's murder, I had instructed the undertakers to retrieve her body from Reginald Drake's dissection room immediately and ready her for her journey home. The good Mr. France, upon hearing my somewhat abridged version of the horrifying truth, had understood the need to keep our name from any connection to Miss Hollis. He had also, with his usual calm efficiency, assured me that he would himself restore her to her family to ensure discretion. It was not an entirely adequate return of the girl to her family—they would no doubt have questions that would never be answered—but considering what was at stake, it was the best I could do.

Two silent hours later, we approached the gates of Charlotte's estate. The apprehension that had clenched my innards since London finally eased; we had found sanctuary. At least for a while.

I gently shook Julia's shoulder. She opened her eyes, blinking away the haze of slumber.

"We have arrived," I said. "It has finally stopped raining."

Julia sat up and peered out the window as we passed the gray-stone Davenport estate gatehouse. The gatekeeper raised a hand in greeting to John Driver, then sounded his horn to herald our arrival. Our carriage crunched and splashed along the gravel driveway, the luggage coach lumbering behind. The old sentinel oaks on either side were still clothed in magnificent autumnal reds, and I spied the estate's small deer herd in the distance springing away from the thud and clatter of our arrival.

"What time is it?" my sister asked, stifling a yawn.

I gathered my fob watch upon its chain and consulted it in the dwindling afternoon light. "Ten past three o'clock," I reported.

"It feels later," Julia said, faint irritation in her voice. She was, I think, more unwell than she wanted to admit.

"It gets dark earlier this far north," I said. "We are just past Wales."

Beside her, Hester stirred under Miss Grant's gentle hand, her eyes fluttering open. She greeted the sight of her love with a smile. Lud, the sweetness of it was so like her brother's expression.

My fear for Evan—never far from my mind or heart—surged

through me. But I had been reminded over the last few days that there was no benefit in living a dread that had not yet happened. It only created exhaustion. I drew a deeper breath and focused on the immediate matter at hand.

"Remember, while we are here you are Mrs. Carter, convalescing widow, and her sister, Miss Dashwood, our dear friends from Bournemouth," I said to them. "Only Countess Davenport knows who you truly are, and she—"

"I know," Miss Grant said sharply. "I made a mistake before, but you do not need to keep reminding us."

Admittedly, my coaching may have been a little too persistent during our journey, but we could not afford any more mistakes. Servants and neighbors liked to gossip, and the true names of a runaway lady and her companion might reach the ears of Lord Deele.

"Lady Augusta is merely concerned for our safety, Lizzie," said Hester, taking Miss Grant's hand in gentle remonstrance. She turned her Belford smile upon me. "We will remember and play our parts."

The carriage took the curve in the driveway and the glory of Davenport Hall opened up before us. It stood at least twice the size of our family seat, Duffield House, and had been built during the first King George's reign, in the Palladian style. The much-celebrated Davenport domed roof crowned the main building, and large wings stretched out on either side: the east for accommodation and the west housing the kitchen and service rooms. Julia and I had stayed here, happily, so many times that we each had our own bedchamber.

We pulled up outside the stone steps that led to the front portico, the luggage coach with Weatherly and our maids coming to a halt farther back, closer to the servants' entrance.

My dear Charlotte stood at the top of the steps, dressed in burgundy and gold lace and flanked by her butler, Hanford. Unusual— the Countess Davenport did not usually come out to greet guests on arrival. Our eyes met, and a smile lit her face. Surely to be met with such warmth was one of life's delights.

Charlotte's footman opened the carriage door, waiting to hand us down. I descended first, taking his arm and arriving on the gravel just as Charlotte did. I curtsied, as did she, and then with a laugh she embraced me in a waft of her lily perfume and arms tight around my shoulders. Even more unusual; Charlotte was not one for displays of physical affection. Was something amiss? I returned the hard hug.

"I was not expecting you so early," she said urgently against my ear. "Prepare yourself because—"

But she had no chance to finish her warning, for a familiar voice called from the top of the steps, "Ah, Lady Augusta, how wonderful to see you again."

Charlotte's arms tightened, bracing my horrified recognition. Dear God, Emelia Ellis-Brant. The Ermine. Exactly the busybody we did not need anywhere near Lady Hester and Miss Grant.

"Porty brought her and her husband from London without informing me," Charlotte whispered against my ear.

Lord Davenport, or Porty to his intimates, was Charlotte's husband and cousin to the Ermine's spouse. While an affable man, Porty was also prone to impulsive and inconvenient gestures of generosity. Particularly when it came to his Ellis-Brant cousin.

I prepared my smile, then drew back from Charlotte's embrace and looked up the steps at the pale blond woman resplendent in orange silk and a red shawl. Oddly, Charlotte kept hold of my hand; did she think I would take to my heels?

"Ah, Mrs. Ellis-Brant, what a pleasant surprise to see you here."

"We came with Davenport now that His Royal Highness has finally gone to Brighton. How jolly to be here all together."

Jolly was not the word I would have used.

"Yes," Charlotte said. Her grip tightened. "An unexpected pleasure. And you will see that Mr. Talbot is here with us too."

Now I understood why she had kept hold of my hand.

Evan, newly arrived at the top of the steps, stood beside the Ermine. He was dressed in the clothes of a gentleman, the first time I had seen him in his rightful garb. Fitted buff breeches that showed the strong length of leg, a pristine cravat, a blue silk waistcoat, and a jacket that seemed molded to his broad shoulders. He had shaved, too, and cut his hair in a fashionable Brutus. Here was Lord Evan Belford, and the sight brought an involuntary flush of heat to my face.

He politely offered his arm to the Ermine and they both descended the steps. She did not seem pleased by his escort—I wondered what he had done to deserve such pinched-nose censure.

By this time, Julia, Lady Hester, and Miss Grant had vacated the carriage. At the corner of my eye, I saw Julia stiffen at the sight of the Ermine, but she managed a smile of greeting. Hester visibly gasped at the sight of her brother. Lud, was she going to give us away at the first test? But no, she quickly turned the involuntary sound into a cough and busied herself with her shawl, maintaining the masquerade. Miss Grant, too, had herself in hand but stared across at me as if this, too, was my fault.

"Lady Augusta and Lady Julia, I believe you are acquainted with my cousin Mrs. Ellis-Brant," Charlotte said. "And may I present Mr. Talbot, who is staying with us to study some of our rare books."

Evan bowed to me and Julia.

I nodded graciously and fleetingly met his eyes: *Study rare books?*

A tiny lift of one shoulder: *Best we could do.*

What was he doing here? He was meant to be far away, safe from Mulholland and searching for the doctor who had attended the duel, if the man still lived. We needed to ascertain whether there was a link between him and the Sally Lawrence who had appeared in the wager book of the Exalted Brethren of Rack and Ruin. Had something happened to stop his search? Or had he decided to do as his sister demanded and take her and Miss Grant out of the country, after all?

Whatever the case, he had put himself in grave danger.

I turned to Charlotte and managed to gather myself enough to attend to the courtesies. "Countess Davenport, may I present Mrs. Carter and her sister, Miss Dashwood." Hester and Miss Grant curtsied. "Mrs. Ellis-Brant and Mr. Talbot, our friends Mrs. Carter and Miss Dashwood."

Bows and curtsies were exchanged once again. All very unremarkable, except for my racing heart and mind. The Ermine had been following the scandal around Lady Hester with relish. What if she put two and two together?

For a wild moment, I considered herding everyone back into the carriage and departing, posthaste, before Tully and Leonard, our maids, unloaded our trunks and boxes from the luggage carriage with the help of Weatherly. But no—it was not feasible. Such a departure would be too odd, and besides, neither my sister nor Lady Hester would be able to manage it. They were at the end of their strength.

"You are all most welcome," Charlotte said. "Hanford will show you to your rooms. Please join us in the drawing room after you have settled in, or do rest if you prefer, Mrs. Carter. We keep country hours here, so dinner will be at six."

I moved to walk beside Evan, but he gave a small shake of his head.

Good Lord, what was I thinking? Or not thinking—it had been more an impulse from my heart than a rational decision. I had to take my own advice and exercise more caution.

I fell back beside Julia, who took my hand, her tight grip mirroring my own strained nerves.

And so the jolly house party moved indoors.

24

Julia paced across my bedchamber, turned on her heel at the window where I sat, and paced back.

"What are we to do, Gus?" she demanded.

"For the moment, nothing, my dear." I would have liked to pace alongside her, but it was best if only one of us was in a whirl at a time.

We were not in our customary rooms; Charlotte, with her usual quick wits, had placed us all in the east wing, as far away from Mrs. Ellis-Brant as possible. I had been given the Chart Room, decorated in eggshell blue, with a pretty cornflower paper on the walls, and silk furnishings. More importantly, it looked out upon the stables, and I could see Evan down below in conversation with Porty, whose stringy stature was in stark contrast to my love's muscular build. *Look up,* I willed, but of course he did not. One must always temper one's romanticism with a dose of reality.

A knock upon the door halted my sister's agitated progress back across the room. Since I had a fair idea who it would be, I said, "Come in."

As expected, the door opened to admit Lady Hester, supported by Miss Grant. Neither had divested themselves of their outerwear and bonnets, and Lady Hester had wrapped a further two paisley shawls over her pelisse to counter the chill of the hall's stone walls.

Miss Grant closed the door. "Are we alone?"

"We are, but—"

"You said we would be safe here," she hissed. "Am I right in thinking that Mrs. Ellis-Brant is the woman who told you about Deele's search for us? The gossip?" At my nod, she pressed her hand to her forehead. "It is a catastrophe. We cannot risk being here. If she discovers who we are she will tell her husband or Lord Davenport, and they are friends of Deele. They will tell him where we are."

"We must go now," Lady Hester said. She swayed upon her feet and Miss Grant tightened her grip upon her beloved's thin arm. "My brother will take us. He has come here to arrange our travel out of England, after all. Why else would he be here?"

Indeed, why was he here? He was not supposed to be anywhere near us.

I stood and motioned for them to keep their voices down. The Ermine was halfway across the huge house in the drawing room with Charlotte, and I had stationed Weatherly to ensure that the woman, or anyone else for that matter, did not come ferreting around our corridor. Even so, extra caution was always prudent.

"I know it is alarming, but we cannot leave immediately, nor in the company of your brother, Lady Hester," I said. "It would be too strange and would alert Mrs. Ellis-Brant. She may be a busybody, but she is not stupid. Besides, where would we go? You can barely stand up."

"We will be discovered," Hester said, terror in her voice. "Deele will come."

"There is no reason why Mrs. Ellis-Brant should find out," I said. "Lady Davenport has prepared the way by telling your story: you are Mrs. Carter, a widow from Bournemouth who has been ill and is convalescing in the company of her sister. It will allow you and Miss Grant to stay out of the woman's way."

Julia stepped forward. "Lady Hester, if you tried to leave now—even in the care of your brother and Miss Grant—I fear you would not get far before you collapsed. Remember how hard this journey has been, and it was done in comfort!"

My sister had tried to persuade Hester with the same truth when we were set upon meeting Evan by the roadside, and Hester had not listened then. Nor did she seem to be listening now. At least Miss Grant was considering our words. "I think Lady Augusta and Lady Julia are right, my dear. We cannot go yet."

"I must see my brother," Hester said, her mouth set into a mulish line. "I must. He will have plans for us."

"He did not last time," Miss Grant muttered.

Hester glanced hard at her companion, something passing between them that I could not catch.

"If you must, I will arrange it," I said. Although how a gentleman was to privately meet a widow to whom he had just been introduced without causing unwanted interest was, at that moment, a little beyond me. I pushed that problem aside and returned to the matter at hand. "For now, go back to your rooms. Do not come down to dinner if you do not feel safe."

"You can take a dinner tray," Julia said. "It will set up a precedent so that you will not need to come from your rooms very often."

Lady Hester stepped back, out of her beloved's supportive grip. "But I cannot stay locked in a room . . . No, no, I cannot."

"You will not be locked in a room," Miss Grant said soothingly. "We will walk the galleries and take the air, as you wish. There will be no locks." She took Hester's arm again and gently steered her to the door. "Come, we will walk now."

As Miss Grant opened the door, Hester looked back, her face stony. "If I see Deele again—if he comes for me—I will kill myself. Or I will kill him."

It was said with such quiet conviction that I was at a loss for words. Miss Grant tucked in her chin; she had heard that grim promise before.

The door closed behind them.

"Dear God, what a mess," Julia said, digging her fingertips into the bridge of her nose. "I am getting a headache."

She did indeed look pale. "Have you had something to drink?" I asked. "Maybe you need something to eat too. I can ring for tea."

"Stop fussing!" She drew a deeper breath. "I am sorry, but I cannot abide fussing."

"It is not *fussing* to be worried about you." Her irritability seemed to be increasing daily. "Go, lie down. The journey has been taxing."

"Do you really think she would kill herself? Or Deele?" Julia asked.

I did, and my sister saw it in my face.

"God help her," Julia murmured. "And God help us."

Once Julia had departed, I donned a woolen shawl and made my way out to the stables. I had guessed Evan would be waiting there, and I was right.

He was talking to John Driver with his back to me when I entered the cobbled stable yard, their conversation pitched for privacy. From the way my coachman was nodding, he was receiving instructions. But for what?

The stables and the coach house doors both stood open. Inside the coach house, Charlotte's pride and joy—an unsuitable perch phaeton with its huge wheels and small double seat—was in prime position, waiting to be hitched on short notice. Inside the stables, the change horses that had brought us here and the Davenport purebreds were being fed in their boxes. I breathed in the familiar and pungent smell of manure and hay. If this had been a normal visit, Charlotte and I would already be planning our rides—including a few illicit gallops astride rather than sidesaddle—and phaeton jaunts around the estate and beyond.

John Driver saw me approach and touched his hat. "Milady."

Evan turned, his smile a wry acknowledgment of the situation. I smiled back, trying to contain my desire to go straight to him. With remarkable restraint, I directed my attention to my coachman.

"You did well to get here so quickly, John. Thank you."

"Helped that we had good teams out of Manchester," he said gruffly. He eyed me and Evan with dawning comprehension—did he feel my longing?—then said, "Well, I'll be getting along, then, milady."

He sketched a bow and headed toward the tack room. Good man.

"Come, this way," Evan said, gesturing for me to follow him into one of the larger outbuildings. He had news; I could tell.

Inside, a large number of hay bales, boxes of winter apples, and grain barrels were stacked in neat order. We made our way farther in, dust motes and tiny pieces of hay flying into the air around us as my gown swept the floor. Evan stopped beside a wall of bales and held out his hands. I took them, wishing I was not wearing gloves. I wanted to feel the warmth of his skin.

"I have found Dr. Lawrence," he said, his excitement palpable. "Well, to be accurate, Dr. McLeod found two Dr. Lawrences: one in London, whom I have already visited and determined is not our man, and one in Blackburn. I have yet to see this Blackburn doctor, but I have every hope he is the right one."

"Oh, Evan, so close!" I said. "But why are you staying here, at Davenport Hall? It is too dangerous."

"Not as dangerous as traveling or sleeping rough around here. There are so many militias in the area."

"I know, I saw them about ten miles from here."

He nodded. "I only came here to solicit Lady Davenport for a meal and more respectable attire before riding on to Blackburn. But then the militia arrived in force to quell the Luddites. Lady Davenport insisted I stay until they moved on. It seemed like a good idea: my description has been distributed widely among the militia. Besides, it would be unlikely they would ever think I would be staying with the Davenports. Of course, they did not move on, and neither Lady Davenport nor I was expecting Porty or the Ellis-Brants to arrive."

"Indeed, it is a bad turn. So, you are not planning to take Hester out of the country? She believes you are here to do so."

"Ah, of course." He rubbed at his forehead. "Damn, she will see me as failing her yet again, for I see no way to do so safely at present."

I could not help a moment of relief. Shameful and selfish, but there it was. "Then you had best tell her, Evan. But do so gently. She is in terror of Deele finding her, and the presence of Mrs. Ellis-Brant is compounding that fear. She has threatened to kill him or herself if he tries to return her to an asylum."

"She voiced such a threat?"

"Yes, and I believe she means it."

"She probably does. The horror of that asylum is now carved into her mind and body, and it will be with her for the rest of her life." He stared at the wall behind me, his own past rising within him. I gently touched his arm, drawing him back. He gave me a quick, reassuring smile. "Do not fear, I will tread carefully, and we must ensure her safety, but for now I must focus upon finding Dr. Lawrence. It could be the path to ultimate safety for us all."

"We must focus upon it," I said firmly. "I will come too."

He shook his head. "A level head is needed here, Gus, especially now that we are so crowded. Hester and Miss Grant must be kept calm and safe. It will be better if you manage them and I visit Dr. Lawrence as swiftly as possible."

"Julia will manage the situation just as well as I can," I said, ignoring the jab of doubt that followed upon the heels of that assurance; lately my sister had seemed more prone to nervous agitation. Even so, the journey to Blackburn would be made in a day if we pushed ourselves.

"Do you think she is up to it?" he asked.

Ah, he had noticed as well.

"I think so. No, I am sure. Please, do not deny me, Evan. Every time we are parted, I fear it is the last time I will see you." I looked away, the stark admission heating my face. "Besides," I said, playing my trump card, "my presence will confound your description as a lone scruffy highwayman, and it will give Dr. Lawrence the assurance of respectability."

"Little does he know," Evan murmured. He took my hand and leaned across, his eyes upon my mouth. "If you think Julia can manage the situation here, then we shall finish this together."

His lips on mine were gentle—still curved into a smile—the kiss raising me onto my toes and into his arms. I pressed myself into his solid strength until the gentleness between us shifted into something far more urgent. All thought narrowed into the sensation of merging into the warmth and scent and sweet taste of his mouth on mine, the heat cascading through me.

"Milady?"

Lud! I flinched at John Driver's call and jumped back. At the corner of my eye, I saw Evan step behind the stack of hay bales as I quickly wiped the intense moment from my lips.

John Driver appeared at the doorway, Mrs. Ellis-Brant by his side.

Good God, that was close.

25

What on earth are you doing in here, Lady Augusta?" the Ermine asked with an arch laugh in her voice. She peered into the shed.

Good question. I scrabbled through my hot daze for an answer.

"I was getting some apples for the change horses. They did such good work getting us here." I paused a beat. Two can play this game. "What are you doing here, Mrs. Ellis-Brant?"

"I saw you go to the stables, and since I wished to speak to you privately, I thought this might be the chance."

"I see." Had she seen me go in here with Evan? And what could she have to say to me that had to be beyond the walls of the hall? "Well, I am on my way back to the house. Perhaps we could go together," I said, moving toward the door. I kept my pace sedate, although I wanted to hustle her out of the doorway as fast as possible.

"What about the apples?" she asked.

She did not miss much. "You are far more important than change horses," I said just as archly. "John can see to them."

I sent him a glance of gratitude: for the warning and the apples. My coachman touched his hat.

At the doorway, I took the Ermine's arm and used all my resolve not to look back at the tall stack of hay bales.

Mrs. Ellis-Brant walked in silence beside me until we had left the stable yard behind and were crunching our way across the large gravel driveway in front of the hall.

"Will you walk with me to the ha-ha?" She waved toward the steep grassy step at the end of the front lawn that dropped down to the beautiful Capability Brown gardens. "I would not wish to be overheard."

"Of course," I said.

We changed direction to walk across the wet grass, our backs now to the hall and anyone looking out a window. Although it was barely four o'clock, the night chill had already arrived and the gray daylight was giving way to impending dusk. If we were to traipse across the landscape, I wished I had thrown on more than a shawl.

"This is a rather delicate subject," the Ermine said, glancing up at me. "I know you are very good friends with dear Charlotte. Perhaps I should start by asking if you are aware of a man by the name of Edward Harley."

I could not help a jolt of surprise. Harley had been Charlotte's lover; he had stolen her letters and, in a way, started this whole adventure.

"Ah, I see you are," the Ermine murmured. "Then perhaps you also know that he was her paramour?"

"Did she tell you about him?" I asked. I could not conceive of Charlotte telling Emelia Ellis-Brant about anything, let alone her dalliances.

"Lud, no. But I have eyes in my head, Lady Augusta. I could see what was going on." She paused for my comment, but since I had none, she continued. "I told him he was a cur and should take himself off, and I think my words had an effect, for he retreated to Bath soon after."

"I see," I said, biting my lip. I rather thought the rock I had slammed into his nethers had effected his hasty retreat a good deal more than her censure.

"I know Charlotte is a great lady, and such sordid associations are not uncommon among the—" She stopped, realizing she was about to criticize my own rank. "Anyway, she does not seem to have learned her lesson. I think she has installed another of her inappropriate associations here, at the hall."

"Really? Who?"

"Mr. Talbot, of course."

I stopped walking, my arm dropping from her hold. "You think Mr. Talbot is Charlotte's lover?"

"*Lover*—dear me, you do not mince words, Lady Augusta. Yes, I do. I have seen them in close conference together. He is clearly not here to study rare books; just look at the man, all brawn and muscle and too charming by far. Besides, there is something inherently untrustworthy about him. Do you not agree? Mr. Harley had the same slippery charm. She must be attracted to such dangerous jackanapeses."

I stared at her, trying not to bristle at the comparison between Evan and the detestable Mr. Harley. "You think Mr. Talbot is untrustworthy?"

"I do, indeed. He may be a gentleman, but he is not being truthful. And neither is Charlotte."

Well, she was right about that.

"I see. But why are you telling me this?"

"I believe we must intervene, for her own sake. She is keeping him right under dear Porty's nose. You know I cannot abide such subterfuge, especially this kind of deceit."

"Indeed," I murmured, battling to keep the irony from my tone. Beyond the absurdity of the situation, I could see an inkling of opportunity. A rather splendid opportunity. "In what way do you think we should intervene?"

"Perhaps you could speak to her?"

I pretended to consider the proposition.

"No, I do not believe I can do so. It is not the manner of our friendship," I said, my mind conjuring an image of Charlotte when I reported this conversation. It was entirely possible she would wet herself from laughter. I sighed gustily, as if thinking further upon the problem. "Perhaps we should keep them apart as much as possible," I ventured. "I could suggest Mr. Talbot and I ride out tomorrow. For the day."

"Yes, that is perfect," the Ermine said gleefully. "We will keep them apart. I knew I could count upon you, Lady Augusta. God's law is God's law, after all, and if Charlotte is too weak to guard her marriage and her soul, then we, as her friends, must take action on her account."

Too weak? The woman's presumption—and her obtuseness—was astonishing.

"We are at the ha-ha," I said, in lieu of my true thoughts. We both looked down the steep step. The impulse to push her off was fleeting but strong. "Shall we go back?"

We turned around, the Ermine taking my arm again. "I am so glad I spoke up, Lady Augusta. Together we will ensure Charlotte does not stray into another unfortunate liaison. Now, let me tell you something I heard about the vicar of this parish. You will be astonished, I assure you."

*I*n the end, I was the only one of our party to go down to dinner. Hester and Miss Grant had arranged to have trays in their rooms, and my poor Julia had succumbed to the migraine. Even so, when I returned upstairs to dress, she insisted on knowing what had happened. I gave her a quick summary of my meetings with Evan and Emelia—my interview with the Ermine raising a wan smile upon her face—then left her in her darkened room under the tender care of her maid, who knew how to manage her headaches. It occurred to me as I changed my gown that my sister was lately suffering far more of these attacks, and in greater violence. Together with her agitations, it was a worrying progression.

I called in on Charlotte in her boudoir on my way down to the drawing room and gave my report once again, this time to peals of laughter.

"Good Lord," Charlotte said, wiping her eyes with a manicured fingertip. "The woman is insufferable. Did she really say she warned off Harley?"

"She did. But her interference will work in our favor this time," I said, and outlined the plan.

"Well, I shall enjoy playing the frustrated lover, and it will have the added benefit of diverting Emelia's attention away from Mrs. Carter and Miss Dashwood," Charlotte said. She picked up the gown her maid had laid out for her to wear—a green silk column with pleating at the bust—and raised a droll eyebrow. "Considering my new role, perhaps I should choose something with more décolletage."

I considered the green silk. "Any more and you may as well forgo the dress completely."

Charlotte snorted. "I am no Caro Lamb. Did you hear about that?"

"I did." Lady Caroline Lamb had literally served herself naked upon a platter at a party to celebrate the birthday of Lord Byron, her lover. Dear Caro had no concept of discretion. I felt sorry for her husband, but one had to admit to a small amount of admiration for her total disregard for convention.

Thinking of flouted husbands, I asked, "What about Porty? It is a poor trick to play upon him. What if he takes exception?"

"My husband is not one for recognizing undercurrents or indeed any kind of emotional nuance," Charlotte said dryly. "Besides, we have an arrangement. I will inform Lord Evan of our liaison before dinner. I am sure he will be interested to know of our affair."

As it happened—or perhaps it was a swift change made by Charlotte—I was seated next to Evan at the dining table. Porty, of course, sat at the head, Charlotte opposite her husband at the other end, and Mr. and Mrs. Ellis-Brant on the other side of the table. A small gathering in such a huge dining room. Due to the party's size, Charlotte declared we were to dine en famille: instead of only conversing to the person beside us as was custom, we could converse across the table too. Although I was not sure that would be to our advantage.

"May I serve you soup, Lady Augusta?" Evan asked as the footman positioned the tureen upon the table.

Charlotte had ordered a fine repast: the first remove consisted of soup à l'oignon, duck rillettes, a casserole of rabbit, a cheese tart, green beans, fricassee of mushrooms, salmon vol-au-vents, and a turbot awaiting its place once the tureen had been withdrawn.

"Yes, please." I tried to keep the warmth from my voice. I was, after all, playing the part of Charlotte's judgmental friend.

Evan took my bowl and ladled out the rich broth, placing it in front of me. "And for you, Lady Davenport?"

"Thank you, yes, Mr. Talbot," Charlotte said, managing an excellent simper. I stared down at my bowl, pressing back a snort of laughter; I had never seen my friend simper before. A glorious sight.

Evan smiled back at his alleged lover and ladled a bowl, placing it in front of her with a small, gallant bow.

The Ermine observed the interplay with narrowed eyes.

"I have had a letter back from Lord Alvanley today," Porty said, his voice overloud in the scarcely populated room. The man did tend to shout rather than talk. "He and Mr. Brummell are presently visiting the Ladies of Llangollen."

Of course; the Ladies of Llangollen were close by in Wales. Only hours away. If things were not so fraught, I would suggest Julia and I visit her friend Miss Ponsonby.

"They are on their way to Alvanley's estate," Porty continued, "so I have invited them to join our party at the end of the week for a few days."

Charlotte looked at me, her face under control, but I could tell she was alarmed. As I was, and no doubt Evan beside me, but I dared not glance at him. Lord Alvanley was as close to the Regent as Mr. Brummell was, and both were leaders of society. They knew everyone and everyone knew them. George, of course, knew about Hester and Deele and had already shown his alliance. Or perhaps his indifference. But the same could not be said for Alvanley. There was every chance he had met Hester before she was incarcerated and I did not have the same leverage of friendship with Alvanley as I did with George to ensure his discretion.

"At the end of the week, you say, Porty?" Charlotte asked, her tone overly blithe.

Porty grunted. "Most likely. He says they will stay until Sunday." He glanced at Mr. Ellis-Brant and Evan. "It is well into the season, but we could get in a shoot. There may be some birds left."

"Excellent," Mr. Ellis-Brant said heartily.

"Indeed," Evan said, and I almost believed his enthusiasm.

"Are you a shooter, too, Mr. Talbot?" Mr. Ellis-Brant asked, clearly surprised. "I thought you bookish types didn't go for sport."

The Ermine's husband was a big, genial man with an infectious laugh and an easy manner; I could see why Lord Davenport favored his company. I did wonder, though, how he rubbed along so well with Emelia. Perhaps his congeniality compensated for her uncharitable outlook on life.

"I enjoy all sports, Mr. Ellis-Brant. Shooting, riding, boxing. As well as my books."

"Well, you're in luck if you want to ride," Mr. Ellis-Brant said. "The stables here are exceptional."

"I agree," Evan said. "Lady Davenport and I have already ridden the perimeter." He took another spoonful of soup, sending a swift amorous glance at Charlotte.

The Ermine was not going to let that pass. "Did you know that Lady Augusta is an excellent horsewoman, too, Mr. Talbot?"

He glanced at me, soup spoon poised again. "I did not."

"You do enjoy riding out, Lady Augusta; is that not so?" the Ermine prompted. She was working hard.

"Yes, there is nothing better than a day's riding," I said. "Perhaps we could venture out tomorrow if that suits you, Mr. Talbot."

"It would be my pleasure," Evan said politely.

"A marvelous idea. I shall enjoy that enormously," Charlotte said.

"But, my dear, you promised to take me to visit your tenants tomorrow morning with charity baskets," the Ermine said silkily. "I was so looking forward to it."

"Did I? Oh yes, of course," Charlotte said. "But you must go riding, Lady Augusta. I would not wish you to forfeit any pleasure." She allowed a nicely judged instant of irritation and disappointment to cross her face. A performance worthy of the great Sarah Siddons herself.

"Well, that is settled to everyone's satisfaction, then," the Ermine said, glancing at me with a smug smile.

I returned my own smug smile.

To everyone's satisfaction, indeed.

26

The next morning, I woke to the sound of Tully drawing the bedchamber curtains and the rhythmic thud of heavy rain upon the windows.

"'Tis a foul day, my lady," Tully reported, her tone implying that the Lancashire sky rained out of spite. "Looks like it has settled in too."

So much for best-laid plans. I rose, receiving my silk wrap from Tully and drawing it close as I walked to the window. A pessimistic squint at the dark clouds and rain sweeping across the stables agreed with Tully's prediction. There would be no riding today. Not unless a miracle happened.

Charlotte kept country hours and so breakfast was not until after nine. Time, then, to dress and visit Julia, if she was awake, and apprise her of last night's fun and games.

My sister was in the process of dressing when Leonard opened her bedchamber door to me.

Julia sat at the dressing table in a white morning gown with a Vandyke collar trimmed with double lace. She always chose an abundance of lace when she wished to invigorate herself. It made her feel better, she said. Which probably meant she was not feeling any better.

"Has your headache gone?" I asked, walking to the windows to check if the miracle had happened in the minute it had taken me to walk along the corridor. No—if anything, the rain was heavier.

"A little," she said as she considered the linen cap that Leonard had fetched from the clothes press.

I glanced at her maid for confirmation. Leonard gave a slight shake of her head.

My sister waved away the cap. "No. The lace-trimmed one, I think." She turned her attention back to me. "So, what transpired at dinner last night?"

I apprised her of the currently untenable plan to ride to Blackburn and the advent of Lord Alvanley and George Brummell at the end of the week.

She clicked her tongue. "That is a meeting we cannot risk."

"No, we cannot. I believe we will have to go before they arrive, but we must consult with Lord Evan. At present I cannot think where we can go."

"And we must consult with Hester and Miss Grant too," Julia said, a little reproachfully, as Leonard pinned on the chosen cap. She glanced at her maid. "I know I do not need to remind you, but none of this is to be discussed, even with Tully."

"Of course, my lady," Leonard said, clearly a little offended at the warning. "Miss Tully and I understand."

I eyed my sister; she must be highly anxious to remind her trusted Leonard about discretion.

"I think we should wait to tell them. The prospect of Lord Alvanley and Mr. Brummell coming will be a little too much for Lady Hester after yesterday's shock," I said.

Julia rose from the dressing table stool. "As you wish."

I had expected a great deal more argument from her, but there was an odd lethargy in her manner. I hesitated to ask after her health again, since it was such an unpredictably prickly subject now, but I could not help myself.

"Are you really feeling better, my dear?"

"I must admit I feel a little odd." She shrugged her shoulders as if her gown was too tight. "Everything is a bit prickly and crawly. I think I am just in need of exercise after the long carriage journey."

"We could walk the long gallery before breakfast."

She nodded, allowing Leonard to place a shawl around her shoulders. I noticed she slid her hand along the dressing table edge as she rose and headed to the door, as if to keep her balance.

I thrust out my arm. "Come, let us walk arm in arm. We have not strolled so for such a long time."

She took the offered support. I smiled, receiving a bare lift of her lips in return. She might deflect my concern at every turn, but something was very wrong with my darling sister.

*T*he long gallery on the second floor stretched the whole length of the main house. It accommodated the Davenport collection of their more second-rate family portraits and overlooked a charming vista of formal garden. Julia, Charlotte, and I had spent many a rainy day walking its length for exercise, and sometimes, when all the servants had been dismissed and no one was around, playing a childish game of tag, full of shrieks and laughter.

As Julia and I slowly climbed the smaller side staircase that led to it, we heard a voice. A shrill voice.

"Oh no, that is Emelia," Julia whispered, stopping upon the landing and therefore halting our momentum. "I cannot deal with her this morning. Let us go back. We are still out of sight."

Then two other female voices reached us. Good God, the

Ermine had cornered Lady Hester and Miss Grant. I glanced at Julia; she had recognized their voices too. And the danger.

"You go back. I'll stay," I whispered. "I cannot leave them with her; she will agitate Lady Hester too much."

Julia, clearly torn, shook her head. "No, I will come too. We can draw Emelia away so they can retreat."

We took the last steps, emerging into the gallery. Although it was early in the day, the wall sconces and side table candelabra had been lit, providing a warm light along its majestic length. The two hearths, however, had not yet been lit, so the air held the chill of morning. Lady Hester and Miss Grant stood about halfway along, swathed in paisley shawls and politely nodding as the Ermine—in a pale blue fur-trimmed mantle—expounded upon what sounded like the game of hoop rolling.

"Ah, Lady Augusta, Lady Julia," Miss Grant called, valiantly trying to keep the relief from her voice. "You have come to walk too?"

Mrs. Ellis-Brant turned. "We have all had the same idea," she said gaily, pulling her mantle more securely around her shoulders. "If Charlotte joins us, it will be quorum."

I smiled, ignoring the misuse of *quorum*. "Indeed," I said as we walked to join them. "A morning walk is aways beneficial. Even on such gloomy days."

We all exchanged curtsies. It seemed we had arrived just in time: Lady Hester gripped the edge of her paisley shawl a little too hard, and Miss Grant was chewing on her lip. No doubt suppressing the desire to scream.

"I was just telling Mrs. Carter and Miss Dashwood about the fun that dear Charlotte always organizes for our amusement," the Ermine said. "Just the thing to help one's convalescence, Mrs. Carter. A little bit of vigorous exercise will chase away the doldrums."

Lady Hester made an incoherent noise.

"I think my sister will need bed rest more than hoop rolling," Miss Grant said.

"Of course, of course," the Ermine said. "You no doubt found London exhausting. If one is not used to city life, it can be a trial. It must be very different from the isolated wilds where you are from. How did you end up in such a place? I cannot imagine anyone choosing to live in a swamp if not forced to do so."

Since we had failed to rehearse a story of how Mrs. Carter and Miss Dashwood had ended up in Bournemouth, we all stared at her, momentarily nonplussed.

"Weymouth is not that isolated or wild, Emelia," Julia finally said.

A beat of nonplussed silence met my sister's comment.

"Weymouth?" the Ermine said, and gave a small giggle. "Do you not mean Bournemouth, Lady Julia?"

Oh no.

She turned to Lady Hester. "Did you not say you were living in Bournemouth?"

"Yes," Lady Hester managed, her alarm plain to see.

For a long, awkward moment, Julia did not answer—I could see her horror at the slip—but she finally rallied. "Of course, Mrs. Carter is from Bournemouth. I misremembered, that is all."

"You? Misremember? But you are famed for your prodigious memory, Lady Julia," the Ermine said archly. "It has always been remarked upon."

"I think yesterday's travel has been hard upon us all," I said quickly. "It was arduous and we are all still a little weary. Perhaps that is enough walking for today."

"Yes, quite," Miss Grant said. "My sister and I will take our leave now to rest before breakfast. Good morning." She ushered

Lady Hester away, casting a wild look back at me as they walked toward the staircase.

"It must be the fatigue of the journey," Julia said. "Of course I know where our friends live. It was just a slip of memory. From fatigue, I'm sure it was just fatigue—"

"Indeed," I said, cutting her off. My sister was, I feared, protesting too much, and the Ermine was watching her with knitted brow. "Good morning, Mrs. Ellis-Brant. We will see you at breakfast."

I took my sister's arm and sedately steered her to the staircase, away from the Ermine's far-too-watchful gaze.

Back in her bedchamber, Julia pressed her hands to her face, close to tears.

"I do not know why I said Weymouth. I know it is Bournemouth. And Emelia pounced upon it. Did you hear that snide remark about my memory? And Hester's face—it has frightened her even more."

I drew my sister's hands down in my own. "Come, you are making too much of it." It was not idle comfort on my part; my sister seemed overwhelmed by the small mistake.

"What if she puts it all together?"

"From that one comment? I do not think so, my dear."

I suspected the Ermine had been more interested in my sister's failure of memory than in what she had failed to remember. Even so, Julia was right about Hester—her fear had been almost tangible.

"Leonard," I called. My sister's maid promptly emerged from the adjoining dressing room. "Go fetch tea and some bread and butter for Lady Julia."

"I do not need tea and bread," Julia said.

"You ate nothing for dinner. Please take something."

She eyed me for a mutinous moment, then sighed. "As you wish."

I nodded to Leonard, who departed on her mission.

Julia grasped my hands, her skin oddly clammy. "You must check on Lady Hester and Miss Grant. They must be so anxious. No, I should do it. To apologize. Yes, that is what I must do."

She drew her hands back but I kept hold of them.

"No, my dear," I said. The last thing we needed was my sister and Lady Hester spinning each other into more agitation. "I will visit them. Now, put this behind you and do not mention it again. Especially to the Ermine. Returning to it will only raise it in its importance."

On that sage advice, I took myself off to Lady Hester.

Her bedchamber was almost a mirror of my own, except painted green, and the bed had a canopy set above four turned posts, one of which Lady Hester was clinging to for support, panting with fear. Miss Grant held her beloved's free hand and rubbed her back.

It appeared Lady Hester did not need any help spinning herself into greater agitation. I quickly closed the door and provided the same reassurances I had given my sister.

"See, Lady Augusta agrees with me, dearest," Miss Grant said firmly. "It was a minor slip. Nothing will come of it." She looked at me over Hester's shoulder, plainly unconvinced herself, but I approved her attempt to calm her love.

"We are all forced indoors today," I said. "Please, if you can bear it, come down for breakfast and then claim the need for rest. Mrs. Ellis-Brant has other fish to fry and I believe this will go unremarked if we do not make it a point of interest."

"How can you know that?" Lady Hester demanded.

"She thinks your brother is Lady Davenport's lover and is trying to interfere."

As I had hoped, the shock of that statement jolted Hester from her track.

"What?" She stared at me for a moment—the information sinking in—and then a glimmer of a smile curled her mouth. "Oh my goodness. Does my brother know?"

"He does. He and Charlotte are playing along in order to distract Mrs. Ellis-Brant. So, you see, she is busy upon her own scandal."

Hester released her death grip upon the bedpost. "My brother is playing along? But surely he would find such a pretense distasteful. He cannot abide anything that is not of an honest nature."

Her view of her brother was, understandably, somewhat outmoded. I'm sure there had once been a time when Lord Evan Belford would not have engaged in such a deception—it would have been too dishonorable—but now it was his only way of survival. And, thankfully, he was rather good at it. "Your brother would do anything, I think, to ensure your safety," I said diplomatically.

I left them discussing that development, but I had no confidence in its distracting them for long. I had ducked Hester's challenge, but she was right: I did not know if Julia's mistake had piqued the Ermine's interest. What concerned me more was Hester's state of mind. And what impact the imminent news of Lord Alvanley's and Mr. Brummel's visit would have upon that state. It was all becoming so tangled and strained.

I stopped at the top of the staircase, suddenly uncertain of where I should go. Back to my sister? To Charlotte? What was the next step? My true desire was to find Evan, but he would be in the bachelors' quarters. No place for an unmarried lady, or indeed any lady. Not with all the servants busy throughout the hall upon tasks.

I looked out the stairwell window at the sodden garden. It had been my idea—no, in truth, my insistence—that brought us here for sanctuary, and now danger was closing in from all sides. We would, I think, have to flee soon. But to where?

Rivulets of water ran down the window glass. The rain had not eased at all. No miracle yet, and we sorely needed one. Hopefully tomorrow it would be waiting for us in Blackburn.

27

My next step, I finally decided, was to have a note delivered to Evan.

I sent a footman to find Weatherly for me, then returned to my room and wrote the message: a brief précis of what had happened in the gallery, the fear around the arrival of Lord Alvanley and Mr. Brummell, and most importantly a proposal to meet in the stables once again.

Before long, I heard Weatherly's particular knock upon my door and bade him enter.

"Good morning, my lady."

I turned from pressing the wafer upon the parchment to seal the note. My butler closed the door and stood watching me, his calm manner always bringing comfort. He had, I noted, dressed in his blue Sunday coat, not his butler black.

"How is it, Weatherly? Is Hanford deliriously happy to see you?"

Weatherly allowed a small smile at the long-standing joke. It was, admittedly, rather singular of Julia and me to travel with our butler, especially to houses that were presided over by their own senior man, but I trusted our safety and comfort to no one else. He had accompanied us on a number of occasions to Davenport Hall, but he was yet to receive any collegial warmth from Mr. Hanford.

Two butlers in one house was clearly an affront to the man—especially, I think, a Black butler—thus Weatherly's slightly less formal attire.

"Actually, my lady, this time I have made some headway," he said. "Mr. Hanford has asked me if I would be willing to valet for Mr. Talbot since neither Lord Davenport's man nor Mr. Ellis-Brant's will see to him. He knows it is a step down so sees it as a great favor. I said I must obtain your permission."

I sat forward in my chair. "Of course you can—it works to our advantage—but why will the other valets not dress Lord Evan?"

Weatherly tilted his head, an amused squint to his eye. "There is some notion among the staff that he is here under false pretenses and is Lady Davenport's lover."

"Good God, we only thought of that last night and it has reached the servants' hall already?" An alarmingly fast transmission of gossip, which brought another concern hard on its heels. "Are they talking of anything else? What do they say about Mrs. Carter and Miss Dashwood?"

"Nothing of import, my lady," Weatherly said. "Two of the housemaids are dressing them and they are keen for the experience so are not talking out of turn. All that has been said is that the widow is frail and the sister most attentive. The general sense seems to be one of sympathy. Other than that, there is some general discontent regarding Mrs. Ellis-Brant's demands."

"Well, sympathy is better than curiosity, I suppose." I sat back in the chair. "We are rather crowded here, Weatherly," I said ruefully. "Not what we expected to encounter or what we need."

"No, my lady. Is the plan to stay?"

"As yet, undecided." I offered the sealed packet. "Please take this to Lord Evan."

Weatherly received the note with unusual diffidence. "I would, my lady, but Lord Evan has ridden out with Lord Davenport and Mr. Ellis-Brant. There is a boxing match in the village and Lord Davenport has insisted on their company. They are to be gone most of the day."

"A boxing match, in this weather?"

"It is in a barn, my lady."

I stared down at the table. Damn. Would it be too marked to send Weatherly or John Driver to the boxing match with the message? I had to reluctantly conclude that it would.

"Give it to him as soon as he returns, then."

"I will, my lady." He paused, the moment holding enough weight that I knew he had something else to say. Something that was not quite proper to volunteer.

"Is there anything else I need to know, Weatherly?"

"The mail has arrived, my lady. I have just delivered a letter to Lady Julia."

"Do we know who it is from?"

"I could not say. Although Lady Julia seemed delighted to see the direction written by that particular hand."

Ah, Mr. Kent.

I met Weatherly's worried gaze: we both knew that was a storm yet to break.

He bowed. "Lady Julia is in the library, my lady," he said. And on that intelligence, he departed the room.

I found my sister in her favorite seat in the Davenports' impressive library. It was tucked away at the far end of the large book-lined room, a leather armchair in a small nook that she had found early in our visits and claimed as her own. She sat with her letter in her hands, staring at it in some consternation, but looked up as I approached.

"There you are," I said.

"Here I am," she responded, smiling a little at the childhood greeting. "I suppose Weatherly told you I had a letter from Mr. Kent?"

"Not in as many words."

"He does like to be discreet," she said dryly. "As it happens, I was about to look for you." She held out the single sheet of paper.

"I can read it?"

"It is too urgent for anything other than words of warning," she said. I did not like the sound of that. I took the letter, finding the paper sturdy and the broken wafer of good quality. Mr. Kent had wished to ensure a secure seal. I read his neat hand.

> *Tuesday, 27th October*
> *1812*
> *Cheapside*

> *My darling Julia,*
>
> *I have been following Mulholland and his men since I quit your house. I believe he is aware you have left London, and most likely knows your initial direction. I trust that Lady Augusta's particular friend is not with you.*
>
> *There is, however, another development that will concern all who traveled in your carriage. Lord Deele has arrived in London, and Mulholland called upon him today. Whether he went upon his own cognizance or was summoned by Lord Deele, I do not know. But such an odd meeting does not bode well.*
>
> *I will continue to follow Mulholland and send word if he or Lord Deele leaves London.*
>
> *I am, for now and ever, yours,*
> *Michael*

The writing blurred before me—I had failed to take a breath, shock locking my chest. I drew a gulp of air. Mulholland and Lord Deele? It was not a meeting I had anticipated. I glanced up at the date again. Written two days ago.

"Is it possible that Mulholland knows we are hiding Lord Deele's sister?" I asked, trying to understand such a dangerous collusion. "He did hear Miss Grant's name before Duffy came into the room."

"Only once and it was a fleeting reference," Julia said quickly. She sat back, rubbing her temple. "Although I suppose it is possible. And if he has made the connection, then he must also realize Lord Evan is brother to both Deele and Hester."

"Or if he does not, he soon will," I said. "But Mulholland is not a man to offer information for free. He will want something from Deele in return for the fact that we are hiding Lady Hester."

"But what?" Julia asked.

"Mulholland wants Lord Evan, but I cannot see what Deele has that would help Mulholland find him. Besides, would Deele give up information about his own brother to a man who is so clearly a shady sort? Deele would know it would be the gallows for Lord Evan if he is taken, so I cannot see him doing that."

"I suppose it depends on how much Deele wants to find Hester."

"Very much," I said. Yet the Deele I had met at Charlotte's ball months ago had seemed adamant that his brother was innocent. "Well, as of two days ago, they have not left London. We have time to make another plan."

"You will think of something," Julia said.

I was touched by her faith in me. I, on the other hand, did not share that faith.

I passed back the letter. "'I am, for now and ever, yours'? It is a big claim. Do you feel the same way?"

She brushed a fingertip over the bold signature. "He is a good man, Gus. This is dangerous for him."

She had not answered, but I did not push the point. Besides, her answer was in every action and every expression. Instead, I said what was truly playing upon my mind. "You do not have to persuade me of Mr. Kent's worth, Julia. But you know Duffy will never countenance such a match. And neither will society. He is too far below us."

She raised her head, mouth mulish. "Michael may be lowborn but he is a man of honor. What about Lord Evan? Do you imagine Duffy will embrace a disgraced nobleman—a convict—into the family just because of his birth?"

I heard the pain in her voice.

"Not at all," I said. "Duffy will not countenance either match. But the difference is, I do not care what our brother thinks."

"No, because I do that caring for you," she snapped. "I am always between you two, building a bridge so that our family does not collapse."

"I have never asked you to do that," I said, bristling a little.

She shook her head, not in negation, but as if she was trying to dislodge her ill humor. "I know. But one's connections are important. We must keep our family together. You, Duffy, and I—we are the only ones left." She sighed. "Still, it is not fair. Everyone wants to tell us who we can and cannot love. Surely I am old enough to love as I wish. I am of no interest to anyone, yet my life is still under scrutiny. Still directed by others."

I thought of Lady Hester and Miss Grant and the suffering they had endured because they loved each other. And yet they persisted.

"I suppose it is what you are willing to give up to claim that love," I said. "Will the love be more than the loss?"

I was not only asking it of my sister. It was the question that I faced as well. Frankly, I felt little regret at the thought of leaving my brother, but could I ever leave my dearest Julia, my ailing twin, to be with Evan?

Even the question brought a clench of pain around my heart. And underneath all the hope of exoneration, I could feel the need to decide bearing down upon me.

28

To their credit, Lady Hester and Miss Grant came down to breakfast and sat with Julia, Charlotte, Mrs. Ellis-Brant, and me. The meal passed without any incident, going some way, I think, to soothing Lady Hester's alarm.

And then came the true test. There is nothing quite like a gloomy, rainy day indoors to set my teeth on edge, particularly outside my own home. The usual indoor occupations of a genteel female guest—needlework, gossip, and artistic endeavors—were far from my favorite activities. If it had just been Charlotte and Julia, the time would have passed tolerably well. I could have read or gone to the stables to view the horses with their blessing. However, in a hurried whispered conversation among the three of us on the stairs before breakfast, we decided to keep Mrs. Ellis-Brant close to us throughout the day. An admirable plan to save Miss Grant and Hester from her presence.

The problem with that plan, however, was that Mrs. Ellis-Brant was close to us the entire day. Although I dearly wanted to escape the confines of the drawing room, I could not, in all honor, abandon Charlotte and Julia to her shrill company. It transpired that Mrs. Ellis-Brant had her own goals: to poke Julia about her health, slander Mr. Talbot in as many insidious ways as possible, and pass uncharitable judgment upon our mutual acquaintances.

By the time it came to dressing for dinner, even Charlotte was a little short with her cousin-by-law. We all parted at the staircase for our various dressing rooms, three of us breathing deep sighs of relief.

As was the custom of country living, the ladies were to meet the gentlemen in the drawing room before being escorted to the dining table. My sister, although still suffering a headache, had elected to come down to dinner. We met upon the landing, ready to descend. She had chosen an apricot silk gown with gold lace, the color adding some warmth to her pallor. I had chosen my favorite royal blue gown, its Grecian column cut swathed in silver net embroidered with stars and well suited to my tall, angular figure. Tully had also added some diamond star clips into my tonged curls, a decoration I had not indulged in for some time.

"I have not seen that gown in a while," my sister whispered as we descended the stairs to the drawing room. "Is it for Lord Evan?"

"Maybe," I said, feeling unaccustomedly coy.

My sister smiled and patted my arm. "Well, you look magnificent, my dear."

The footman opened the drawing room doors to the sound of male voices.

"Ah, Lady Augusta, Lady Julia," Porty said loudly.

The conversation stopped as we entered. A scan of the assembled gentlemen brought first the warm welcome of Evan's gaze—my heart beating a little harder at that brief connection—then Mr. Ellis-Brant's genial countenance, and then two faces I did not know. Two faces and two red uniforms.

"Allow me to introduce Captain William Morland and Lieutenant Henry Powers," Porty continued, "currently in charge of the company who are dealing with the Luddites in the area."

Good God, soldiers. No, worse. Officers, who may have received the description of a desperate criminal known as Hargate. Evan was still a wanted man, and not only by the murderous Mulholland. I glanced at him again. To all other eyes he no doubt seemed serene, but I saw the strain around his mouth.

The captain and lieutenant bowed, along with Evan, Porty, and Mr. Ellis-Brant. Julia and I curtsied our own greeting, and I could feel the same tension that gripped me radiating from my sister.

The captain was absurdly young: fresh-faced, with barely a beard. Probably a younger brother in a good family making a career in the army. For all his youth, however, he had shrewd blue eyes and a hint of humor about his mouth. His lieutenant was a little older—mid-thirties, perhaps—which must make for an interesting dynamic between them. He possessed a long, bony face that seemed settled into a morose expression, rather like a scent hound.

"Ah, you are already down," Charlotte said behind us. She herded Miss Grant and the Ermine into the room. "Captain Morland, Lieutenant Powers, allow me to introduce Mrs. Ellis-Brant and Miss Dashwood. Mrs. Carter is not well enough to join us tonight, so I believe we are all here now." As she spoke, Hanford arrived at the doorway, signaling with a bow of his head. "And I see that we are ready to dine. Shall we?"

Lord Davenport immediately offered his arm to me, Mr. Ellis-Brant to Charlotte, Evan to my dear Julia, the captain gave a smart salute to the Ermine, and Miss Grant took the lieutenant's arm. A nicely balanced table, and one that I wished Evan was miles away from.

It transpired that Captain Morland was, indeed, the younger son of a nobleman who was also a particular university friend of Porty's, thus the invitation to dine. They had met at the end of the boxing match, where the captain and the lieutenant had been keeping a close eye upon the assembled spectators.

"Are you expecting trouble?" Mr. Ellis-Brant asked, helping himself to the cheese tart. He sat next to Miss Grant and offered her a slice with a kindly smile. "I remember there was some problem in Yorkshire earlier this year."

If Mr. Ellis-Brant meant the British Army gunning down some weavers at a mill near Huddersfield in March, then yes, there had been a problem. The weavers' protest had been declared a deplorable situation—wanton destruction of machines and injury to innocent people—but I had rather thought the shooting of one's own citizens who were fighting to maintain a livelihood just as deplorable. Not a popular opinion, but in my mind such violence set a dangerous precedent.

"There was some unrest in Yorkshire, and in Manchester," the captain said, beside me. "And we have received intelligence that there could be more trouble here." He looked around the table, realizing the effect of his words upon Miss Grant and my sister, who had both ceased to chew. "However, I would not wish the ladies to be concerned in any way. I doubt there will be any unpleasantness this far west. Besides, the Yorkshire outcome significantly dampened their activities."

"Yes, I am sure it has dampened their activity," I said dryly. "Men and women were shot, or rounded up and will be either hanged or transported."

"Well, they are criminals," the Ermine said, nibbling at a sweetbread. She sat beside Evan, who, understandably, had been rather taciturn during the first remove. "They should bear the consequences of their actions."

"They are fighting to survive," I said. "The machines are destroying their livelihoods and their rights."

"They killed a man trying to protect his mill," the captain said mildly, spooning out peas from the silver bowl. "I am sure you do not support such violent action, Lady Augusta."

"Of course not," I said, although considering the past few months, perhaps I was not the best candidate to condemn violent action. "But as I understand it, they attempted to negotiate in a peaceful manner, but no one—neither mill owner nor government—would listen to their concerns. It seems they have been driven to extremes."

"Well, I feel any minute you might stand up from the table and join their cause. Such vehement defense of the indefensible," Mr. Ellis-Brant said jovially, but with some censure in his voice as well. "You are misguided by your womanly compassion, Lady Augusta."

I gritted my teeth. Why was it that any analysis made by a woman was attributed to emotion rather than logic and therefore demeaned?

"I do not defend, Mr. Ellis-Brant, merely debate," I said, stabbing at a recalcitrant carrot. "What is your opinion on the matter, Captain?"

"It is not for me or Lieutenant Powers to have private opinions about our orders or, sometimes, I think, opinions at all," the captain said drolly. His subordinate allowed a wry smile to touch his lips. "However, the Luddites have been marked as a danger to our way of life, and so the British Army has been sent to address that danger."

Porty waved over the footman with the wine decanter. "Good thing too. We don't want a situation like the French, do we? Killing their king and replacing him with a devil like Bonaparte." He waited for his glass to be filled, then picked it up. "A toast, to the brave efforts of our soldiers here"—he angled his glass first at the captain and then at the lieutenant—"and on the Continent."

We all picked up glasses, lifted them, and drank.

I looked across the table at Evan: *They are here for the Luddites, not you.*

He tilted his head: *Maybe, but this is a little too close for comfort.*

True. But Evan could hardly absent himself from the table without causing unwanted attention.

"What kind of trouble do you anticipate, Captain?" Evan asked politely. A seemingly innocuous question, but he was probing. "Has there been some activity?"

"We have agents in the area, Mr. Talbot. They have infiltrated some of the groups and report back to us. At present, all is quiet, so we do not anticipate immediate action."

"And you are here, too, for our protection," Miss Grant said, smiling across the table. "Do you intend to stay for long?" Her demeanor was almost flirtatious, an unexpected direction.

"Indeed we do, Miss Dashwood, and in good number."

On that reassurance, and the arrival of more sweet dishes, the general conversation broke up into more private discussions.

"When you say agents, do you mean agents provocateurs?" I asked the captain.

"A provocative question in itself, Lady Augusta," he said.

For all the threat of him, I rather liked Captain Morland.

"I have heard that the government has employed such creatures," I said.

"From whom? I would not wish to think such matters are the subject of idle gossip." Although asked in a nonchalant way, it was a pointed question. A sword drawn.

"At a salon where Lord Sidmouth was speaking about such matters," I said. Not entirely the truth, but close enough.

He smiled, knowing I had parried his sword. "Not idle gossip, then?"

"No, although there would be those who would consider the new prime minister idle," I returned. "But what do you think of such a possibility? Is it right that people of little means and less hope are incited into breaking the law?"

He gave a small bow. "As we have already established, Lady Augusta, I have no opinions." He picked up a plate of dessert. "May I offer you some flummery?"

I bit back a laugh but could not hide my smile of appreciation. "I believe I have had my fill, Captain."

The captain returned the smile and helped himself to the dessert.

How easy it would be to dismiss such a young man as a product of nepotism rather than skill and talent. A mistake that, no doubt, many had made to their disadvantage. Captain Morland had the self- possession of a man twice his age, and I suspected his mind was as keen as his wit. And more often than not, wit and intuition traveled hand in hand.

The captain clearly received a great deal of information from his sources. Maybe I could discover how much danger truly surrounded Evan. A tantalizing prospect, but did I dare ask the captain about a certain escaped convict? Was it too much of a risk? A question might—if it was maladroit—unintentionally focus such a keen mind upon the subject of criminals and then possibly upon the man with a scar who sat opposite him. Admittedly it was a small risk. Who would, after all, think the well-dressed gentleman— who sat at Lord Davenport's dinner table—could be a desperate criminal? Even so, a risk.

It seemed I could dare. With as much sangfroid as I could muster, I selected a macaroon from a plate and asked, "Does that quietude extend to the roads, Captain? If the weather improves, I intend to ride out tomorrow and I have always believed the roads here are safer than those near London. Yet there have been so many reports of highwaymen and ruffians in the papers. I have even read there is an escaped convict roaming the countryside. I do not wish to come upon such danger."

I knew Evan was listening, his chin angled toward our conversation, his relaxed attitude belied by the clenched fist around his fork.

I tried not to hold my breath as I offered the captain the plate and he chose his own fancy. "We have received a dispatch about an escaped convict turned highwayman," he said, placing the biscuit neatly on his plate and nodding his thanks, "but that is a countrywide alert. He is unlikely to be this far west. Even so, if you are concerned about such dangers, then perhaps it might be prudent to stay within Lord Davenport's extensive grounds."

The main danger I could see was the man sitting beside me currently biting with some appreciation into a macaroon, but I managed to smile.

"A good thought, Captain."

I glanced at Evan, but he was in polite conversation with Miss Grant, the very epitome of a well-bred gentleman, with his face—and scar—turned from the view of Captain Morland and Lieutenant Powers.

29

Overnight the rain stopped and I'd had the rather obvious realization that Evan and I would be riding to Blackburn to face a man who might be a murderer. Admittedly it was a late realization, mainly because all I had seen ahead was a possible pathway to exoneration for my love. But if Dr. Lawrence had killed once, then perhaps he could kill again.

On that sobering thought, when Tully arrived to open the curtains, I asked her to sew the sheath of my silver knife into the sleeve of my riding habit. She met the request with her usual equanimity and got to work. On the face of it, the operation should have been straightforward, but it took both of us some time to figure out the engineering of easy access. As Tully remarked, it would help no one if I drew my weapon and sliced open my own artery on the way out.

Thus, when I finally walked into the bright morning room, Julia, Charlotte, the Ermine, and Evan were already seated at the table. Porty and Mr. Ellis-Brant, I was promptly told by Charlotte, had already finished their repast and gone to view some rain damage on a tenant's farm, and Mrs. Carter and Miss Dashwood were taking trays in their rooms.

"I am sure an unmarried lady never took breakfast in her room here before, Charlotte," Mrs. Ellis-Brant said archly.

"The breakfast trays were my suggestion," Charlotte said, quashing any further comment.

The morning meal was laid out on the sideboard: I picked up a plate and investigated the offerings as a footman lifted each silver cloche, deciding upon glazed ham, a hard-boiled egg, cheese, and bread. With my plate so laden, I took my seat at the table.

"Did you wish for *The Times*, Lady Augusta?" Charlotte asked.

"No, I would like to start riding as soon as I have finished breakfast," I said. "If that suits you, Mr. Talbot?"

"It does, indeed," Evan said.

He had a pile of ham on his plate and was addressing it with vigor. I liked sitting across from him, the ordinariness of taking breakfast together. I knew we dealt well together in times of crisis, and we had built a certainty around that relationship, but what about a conventional life? Would we deal just as well taking breakfast together every morning ad infinitum? I pulled myself up; was a conventional life with Lord Evan Belford what I really wanted? Could I really relinquish my independence? I had not thought much beyond the struggle for Evan's exoneration, but if we were eventually successful and a proposal made, it was not going to be a straightforward matter. At least not for me. A woman lost not only all her assets within a marriage, but also her individual identity and, to a disturbing degree, the ability to steer her own life. A troubling dilemma.

"I do hope you enjoy your ride, Lady Augusta," Charlotte said, pulling me from my thoughts. She dabbed at her mouth with her serviette. "If you are finished, Emelia, I would like to start upon our belated visits. I have ordered the gig to come round."

"Of course," the Ermine said, casting me a knowing look as the footman pulled back her chair.

"Will you be out all day, Mr. Talbot?" Charlotte asked, adding a little edge to her tone.

"I believe so," Evan said.

"I have arranged Callista for you to ride, Lady Augusta," Charlotte said. Our eyes met fleetingly; Callista was one of her best, with excellent stamina and good speed. With some care she would manage the distance to and from Blackburn.

"Thank you, Lady Davenport."

With one last lingering look at Evan, Charlotte departed. The Ermine followed, her own last look directed at me and full of smug collusion. I smiled conspiratorially over the rim of my coffee cup. I suspected Emelia Ellis-Brant had never had help in her meddling before and she was delighting in a comrade in harm. Although I did not like the woman, it was, in truth, a little sad.

"You may go now, thank you," I said to Hanford, the butler, dismissing him and the three footmen.

With bows, they left the room.

As soon as the door closed and we were alone, Julia sighed and rubbed her forehead. "Thank goodness Emelia is gone. Her voice is so . . . so shrill." She took her gold pillbox from her lap. "Last night's guests were rather unexpected: Captain Morland and his lieutenant. I was so strained throughout the whole meal."

I had already discussed the evening with my sister, after we had retired to bed, but clearly she still had some residual fear.

Evan looked up from his ham. "I agree, it was a difficult meal, but I have now spent an entire evening with them—including an extended after-dinner port session—and they have not questioned my identity."

"The captain is not stupid, though," I said. "I think it best to avoid him."

Evan nodded his agreement. "I cannot foresee meeting him again."

"How long do you think it will take you to find Dr. Lawrence?"

Julia asked, flicking open the box lid and tapping out one of the bright blue pills.

"I would say we will get to Blackburn in under four hours," Evan said, eyeing the pill in her cupped hand. "May I ask, is that a blue mass tablet?"

"Yes," Julia said, then added quickly, "Prescribed by Dr. Thorgood."

"Does Dr. McLeod concur with that prescription?"

Julia looked pointedly across at me. "I am not Dr. McLeod's patient," she said crisply. "Nor am I yours, Mr. Talbot." She placed the tablet in her mouth and, with a swift swig of tea, swallowed it.

Evan subsided. He recognized an explosive subject when he heard one. "If all goes as it should, we will be back for dinner," he said.

"What if you are not?" Julia demanded, her tone overly forceful.

"Then we will be late," I said. "We will make an excuse. Do not worry."

"Of course I will worry." She drew a shaking breath. "I beg your pardon. I am being as shrill as Mrs. Ellis-Brant. I am still feeling a little worn down by the travel."

"It is my fault. I pushed us too hard. I fear Lady Hester has suffered from our speed too."

Evan nodded. "I saw my sister and Miss Grant this morning— Miss Grant sent a note to meet them in the garden as they walked. I told them about the visit from Lord Brummell and Lord Alvanley and, as you can imagine, Hester and Miss Grant are extremely uneasy. I have asked them to endure for another day and then we will take steps to find them a permanent safe haven."

"I think we could depend on Mr. Brummell's discretion, but I am not sure about Lord Alvanley. Has he ever met Hester?"

"According to Hester, they have met once or twice," Evan said. "Who knows if he would remember, but we cannot take the chance."

"Where do you propose to find this safe haven?" I asked. "Out of England?"

"I think it must be so," he said slowly. "Even if today proves fruitful, our brother will not politely stop looking for Hester while I attempt to exonerate myself."

I sensed Julia's eyes upon me; the question of what I would do if he really left this time was palpable between us. But I still had no answer for Julia or Evan, or even myself.

"Would you check on them during the day, Lady Julia?" Evan added. "A friendly face would no doubt calm their nerves."

"Of course," Julia said. "But you both must take care. If this Dr. Lawrence did, indeed, kill Mr. Sanderson, then you are dealing with a murderer."

Beneath the table, I touched the reassuring length of knife and sheath stitched into my sleeve. "I know, but we are prepared."

"I will not let anything happen to your sister," Evan said.

"Like getting stabbed?" Julia said dryly. I opened my mouth to protest, but she waved away the necessity. "Just do not get hurt. Either of you. My nerves cannot take it."

"We are only speaking to the man," I said, glancing at Evan. "I am sure we will be safe."

Of course, I could not promise such a thing and Julia knew it. There was only one certainty in the situation ahead, and that was that I trusted Evan with my life. I had already done so on at least three occasions.

Mind you, all things being equal, it would probably be better if we did not test that certainty quite so often.

I looked up at the sky. Cloudy but no sign of rain—a blessing for such a long journey. We were making good time, the horses ready for the lengthy ride, and the road reasonably dry and in good repair. So far, we had not met anyone else traveling along it, although a few miles from Charlotte's estate we had seen a couple crossing a field in some haste, the woman clad in a country cloak of scarlet and the man pulling her along by the hand. I had suggested secret lovers. Evan had laughed and said they would have a hard time finding a haystack at this time of year, which had made my imagination leap back to that alleyway in Covent Garden.

I glanced across at him, his body moving with relaxed grace in time to the horse's gait in an undulating rhythm, the strong line of his thigh close to mine. I hurriedly looked forward again; my mind, it seemed, was determined to turn everything he did into some kind of carnal distraction.

It did not help that we had, for some time, ridden in heavy silence, my awareness of his body beside mine growing with every mile. Whereas his attention seemed firmly fixed ahead, brow furrowed in thought.

What had prompted such inwardness? Had it been something I said?

I picked over my memory of our conversation; it had mainly been about the interview ahead: what we might discover and the steps we might take afterward, namely, a petition to the courts for a pardon or even an overturning of the original judgment. Perhaps it was the possibility of exoneration that had silenced him. Or maybe he was thinking upon the problem of Hester and where, exactly, we could find a safe haven. I had not brought it up myself; my mind had been going around in circles upon the subject for too long without any result. Besides, if the doctor provided information we could use, then surely Evan must stay in the country to pursue true justice.

I said as much, breaking the silence between us.

"There is that," Evan conceded, "and I am not convinced Hester would survive a sea journey. Yet moving her from one situation to another in England will not keep her from my brother for long, nor me from Mulholland. I do not like it, but we must try to sail. Ireland would be the most obvious destination for its proximity, but there are too many of our acquaintances there. I think it must be Sweden. They are not allied with Bonaparte and we could live in obscurity."

Sweden. Good God, so far away. And through the dangers of Napoleon's Europe.

"I will come with you," I said abruptly.

Finally, a decision, dragged from me along a path of anticipated loss so intense it took my breath away, and bringing as much pain as it did resolution. Could I really leave Julia? Yet I wanted to go. I wanted to be with Evan. With him, I was truly myself. A self that was better. I could not give that up—or him. And if that meant leaving England, then so be it.

Then I realized my announcement had been met with silence.

He was looking at me, but there was no glad smile upon his face, or even a smile at all. "That is, if you wish me to accompany you," I said. Good God, did he not want me to go?

"Tell me—" he began.

I braced myself.

"Did the HMS *Triumph* and HMS *Phipps* make the newspapers here two years ago?"

Not the direction I was expecting.

"The *Triumph*?" I echoed. Why was he talking of ships? Yet the name was familiar. I searched my memory. "They were involved in an accident, were they not?"

"Not as such," he said. "Both ships salvaged a cargo of elemental mercury in kidskin bladders from a wrecked Spanish ship near Cádiz. However, when the bladders were taken on board, they ruptured and the mercury spread around the ships as both quicksilver and vapor. The sailors were struck down with tremors, nervous agitations, heart complaints, tooth loss, and even paralysis."

"How awful."

"Indeed. I read a medical article by the *Triumph*'s surgeon and it concluded that it was the mercury vapor that caused the crew to fall ill. Not many subscribe to that conclusion, mind you. Mercury is the most popular cure for . . ." He stopped. "Well, for the French disease. For me, however, it sounds a warning bell."

"Indeed," I said. "Most interesting, but why are you telling me this?"

"Because your sister is taking blue mass pills, and they are made of mercury."

For a second, I did not quite take his meaning. "But they are not vapor or quicksilver."

"Even so, it is still the same element."

The full import of his words finally landed upon me. "You think the pills are poisoning her?"

"If just breathing in mercury or touching it causes such illness, then what would ingesting it do?"

"Dear God." I looked over my shoulder at the road we had just traveled, every impulse in me to turn and gallop back to Davenport Hall. "I must tell her."

"You must. Thankfully she is only taking a tiny amount, but I think we have both already noticed changes in her demeanor: agitation and irritability."

"Headaches and faintness too. Dear God, she has already taken today's dose." The knowledge clenched my innards.

"I know. Tell her when we return—she may listen to you, and I know young Dr. McLeod refuses to prescribe blue mass, so he may be able to add another voice."

"So all of her deterioration could be those pills?" Part of me was appalled but another part held a sudden hope that Julia's tumor was not actually worse at all.

"I cannot say with any certainty, but at the very least, I would say they are not helping her condition." He leaned across and touched my arm, a gentle reassurance. "You cannot change what has gone before, but you can stop any more harm. And I think perhaps you will not wish to leave her."

I stared at him, the same realization lodging in my chest like a howl. "I cannot leave. At least, not for the time being."

"I know."

I could not think upon that heartbreak hurtling toward me. Not yet. It was too much.

"Let us pick up our pace," I said, and urged my horse into a trot. The sooner we got to Blackburn, the sooner I could return and destroy every blue mass pill in my sister's possession.

30

~~~~~

*W*e rode into Blackburn, over the river Darwen. I had thought we would see the new canal that had recently opened, part of the progressive Liverpool-Leeds canal network, but we had come into the town a good mile or so from it. Or so the new signs told me as we passed. Instead, we made our way past a solid brick house of corrections. A rather grim welcome to the town.

"What is Dr. Lawrence's address?" I asked.

"McLeod told me it was Market Street Lane," Evan said. "That was all the information he could obtain."

I looked around for a likely candidate for directions and found a neatly dressed young woman, basket laden with cloth, idling outside a storefront window full of haberdashery. I suspected the attractive display of bonnets held her attention. I drew my horse up nearby.

"Good day," I called.

The girl jumped at my greeting, then turned, her bright brown eyes wide with startled guilt. Clearly caught in the act of loitering rather than working. She managed to bob into a curtsy.

"Can you tell me the way to Market Street Lane? We are seeking Dr. Lawrence."

She gave a nod and took a breath, clearly trying to retrieve some self-possession. "It ain't far, milady. A bit farther along and turn left opposite the church. Ye'll find the doctor's cottage at the end, near the lane."

"Thank you." I eyed the window display. "The pink-trimmed straw would suit you very well."

She blinked, then grinned, bobbing into another curtsy.

I turned back to Evan and pointed along the street with my crop. "This way."

We followed the directions, passing the Church of St. Marie, then turning into Market Street Lane. The doctor's cottage stood near the corner of the appropriately named Back Lane.

It was a reasonably sized abode—two stories—made of brown stone with well-proportioned windows, the frames painted a fresh white. A brass plaque upon the white front door proclaimed it was the residence of Dr. P. Lawrence. We had finally found our man, and he was, it seemed by the upkeep and position of his house, of good standing in the town.

Evan dismounted, tied his horse to a nearby post, then held out his hands to help me down. I levered myself from the saddle, his hands finding my waist and catching my descent. For a second, our faces were only inches from each other. Our eyes met, acknowledging the importance of what lay ahead, and then I was back upon on my feet, a decorous gap between us.

I secured my own mount to the post and spied a pale feminine face at the window watching our arrival. At my return scrutiny, she ducked away, leaving only the flick of a blue curtain. A maid? Or perhaps the lady of the house. It all seemed very genteel and quiet.

We were both silent as I undid the saddlebag and withdrew my silver card case. Evan stood aside for me to approach the front door, his expression somber and his finger and thumb rubbing together, the only sign of his anticipation about the interview ahead.

I grasped the brass door knocker—in the shape of a garland—and rapped it twice upon its plate.

Only a few seconds passed and then the door opened and the face I had seen fleetingly in the window peered out. The girl curtsied. A maid, then. And one kindly kept, for she was neat and smiling and had been allowed a blue-ribbon bow upon her linen cap.

"Good day," I said. "I am Lady Augusta Colebrook and this is Mr. Talbot. We wish to see Dr. Lawrence."

She took my offered calling card but did not read it—she likely did not have her letters—her smile shifting into consternation. "Is it an urgent medical matter, my lady?"

Although I wanted to say yes to ensure our audience, I also did not want to start the meeting upon a lie. "It is not," I admitted. "It is a personal matter."

"The doctor and mistress ain't currently in, my lady."

"I see. We will wait, then."

She considered this development. "Doctor could be a while, my lady."

"Even so, we will wait."

Since I was clearly not going to go, she stepped back to allow us to enter. We followed her into a well-appointed foyer with a good rug underfoot and a narrow staircase that ascended to the next floor. I looked up to see a little boy and girl—both under ten years of age, with dark curls—watching us through the banisters. I smiled up at them, but they disappeared like startled deer. The doctor's children? Probably, although he would most likely be in his fifties or more by now. Not that a man's age had anything to do with his ability to procreate. Perhaps his wife was much younger than him, or she was a second spouse.

I glanced back at Evan. He had seen the children, too, his expression somewhat stricken. Odd.

"May I take your hat, sir?" the maid asked.

Evan relinquished his hat, which was placed carefully upon a sideboard.

"Is there a stable nearby for our horses?" he asked.

"We have a stable, sir," she said with some justified pride. Not every country doctor could afford to keep a horse. "I'll get our boy Sully to look after yer horses."

She then opened a door and stood aside, ushering us into a good-sized drawing room. The walls were papered in fashionable eggshell, a good velvet sofa in rose pink was positioned before a brick hearth, and two silver candlesticks sat upon the mantel. The dagger up my sleeve seemed somewhat ludicrous in such surroundings.

With another curtsy, the maid withdrew, closing the door behind her.

I looked across at Evan. He was contemplating the spines of the books, or so it appeared; by the angle of his head, I knew he had, in fact, turned inward again. Not surprising, I supposed. How would it be to face the man who had stolen twenty years of your life and ruined your name? It would send even the best man into a dark place.

"A pleasant abode," I said, hoping to draw him from his grim ruminations. "The doctor is doing well for himself."

He did not answer, so I tried again. "It is a pleasant home."

This time he turned to face me. "But is it the home of a murderer?"

Well, that was to the point. Since I had no answer to that question, I decided to address the next pertinent one. "Indeed. And what if he is the instigator of all you have endured? If I was face-to-face with the man who had sent me to prison unjustly, my thoughts might turn to revenge."

He met the unsaid query with a shake of his head. "For twenty years I have thought that I killed Sanderson in that duel. My main emotion on discovering that I may not have killed a man is one of relief. Not revenge."

"But you have lost so much. Suffered so much."

"True." He cocked his head, a wry smile curling the corners of his mouth. "Are you trying to talk me into wreaking vengeance, Lady Augusta?"

I smiled. Here was my Lord Evan. "Not at all. But it would be understandable if you felt violence toward the man."

He crossed the room to me. "Do not fear, my love. I am not going to kill the man who may be the key to my exoneration." He took my hand and lifted it to his lips, pressing a firm kiss upon it. "If I am, indeed, not a murderer, I would prefer to stay that way. For many reasons."

I closed my hand around his in a sudden sweep of emotion. Yes, so much was at stake.

Through the window, I saw a young man—Sully, the doctor's stable hand, presumably—untie the horses and lead them in the direction of the back of the house.

Evan released my hand and took a seat before the hearth, but I could not sit still. We might soon have a way to clear his name, and the prospect buzzed through my body. I wandered the room, noting a vase of fresh roses, a collection of poetry, a needlework box. The doctor's wife had refined taste.

The mahogany mantel clock ticked away the minutes.

Evan had withdrawn again—his head bowed, fingers steepled—but this time I left him to his thoughts. If I was feeling the strain of what was to come, then he must be feeling it ten times over.

After forty minutes, a gig finally pulled up outside the house, drawn by a glossy chestnut, its driver dressed in a black coat and a black Clericus hat, a doctor's ensemble. Sully, the stable hand, emerged to take the horse's head, clearly reporting our arrival to his master; the black-clad man nodded and cast a surprised look in the direction of his house. He sprang down from the gig with a great deal of vigor.

A young man's vigor.

"Is that Dr. Lawrence?" I asked.

Surely not.

Evan came to stand beside me, but the man was already entering his front door and obscured from our view. We both turned at the sound of the front door opening and closing and the muffled sound of a male voice giving instructions.

Then footsteps, and the drawing room door opened.

The man who entered—without a hat but with a smile—was of medium height, with the same dark curls as his children, brushed back into a fashionable style. His brown eyes were kind—the sort of eyes one wanted in a physician—and, at that moment, curious about these two strangers in his house. But most pointedly, he could be no older than thirty years of age. Far too young to be the Dr. Lawrence who had attended the duel so long ago.

We had found the wrong Dr. Lawrence. I glanced at Evan, seeing my own dismay reflected in the slump of his shoulders.

"Good day," the doctor said, his voice professionally pleasant. He bowed. "Lady Augusta Colebrook?"

I nodded my greeting. "Indeed. And allow me to introduce Mr. Talbot."

The two men bowed to each other.

The wrong Dr. Lawrence closed the door. "My maid said you have been waiting for me? How may I be of assistance?"

There could be no assistance here, but how best to make a gracious exit? The truth was probably best.

"I am afraid we have made a mistake," I said. "We are seeking another Dr. Lawrence. A Dr. Paul Lawrence from London. He had some information we were hoping to obtain. Please accept our apologies for any inconvenience."

"Paul Lawrence? From London?" The doctor had stilled, his eyes wary.

"Well, I met him in London," Evan said. "Briefly." He glanced at me, the wry addition for my benefit.

The doctor drew a breath. "Lady Augusta, Mr. Talbot, are you, by chance, associated with Lord Evan Belford?"

We both stared at him.

"Who?" Evan asked, at his most dangerously pleasant.

The doctor licked his lips. "If you are associated with Lord Evan Belford, then you are seeking my father."

"Your father is Paul Lawrence?" I repeated, not from any misunderstanding but from the sudden leap of hope. Had we found our man, after all? Our way to Evan's exoneration?

"He told me that if strangers—noble strangers—came calling, then it was probably Lord Evan Belford or his friends."

I looked at Evan, but he was motionless. Unable, I think, to acknowledge who he was to this stranger; there had been too many dangerous years of denying his true identity.

So I said, "We are, indeed, associated with Lord Evan."

"Ah." Dr. Lawrence drew himself up. "I am Dr. Phillip Lawrence. My father knew this day would come."

"Where is he? May we speak with him?" I asked, unable to contain my urgency.

The young man shook his head. "I am sorry, Lady Augusta. My father died four years ago."

31

✤

$\mathscr{I}$ felt as if all the air had gone from my body. Everything around me grayed, my chest aching from the loss of hope.

"Lady Augusta, are you quite well?"

Evan's voice brought me back to the room. I drew a gasping breath, the blessed air easing the pain. Two pairs of alarmed medical eyes were scrutinizing me.

"I am quite well," I managed.

Dr. Lawrence crossed the room and poured a glass from a decanter. "Here, take some brandy."

I took the offered glass and sipped, the liquor burning its way down my throat and lighting a small flame of warmth in my innards.

"I am sorry for the shock," the doctor said.

I looked at Evan. He was the one who should be swigging brandy. Yet he seemed abnormally composed.

I took another sip, trying to focus through the crushing disappointment. "We were hoping to speak to your father on a matter of great importance," I said.

And now all hope was gone. The man was dead.

"I know," Dr. Lawrence said. He turned to Evan. "Sir, am I, in fact, addressing Lord Evan Belford?"

Evan considered him for a tense second, then sighed. "I have not gone by that name for many years."

"My lord." The doctor bowed. "My father described you to me. I did not think I was mistaken."

Evan inclined his head, the marquess's son appearing in just that simple gesture.

Dr. Lawrence motioned us to the sofa. "Please, sit. There are things I must tell you."

As we took our seats, he asked, "May I offer you refreshment?"

"No, thank you," I said. The brandy had been quite sufficient.

Evan politely waved away the offer. "What is it that you must tell us?"

Dr. Lawrence took the seat opposite us in the armchair but sat forward as if the information he held bowed him over. "My father died of a short illness. On his deathbed, he told me about the duel twenty years ago." He looked at Evan. "He made me promise that I would relate the truth to you if you were ever to come looking for it." A fleeting expression of anguish crossed his face. "I must say, I do not wish to do so. There is a great deal of pain within this story, and it brings shame upon my family's name. Even so, I made a vow and I will honor it."

Pain not only for his family, I thought.

"Twenty years ago," he began, "my father had a flourishing practice, a wife, two daughters, and two sons. One of the daughters, Sally—"

I sat up slightly—Sally Lawrence, the name in the wager book. I glanced at Evan. He nodded his own recognition.

Dr. Lawrence saw our exchange. "You know my sister's name?"

"We have come across it," Evan said. "But please, go on."

"My sister Sally was beautiful in countenance and in spirit. She was also headstrong and a little too romantic for her own good. She thought her destiny lay beyond marrying a man chosen for her and ran away to London, thinking to become a lauded actress like Sarah Siddons. Her destiny, however, was to come into the path of a man by the name of Sanderson." He looked at Evan. "As was yours."

"Destiny?" Evan said. "I would not call it destiny."

Indeed, not after what we had found in the Rack and Ruin Club.

Dr. Lawrence gave a small shrug. "Whatever you call it, their meeting was the greatest misfortune of our lives. We searched for her—my father, brother, and I—but London is a big place when someone does not wish to be found, and there are so many young women without family or protection. By the time we did find her, she was with child and adamant that she would stay with Sanderson. She loved him, she said, and he loved her, although he was conspicuous in his absence. My father, in a fit of rage, disowned her right there in the front room of the hovel where Sanderson was keeping her, an act that haunted him to the end of his days.

"It was at this time that I went to Edinburgh to study medicine. I should have stayed, but I was young and keen to start my own life. The events that unfolded from there on were related by Father upon his deathbed and sworn by me to keep secret from everyone except you, my lord, or your associates."

He paused and rubbed his forehead as if considering how to continue. Finally, he looked up, his gentle brown eyes pained.

"Forgive me for what is about to come, Lady Augusta. It is shocking."

"I have heard and seen a great deal, Dr. Lawrence."

With a resigned nod, he continued. "My father—a conscientious professional—attended lectures at Bart's. On one such occasion he decided to attend a dissection. It was to be of a pregnant woman . . ."

I drew in an audible breath. "No," I whispered, hoping to ward off the horror of where this story was heading. "Surely not."

The young doctor nodded slowly. "I am afraid so. The corpses upon the table were my sister and her unborn child. My father's daughter and his grandchild, split open." He stopped, overcome for a second.

"*Mon Dieu,*" Evan murmured.

The doctor wet his lips. "As you can imagine, the sight was too much for my father. He collapsed and was brought home. For two days he literally could not speak, and when his voice finally returned, he refused to speak of what he had seen. Not to my mother, my siblings, or even me when I returned home. He alone carried the burden of that horrifying sight and its consequences for sixteen years, until he confessed all to me on his deathbed. I believe it unbalanced him, for he was never the same again after that terrible day."

"Surely he could have informed the magistrate," I said.

The doctor nodded. "He did try. First he confronted Sanderson— knowing he must be somehow involved in the deaths—but Sanderson merely shrugged off my father's accusations. He said that no one would be interested in a dead whore and her bastard. My father soon found out Sanderson was correct. He received no help from the magistrates. No help from anyone. And so he decided to exact justice himself."

"Justice?" I echoed. "Do you mean murder?"

"I do," the doctor said soberly. "It became an obsession. A way to redeem himself for abandoning his daughter. He turned his back upon his patients and his practice, even his family to some degree, to follow Sanderson and discover the moment he could strike." He looked across at Evan. "He found that moment at your duel, my lord."

"How did he manage it?" Evan asked quietly.

"He offered to take the place of the doctor who had been engaged. Since attending a duel was illegal, the other doctor was happy to pass on the task to him. My father disguised himself—for Sanderson knew what he looked like—and waited. His chance came when you wounded Sanderson across the chest. My father used a stiletto knife to nick the man's heart through the same superficial wound you had inflicted."

Evan nodded. "Clever."

Not the adjective I would have used: *diabolical* was more accurate.

The young doctor paused. "I wish I could say that my father had no intention of falsely incriminating you, my lord, but when he realized you were charged with murder, he did not step forward. In fact, he took it as a sign that his vengeance had been blessed by God."

"A convenient belief," I said. "Your father sentenced Lord Evan to half his life in a penal colony."

"I am sorry, my lord," the doctor said. "If it is any consolation, I believe my father lived in his own purgatory of guilt. It was his dying wish for me to tell you, or anyone who came on your behalf, the truth and to ask for your forgiveness."

For once, I could not read Evan's expression. He looked up at the ceiling, perhaps collecting his thoughts or maybe even praying. Finally, he drew a deep breath and exhaled as if a heavy burden had been lifted from his shoulders. "I hold no grudge against your father, Dr. Lawrence. It is clear to me that he acted out of great pain and love for his daughter. As for forgiveness, only God can forgive the sin of murder. I thank you for honoring your father's dying wish and relieving me of the belief that I had killed Sanderson. I consider this terrible affair to be at an end."

At an end? Surely not—we had a plan. I tried to catch Evan's eye, but he would not look at me.

"But that is not the end of it, is it?" I said, as much to him as to the doctor. "Surely you will right this wrong, Dr. Lawrence. If you report your father's confession to the courts, Lord Evan could be exonerated. He will be able to take his place once again in society." I looked at Evan for support. "Is that not so, Lord Evan?"

The doctor straightened in his chair. "Lady Augusta, I have a wife, two young children, and a practice. My brother and remaining sister are well settled. To go to the courts and name my father as a murderer would ruin my family's name. Ruin all of their lives." He shook his head. "Forgive me, but I cannot. I will not. I have discharged my duty."

"No, you must! Your family owes Lord Evan his life back."

"I do not ask Dr. Lawrence to ruin his and his family's life, Augusta," Evan said. "Sanderson harmed too many women and children when he was alive. He will not do so dead. It ends here."

"No!" I stood, my confusion rapidly climbing into fury. "You owe him, Doctor. I thought you were an honorable man, but I see no honor here!"

The man hunched in his chair. "Forgive me, I cannot place the past over my family's future."

"But—"

"Augusta, no," Evan said, his voice implacable. He stood and made a small bow. "We will take our leave of you, Dr. Lawrence. This terrible secret that has bound your life to mine is now resolved. From here on, you do not know me, nor I you. Live your life in the knowledge that your father's sin will not be visited upon you or your family. You have my word upon it."

I stared at him. He had given his word. His unbreakable word. All hope of exoneration was gone.

32

You are angry," Evan said, after we had ridden for twenty minutes in silence. "Please look at me."

I craned my neck back and looked up at the sky. The afternoon clouds had cleared and dusk was approaching, an early crescent moon visible. It would not give us a great deal of light when night settled, but enough to make our way along the road. Back to exactly the same problems we had left, but this time with no way forward.

"I do not believe that you would wish me to force the doctor into giving testimony and thus ruining so many innocent lives," Evan added. "I know it is disappointing—"

"Disappointing?" I said, finally looking at him. "Do you not see? We have no testimony. No usable evidence. You cannot be exonerated. Mulholland will keep coming and you will never be safe."

"I am quite aware of that," he said soberly. "And although I know you wish it to be otherwise, you cannot keep everyone safe, Gus. It is impossible."

"You are very calm about it. Did you never believe the doctor could exonerate you? Did you come here without hope?"

"I hoped. Of course I hoped. But I also knew that there was little chance of it working out as we wished." He paused, navigating his horse around a large hole at the side of the road and coming up beside me again. "You have so much hope and so much passion, Gus. You believe you can set things right, even when the odds are insurmountable."

"Naïve," I said bitterly.

"No," he said with some force. "Hope is essential. Without hope, we do not seek a way out of impossible situations. Your hope is your strength. And it is one of the many, many reasons why I love you, my darling Renegade."

Love.

He had never spoken the word before, but then, neither had I. Of course, the word had been written in our letters, implied in our every action, felt within our kisses, but never the actual word stated itself.

The irretrievable declaration.

We were a few feet apart, on horseback, and navigating a bad road, and yet I had to touch him. I reached across and found his hand waiting for mine.

"I will not stop trying to clear your name," I said. Then added, "My love."

My own irretrievable declaration.

He smiled. "I know you will not, and we will find a way."

We released hands, more from practicality than from any wish to do so. I looked ahead, fighting back a rise of tears. Absurdly happy and heartbroken at the same time. "So, you must go. You must take Hester and Miss Grant and find somewhere safe."

"Yes, and I think it must be done in the next day or so." There was apology in his tone.

"I agree. Before Alvanley arrives." I pushed away the pain of our imminent separation. There would be enough time after to wallow in heartache. "Will you go out of Bristol?"

"No, too far away. I know a Welsh smuggler who sails out of Ceredigion. I should be able to organize something with him and his crew."

Of course he knew smugglers. He had probably even smuggled goods himself. It was not the passage I would have chosen for Lady Hester in her current state, but if anyone could dodge the coastal defenses and warships, then it would be the smuggling fraternity.

And so, as dusk darkened into cold, clear night, we settled into the ride and planning an escape route through Bonaparte's Europe.

*A*bout a quarter of an hour from Charlotte's estate and a much-longed-for wash and dinner, we rounded a curve in the road to find a small troop of militia marching in the same direction as us, their progress a muffled clank of weaponry and thud of feet upon the damp dirt road. By my reckoning at least ten men, their uniforms dulled in the meager moonlight but still recognizable as red with blue facings.

Beside me, Evan stiffened in his saddle, his breath releasing in a long, misted hiss. "Ah, this is unfortunate," he said.

They were a good distance ahead of us. Perhaps we could go around them. Even as the thought rose to my lips, the troop stopped. One of their number had clearly noticed us and apprised his leader, for the man motioned us to halt too.

We reined in as the troop turned smartly and marched back toward us. Callista shook her head in protest at the oncoming commotion, the rattle of her tack a chiming counterpoint. I peered into the dim light. The way the leading figure ahead walked seemed familiar, as did the lankier subordinate beside him, but I could not make out the man's features beneath the visor of his shako hat.

"Is that Captain Morland and Lieutenant Powers?" I asked Evan.

"I cannot be certain," he said, then added in an undertone, "If they are coming for me, I will head into the woods. You must not follow me, my love."

"But they will shoot at you!"

"Exactly why you must not follow me."

I tightened my grip around the reins. I might not follow, but nor would I stand by while men shot at him.

The troop came to a standstill a few yards from us. They were all fully uniformed, carrying rifles with bayonets and on high alert, for most of them continued to scan the surrounding woodland.

The captain walked up to us, removing his shako. It was, indeed, Morland, his youthful features made harsher in the moonlight. Or perhaps it was the task they were on that made him seem older.

I smiled warmly at him, although it felt like a rictus.

"Ah, I thought it was you, Lady Augusta." He gave a quick, courteous bow. "Good evening. And to you, Mr. Talbot."

Thank God, Evan was still Mr. Talbot. His horse bobbed its head and shifted to the side, no doubt from the ease of tension upon its reins.

"Good evening, Captain Morland," I said, and nodded a greeting to Lieutenant Powers, who had stayed back with the men. "Has something happened?"

"There's been some Luddite activity in the area. We are looking for a young man and woman—weaver types," the captain said. "Have you been traveling far along this road?"

"A fair way," Evan said. "That is why we are so late on our return."

"Beyond the junction at Ashton-in-Makerfield?"

"Yes," I said.

"Did you see anyone on the road or the surrounds?"

I recalled the man and woman crossing the field. Not lovers, then, but Luddites.

Evan shook his head. "Not a soul."

"No, indeed," I added. "What have these people done?"

"They are part of a Luddite group who are targeting mills and the houses of business owners in the area," the captain said. "They have already set fire to one miller's house and injured innocent people. We have reason to believe they will be targeting another tonight."

"Well, I hope you find them before they do so, Captain," Evan said.

"Thank you, we will." He looked at his troop, then back at us. "Allow me to provide you with two of my men to escort you to the estate. I would not rest easy if friends of Lord and Lady Davenport came to harm under my watch. And if Lord Davenport wishes it, my men can stay and protect the gate."

He signaled to his lieutenant, who gave an order to two of the front men of the troop. They stepped forward.

I gripped my reins more tightly. Before Evan, I would have considered such an escort a prudent precaution. Now the last thing we needed was a guard at the gate or Hester and Miss Grant seeing us arrive under the escort of soldiers.

"That is very thoughtful of you, Captain," Evan said smoothly. "But I am accompanying Lady Augusta for that very reason."

"Even so," the young man said. "I think—"

"Thank you, Captain," I interrupted, "but I would not wish to take any men away from your endeavors to protect people and property. You have such a large area to search and we have such a short distance to travel. We will be quite safe, I am sure." He frowned, about to argue the point, but I surreptitiously urged my horse to take an impatient step. "I insist, Captain. We are on horseback and near our goal. Your men are on foot and will only delay our progress. We will be safe."

The captain conceded my reasoning with a tilt of his head. "As you wish." He waved his two men back into formation. "However, I do suggest you go carefully, Lady Augusta." He gave a smart bow of his head and stepped back.

I raised my crop in acknowledgment and clicked my tongue, pressing my tired horse into a trot. "We will."

Evan raised his hand in salute and followed, bringing his horse alongside mine.

We rode in silence for a minute or so, listening to the sound of orders shouted and the clang of troops marching again. Finally, I murmured, "Are we beyond their sight?"

"I do not know, but do not look back," he replied, forestalling me from that very action. "Guilty people look back."

I kept my gaze fixed upon the dark road ahead, straining to make out the sounds behind us. Finally the clang and thud of troops marching was no longer audible.

Evan glanced over his shoulder. "We are clear."

I looked back, too, seeing only the shadowy, moonlit curve of road. "You lied about seeing the couple."

Evan looked at me, amused. "So did you." He leaned forward and patted his horse's neck. "I do not help a redcoat on principle, and I think the Luddites have a just cause, but what is your excuse?"

"It must be your bad influence," I said.

"Perhaps." I caught the edge of his rogue's smile. "Or perhaps it is because you are an outlaw at heart."

I was thinking up a suitable retort when I heard the sound of galloping hooves coming toward us. One rider, at full speed. Dangerous along such a dark road. Evan must have heard it at the same time, for he reined in his horse. I drew Callista to a halt alongside.

"Someone is in a hurry," Evan said. He flipped open his saddlebag and drew out a pistol.

My heart quickened. "Mulholland?" I asked, gathering my reins, but even as I said it, I knew it could not be so. Mulholland would never travel alone.

Who, then, was hurtling toward us at such speed?

The horse and its rider—dark silhouettes against the moon-silvered road—thundered into view. At the sight of us, the rider sat back, half halting upon the reins until the horse slowed. The wild gallop toward us shifted into a slower gait. Whoever it was certainly knew how to manage a horse.

The rider—now clearly a man in a greatcoat—eased his horse into a trot. He raised his hand, a commanding wave signaling us to stay where we were, and with that action I finally recognized the broad-shouldered figure.

"It is Mr. Kent!"

"Are you sure?" Evan demanded, but before I could answer, the distance between us and the rider had dwindled enough for Evan to recognize the Runner too. He lowered his pistol. "I thought he was in London. What is he doing here?"

A good question, and clearly about to be answered since Mr. Kent was already reining in. Both man and beast were panting, their breaths puffing into mist before their mouths.

"Thank God I have found you," Kent managed, walking Caesar up to us. "Your sister sent me."

"Julia? Is something wrong?" Good God, had she collapsed again?

"No, nothing is wrong with your sister, I assure you. But Lady Hester and Miss Grant have run away from Davenport Hall."

Evan straightened in his saddle. "Damn." He gathered his reins. "Which way did they go? Are they on foot? We must find them. Hester will not last long in this cold."

"Wait," Mr. Kent said. "It is worse. I am here because I followed your brother, Lord Deele, to Davenport Hall, and he has brought Lord Duffield too."

Deele and Duffy were here? "They came together? In the same carriage?" I asked.

"Yes, Deele visited your brother after Mulholland met with him. I can only imagine Mulholland told him about seeing Miss Grant in your drawing room. There was no use sending a note to you because they left almost immediately, and so I followed."

"What about Mulholland?" I asked.

Kent shook his head. "I don't know, but I could not leave you and Lady Julia to face Deele alone. Well, I thought you were alone." He eyed Evan. "What are you doing here?"

"Looking for the doctor from the duel."

I frowned, trying to rapidly piece together the reasons behind these unlikely alliances. "I think we must assume Mulholland is here too. Why else would he send Deele here to flush out Hester? She is bait for you."

"But he doesn't know I am here," Evan said. "For all he knows, I am still in London."

"My darling," I said, "wherever Hester is, you are, too, or soon will be. Mulholland knows that."

He considered the logic. "That gives a lot of credit to him. Do you really think he is that strategic?"

"I do. Or if not Mulholland, then whoever is pulling his strings."

"I did not see him or any of his men following," Mr. Kent said. "But I think you are right."

Evan waved away the problem of Mulholland. "Whether he is here or not, I do not care. Hester and Miss Grant must be our priority. If Deele gets hold of Hester he will not let her go, and as her legal guardian, he has the law upon his side."

"Deele is pursuing Lady Hester in his coach. Lady Julia sent me to find you to bring you back as quickly as possible."

Evan shook his head. "Too much time will be wasted if we return to Davenport Hall. I must go after my brother now."

"Your horses are spent," Mr. Kent said. "You'll have to change them before we start our search."

Evan glared at Kent, the fear for his sister warring with practicality. Finally, he nodded. "We'll change horses."

"We will do better than that," I said with some anticipation. "We'll take Charlotte's racing phaeton."

33

The stables were lit up with lamps and torches when we finally clattered tiredly across the cobbles. I did not wait for a groom but dismounted upon the mounting block, my back aching and my legs a little wobbly. I had not ridden for such an extended time in a long while. I stroked Callista's warm muzzle, murmuring my thanks, then handed her reins to the groom who had emerged from the stables.

I stretched into a burning backward arch—both unladylike and mortifyingly stiff—finding brief relief for my muscles, then turned to see Evan and Mr. Kent also on the ground. Evan had handed over his horse for the stable, but Kent had given one of the grooms Caesar's reins to walk him around the yard to keep warm.

"Augusta!"

I turned to see Charlotte and Julia emerging from the stables. Charlotte was in full dress for dinner with a hurried blue shawl around her shoulders that did not match her emerald green silk gown. My darling sister was in her heavy wool riding habit, gloves, and a firmly tied bonnet. Ready for the search.

I met them in the middle of the stable yard, the two men joining us. From the corner of my eye, I saw Julia clasp Mr. Kent's hand and briefly raise herself upon her toes to whisper something in his ear. He turned his head into her words, his expression tender. And then my attention was claimed by Charlotte.

"Augusta, dear, I am having the phaeton harnessed for you and Julia," she said. Her movements held the quick decision of battle and her cheeks were flushed. I suspected this trouble had brought a great deal of discord into her house. "It will give you a chance to catch up to Deele."

"Thank you." I touched her arm to press home my gratitude. "I hoped you would lend it to us."

"It is a pretty pickle, indeed." She covered my hand with her own. "We think Lady Hester and Miss Grant took one of the horses when the grooms were at their dinner. Then Deele and your brother arrived, demanding Hester be handed over. I've never seen Porty so disconcerted—Deele is one of his Eton cronies, you know. That is when we discovered they were gone."

"So they do not know Deele is here and following?" I asked.

Charlotte shook her head. "We think they left at least an hour before Deele and your brother arrived."

"They must have been planning it," I mused aloud. "Not a spontaneous decision."

Julia released Mr. Kent's hand to stand at my side. "Probably prompted by the presence of Porty and the Ellis-Brants, and the imminent arrival of Brummell and Alvanley," she said.

"Deele is following in his coach?" Evan asked.

"Yes, but he took the rested change horses and left his own spent team. Another horse is being saddled for you, Lord Evan," Charlotte said. No more pretense of Mr. Talbot, then. "Where is that damn phaeton?" She turned to check on the harnessing. The equipage was out and one of the horses in the traps, the other being hitched. "My matched bays should give you some chance of catching up," she added.

"Our brother is in the drawing room, Gus," Julia said quietly to me. "He didn't go after Hester with Lord Deele. Apparently

Deele insisted Duffy come here with him to make us hand over Hester. As you can imagine, Duffy is in quite a mood. Shouted at me in front of Porty and the Ellis-Brants."

My poor girl—facing Duffy's rage without me. Our brother rarely shouted at her, and when he did it always upset her more than it should. Moreover, to receive a scolding in front of the Ermine: beyond humiliating.

"I can imagine," I said, sliding my arm across her shoulders for a quick, consolatory hug. "However, his fury will have to wait."

I waved over one of the young grooms. "Go find Mr. Weatherly and ask him to come here, ready for travel. As quick as you can," I instructed. The boy ran off toward the house.

"Weatherly?" Julia asked. "You know he is not yet confident on a horse."

It was true. Our butler had come to horse riding only a month ago and was not yet comfortable in the saddle. Of course, not many butlers, and even fewer Black butlers, knew how to ride— their station in life did not allow or require it. Even so, I had asked Weatherly to take lessons with John Driver, in case of . . . well, in case of situations exactly like this.

I pretended not to hear Julia's comment—mainly because my plan did not involve Weatherly riding or Julia accompanying me— and turned to Charlotte again. "Do we know in which direction Lady Hester and Miss Grant have gone?"

"The gatekeeper thinks he heard a single horse head in the direction of Chester."

"Thinks?" Mr. Kent echoed.

"It is the best we can do," Charlotte said. "But he has manned the gate for twenty years and so knows the sounds of travel along the road."

"We rode in from the other direction and came upon Captain

Morland and his troop," Evan said. "He and his men are looking for Luddites. I hope they do not mistake my sister and Miss Grant for rioters."

"Luddites?" Charlotte said. "Is there trouble?"

"Not yet, but the captain said they have reason to believe there may be some activity," I said.

"If Lady Hester and Miss Grant took only one horse, they will be riding double," Mr. Kent said.

"They took Bruno, one of our steadiest horses," Charlotte said. "They are riding with a bridle but no saddle, as far as we can tell."

I knew Bruno: a big gelding with a small white diamond blaze and a big heart. They would be able to ride double on him for quite some way; Miss Grant was a small woman and Hester was well below normal weight.

"I assume Miss Grant will have control of the horse. Is she a good rider?" Mr. Kent asked.

Julia and I looked at each other. To our shame, we hardly knew anything about Miss Grant's abilities. "We do not know," Julia admitted.

"Hester is, or at least was, a good rider," Evan said. "But she is so weak." He drew his hand down his face. "What if she falls . . ."

I placed my hand upon his shoulder. The muscles under my palm were rigid with tension.

"Any idea where they might be heading?" Kent asked.

"None," I said. "Hester has been talking of leaving the country, but I do not see where that might lead them."

"Holyhead," Charlotte said, with a decisive nod. "It is a long way but maybe they are trying to get to Ireland. They would be able to find passage at Holyhead."

Evan considered Charlotte's theory. "I agree leaving the country will be their goal. And if they did not go in the other direction to Liverpool, then Holyhead is, indeed, the rational choice."

"That is something we do know about Miss Grant," Julia said. "She is a rational woman."

"Finally," Charlotte said, motioning to the fully harnessed phaeton. "Augusta, it is ready."

Charlotte's perch phaeton was a sleek four-wheeled, two-horse affair, with only one nod to propriety: a groom's seat set behind the two-person high-slung cabin. Not that Charlotte and I ever brought one of the grooms along with us on our jaunts. Frankly, the carriage was too light and too fast, and one had to corner carefully if one did not wish to upend the entire equipage. An adventure every time we took it out.

"You are going to drive that?" Mr. Kent asked.

"Indeed, she is," Charlotte said. "Augusta is as good with the reins as I am." Quite some endorsement, since Charlotte was an acclaimed driver.

I drew Julia to one side by her arm. "I do not think you should come. I'll take Weatherly."

"What?" She frowned under the stiffened curve of her bonnet visor. "Do not be ridiculous. Of course I am coming. I am to blame as much as you are for their flight—perhaps even more so after that stupid Weymouth business. We took on the responsibility of their safety and we have patently failed. We need to find them and then find somewhere truly safe for them."

"Blame? Really, Julia, neither of us is to blame," I said, then waved away my irritation; it was no time to argue that point. "Frankly, you are not well enough for the pursuit, dearheart. Lord Evan says that those blue mass tablets you are taking are poisoning you."

Julia eyed me, her mouth pursed. "Poisoning me? Why would Dr. Thorgood give me something that would poison me?"

"Because he does not know it is poison. No one does."

"Then how does Lord Evan know?"

A good question. It was, after all, just a hypothesis. "He read about it in a medical paper." Clearly not enough evidence for my sister, for her jaw had shifted into Colebrook mulishness. "Do not give me that look, Julia. Even if it has just the smallest possibility of being true, you must stop taking them."

"You are always telling me what to do," my sister snapped. She shook off my hand and walked to the carriage. "What I must do is get into this phaeton and find Lady Hester. Are you going to drive or not?"

A few yards away, Lord Evan and Mr. Kent were already mounted, Lord Evan leaning down to receive a lamp and instructions from Charlotte. No doubt the direction to Holyhead. Both men had pistols in saddle holsters, and Mr. Kent had a rifle. A Baker, if I was not mistaken, which stood to reason since he had been a soldier.

"Well, are you coming?" Julia demanded as a groom handed her up into the phaeton.

It seemed Julia was adamant. Still, I wanted Weatherly with us. It would be a squeeze for him in the groom's seat, but it would have to do.

"I am coming," I said, taking the hand of the groom waiting for me.

Finally Weatherly, clad in his greatcoat and tricorn hat, jogged into the stable yard with our coachman's blunderbuss in hand.

I waved him over, then climbed up onto the right step and swung into the driver's seat, the well-slung cabin rocking into balance under my weight as I gathered the reins. The groom handed me the long whip and stepped back, making way for Weatherly to climb into his higher perch.

"My lady, John Driver insisted I bring Hades with me. Just in case," he said, folding his long body into the small, raised seat and laying the blunderbuss across his thighs. The gun had accompanied us on many of our adventures and survived an unceremonious dumping in a horse trough. It had, to some degree, become a lucky talisman. The groom handed up a lamp to Weatherly, the yellow light catching upon the long metal barrel in a dark glint.

"Are you set?" I asked. He nodded. I looked across at my sister. One last attempt to get her to see reason. "I do not always tell you what to do, Julia. But if I do say something, it is because I am worried for your safety. Are you really sure you are up to this?"

"Oh, for heaven's sake, Gus, just drive," she said, staring ahead.

A good idea, since in the distance I could see a familiar figure stalking down the front steps of the hall. Our brother jabbed his flat hand high in the air, commanding us to wait. I had no idea why he thought I would obey.

"I'll take care of it," Charlotte called, her hand raised in farewell.

"Thank you. For everything," I called back.

I signaled to the groom at the head of the eager offside horse to let go of the bridle. He jumped back, and with a flick and release of the reins, we clattered across the cobbles, then onto the gravel driveway, with Evan and Mr. Kent following on horseback. I could not see Duffy's face as we passed—the distance too great and the light too dim—but I had felt his outrage many times over the years and had to admit, I felt rather shamefully pleased that this moment would probably top them all.

Our speed added to the chilled night breeze, the rush of cold air nipping at my nose and lips. I braced my feet more securely against the footboard and settled into managing Charlotte's excellent pair of bays and the task at hand.

Somewhere out there were our runaways. Beside me, Julia clutched the gold cross around her neck, no doubt praying that we would retrieve Hester and Miss Grant before Lord Deele found them. Since I could not add a prayer, I briefly looked up at the cold, star-filled sky as we drove along the gravel drive. There might be no God, but there was a fast phaeton, five committed people, and a sense of true justice that burned through us all.

34

꧁

"ood God, Gus, slow down," Julia shrieked in my ear as one of the large back wheels left the road on a particularly bumpy stretch.

I steadied the horses, the phaeton bumping back down onto its four wheels. Julia gasped at the jolt and braced her feet wider on the footboard beside my own. Ahead, Evan and Mr. Kent galloped in tandem, the glows from their lamps seesawing across the dirt road and dense woodland on either side. Our lamp had gone out about a mile back, and now Weatherly grimly clamped it between his knees while hanging on to the blunderbuss and the edge of the groom's seat.

"Still there, Weatherly?" I yelled over my shoulder.

"Still here, my lady," he yelled back.

We had all caught sight in the distance of a horse without a rider standing on the road, and increased our speed. Was it Hester and Miss Grant's horse? And if so, why was it abandoned?

"I do not see anyone near it," Julia said over the sound of our wheels and hooves. "Do you think they are on foot?"

"Duck!" I ordered, unable to avoid a low arch of overhanging branches. We all ducked, the bare twigs scraping along my riding hat. I glanced back at Weatherly. He was bent double over the gun across his thighs but had lost his own hat.

"Sorry," I yelled over my shoulder.

"Only so far I can duck down, my lady," he replied, at his driest.

Understood. Unless I wanted a headless butler, best to avoid the branches. A six-foot man was not meant to sit in a groom's seat.

Evan and Mr. Kent had slowed their momentum into a trot, no doubt in an effort not to spook the horse ahead. I drew on the reins in my hand, slowing the bays to a trot, then a walk. Ahead, I saw Evan dismount and hand his reins to Mr. Kent. The abandoned horse must be near.

I drew the phaeton to a halt. "Weatherly, go to their heads." The phaeton rocked as our butler clambered down from his perch. "Do you feel up to taking the reins, Julia?"

She narrowed her eyes at me, then expertly looped the offered reins in her left hand and took the whip in her other. "For heaven's sake, Gus, you taught me yourself."

Clearly, still annoyed with me. And she was indeed a competent driver, if not an enthusiastic one.

I waited until Weatherly had hold of the pair's harness, then gathered the skirts of my habit and found the step down. It was a bad stretch of road: holes and rocks under a canopy of trees that, although autumn-leaf depleted, still blocked some of the meager moonlight.

Ahead, Evan was closing in on the horse. The animal stood alert, watching him approach. It was hard to judge color in the moonlight, but I saw a diamond blaze and no saddle. Without a doubt, Bruno.

I walked to Mr. Kent, still mounted and holding the reins of Evan's horse as he studied the gloomy woodland on either side.

"Anything?" I asked.

"No signs of trampling through the undergrowth," he said.

"May I take your lamp?"

He passed it to me and I continued onward, picking my way around the rocks and ruts in the warm circle of its glow. Evan had masterfully caught Bruno and was stroking the horse's muzzle. I raised the lamp as I approached, studying Bruno's legs and chest.

"He looks unhurt," I said, glancing at Evan for confirmation.

"His gait is sound. His reins were hanging, but as far as I can tell he is not blown."

I walked to the edge of the road and peered into the dark woodland beyond, holding up the lamp. The bright arc of my search swept across bushes, lichen-patched tree trunks and, beyond, a stone stacked fence.

"Any sign?" Evan asked. "Do you think they are walking now?"

"If I had a horse and someone who could not go far on foot, I would not abandon my mount. Even if he were spent. And Bruno is not spent." I paced a few yards onward. The undergrowth here was undisturbed too. I swung around and studied the road but could find no sign of fracas: no churned dirt or new wheel ruts. The anticipation I had felt at finding the horse chilled into foreboding. I turned back to Evan. "Hester is not up to walking across the fields. I think Bruno has come back on his own. We need to ride on."

With that decision made, we returned to Mr. Kent with the loose horse in tow. Kent volunteered to lead Bruno; he'd had a great deal of experience doing so on the Continent, he said, whenever one of his fellow cavalrymen had fallen in battle. Evan and I looked at each other, not knowing what to say. Mr. Kent clearly had a great deal more history than we had suspected. But then, did not everyone?

Evan handed over Bruno's reins and I returned to the phaeton, reporting our finding—and lack of finding—to Julia and Weatherly and retrieving the reins and whip from my sister.

From the seat behind, Weatherly bent close to my ear. "You think there is serious trouble ahead, my lady?" he asked.

"Always," I said, flashing a wry smile back at him.

He settled Hades more firmly across his thighs.

"Walk on," I called to the bays, and we jolted once more into motion behind Evan and Mr. Kent. We did not travel as fast this time, more trot than gallop, for the sake of caution and to save the horses. We did not know how far Bruno had wandered alone.

The answer was not long in coming.

"Look!" Julia said, pointing ahead.

Evan and Mr. Kent suddenly accelerated, pulling Bruno with them into a gallop. Beyond them I saw the reason why: a dark, huddled form upon the road.

I flicked my whip over the heads of my pair.

"Dear God," Julia said, leaning forward as we lurched into a slow gallop. "Who is it? Are they dead?"

Evan, unencumbered by the extra horse, dismounted in one swinging move and ran over to the hump of dark cloth as I pulled up the bays. His horse stood where he had left it: thank God Charlotte always trained her horses well. I thrust the reins into Julia's hands again and climbed down the step, almost tripping upon my hems as I found the ground.

"Hold them," I said.

"Wait—" Julia started.

But I had already launched myself across the stony ground, skirts hauled up above my ankles. At the corner of my eye, I saw Weatherly climb out behind me, scouring the shadowy woods on either side of the road, blunderbuss ready.

"It is Miss Grant," Evan called, crouching at her side.

She had uncurled a little by the time I reached them, one hand clutching the capes upon Evan's greatcoat, the other held awkwardly against her chest.

"He has her," she said. Tear tracks striped her pale face. "Lord Deele has her."

"Are you hurt?" Evan asked.

"My arm," she said. "I couldn't catch the horse."

"May I see?" Evan gestured to her cradled arm. "Gus, can you help her sit up, please?"

"Do not worry about me. We must find Hester," she said. "We must go after them."

"First your arm," Evan said, although I knew he, too, wanted to be on a horse and after Hester.

"What on earth were you thinking, taking Hester out on a horse at night?" I said, a little too sharply. I crouched behind her and settled stiffly onto my knees. "Where did you think you were going?"

She rallied a little at my tone. "I had to do something. Hester was going to do herself harm if we didn't act on our own account. You kept on promising we would go and then nothing happened. You saw how frightened she was and yet all you did was tell her to wait." Her scathing glance took in both myself and Evan.

He raised his brows at me: *She has a point.*

"Lean into me," I said, drawing her back against my body. "The sooner you let him examine you, the sooner we will be after Hester. Remember he is a Belford, too, and nothing stops them."

She managed a wan smile at my conciliatory tone: the two of us, loving our stubborn, brave Belfords. Finally, a point of affinity.

Farther back, Mr. Kent dismounted and called over Weatherly, exchanging the reins of the three horses for Weatherly's blunderbuss. Evan carefully dug his fingertips along Miss Grant's right arm. She gasped when he reached her elbow.

"I take it that is painful," he said.

"Yes," she managed.

"My apologies, but the good news is that it is only wrenched and bruised. Not broken."

Mr. Kent jogged up to us. "What happened?"

"Deele's man pulled me from the horse," Miss Grant said. "Then they grabbed Hester and bundled her into the carriage."

A dangerous maneuver that could have killed both women. "And Deele left you on the side of the road, injured," I said, trying to come to terms with such villainy.

"How long ago?" Kent asked.

Miss Grant shook her head. "I cannot be sure. No more than fifteen minutes."

"We can pursue." I looked at Evan for accord, then at Kent, drawing him into the discussion. "The three of us on horseback. We have guns; we can stop the coach. Julia can drive the phaeton behind with Miss Grant and Weatherly."

Evan gave a nod and stood, brushing road grit from his hands. He offered his hand to me. I took his firm grip and felt my not-insubstantial self pulled to my feet. My face heated: his easy strength always did unseemly things to my innards.

"The three of us?" Kent echoed. "You cannot think to come, Lady Augusta. It will be far too dangerous."

"Save your breath, Kent," Evan said. "If Lady Augusta says she will come, then she will come." He allowed a grim smile. "It would seem you are both joining me on the high toby."

"But this is not highway robbery," Mr. Kent said.

"No, it is worse," Evan said. "It is abduction. My brother has the right to take Hester back."

"God's blood, I knew I would end up hanged," Mr. Kent muttered.

"This is my area of expertise," Evan said, with a side glance at Mr. Kent. "It will be too difficult to stop my brother's coach from behind. We must circle around in front of it. Once we sight it, we will cut across fields and meet it farther along."

He outlined the plan: a mad mix of strategy, knowledge of his brother, and derring-do.

"Now I know why you have never been caught," Mr. Kent said. "Does your brother know you are in England? In the vicinity?"

"A good question," Evan said. "I have no idea."

He glanced at me, but I answered with a shrug. Mulholland could have told him, but then again, it was just as likely he did not. Hester, too, might let slip the information in extremis.

"He must know Julia and I are involved, since he brought our brother to force us to hand over Hester," I said, "but that does not necessarily mean he knows Lord Evan is here."

"And I do not know how he will react when he discovers I am the one stopping his coach," Evan added. "He has not hesitated to enact violence upon our sister, so I would assume he would have no compunction shooting me."

"Excellent," Mr. Kent said dryly. "Do I need to add that it would be better if we do not shoot a lord of the realm?" He fixed a stern gaze upon me from under his brow. "You may wish to ride with us on this mad enterprise, Lady Augusta, but Lady Julia must not be exposed to such danger. She is, I think, more gente—" He stopped, clearly realizing he was about to insult me.

I eyed him for a long moment; he still had a lot to learn about my sister. Nevertheless, I did agree with him about Julia's safety.

"Let us help Miss Grant to the phaeton," I said. "She and my sister can follow at a judicious distance."

"No, they should not follow," Mr. Kent said. "They should go back to Davenport Hall. Miss Grant is hurt."

"Absolutely not," Miss Grant said vehemently. "I could never abandon Hester."

"Of course not," I said. "Besides, we will need the phaeton to carry Lady Hester once she is retrieved."

In truth, our options for Hester's safety had now dwindled to one possibility: the two women, and most probably Evan, must flee the country via boat. I pushed away the familiar burst of anguish that squeezed my heart. Evan would have to go; he could not let them travel unaccompanied. As it stood, Hester could not go back to Davenport Hall; we had already brought too much trouble upon Charlotte, and even if we did return, Porty would probably just hand her over to Deele. Nor, it seemed, could we find a safe haven from them elsewhere in the country. Holyhead was too far away, so we were left, then, with the closest port: Liverpool. In her current state, Hester might not survive a sea journey, but I could see no other course of action.

Evan helped Miss Grant to her feet, the maneuver draining her face into a pasty gray. She did, indeed, look very bad, but took a gulping breath and stalwartly continued to walk with the support of both Evan and Mr. Kent.

At the phaeton, I told Julia our plan to stop Deele's coach as Miss Grant leaned upon Evan's shoulder and gingerly levered herself into the seat beside my sister. The well-sprung carriage rocked under her arrival, the horses shifting in the traps.

"Are you sure you are up to managing this pair?" I asked.

"Have I not already said so?" Julia said. "More to the point, you have been in the saddle all day. Are you sure you can ride all night too?"

"Indeed, there is no sidesaddle for you, Lady Augusta. Perhaps you should ride in the phaeton too," Mr. Kent said as if it were some kind of fait accompli.

"For heaven's sake, I am not in my dotage," I said to my sister, then sent her a swift, silent apology; she was not going to like this next admission. "And I will ride astride on Bruno. Charlotte and I have been riding astride at the hall for years, when no one was watching."

Julia clicked her tongue, no doubt mourning my last shred of ladylike dignity. Thank heavens I had worn my full knitted pantaloons under my habit.

"Of course you have been riding astride," Evan murmured, allowing a glint of amusement to show through his urgency. "Are we ready? Do we know our parts?"

We did. Now it was up to our nerve, my beloved's skill, and a good dose of luck.

With excitement thrumming through my body, I followed Evan over to Weatherly, who still held the other two horses. Perhaps it was unladylike to feel such invigoration at the prospect of holding up a coach, but I could not help it. Nor could I help the anger that burned in my innards; Lord Deele had caused immense anguish and pain to his sister, and now he wished to do so all over again.

Evan leaned down beside Bruno and offered his laced hands as a mounting step. I placed my booted foot onto his outstretched palms and swung my other leg over the horse's unsaddled back, dragging my skirts and petticoats up in a most indecorous manner. I wrenched them into a more demure arrangement, the warmth of Bruno underneath me almost canceling the chill of the night air on my stockinged legs. I looped the reins and settled into my seat.

Evan looked up at me, and I could see him carefully not noticing my exposed calf. "Is it worth me asking you to retreat if they start shooting?"

"Only if you do."

He sighed. "Just do not get shot. I could not bear it."

"Nor could I," I said dryly. Still, the danger was very real. "I should have brought a pistol too."

"Do you wish for the blunderbuss, my lady?" Weatherly asked, holding out the big rifle.

It was tempting—if only to horrify Mr. Kent—but I shook my head. "Keep it to protect Lady Julia and Miss Grant."

"Of course, my lady."

He bowed and jogged back to the phaeton, the blunderbuss still in hand.

"I brought two pistols; you can have one of mine," Evan said.

Mr. Kent stared at him. "You are going to give Lady Augusta a pistol?"

"Well, not until we are closer," I said, flashing a smile at Evan. "I do not have a saddle holster."

Evan snorted and swung up onto his horse.

"We'll all be hanged," Mr. Kent muttered as he mounted his horse.

We looked at one another—a shared moment of resolve—then the three of us sprang our horses, leaning forward into the building rush of the gallop. We had lost at least another ten minutes behind Deele, but hopefully he would not be pushing his horses now. He had his prize in hand and would not be expecting his outlaw brother to be riding hard behind.

35

Dark clouds had momentarily blocked the pale moonlight. I bent over Bruno's neck, straining to see any treacherous holes he might catch his hooves in. My heart pounded in time to the thud of his gallop, my breath coming short and hard, my thighs aching from keeping balance and control upon his unsaddled back. Although it was a freezing night, sweat dampened the front of my chemise and gathered under my cravat, as much in anticipation as exertion. And perhaps a little fear.

A mile back we had spotted Deele's coach lamps, and now Evan, Kent, and I were making our run to overtake him. A foolhardy gallop across a field on a cloudy, crescent-moon night. Absolute madness, and ridiculously exhilarating.

Ahead, Evan sat back up in his saddle, slowing his horse's gait into a trot. He held up his hand. In the gloom beyond him, I made out the low jagged shape of a stone stacked fence with a breach in its length of broken slate and tumbled stones.

I drew upon the reins, leaning back into the request to slow our momentum. Bruno obeyed, dropping into a trot, until I could bring him around to stand beside Evan and Kent.

"This is our place," Evan said, the misted breath upon each word curling in front of his mouth. "I would say we have about five minutes before the coach comes around the turn." He drew a pistol out of one of the holsters and handed it to me, grip first. "It is loaded."

I ripped off my glove and took the gun, its metal weight heavy and cold in my bare hand. Beside me, Mr. Kent passed his Baker rifle to Evan, as planned, then drew out his own pistol.

"Should we wear our kerchiefs up around our noses and mouths, like all good highwaymen?" Mr. Kent asked. "I would not wish to break the highwayman code on my first time out."

Evan was clearly not in the mood for levity. "You do what you must do," he said, slinging the rifle strap over his shoulder. "I will be showing my face. My brother will know who is stopping his treachery."

Kent glanced at me, somewhat abashed. "My apologies, Lord Evan. I did not mean to belittle your sister's peril."

Evan gave a curt nod.

"Once we have Hester, I think our only choice is to head back to Liverpool," I said. "Ceredigion Bay is too far. In Liverpool you can always find a ship that is leaving on the next tide."

Evan blinked at the use of *you*, then sighed. "I think you are right."

We looked at each other: a question asked, an answer given. I could not go.

"We should get out there," Kent said, breaking the tension between us.

We filed out onto the selected section of road—a straight length after a curve to slow them down—and took our positions: Kent riding into the trees closer to the curve; Evan, with the Baker rifle, and I ranged across the road.

Bruno shifted underneath me, no doubt feeling my tension. I held my breath, straining to hear the sound of the approaching coach, my vision narrowed to the rutted and rocky stretch of road ahead. Ah, there it was: the unmistakable jangle of tack and thud of hooves. By my reckoning, an easy pace; no alarm in the momentum of the team of four. I raised my pistol, steadying it. Only one shot: I hoped I would not have to fire it.

The rhythm of hooves slowed as they took the curve, and then the team and coach were coming at us.

"Stand!" Evan bellowed, and shot the rifle above the heads of the driver and footman. "Stand or be killed!"

I saw a flash of the driver's face—eyes and mouth wide—then he wrenched upon the reins. The four horses, already startled by the shot, plunged and reared in the traps as they were hauled to a stop, haunches straining. The coach behind them rocked upon its springs, swinging and spraying dirt as it came to a cumbersome halt.

Evan slung the spent rifle back over his shoulder and pulled out his pistol. "Hands where we can see them," he yelled to the driver and footman, the pistol aimed at them. They raised their hands, their fear shifting into disbelief at seeing me beyond him.

"It's a woman," the driver said.

I urged Bruno forward, still pointing my gun at them. "It is, and I'll take your head off if you move." I was rather pleased with the steel in my voice.

Mr. Kent broke cover just as the door of the carriage swung open and Deele poked his head and hand out, a pistol aimed at Evan.

"Drop it, or I will shoot!" Kent ordered, coming up from behind him.

Deele looked over his shoulder and, upon seeing Kent's pistol pointed squarely at his head, lowered the gun.

"I said drop it," Kent ordered again.

"Damn you!" Deele tossed the gun to the ground. "Do you know who I am?"

"Indeed I do, brother," Evan said. He dismounted as Deele jerked around to face him again.

"Good God!" Deele sounded genuinely flabbergasted. "Is that you, Evan?"

"Go see to the driver and footman," Evan said to Kent. As the Runner passed him, Evan handed back the Baker rifle.

That was my cue. As soon as Kent took over guarding the two men at the front, I slid off Bruno, my cold feet jarring upon the hard road, ready for my part.

"What are you doing here?" Deele said. "Why are you pointing a gun at me?"

"I am saving our sister," Evan said.

"Saving her? What do you mean? I am saving her."

Gun in hand, I skirted the blowing horses and made my way around to the other side of the carriage. It was a large traveling coach, with windows set into the door as well as either side of the cabin. Carefully, I peered into the bodkin window, gun at the ready.

On the other side of the carriage, I heard Evan say, "How can you think consigning our sister to a madhouse is saving her in any way?"

Hester sat propped next to the window I looked through, either asleep or, more likely, unconscious, for no one could have slept through that tumultuous halt. Either she had been drugged or the ordeal of being snatched by her brother had been too much. Extracting her from the coach would be more difficult than anticipated.

Deele caught sight of me through the window. He turned, peering intently across at me, the physical similarity to his brother uncanny: a younger version of Evan but without any strength or character carved by hardship in its lines. "Lady Augusta Colebrook? Is that you? I was told you were interfering in my affairs!"

So Mulholland had told him that Hester was with us but had not told him about Evan's return. Unsettling, yet I did not have time to trace that dangerous map of motivation.

I opened the carriage door. "I am not interfering in your affairs, Lord Deele," I said. "I am helping Lady Hester escape your brutality."

"This is none of your business, Lady Augusta. You have no idea what my sister has done."

"All she has done is love someone," Evan said. He must have crossed the short distance between them, for now he stood at arm's length—and a gun's length—from his brother. Through the carriage, he met my eyes, a swift confirmation that I had all in hand. Then he saw his sister, unconscious in the corner. "Good God, Charles, what have you done to her now?"

"Just laudanum. I did not want her to attack me and my men again. She is violent, Evan."

"Balderdash!" Evan said. "If she fought you, it is because she is fighting for her survival."

"Is that what she told you? You should know she has been bewitched by a woman," Deele said. "A woman. It is ungodly. A monstrous thing." He shook his head. "I tell you, we Belfords are cursed, brother. First you, a convict, then our father's debts, and now Hester."

"Our father's debts?" I heard the flex of disbelief in Evan's voice. "He was never one for cards or the bones. What debts?"

"After you were transported—his beloved firstborn—all he did was gamble. Then he died, and I"—Deele thumped his chest—"I had to pay back all his IOUs. It nearly ruined me. I had to use everything in the estate and borrow too."

"Everything?" Evan demanded. "Did you use Hester's portion as well? Is that why you put her away?"

"That is not why I committed her. She is mad. Anyway, I am her guardian; I can use her and her portion any way I wish, and I used it to drag this family out of disgrace."

"There is only one disgrace here, brother, and it is you," Evan said coldly. "Look what you have done to our sister." He motioned with the gun at the prone Hester. "She is not mad. And yet you abandoned her in a madhouse. When we found her, she was near dead!"

Deele lifted his Belford chin. "Better she is dead than without the grace of God or bringing more scandal upon our name."

I sucked in a breath. Such a terrible thing to say—did he truly mean it?

Evan stared at him. "What has happened to you, Charles? Your piety is all twisted and foul. I do not recognize you."

Deele was about to answer but stopped at the sound of hooves and wheels approaching at speed. I could see the anticipation within him; perhaps this newcomer would offer an opportunity to overcome us.

I had to admit to a second of malicious pleasure at what was about to arrive.

The phaeton emerged from around the curve at a smart trot, Julia fixed intently upon handling the reins, Weatherly with blunderbuss at the ready, and Miss Grant sitting forward, searching the road. At the sight of us, Julia deftly maneuvered the phaeton to one side and drew the horses to a stop, just in time to avoid Miss Grant's going under the wheels as she clambered down from her seat and ran forward, injured arm clutched to her chest.

"Hester!"

I held up my hand, halting her headlong dash toward us. "Miss Grant. Wait!"

She stood, stranded between the phaeton and the coach. I did not want her to distract Evan or come between any guns.

"You!" Deele said to Miss Grant, his voice deep with loathing. He turned back to Evan. "You are helping the creature who is dragging our sister into perdition?"

"Come this way," I said, waving Miss Grant over to my side of the carriage. "You, too, Weatherly. Help me get Hester out of the carriage."

"What is wrong with her?" Miss Grant asked as she obeyed my urgent summons. "Did he hurt her?"

"Drugged," I said, opening the door. We both looked inside at Hester: still insensible. It must have been a hefty dose of laudanum. At the corner of my eye, I saw Weatherly climb down from the groom's seat and hand Julia the blunderbuss. It seemed my sister always ended up with Hades in hand.

Miss Grant glared through the carriage at Deele. "You are despicable. All you do is hurt her!"

"Me, hurt her? You are destroying her chance of salvation," Deele hissed back.

"She hates you!" Miss Grant lunged forward, as if to launch herself through the carriage. "Hates you!"

I grabbed her shoulder and pulled her back from the door. "There is no time for this. We must get Hester out now!"

She drew a quivering breath. "Of course."

At the front of the coach, the clink and jangle of tack told me Mr. Kent was well on the way to achieving the next part of the plan: unhitching the lead horse from the coach and letting it loose farther down the road to delay pursuit.

Weatherly jogged up to us. "Did you wish me to retrieve Lady Hester, my lady?"

At the other side of the carriage, I heard Deele's profane outrage as he saw his horse free from the harness.

"No, not a man," Miss Grant said abruptly. "I am sorry, Mr. Weatherly, but she would not like to be touched by a man."

Indeed, Hester had suffered so much at the hands of the brutal basketmen and mad doctors at the asylum, and by her own brother forcing laudanum down her throat. We could not subject her to more. Even the kindly hands of Weatherly.

"I'll pull her out," I said, and found a firm foothold upon the coach step. I levered myself halfway into the carriage. "Hester? Can you hear me?"

No response, but I had not expected one. I dug my hands between her lax arms and slumped body and pulled her upright by her armpits. With a heave, I dragged her off the seat and into the doorway, her head lolling over my shoulder, her arms hanging inert. Although malnourished and bone thin, she was still a deadweight, the imbalance upon my chest teetering me on the coach step.

"Steady," Miss Grant said, and I felt her hand pressing the middle of my back, guiding me as I felt for the ground, pulling Hester with me.

"I think you will have to carry her to the phaeton, Weatherly," I said. "I am sorry, Miss Grant, but she is too heavy for me and we cannot delay."

Miss Grant hesitated, then gave a reluctant nod.

I swung Hester around as if we were in a drunken dance, and Weatherly neatly gathered her up into the cradle of his arms.

"Do you think this is going to change anything?" Deele demanded. I could no longer see any resemblance to my love: Deele's teeth were bared, his face puffed and dark with choler. "I am not going to stop until she is far away from that woman. I am her guardian and she will submit to my will. She will not ruin our name again!"

"If you do not stop, brother, then neither will I," Evan said. "You will not ruin Hester's life again."

I slammed the carriage door shut and followed Miss Grant and Weatherly—carrying his burden with infinite care—to the phaeton.

I believed Deele; he would not stop his relentless persecution of Hester and Miss Grant. Ever. We only had one choice now. Liverpool, and a ship that would take them as far away from him as possible.

36

~~~~

$\mathcal{W}$e left Deele's coach still under the aimed guns of Evan and Kent. Miss Grant and Hester were crammed in the narrow groom's seat behind Julia and me—not the arrangement I had favored, but the high-seat squeeze did keep Hester upright. Beside me, Julia was handling the reins nicely, keeping the pair at a brisk trot. I had Hades across my knees, ready to fire if anyone followed. I really should have been driving, but I was a much better shot than Julia.

We drove in silence for a few miles, my reticence due to a deep wash of fatigue, and Julia's, I think, due to concentration. The road was treacherous. Finally, we saw a crossroad up ahead.

"Turn left here," I said over the rumble of our wheels. "This road can take us back in the direction of Liverpool."

"We are not going to Liverpool," Julia said.

I dug my feet against the footboard as we bounced over a series of ruts. Of course, Julia did not know the new plan.

"We are not going to Holyhead now. It is too far away," I said. "We are going to Liverpool—it is much closer and we'll be able to find a ship sooner."

I forced down the rising misery of Evan's departure. I had been living with the possibility for months. Surely I should be used to the hollow sense of loss by now.

"We are not going to Liverpool either." Julia glanced across at me, her face set into determined lines. "We are going to Llan-gollen."

"What?" I said, trying to move my thoughts beyond the obvious stupidity of the plan. "You cannot be serious. Brummell and Alvanley are there! We agreed Alvanley is a danger."

My sister's expression, however, was very serious. "Things have changed, Gus. This is the best course of action now."

"No, it is a terrible idea. Take the turn! We have to go to Liverpool."

Her hand tightened on the reins. "We are going to Llangollen, and as fast as possible; time is of the essence. Miss Grant and Hester will stay with Miss Ponsonby and Lady Butler, if the ladies are willing to take them in. And I am sure they will be."

"Deele will just find them and take Hester back," I said. How could Julia not see that?

"He will not. I am sure of it."

"Sure of it?"

I looked over my shoulder at Miss Grant, grimly holding on to Lady Hester. The racing suspension of the phaeton was more intense between the two larger wheels and Lady Hester had slumped sideways across Miss Grant's lap. "Neither you nor Lady Hester knows the ladies, do you?"

Miss Grant shook her head.

I turned back to my sister, my confusion shifting into anger. "They are not even acquainted, Julia. There is no guarantee the ladies will take them in. Besides, Evan and Kent will not know where we have gone!"

"Weatherly knows the plan. He will tell them. I have told him to do so within Deele's hearing."

"What? In Deele's hearing?"

Had she gone mad? Had the mercury done something to her brain?

Julia leaned forward, loosening the reins and urging the horses into a canter, clearly meaning to drive past the intersection of roads.

"Julia, you are making a mistake. This is a terrible idea. Take the turn!"

"No!"

We were almost upon the crossroad. "Julia, turn!" I acted before I fully knew what I was doing: the worst transgression of carriage etiquette. I leaned over my sister and wrenched the reins out of her hand.

"Gus, what are you doing?" Julia yelled, grabbing back at the reins.

The odd feel of the reins made the horses turn sharply. The phaeton swung wildly to the left, jolting Julia hard against me. Behind us, I heard Miss Grant shriek as the horses broke into a confused gallop. Dear God, what had I done?

I slapped away Julia's hands and let the pair have their head for a few strides, then eased them back, letting them know someone was in charge, my heart pounding as I drew them gradually down into a walk and, finally, a stop.

I looked sideways at my sister. She sat ramrod straight, her jaw set into a hard line of righteous fury, her chest rising and falling in hard, quick breaths.

"How dare you take the reins from me, Augusta," she said. "How dare you." She turned in her seat to face Miss Grant. "Are you and Hester unharmed?"

"Yes." Miss Grant's voice wavered upon the word. I turned to meet her glare. Her arms were tight around the still insensible Hester. "But barely. I nearly lost hold of her."

Julia turned back to me. "What possessed you? That was dangerous and completely unnecessary!"

At her scathing tone, my hot shame shifted into fury. "What possessed me? What possessed you to inform Deele of your idiotic plan? If you take Hester to the Ladies of Llangollen, she will be back in Deele's control before you know it! Especially since you are telling him where she is!" I shouted the last, the fright and confusion of the last few minutes bursting out of me. The horses shifted, jolting the phaeton.

"You don't always know best, Gus!" Julia yelled back. "Other people have good ideas too. It is not up to you to solve every problem. You are not responsible for everything!" She drew a shaking breath. I opened my mouth to protest, but she gave an angry shake of her head, not finished yet. "You have to let people live their own lives. Make their own choices. I know it is the way you show that you care, but you are being too high-handed. Too interfering. I am sorry, but that is the truth."

High-handed? Interfering? I stared at her, a dry ache welling up into my throat. She did not, I think, mean only for Hester and Elizabeth, but herself too.

I shook my head. She did not understand what I was trying to do.

"My plan is good," she added defiantly, "and Elizabeth thinks it is the best way to go ahead. It is her choice and it is what we are going to do."

So, it was Elizabeth now: it seemed Miss Grant and my sister had suddenly become intimate friends.

"Oh, so that is what Elizabeth thinks, is it?" I said, unable to temper my hurt. "And how is leading Deele straight to Lady Hester the best way to go ahead?"

"If you let me explain, you will know!"

I returned my sister's belligerent stare. "Tell me how this idiocy is going to work, then."

She drew a long breath through pinched nostrils. "When we were following you in the phaeton, Elizabeth told me about Deele and his obsession with reputation. He is just like Duffy, Gus. Everything is sacrificed upon the altar of the family name. It is what drives him to treat Hester so badly; she must not sully the family's reputation in the eyes of good society. Not after he has worked so hard to reinstate it."

I had to admit, I had heard him say as much to Evan just minutes before. But I was not ready to concede the point gracefully.

"So?"

"We turn the situation upon its head," Julia said. "We show Lord Deele that the bon ton accepts Hester and Elizabeth and condemns any bad treatment of them. More to the point, his treatment of them."

"How do you propose to do that?"

"The bon ton is basically staying with the Ladies of Llangollen, Gus. Mr. Brummell and Lord Alvanley are society. Well, the leaders of it, anyway. What they do and think will be what everyone else will do and think. And by staying with the ladies, are they not declaring their support of that singular arrangement? The same arrangement that Elizabeth and Hester wish to achieve?"

I tilted my head; this point I had to concede. "It is true for Brummell, but we cannot know Alvanley's thoughts. He is a friend of Deele's."

"Brummell is all that matters, Gus. Even Lord Alvanley bows to Mr. Brummell; everyone knows that. Once Lord Deele realizes he would be condemned more for interfering with Hester than for leaving her alone, I believe he will back down."

"You *believe* he will? That is quite a risk, Julia."

"I understand how people think and feel, Gus. Better than you do. You have said so yourself. Besides, every plan you have devised for Miss Grant and Lady Hester has come with risk, often without consultation." My sister paused upon that accusation, then continued. "This is a risk they know about and are willing to take. Is that not so, Elizabeth?"

"I cannot speak for Hester," Miss Grant said, tenderly stroking Hester's hair, "but I believe Lady Julia is right. Reputation is what is important to Lord Deele, and he will not wish to go against society."

"Do you see, Gus? It would never have worked before because we were trying to keep Hester's whereabouts and our involvement a secret. But we no longer have to obscure either of those. Deele knows both, and we can—no, we must—reveal Hester to Mr. Brummell and Lord Alvanley."

I sat back in the phaeton seat. It was a good plan. A clever plan. Even so, I said, "There are a lot of ifs."

"Perhaps, but taking Hester to Liverpool to board a ship has just as many, and, frankly, she is too frail to make a sea journey."

That was true, and besides, this new plan might mean Evan would not leave the country quite yet. I handed Julia the reins.

"To the Ladies of Llangollen, then."

Julia nodded. "I think it would be best if you drive now. We must put a good amount of ground between us and Lord Deele so that we can speak to the ladies and prepare for his arrival."

"So you want me to take over now?" I asked, a little petulantly.

"Only the phaeton," Julia said dryly.

She handed back the reins. And with them, a brief touch upon my hand. "This will work, Gus."

I was not entirely convinced, but I had been outvoted. And besides, if this did not work, we could always flee back to Liverpool.

37

The village of Llangollen held the crisp silence of an autumn evening as I drove the phaeton along the main street. The windows of the white cottages upon the roadway were mostly dark, with only the torches outside the Hand Inn, the major hostelry, providing light as we passed.

A few minutes before, we had crossed the handsome Gothic arched bridge over the river Dee and asked directions of a lone man upon the road. He had given us the name and pointed the way to Plas Newydd, the ladies' residence, yet I was still unsure of the turning.

"Did he say beyond the inn and the church?" I asked Julia, slowing the tired pair to a walk.

"I believe so," my sister replied. I heard the fatigue in her voice. "The road we are looking for is Cross Lane. On the right."

I looked behind me at Miss Grant, barely awake, and Lady Hester, slumped in her lover's arms and still insensible, though it had been two hours of bumpy traveling since we had bundled her into the groom's seat. How much laudanum had her brother forced down her throat? Neither of them would have been alert enough to hear the man's directions and so could not concur with Julia's interpretation of his delightful but somewhat incomprehensible Welsh lilt.

Evan and Mr. Kent had not yet caught up to us, although I had expected them to do so about an hour into our drive. Had something gone awry? Moreover, I could not help the thought that maybe Mr. Brummell and Lord Alvanley had not dined with the ladies this evening. Or perhaps they had already done so and left, for surely two gentlemen would not lodge with the ladies but take rooms at one of the two inns in the town. So many ifs and all of them capable of ruining the plan. I shook off my rising apprehension and concentrated on finding our turn.

"There," Julia said, pointing to the entrance of a rough track. "This must be it."

"It is not marked," I said, but I turned, hoping for the best.

The weary horses took the hill, climbing into dense woodland on either side. I was beginning to feel that creeping uneasiness of a wrong turn when the glow of man-made light appeared to our left through the trees.

"Thank God," Julia said.

We drew into the short drive of a small but perfectly formed Gothic-style cottage: white walls and a Gothic wooden porch with wood-canopied windows on either side, lit by candlelight. I had heard that the Ladies of Llangollen had a penchant for carved wood and stained glass—often reclaimed from churches—and here was proof of that predilection. The front of the house and the porch were clad in heavy, bold carvings, and the two windows on the second floor were set with a magnificent design of yellow and blue diamond glass. As I halted the phaeton outside the porch, I saw the shapes of four people seated at a dining table. Was it the ladies dining with Brummell and Alvanley? I could not tell—the distortion of the old, thick glass set into small square panes obscured any detail. I did see, however, their four heads turning in unison at the sound of our wheels upon the gravel. I could just imagine the exclamations—who could this be? had something happened?—for only bad news arrived unannounced at this late hour.

And in a way, we were bad news. Or at least complicated news.

I drew the pair to a halt outside the front door. Without a footman on board, one of us would have to knock and offer our credentials. I had left my calling-card case in the saddlebag, but I suspected we were a little beyond presenting a card for the call anyway. I glanced at Julia, strained and pale. Did she have the strength to carry through her plan? I considered asking her if, indeed, she was up to the task, but I stopped myself from voicing the inquiry. I had to trust that she did have the wherewithal, just as she had trusted me over and over again.

Instead I asked, "Shall I go?"

"Yes. Please," Julia said.

I passed her the reins, flexed my cold, stiff fingers, and climbed to the ground.

A saint of some kind glared at me from the center of the heavily carved door. I rapped upon the wood, then took a step back. The door was opened almost immediately; the footman had clearly been waiting on the other side, his face stiff from the struggle of suppressing his curiosity. The warm air from the hallway brought the smell of roasted beef and horseradish, the savory combination striking at my innards. I had not eaten for some time.

"Good evening," I said. "Is this the residence of Lady Butler and Miss Ponsonby?"

"It is," the footman said, his eyes darting across to the phaeton.

"Please tell your mistresses that Lady Augusta Colebrook, Lady Julia Colebrook, Lady Hester Belford, and Miss Grant have arrived and wish to speak to them most urgently on a matter of"— I hesitated but decided I would not be overstating the case—"life and death."

The footman bowed. "If you will wait, I will—"

"Oh, for heaven's sakes, let them in," a female voice called from farther up the hallway.

The footman opened the door to reveal a dim corridor and the heavyset silhouette of a tall woman. She strode forward. "Lady Augusta, is it not? I am Lady Eleanor. Do come in. All of you. It is a freezing night."

She had a brisk manner, her face built on strong bones, with the skin slackened by age. Her gray hair had been cropped short like my own style, but powdered in the old-fashioned way. Also like myself, she wore a dark, well-cut riding habit. If I was of a whimsical nature, it might have been a look into my future.

"I am afraid Lady Hester is currently incapacitated," I said. "Would it be possible for your man to assist Miss Grant to carry her inside?" Miss Grant would not like the assistance of another man—especially a stranger—but practicality had to win out again. Otherwise we would not get Lady Hester into the house.

Lady Eleanor waved her footman outside. "Of course, of course. We will take her directly to a bed upstairs." She raised an eyebrow. "It seems you come with quite a story, Lady Augusta."

"We do indeed. I am sorry to intrude upon your evening and your—"

My apology was cut short by another female voice. "Did I hear that Lady Julia Colebrook is here?"

A smaller, slightly slenderer version of Lady Eleanor emerged from the room on the left, the dining room, if I was not mistaken. Without a doubt, this was Miss Ponsonby, her features more delicate than her companion's but her hair and habit in exactly the same style. Following her came the lean figure of Mr. Brummell and, behind him, the wider dimensions of Lord Alvanley, both impeccably dressed for dinner in black jackets and white silk knee breeches.

"You are here!" I said, unable to contain my relief at the sight of Brummell and Alvanley.

"Indeed, and so, it seems, are you," Mr. Brummell said, a droll slant in his voice.

Belatedly I curtsied to the assembled company, who all returned the honor.

The commotion of extracting Lady Hester from the phaeton interrupted the reunion. Alvanley, a good deal shorter than Brummel and me, peered around us through the doorway, his genial countenance knitted with concern.

"I do not think your footman is quite up to the task, Lady Eleanor," he said in his lisping drawl. "If you will allow me to expedite the situation, Lady Augusta?"

I smiled my gratitude. "Please do."

He edged past us all and crossed the gravel to render his assistance.

"Lady Hester Belford, is it? Are we to expect Lord Deele?" Brummell murmured, the question for my ears only.

The man was too astute by half. "And Lord Evan Belford and Mr. Kent, a Runner."

He considered me for a long moment, then turned his attention to Alvanley, who was manfully carrying Lady Hester into the house, trailed by Miss Grant, Julia, and the footman. With some care, he negotiated the dimly lit hallway and then walked up the steep staircase. We all followed, and in a short time the invalid was settled upon the bed in a small bedchamber with Miss Grant in attendance on a seat beside it, and the rest of the company back downstairs again.

We assembled in the library. It was a most pleasant room with even more carved wood in evidence. The walls were made of carved bookcases, a round table—its legs and underpinnings also heavily carved—displayed a number of interesting objects, and a large tabby cat, not carved but seated upon a carved stool, watched us all from beside the hearth.

"Should we send for the doctor?" Miss Ponsonby asked. She sat on the sofa beside Julia. "We have one in the village."

All eyes fell upon me. Apparently this was my decision.

"Is she breathing well? Is her color good?" I asked Julia. My sister nodded. "Then I think not. The fewer people who know of our visit, the better. Her elder brother, Lord Evan Belford, will be here soon, and he has medical training."

"Heavens, Lord Evan Belford," Lady Eleanor said from the armchair opposite mine. "That is a name we have not heard nigh on twenty years." She crooked a finger to her maid. "We will have our coffee here, and biscuits too."

I would have liked a good lump of that roast beef that I could smell, but courtesy kept me quiet. Biscuits would have to do.

The two men had taken up positions on either side of the generous fire, Brummell and the cat eyeing each other with identical hauteur. I surreptitiously angled my feet toward the warmth, finally able to stretch my frozen toes into some kind of comfort within my half boots.

"It is so good to see you again, Lady Julia," Miss Ponsonby said into the sudden awkward silence, too polite to demand an explanation for our sudden arrival with a drugged woman, although they had every right to do so. "I have enjoyed our correspondence."

"As I have," Julia said. She sounded bright and energetic, but I knew she was drawing upon deep reserves. It was in the angle of her body and the way she had drawn some of the cloth of her gown into her hand, as if to anchor herself. She leaned closer to Miss Ponsonby. "You must be wondering what on earth is going on. Would it be possible for me to speak to you and Lady Eleanor in private about our friends upstairs? I can explain everything." She glanced at me as she waited for their reply, her eyes flicking to Brummell and back again: *Ask him.*

I tilted my head with a frown: *Yes, yes, I know what to do.*

The Ladies of Llangollen looked at each other. I saw the same kind of silent conversation between them that Julia and I had just conducted—a kind of language born from love and a long time in each other's company—and then Lady Eleanor nodded. "Of course. Come with us."

"You are not going, too, Augusta?" Brummell asked as the three women rose from their chairs.

"No, I will stay." I waited until my sister and the ladies had left the room, and then said, "In fact, Lord Alvanley, would it be too much of an imposition if I spoke to Mr. Brummell in private?"

Lord Alvanley—a man of consummate civility—immediately bowed. "Not at all. I shall return to the dining room and reclaim some of Lady Eleanor's excellent claret."

As the door closed behind him, George and I contemplated each other. If he did not agree to what I was about to request, the plan would be over.

"I know you have granted me a lot of favors in the past, George," I said. "But I am going to ask for another. One that vastly exceeds all the others in importance."

He raised his elegantly arched eyebrows. "Indeed? Go ahead."

"I believe you are aware of the situation between Lord Deele and Lady Hester."

He inclined his head.

"Deele will be arriving soon to wrest back his sister from the company of Miss Grant. Lady Julia is, at this very moment, asking Lady Eleanor and Miss Ponsonby to take them in for a few months. If the ladies agree, then the favor I ask of you is to support this arrangement in front of Lord Deele and to condemn his treatment of Lady Hester. I think you know the treatment to which I refer."

His mouth pursed in sympathy. "The asylum. Is she actually mad?"

"Most definitely not. You should have seen what they did to her, George. We barely got her out in time."

"So I have heard." He saw my consternation. "Yes, I am aware of the escapades that you and your sister have been involved in over the last few months. There are others who have noticed too."

That sounded rather alarming. "Others? Who do you mean?" I asked.

He gave a languid wave of refusal. "That I cannot divulge. Go on."

I considered pushing for an answer, but it was taking us too far from the urgent matter at hand.

"You are the leader of society, George. Whatever you do, or publicly support, will be followed by everyone else. I want you to tell Deele to leave Lady Hester and Miss Grant alone or you will turn society against him."

He did not demur at the statement of his power. "You are asking me to interfere in a private family matter."

"I am. And I am also asking that you persuade Lord Alvanley to do the same. I know he is friendly with Deele, but his support would count for a lot too. As would his condemnation of any further incarceration in an asylum."

"I see."

"I would also ask that you and Lord Alvanley do not, in any way, report the fact that you will have seen Lord Evan." I thought it prudent to be totally honest. "He is wanted, you know."

"I am aware."

I was tempted to ask how he obtained all his information, but I knew I would just receive that languid wave again.

He stared down at his perfectly polished black boots, brow knit, patently considering my proposition. I held my breath. The cat must have sensed the tension, for it stood and stretched, then settled back to lick its paw to defuse the situation.

Finally, George looked up, an uncustomary sober look upon his handsome features. "I will do as you ask, Augusta, and I can guarantee Alvanley's support and discretion in regard to Lord Evan too—" I rose, elated, to seal the deal, but he held up his hand. "Wait, there is more." I sank back down to my seat. "As you know, I am a collector of favors, always with a view to claiming a return at some future time. That time has come for you, my dear. I will soon be asking a favor of you and your sister, and like yours, it is an important favor."

"What is it?"

"I cannot say. Not yet, anyway."

"You want me to agree to a favor that I know nothing about?"

"I do. But you are a risk-taker, like me, Augusta. And I also know you are a woman of honor. This will be the return of all those favors I have done for you. Your slate, so to speak, wiped clean."

From his grave expression, this was a large favor, indeed. And I did not like the idea of promising something I did not yet know about. Still, I could not refuse. Too much depended upon my agreement.

"I can promise for myself, but not for my sister," I said. After our roadside confrontation, Julia would be incandescent if I volunteered her for something, particularly something I knew nothing about.

He gave a small bow. "The promise of your involvement is sufficient enough."

What did that mean?

"Now, let us find Alvanley," George said. "I will apprise him of our discussion and his role in it. We will then drink some excellent smuggled claret and await our hostesses' decision regarding Lady Hester and Miss Grant."

"And the arrival of Deele," I said, rising from my seat and joining him at the door.

"Indeed, why else do you think we wait in the dining room? It has a view to that arrival," George said. I glanced narrowly at him as I passed into the cooler air of the hallway; always the strategist. I wondered what that meant in terms of the favor I had just granted.

"It will be an interesting reunion," he added, then sighed. "I do hope there is not a surfeit of emotion—it would quite ruin my digestion."

38

About ten minutes after George and I joined Lord Alvanley in the dining room, we heard voices approaching from the hallway, the discussion lively but inaudible through the thick stone walls.

I took a sip of claret, for courage, and watched the door. George and Alvanley stood near the hearth—behind the dining table, which still held the remains of the dinner we had interrupted—their own intense conversation suspended as they, too, waited for the door to open.

Julia entered first, and the relief on her face was declaration enough: the ladies had agreed to take in Hester and Miss Grant.

"We know what it is like to have the life we wanted forcibly refused by our family," Lady Eleanor added after announcing the news. She looked fondly at Miss Ponsonby at her side. "It is hard to stand against such intervention. One needs resources and, of course, the help of friends and kind people. However, our support does come with one caveat. We cannot stand in the way of the law. Lord Deele is Lady Hester's guardian, and if he insists on taking her from this house, I am afraid we cannot stop him."

"Lord Alvanley and I have the same caveat," Mr. Brummell said.

Beside him, Alvanley nodded. "However, we will do everything we can to assist up to that point."

"We understand," Julia said. "Thank you all, so much."

The relief of their agreement seemed to pull all the energy from my limbs, my body as heavy as lead.

Julia skirted the table to stand beside me as the ladies joined Brummell and Alvanley at the hearth.

"If you agree, we will pay for their lodging," she murmured close to my ear, her words barely above a breath. "Miss Grant has some money left from an inheritance, but she should keep that in the event that they can set up their own household. Besides, from what I have heard among society and what Lady Eleanor has intimated tonight, the ladies have a very limited source of funds, so this will help them as well as Lady Hester and Miss Grant."

"Of course we will pay," I said. The economics of independence was always fraught for women, whether they were of high station or low. Julia and I knew control of one's own money meant control of one's own life, which was probably why men kept it from women in every way conceivable.

"What do we do if Deele insists on taking Hester?" she asked.

But I did not get a chance to answer, for a clatter of hooves sounded outside. We all peered through the old glass at the smeared whirl of activity in the drive. As far as I could tell, not a coach, but three horsemen.

"Is it Mr. Kent and Lord Evan?" Julia said, the anticipation in her voice mirroring my own rise of hope. "They have been so long!"

We both moved to the window, although proximity did nothing to improve the clarity of our view. From the hallway, I heard the front door opening, some muffled instructions in the voice of my beloved—my heart suddenly lighter at that dear sound—and then the footman knocked upon the dining room door.

"Come," Lady Eleanor said.

The door opened and the footman announced, "Lord Evan Belford and Mr. Kent, my lady."

And Weatherly, for I could see him standing in the hallway too.

Evan and Kent entered and bowed. We all returned the honors although all I wished to do was run to my love. I could see the same impulse barely contained in my sister's curtsy.

Evan's eyes found mine, his wry smile warm but tired: *This is an unexpected solution.*

I shifted my own smile into a moue of doubt: *I hope it works.*

Both he and Mr. Kent had divested themselves of greatcoats and hats, but they were road-stained, with dust smeared upon their faces and fatigue dark around their eyes. Kent had dried leaves caught in his hair and in the collar of his jacket, as if he had been dragged through a bush.

"You are most welcome, gentlemen," Lady Eleanor said. "I am pleased to see you again, Lord Evan."

Evan bowed. "Lady Eleanor, Miss Ponsonby, allow me to introduce Mr. Kent."

The two ladies inclined their heads graciously.

"It has been a long while, Belford," Lord Alvanley said with some warmth. "I am glad to see you well."

There was, I think, a hint of relief in Evan's return smile. "Thank you, Alvanley. May I introduce Mr. Kent, lately of Bow Street."

Mr. Kent bowed again, apparently unmoved by an introduction to the most powerful men in society. "How do you do."

"We are very pleased that your sister and Miss Grant will be staying with us, Lord Evan," Miss Ponsonby said. She bit her lip. "All proceeding as we hope, of course."

"Indeed." Evan bowed again. "And I thank you for your generosity. May I see my sister?"

"Yes, yes, come this way," Lady Eleanor said, leading the way out of the room. "She is well enough and almost awake." Evan looked over his shoulder at me. We would confer later. I nodded.

"You are covered in leaves, Mr. Kent," Julia said, crossing to him and gently picking the offending foliage from his collar.

Mr. Kent smiled, their eyes meeting in such a full, raw connection that I looked away. "I took Deele's horse into the woodland beside the road. It was not pleased about it," he said.

Across the room, I saw Mr. Brummell note the intimacy with a lift of an eyebrow. Did nothing get past the man?

"Weatherly," I called, making my way past my sister and her swain to the hallway.

"Yes, my lady?"

He was more worse for wear than Evan and Mr. Kent, his greatcoat wet and muddy in patches, and a graze upon his cheek. He saw my evaluation.

"I came off a few times," he said ruefully. "I think the horse knew I was not a skilled rider."

"Are you hurt, beyond—?" I motioned to his face.

"No, my lady. Lord Evan checked me, but I think I may have slowed down our progress. I am sorry."

I waved away the need for apology. "Do you think you are up to another task with the horses? It will be in the phaeton."

He straightened, a small smile appearing. "You want me to drive the phaeton?"

Weatherly might not yet be skilled in the saddle, but he was an excellent carriage driver. "I need you to take Lady Davenport's team and the other horses to the Hand Inn. Rouse the publican, any way you can, and tell him Lady Augusta Colebrook wishes for a change of horses. Try to get a matched pair for the phaeton—I want to get back to Davenport Hall tonight—but I suspect we will have to take what we can get."

Or ride with all speed to Liverpool. Either way, fresh horses were essential.

"Of course, my lady."

I handed over my bag of coins. "Make sure he knows he is stabling Lady Davenport's best team until she reclaims them. Press upon him that he must not let anyone else use them in the meantime or he will have hell to pay from Lord Davenport. Give him double what he asks."

"I will, my lady." He hesitated. "Will Lord Evan and Mr. Kent be coming back with us?"

A good question. The problematic collusion between Mulholland and Deele was still unanswered. Was the thieftaker nearby? Surely he could not know we were here in Wales. And if we did end up returning to Davenport Hall, Julia and I would be coming face-to-face with Duffy again. A confrontation that would be even more complicated with Evan and Kent in tow. Particularly since I suspected Julia was no longer in the mood to be conciliatory toward our brother.

But that was all too far in the future.

I shook my head. "I do not know."

I felt a touch upon my shoulder and opened my eyes, somewhat disoriented by the last remnants of sleep. I still sat at the dining table, Evan in the chair beside mine, his arm around me and my head nestled quite comfortably in the hollow of his shoulder. I had no recollection of how that had happened.

"I just heard the lookout return," he said. "Deele must be coming."

The last I remembered was discussing Hester's condition—reasonable, considering what she had been through—and eating the very welcome selection of cold meats, bread, and cheese that Lady Eleanor had supplied for an impromptu supper. Apparently, I could not withstand a full stomach, a warm hearth, and one, admittedly large, glass of claret. Nor, it seemed, Evan's shoulder. Using him as a pillow was becoming quite a habit and one in which I found a great deal of comfort. I never felt safer than when I was in his arms. I turned more into his shoulder, feeling the broad muscle beneath my cheek and breathing in his scent: a mix of soap and saddle leather and earthy male skin.

The door opened to admit Mr. Brummell. "Deele is coming up the hill," he announced. Upon seeing me still leaning against Evan, he raised his quizzing glass upon its riband to view the tableau. I eyed him back, daring him to make one of his bon mots, but he merely smiled. An oddly satisfied smile. "Lady Eleanor wishes us to assemble in the library," he added.

I chose to take the smile as a sign of his approval and glanced at the mantel clock. Just past midnight: I had slept for over an hour and a half and felt a great deal better for it. A tight squeeze of my eyelids cleared the last of my slumber.

I extracted myself from the dining chair and Evan's arm. "I sent Weatherly to change the horses at the inn," I said. "Fresh enough to get to Liverpool if you should need to flee."

Evan nodded and stood, massaging his shoulder. The dear man must have remained in the same position for the entire hour and a half. "Thank you. I hope it will not come to that."

If it did come to it, if Deele insisted upon taking Hester, what would Evan actually do? Would violence ensue? I suspected it might, for I could not see Evan allowing his brother to lay hands upon their sister again.

We joined Julia and Mr. Kent, Lord Alvanley and Mr. Brummell, and Lady Eleanor and Miss Ponsonby in the library. Miss Ponsonby and Julia were seated, Lady Eleanor stationed at the door, and the men ranged alongside the hearth. Julia waved me over to sit beside her on the sofa.

"Your hair is all squashed," she said, reaching over to tease out a flat curl. She twisted the offending lock around her forefinger and let it loose. "There."

Apparently, it was important to have symmetrical hair when one was confronting a furious adversary.

A loud thumping upon the front door echoed through the cottage. A fist, I would say, four times upon the wood. I shifted a little more to the edge of the sofa. I did not want to recline too much; facing Lord Deele required a stiff spine and the ability to rise from the seat at any given moment.

"Where is she? Where is my sister?" Deele's voice boomed through the hallway. "Get out of my way, you stupid slut!"

I hoped the poor maid managed to dodge out of the way of his wrath.

Lady Eleanor glanced around the quiet room: were we all ready? Everyone nodded: we were.

She opened the library door and said, "What is this commotion?"

"Lady Eleanor! Where is my sister? I know my brother has brought her here. I demand you take me to her now!"

"Ah, Lord Deele, do come in," Lady Eleanor said graciously. She stepped back into the library, forcing him to follow.

He stalked into the room, his rage obliterating any civility. The fury had reddened his face, a vein pulsing at his temple. He cast a hard glance about the room, then rocked back upon his heels.

"Alvanley, Brummell, what are you doing here?"

"We are on our way to Underbank Hall," Lord Alvanley said mildly.

"Do you know what is going on here?" Deele demanded.

"We do," Mr. Brummell said. He lifted his quizzing glass and viewed Deele through it.

A less furious man might quail under such observation, but Deele turned his glare upon Evan, standing beside Alvanley. "Then you know my brother here is aiding our sister to run away with her female companion! It is monstrous!"

Lady Eleanor cleared her throat.

"Really, Deele, do take note of where you are," Brummell said.

Deele looked from Brummell to Lady Eleanor, coming to a somewhat belated understanding of whose house he stood in. "Well, I did not mean to say—" He huffed, flailing somewhat.

"Lady Eleanor and Miss Ponsonby have kindly agreed to host Hester and Miss Grant over Christmas and New Year," Evan said, interrupting his protestations. "After which, our sister and her friend will find themselves a residence and set up their own household."

"No," Deele said. "You cannot come back into the country and take over. I am Lord Deele. I am our sister's guardian and she will not live with that woman. I forbid it and I have the law on my side. Where is Hester? I will take her from here now."

"I am here, Charles," Lady Hester said from the doorway. Her gaunt pallor held a fierce majesty, and although she leaned heavily upon Miss Grant, she stood firm, ready to fight her own corner.

"You may have the law upon your side, Deele," Brummell said. "But you do not have Alvanley or me on your side."

Deele swung back to face him. "What do you mean?"

"I mean that we are aware of Bothwell House and your subsequent treatment of Lady Hester. Incarcerating your own sister in such a place cannot be tolerated, nor can taking her from her friends by force and laudanum. Leave Lady Hester and Miss Grant alone. Otherwise you and your wife will find yourselves suddenly lacking entrance to all bon ton homes. And I do mean all of them."

Deele stared at him, aghast, then sought Alvanley's gaze. "Surely you do not agree with this, Alvanley. It is coercion!"

"You have acted in a way that no gentleman would, Deele," Alvanley said somberly. "I had thought you better than this."

It was as if Alvanley had struck him in the face. The most gentlemanly man in all society had condemned his behavior.

"All you have to do is leave them alone," Alvanley added. "Nothing else. Let them live their own lives and make their own choices. Just walk away, man."

I swallowed, a sudden sour realization drying my mouth. I had, in effect, been doing the same as Deele: making choices for Hester and Miss Grant, and my sister as well. Overriding their views with my own. I clasped my hands together, trying to quell the rush of understanding. But my past actions rose inexorably into wretched knowledge. Even Deele's motivations were not so far from my own: he believed he was saving his sister, keeping her safe, just as I wanted to keep everyone safe. Of course, Deele's idea of safety was misguided, heinous and brutal, bound up with his own selfish fear for his reputation. Even so, I could not deny the parallel. How many times had I thought I knew best? How many times did I not listen to my sister or Miss Grant? Their protests and ideas? All under my own belief that I was responsible for all. That I could keep everyone safe. Julia had said as much upon the roadside. Evan too. And I had not listened. I bowed my head, feeling a hot wash of shame.

Hester's hoarse voice brought me back from my own agony. "I am thirty years old, Charles," she said. "I must be allowed to navigate my own life. I will never give up Miss Grant. Not for you or for anyone else."

At the corner of my eye, I saw Miss Ponsonby bring her fingertips together in a tiny, silent clap.

Deele looked around the room, teeth bared. His fury settled upon Alvanley, whose round, genial face held an implacability I had not seen before. "You give me no choice. All right, then, I will walk away. Forever." He rounded on Hester. "You are no longer part of this family and you will have no money from me. We will see how long your unholy attachment survives poverty and debasement!"

"She will have money from me, Charles," Evan said. "Hester and I are family, and I think it is you who are no longer part of it."

Deele stared at him for a long, savage second. "You ruined this family, you know. Father always said you were the better man, and nothing I did was good enough. Well, I am not a convict riding around the countryside, robbing people." He looked around the room at our new friends. "I hope you realize who you are colluding with."

On that, he turned and stalked from the room.

"Wait," I called, but I knew he would not do so. I ran after him, following him down the dim hallway and out to his carriage. His footman opened the coach door. "Wait, Lord Deele. Please!"

He turned and snarled, "What do you want?"

"Back in London, you received a man by the name of Mulholland. A big man with sandy hair and whiskers."

"How do you know that?"

"Did he tell you that we were helping your sister? And that your brother was with her?"

"Why do you think I would give you any information?" he said, the fury still in his voice.

"Because he has been hired to kill Lord Evan."

He snorted. "What makes you think that?"

"He told me," I said flatly, pushing away the memory of the man's hands upon my breasts. "Did he say who had sent him to you?" I closed my hands into fists, trying to contain the urgency in my voice. From what I had observed, Deele would withhold the information if he knew how important it was to me. And to Evan.

"I repeat, why would I tell you anything? After what you and my brother have done."

"Because Mulholland has used you as a way of getting to your brother. He tricked and manipulated you, Lord Deele. A common thieftaker. He is probably still laughing about it now."

Deele drew a breath through his teeth. Was it more rage at me, or at the thought that a man of Mulholland's station had manipulated a marquess? I hoped, with all my being, it was the latter.

"Whitmore," he finally said. "He said Charles Whitmore had sent him." He turned and took the step into the carriage.

I stood with my hands still clenched as the name tolled through me. Charles Whitmore. Undersecretary of the Alien Department. Why had he hired Mulholland?

The footman closed the coach door, flipped up the step, then climbed into the seat beside the driver. With a snap of the whip, the carriage jolted forward, wheels and hooves grinding across the gravel.

I turned to go back into the house and saw Evan standing in the shadows of the doorway, arms wrapped around his body. He had followed me.

"I heard," he said. "Charles Whitmore. I do not understand. I have never met the man."

I slid my hand into his, my cold fingers curled into his warmth. "Well, at least we have a name now."

But it was a name that did not make sense. Whitmore was at least ten years younger than Evan and would have been a child when the duel was fought. Why on earth did he want Lord Evan Belford dead?

39

The victory celebration for the emancipation of Lady Hester from her brother's tyranny was necessarily short. Both she and Miss Grant were exhausted, and the ladies had hosted too many people for far too long.

After a toast, we bade our good-byes. Correspondence and visits were promised, and then Julia, Weatherly, and I were back in the phaeton, with Evan and Mr. Kent riding beside us. George and Lord Alvanley followed in the gig they had hired from the Hand Inn, where they were staying.

We parted company at the gates of that hostelry, George touching the brim of his impeccable beaver hat to me as they clattered across the cobbled courtyard.

Which reminded me of the odd promise I had given to Mr. Brummell. I told Julia and Weatherly what had transpired.

Julia sat upright. "You gave your word without knowing what you had promised?"

"I did. But I did not promise for you."

"Well, thank heavens you learned that lesson in time," she said, but leavened it with a smile. "I wonder what he wants you to do."

"If I may say so, my ladies, Mr. Brummell is not what he seems," Weatherly said from the groom's seat behind us.

"I agree, but what makes you say that?" I asked over my shoulder.

"When I was at the Hand Inn changing the horses, I saw a man arrive. Very downtrodden, my lady, and he still wore an old parish beggar's badge."

"That is odd." The requirement for beggars to wear a badge to be given alms had been repealed two years ago.

"I thought so, too, my lady. He said he had a message for Mr. Brummell but would not leave it for him. Instead, he insisted he would wait. The landlord was not keen on him staying, but the man would not budge. It made me wonder what business a beggar had with a man like Mr. Brummell."

I could not even imagine George getting close to a beggar, let alone accepting a message from him. What was George involved in, and what was he about to involve me in too?

We drove in silence, Evan and Mr. Kent riding ahead, both slumped slightly in the saddle, even their excellent seats compromised by fatigue.

This was, perhaps, a good time to try to make amends.

"Julia, I have an apology to make. To you and to Lady Hester and Miss Grant, but they were too tired tonight so I will write to them." I wet my lips. "When I was listening to Deele trying to stand his untenable ground, I realized I have been just like him, dealing with you and his sister in the same high-handed way. I am sorry for it."

"You are nothing like Deele," Julia said firmly. "His pigheadedness comes from a place of judgment and bigotry." She leaned across and gently squeezed my shoulder. "Your pigheadedness comes from a place of love and a strong sense of justice. Of course I forgive you."

"Thank you." I caught her hand and awkwardly held it for a moment, squashed together with the handle of the whip I held.

"To be fair, I let it go on for too long," she said. "You may think you are unstoppable, dearest, but you are not." Then I heard the tone of her voice shift into a new gravity. "We have important choices ahead of us, Gus, and we must each make them alone. You must make the best choices for you. And I must make the best for me. Maybe our paths will be together, maybe they will not, but we cannot make them for each other or, indeed, because of each other."

"I know. I do not like the fact of it, but I know it is true." I looked at the two men riding ahead. "Different paths. Different lives."

Julia leaned against me, her head upon my shoulder, an acknowledgment of this probable fork in our paths, and the bond between us.

$\mathcal{S}$ometime later, Julia yawned and chafed her gloved hands.

"I should have thought to bring rugs," she said. "I am chilled to the bone."

I did not look at her, for my attention was fixed upon the road and the pair of hacks that the Hand Inn had supplied. The nearside gray was at least three hands taller than the bay, which had been causing a mismatch in their gait for most of the journey, particularly now that they were tired. "I would say we are not far from Davenport Hall. Half an hour at the most."

Julia sighed. "I wish we did not have to go back."

"Where do you propose we go otherwise?" I asked.

"I was only wishing. We have to go back or Duffy will have the whole estate out looking for us."

"I do not fancy our audience with him." I had the horses in a reasonable trot and smiled across at my sister. "Perhaps we could slip away before breakfast."

"I am so tired I do not think I will be out of bed for a week, let alone before breakfast," Julia said. "He is going to be so self-righteous and outraged."

I nodded glumly and returned my attention to the road.

After another ten minutes or so, Mr. Kent suddenly sat forward in his saddle. He had plainly seen something. I peered along the dark road but saw only the moon-silvered woodland on either side and beyond it the vast, rolling moorlands. Both he and Evan pulled up their horses, waiting for us to halt between them.

"What is it?" Julia asked.

"Soldiers," Mr. Kent reported. "They are combing the woodland on either side of the road up ahead."

I still could not discern them, but he had soldiered for many years on the Continent before becoming a Runner, so he no doubt knew what he was talking about.

"It is probably Captain Morland, still searching for Luddites," I said. "He will be surprised to see us again."

Evan drew his mouth to one side, considering the potential problem. "I do not think it matters. What Lady Augusta and Lady Julia choose to do is no concern of the British Army. And Mr. Talbot and Mr. Kent and your footman are riding with you for safety's sake."

I was not entirely convinced. Captain Morland was not a fool, by any measure. To see us twice in one night coming from different directions might pique his curiosity.

Even so, we had to pass.

"Walk on," I called to the horses, a short snap of my whip above their heads pressing home the command.

We continued, at a slower pace, Evan and Kent remaining on either side of the phaeton rather than riding ahead. I finally saw what Kent had seen much earlier: the flash of metal and the rustle of movement in a denser patch of woodland. Even with such knowledge, I flinched when a soldier stepped out in front of us and called, "Halt!"

We halted.

More soldiers emerged from the woods to stand upon the road. Finally, a pair of very familiar figures stepped out, the slighter man approaching our phaeton.

"Captain Morland, we meet again," I said.

"It would seem so, Lady Augusta. Two times in one night." He stopped at my side of the phaeton and bowed. "Well met, Lady Julia."

"How pleasant to see you again, Captain," Julia said, at her most charming.

Morland tilted his head back to observe Evan through those shrewd eyes. "And Mr. Talbot."

Evan nodded his greeting. "Captain. Allow me to introduce Mr. Kent."

The two men acknowledged each other.

"A Baker," Morland said, gesturing to the rifle in Mr. Kent's saddle holster. "You were rifle brigade?"

"Cavalry," Mr. Kent said. "Light Dragoons."

His answer clearly impressed the captain, for he made a small grunt of collegiality. "On the Continent?"

"France."

That elicited raised brows and a nod: even more impressed. Mr. Kent was lending us a great deal of credibility.

"Are you still seeking Luddites, Captain?" Evan asked, and although it was said in his usual measured manner, I knew he wanted

to move us along. Away from the captain's keen eyes and cleverness.

"We are. There has been some report of a fracas upon this road.
I do not suppose you have seen any unusual activity? Apart from
yourselves, of course." He smiled, but it was the smile of a man
who knew something was awry.

"None at all, Captain," I said. "We are returning from delivering friends to their home, but it has been a quiet drive, has it not,
sister?"

"Indeed, very quiet," Julia said. She pointedly chafed her
gloved hands again. "And very cold, Captain."

"Of course." Morland bowed and stepped aside. "We will not
keep you any longer from the warmth of Davenport Hall." As I
raised my whip in salute, he added with a dry underpinning,
"Perhaps I will see you again this night."

"I hardly think so, Captain," I said, and urged the horses
onward again. We passed the soldiers on either side of the road,
their tired eyes following our progress.

Mr. Kent and Evan rode past us to take positions a little ahead,
any sign of fatigue gone from their bodies. There was nothing like
an encounter with the British Army to galvanize one into new
energy. I felt it myself, suddenly far more awake than I had been a
few minutes ago.

I snapped the whip over the horses' heads. The sooner we removed ourselves from the vicinity of Captain Morland, the better.

40

⤳

No more than half a mile later, the sound of galloping from the direction of Davenport Hall tightened my grip upon the reins. What now? I ducked my head forward, trying to make out who or what was coming our way.

We had come to a part of the road where the woodlands on either side shifted into the edge of the thick Clwydian Range forest, the wild winter boscage extending far back into gloomy darkness. At the corner of my eye, I caught movement within the wilderness, deer, perhaps, or foxes, but it was too dense to make out any particular animal. The horses were especially unsettled, though, so it must be foxes, I decided, or, more dangerous, wild boar.

Evan looked over his shoulder at me and held up his hand. His expression was hidden in the shadow of his hat brim, but from the tension in his body I knew he was alert to new danger. Could it be Mulholland this time? I halted the phaeton again, the two horses shifting and bobbing their heads. Evan and Mr. Kent both reached for the pistols in their saddle holsters.

"Weatherly, get Hades ready," I said.

"Yes, my lady." At the corner of my eye, I saw him settle the butt of the big blunderbuss against his shoulder.

Julia sat up straight. "Who is it?"

"I have no idea," I said. "Nor does Lord Evan. And that is the problem."

Julia flexed her hands in her lap. "I feel as if I should have a gun too," she whispered.

"Do you want the whip?" I asked.

I was loath to give it up, but if it reassured Julia to be in charge of it, I would hand it over. Otherwise, I only had my little silver dagger still hidden up my sleeve; not much use in this situation.

"No, you may need it," Julia said. "This is a terrible pair."

The terrible pair had become even more unsettled. I allowed them to walk forward a few steps, the gray blowing its dissatisfaction.

A rider appeared a distance ahead, no detail visible: only a shadowy shape, the fact of movement, and the jangle and thud of swift approach. Only one person. Not Mulholland, then. The horseman was covering ground fast. Had he seen us? As he neared, the disparate elements coalesced into a man upon a thoroughbred, riding with a great deal of elegance.

Oh no, I recognized that well-tutored seat.

Duffy.

Good God, what was he doing here?

"That's Duffy," Julia said, a second behind me.

"Weatherly, put Hades away," I said, then called to Evan, "It is our brother."

Upon that gloomy identification, all guns were lowered.

"Stands to reason," Evan commented, although he did not holster his pistol. "You left Davenport Hall in some haste and in the company of two men he does not know. If Hester had ever done the same, I would be out searching too."

Duffy eased his mount into a trot as he approached, his face puffed and shiny with rage. "Where in God's name have you been?" He pulled up his horse, the animal snorting at the rough halt. "I have been up and down this damn road looking for you for the past three hours. Lady Davenport said you went in the direction of Liverpool. Lord Davenport, Mr. Ellis-Brant, and I damn well rode nearly all the way there! They gave up an hour ago and, damn it, I don't blame them."

Three *damn*s in four sentences: Duffy was seriously displeased. I sent a wordless thanks to Charlotte for giving them the wrong direction.

"We did not ask you to follow us," I said. Possibly not the most politic of answers, but I had no time for his overbearing tantrums.

"And what was I supposed to do?" he said through his teeth. "You go charging off in a phaeton, for God's sake, with two men who, I discover, you blatantly lied to me about in London!" He cast a scathing look at Evan. "Oh yes, I know who you are now, Lord Evan Belford or Mr. Talbot or whatever you call yourself. Mrs. Ellis-Brant worked out the truth, and with her mouth that will not stay a secret long."

Of course the Ermine worked it out. And Duffy was right; she would have the whole affair around the bon ton in no time. Even Charlotte would not be able to contain it.

Duffy's attention snapped to Mr. Kent. "And you, a Runner, helping the very man he is supposed to bring to justice. Good God, I cannot believe my sisters even know such men." He turned back to Julia and me. "You debase yourselves."

Julia straightened at that, her hands clenched in her lap. "I beg your pardon. We do not debase ourselves. Mr. Kent has more manners and courage than any other man I know."

Duffy ignored her staunch defense. "And why on earth are you helping Lady Hester defy her brother? Who do you think you are? Your behavior has made me ridiculous in the eyes of Lord

Deele—I did not even know that you were harboring his sister. He is her lawful guardian and you—you two stupid, meddlesome old women—have no business interfering in his decisions regarding her situation."

"Since I am Lady Hester's other brother," Evan said coldly, "I have every right to help my sister. Lady Augusta and Lady Julia have kindly assisted me."

"No, you do not have any right to do anything. You gave up all rights when you killed a man," Duffy said, shortening his reins as his mount danced to one side under his tense hold. "You have as little authority to interfere with Lord Deele's business as my foolish sisters do."

"He did not kill Mr. Sanderson," I said, although the point was probably irrelevant. Still, I could not have such a falsehood repeated. "He was transported for no reason."

"Well, there is reason enough now, isn't there?" Duffy said. "Absconding, highway robbery, abduction. Enough for the gallows."

"And I suppose you will turn him in," I said.

"You have placed me in an impossible situation, Augusta. You are complicit in this man's crimes. If I turn him in, I turn you in too. And your sister as well. Yet I am a magistrate and it is my duty to arrest him."

Right at that moment, I despised Duffy with all my heart. I turned to Evan. "It is time we parted ways again, my love. You should go. Now."

"Love?" Duffy sputtered. "Love? Are you telling me you have compromised yourself with this man, Augusta? This convict?"

"Not as compromised as I would like," I said.

Admittedly, it was a little vulgar, but it did achieve its aim: spitting outrage from my brother. I heard Evan snort back a stifled laugh.

"And I love Mr. Kent," Julia said, lifting her chin. "Yes, love, Duffy!"

This apparently was the first time Mr. Kent had heard that declaration, for he looked just as shocked as Duffy.

"Julia," Duffy said. "You cannot be serious. He is too low for you. You will be shunned by every decent—"

Evan raised his voice over my brother's harangue. "I will go, Gus, but first I will accompany you back to Davenport Hall."

My brother glared at him; he was not used to having his opinions interrupted, let alone talked over. "Gus? You are calling my sister Gus?"

"I agree," Mr. Kent said, ignoring our brother's horror at Evan's familiarity. "We will escort you both back to Davenport Hall and then go." His eyes were fixed upon Julia. Both of them were smiling at each other a little foolishly. So, that was what mooncalving looked like. I suspected Evan and I looked at each other in the same way. As if the whole world was contained within the beloved face of the other.

"Is there any use insisting you go now?" I asked.

"No," both men said in unison.

"To the gate, but no farther," Julia said to Mr. Kent. "I will not have you in any more danger."

"Well, that is settled, then," I said, and snapped the whip over the pair's heads. "Get out of the way, Duffy. It has been a long night and we wish to get back to Davenport Hall."

With as much bravado as I could muster, I drove the pair past my furious brother.

The road through the forest stretched before us, the air colder than ever and the pale light from the sliver of moon hidden behind a dense overhang of trees. Although I would have dearly loved to leave Duffy behind at a jaunty trot, I dropped the pair into a walk, for I could not see beyond a few feet ahead and it would be madness to bowl along such a dark, ill-made road at speed.

"Debased," Julia murmured beside me. "I will show him who is debased."

Fighting words from my sister, but they did not change two sobering facts: Duffy now knew we were adventuring, and he would not sit by while his two sisters brought scandal and shame on the family by attaching themselves to a convict and a disgraced Runner.

Our judicious decampment did not last long. I heard hooves coming up alongside me, then saw Duffy, his usually perfect seat somewhat undermined by his anger, at the corner of my vision. I kept my gaze fixed ahead, unwilling to give him the satisfaction of my attention.

"I will not be ignored, Augusta," Duffy said, keeping his horse in pace with the phaeton. "Do you have any idea how ridiculous you will appear to those around you? Two women well beyond the age of such infatuations and foolish misadventures. I only hope it is laughed away and does not become a scandal."

Julia leaned out from behind me and fixed him with a glare. "Well beyond the age? We are only forty-two, Duffy, not in our dotage."

He looked past me, his expression one of kindly condescension. "I do not blame you, Julia. You are still suffering the sorrow of your betrothed's death and easily led by Augusta. I am sure the novelty of such admiration will wear off once Kent's base nature shows." He returned his gaze to me. "It is you I am most concerned about, Augusta. I offered to forgive your absence at my wedding and you threw it back in my face, and now you are leading Julia into danger. This bizarre behavior must stop. I think, perhaps, you are a little unbalanced. Harriet tells me that it could be the older time of a woman's life that is affecting your mind. Whatever the case, we are deeply concerned."

"Concerned, Duffy?" I asked. "Or just irritated that I am not listening to you?"

"I am so concerned, Augusta, that I have engaged a doctor to visit you upon your return to London."

"Ha! As if I would see any doctor you sent," I said, and snapped the whip, setting the pair into a trot, away from his infuriating self-importance.

Julia clutched the side of the phaeton. "I think he means a mad doctor, Gus," she said, her exhausted face tight with sudden fear. "I think he has been talking too much to Lord Deele."

"Nonsense. He would not dare."

"I think he would dare. He believes he is the arbiter of our moral conduct and he has always thought your independence a sign of a wanton mind." She looked over her shoulder. "Here he comes again."

I risked taking my attention from the road to look him straight in the eyes. "You do not control our lives, Duffy. We are well beyond anyone's guardianship other than our own. You are sadly mistaken if—"

"Gus!" Julia shrieked.

Three men. Standing across the road. Guns aimed. In reflex I wrenched at the reins, the two horses bunching back upon their haunches, shrilling their distress. Beside me, Duffy's horse reared. I heard him yell "Christ" as I struggled to hold my pair, the phaeton lurching back, beginning to tip. I saw Evan run past me, off his own mount and heading for my plunging pair. He caught the bridle of the nearside horse and brought its head down. The two horses surged forward, but I held them firm, Evan deftly bracing against their fear.

"All is well, all is well," he chanted to the quivering horses.

"What on earth is this outrage!" Duffy demanded from behind us.

Panting, I checked on Julia—still beside me, hanging on to the edge of the now stable phaeton for dear life. And then all I could see were the rifles aimed at us, the men behind them a blur of worn coats and battered hats.

"Who are you?" Duffy's voice again.

I looked over my shoulder. Three other men in worn military greatcoats, one struggling to hold Evan's frightened horse, the other two with pistols aimed at Kent and my brother, who were both still mounted. Kent had clearly attempted to draw his Baker, for he had it half out of its holster, his hand still upon its grip. In the groom's seat behind Julia and me, Weatherly had raised Hades but had never got the blunderbuss braced. He held it half-raised, his eyes fixed upon another scruffy man on the ground with a pistol aimed at his head.

"Get their guns."

I knew that voice, the sudden recognition squeezing the breath from my lungs.

Mulholland.

41

⤴⤴⤴

He stepped out from the dark shadows at the side of the road: a tall, muscular figure holding his rifle under his arm, as if he were on a pheasant shoot.

"Dear God," Julia whispered. She seemed about to crumple.

"Stay still," I murmured. We could not show our fear to this man.

From my seat, I looked down at Evan. He held the bridle of the nearside horse, his eyes fixed upon me.

A tiny jerk of my chin: *Step back. I can run them down.*

An infinitesimal shake of his head: *Too many men.*

And too many guns. Besides, I could not trust these horses and the attempt might get Julia or Evan shot.

I sighed and gave a slight nod: *Too many men.* Still, we had to do something. I scrunched my toes to rid my body of the abandoned plan and its desperate energy.

Two of the men, one of them Pritchard, for I had now recognized Mulholland's henchman, had collected the Baker and pistols from Kent's saddle and were now beside Weatherly. With a jeer, Pritchard jerked the blunderbuss from his grasp.

The man holding Evan's horse removed the pistols from its saddle. Eight men in total, including Mulholland. Now all armed with multiple guns. Mulholland was not taking any chances this time.

"His sword too," Mulholland instructed his man, gesturing to the saber my brother wore buckled at his waist.

"I beg your pardon!" Duffy said, drawing himself up into all of his importance. "Do you know who I am?"

"I do, my lord. Do you know who I am?"

"Of course I do not," Duffy said with magnificent disdain.

"Allow me to remind you, then. I am James Mulholland. We met at your sisters' house."

Duffy frowned down at him from his saddle, recognition dawning. "The thieftaker?"

"That is correct, Lord Duffield," Mulholland said. "Please give my man your sword."

Since Pritchard had a pistol aimed at him, Duffy complied.

Upon seeing the last weapon collected, Mulholland strolled past Duffy. I drew a steadying breath, for he was making his nonchalant way to the side of the phaeton.

He looked up at me and bared his yellowed teeth into the wolf smile I remembered from the drawing room.

"Still not afraid, Lady Augusta?" he whispered. "You really should be."

He continued on to Evan and murmured, "Make any move, and my men have orders to shoot Lady Augusta and Lady Julia. In the guts. As I'm sure you are aware, a very long and painful death."

He turned back to Duffy and said loudly, "Your sister told you that this man was her groom. But he is not. He is Lord Evan Belford."

"I am already aware of that," Duffy said condescendingly.

"Then you must be aware he is a wanted man, my lord. I have

been waiting for another chance to bring him to justice, since you interrupted my last effort."

"Well, I was misled," Duffy said, glancing across at me. "I do not see why you have taken my sword, Mulholland. This is a very irregular arrest."

"Duffy," I said urgently. "This is not an arrest. He is going to kill Lord Evan. Charles Whitmore has ordered it."

At Whitmore's name, Mulholland squinted up at me with an odd smile upon his face. I glared at him: *Yes, Mr. Mulholland, I know it all.*

"Do not be ridiculous, Augusta," Duffy said. "Whitmore is an Oxford man and a trusted member of Liverpool's government. You cannot fling around preposterous accusations about men of good standing."

"Your sister is telling the truth, Lord Duffield," Evan said. He moved to take his hands from the horse's bridle, but one of the riflemen stepped closer to me, the barrel of the gun aimed squarely at my midsection. Evan froze.

"My sister is delusional, Belford, and you are taking advantage of her," Duffy snapped. "I am a magistrate, Augusta. Mr. Mulholland is hardly going to murder a man in front of me."

"As his lordship says, my lady, I am hardly going to murder a man in front of him." Mulholland's wolf smile appeared again. He scratched his sandy-red stubble as if making a decision. "I will take Mr. Kent, too, my lord. He has assisted Belford and so must answer for that crime back at Bow Street."

"No!" Julia said. "Duffy, you must see something is wrong," she implored. "Mr. Kent is a Bow Street agent. Not a criminal."

"All I see are two desperate men who have been using my foolish sisters for their own nefarious ends," Duffy said. He had, it seemed, settled upon our womanly weakness as an explanation. "Where do you take them, Mulholland?"

"To Wrexham. It has a lockup house. We will take a shortcut through the woods."

Duffy waved them into action as if he were in charge. "Go about your business, then. We will be on our way too."

Mulholland nodded, as if receiving the order. He knew how to manipulate a man as pompous as my brother. "Thank you, my lord." He nodded to his men. "Bind Belford and Kent."

One of the riflemen brought out rope and stepped closer to Evan.

"Hands behind your back," he ordered.

Evan's jaw muscle bulged with his desire to turn and fight, but he complied, his eyes upon me: *Do not follow us.*

I drew a breath through my teeth: *Try to stop me.*

He lurched back a step as the binding wrenched his shoulders back, but his eyes still did not leave mine. His lips curved into the smallest of smiles: *My darling Renegade.*

I drew a shaking breath. Good God, that was a good-bye.

I shook my head: *No, I will find you.*

Julia had twisted in her seat, her hands clenched on the sides of the phaeton. "Duffy, Mr. Kent is a Runner! Please—"

"Be quiet, Julia. You are embarrassing yourself," Duffy said.

Mulholland leaned against the side of the phaeton. "No bleating on behalf of your own man, Lady Augusta?" he asked me sotto voce. "Maybe you don't really care."

"If you hurt him, I will kill you, although you will wish I had."

He ran a surreptitious finger along the outside of my thigh, the light pressure sending a sickened blaze of fury through my body. "Follow me and my men, Lady Augusta, and I will finish what I started in the laneway, and let my men have their turn too. And I will not kill you, although you will wish I had."

I thrust his hand away. "I know who has ordered this," I said. "I am not going to give up."

He lifted his heavy shoulders into a shrug. "You cannot win, and right now you are irrelevant. I advise you not to become relevant."

He levered himself lazily from the phaeton. "Take their horses," he ordered his men, jerking his chin at Mr. Kent's and Evan's mounts. "And give his lordship back his sword."

Duffy received his sword and inspected the blade to make sure no harm had come to it.

"My apologies for the unusual method of detaining Belford and Kent, my lord," Mulholland said, bowing. "I hope we did not inconvenience you too much."

Duffy waved away the apology. "It was unusual, but I do not take offense."

Dear God, how could my brother be so foolish and misguided?

"Do something, Gus, do something," Julia said. But a lone rifleman still had his gun aimed at us. More precisely, at Julia. All I could do was watch as Evan and Mr. Kent, their hands bound behind their backs, were surrounded by Mulholland's men and pushed toward the dense, dark woodlands. And, without a doubt, their deaths.

The lone rifleman stayed, watching us along the barrel until the sight and noise of his compatriots making their way into the depths of the forest disappeared. Then, with a sure-footedness that spoke of some kind of training, he backed into the darkness and was gone too.

My body slumped, the strain shaking through every muscle.

For a second, my gorge rose. I forced down the sour nausea. Beside me, Julia slammed the flat of her hand over and over again against the phaeton's dash rail, the thuds startling the horses again.

"Julia, stop that," I said, steadying the pair. "You'll have them off again."

"I cannot bear it. That man. What are we going to do? We must do something." She whirled upon me. "You must have a plan. You always have a plan."

"Plan?" Duffy echoed. He had walked his horse up alongside the phaeton. "The only plan you have is to return to Davenport Hall and apologize to Lord Davenport for the upset you have caused."

"You are an idiot, Duffy," I said, which did nothing to conjure a plan but did much to relieve my feelings. "How could you ignore the fact that Mulholland had us at gunpoint the entire time? They are not going to march Lord Evan and Mr. Kent to Wrexham. They are going to shoot them in the woodlands and bury them."

"Oh, Gus, no," Julia said, pressing her hand over her mouth.

We were outmanned and outgunned. I felt a rise of despair. We had three people—for I did not count Duffy—and no weapons. When in fact, what we needed was an army to—

Dear God. That was exactly what we needed.

I thrust the reins and whip into Julia's hands and found the step with my toe, swinging to the ground. "Weatherly, help me turn the phaeton."

Weatherly immediately climbed down. We ran to the offside horse's head. I took hold of the bridle and Weatherly grabbed the collar and together we half led, half pushed the recalcitrant beast around, the other horse and the phaeton following slowly with it. The road was just wide enough to manage the turn without going into the ditch.

"Get out of the way, Duffy," I said.

He walked his horse beyond the phaeton. "Augusta, what are you doing?"

I ignored him and looked up at Julia. "Drive back to Captain Morland and tell him Mr. Talbot and Mr. Kent have been taken by armed Luddites and need their assistance."

"Luddites?" Julia echoed. "Why would Luddites take them?"

"It does not matter. The troop will come at just the whiff of the word. Bring them back here and point the way." I hoped it was true. It had to be true. I wrenched my riding hat off. "I'll leave this as a marker. Make sure they know that we are in the woods—"

I realized I had not actually asked Weatherly. "Will you come with me? You do not have to. It will be dangerous."

"Of course I will, my lady."

I touched his arm for a second in thanks and continued my instructions to Julia. "Make sure they know that Weatherly and I are in the woods too. We do not want to be accidentally shot. Do you have that?"

"I do," Julia said.

The phaeton was finally pointing back toward the army we needed.

"I forbid this," Duffy said, bringing his horse around. He raised his voice. "Julia, stop! Do as I say! Augusta, you cannot be seriously planning to go after those men!"

"As fast as you can, dearheart," I said to Julia. "Keep an eye on that gray, it will try to take you to the right."

She gave a tense nod and snapped the whip, the phaeton lurching into motion.

I turned to face our brother. "Give me your sword, Duffy."

"No. I will certainly not," he said.

"So you are going to let me go into the woods unarmed?" Not

entirely true; I still had my little dagger, but a sword would be far more reassuring.

"I am not going to let you go into the woods at all." He held out his hand. "Get up behind me. We will follow Julia. Stop her from reaching Captain Morland and making a fool of herself."

I eyed the sword—too dangerous to try to wrest it from him while he was on horseback, and I could not waste the time to argue it out of him. I drew my fob watch out upon its chain. A quarter past three. Morland and his men were about ten minutes away if they had not marched on, and then give or take time to persuade him, another fifteen to twenty minutes to return here. Half an hour until help arrived. If it did arrive.

"Weatherly, we must go."

"I am ready, my lady."

I flashed him a smile, which he returned. We were no longer mistress and servant, but comrades in arms. Well, not enough arms, as it happened. Together, we headed toward the edge of the forest, where Mulholland and his men had forced a way through. Hopefully their path would not be hard to follow; Mulholland had two horses as well as seven men and no belief that we would dare enter the forest behind them.

"Augusta!" Duffy bellowed behind us. "Come back this instant. You will get lost, you stupid woman."

And on that message of good luck, Weatherly and I pushed our way through the scraggly roadside undergrowth into the forest.

42

As soon as we left the road, the temperature dropped into a bone-aching chill, and the rich odor of damp earth, distant smoke, and leaf decay filled my lungs. The smell of October.

Ten or so yards beyond the roadside, the low grassy undergrowth shifted into a thick maze of trees. Mainly ash mottled by lichen, interspersed with hazel and oak. A good canopy of leaves still clung to their branches, although the forest floor was carpeted with the autumn drop. Very little moonlight penetrated the branches above us, but I could just make out the trodden pathway of our quarry through the scrub and spiky gorse. No sounds of human or horse progress, though. Mulholland was some distance ahead.

"Do we have a plan, my lady?" Weatherly asked beside me.

I was struggling to free the hem of my riding habit from a sharp, pointed branch that had fallen among the scrub and leaves. A yank liberated the wool and linen, sending the branch shivering back in a thudding, cracking release. "We follow them—as quietly as possible," I said dryly, "and stop them from killing Lord Evan and Mr. Kent until Captain Morland comes."

"Excellent," he said. "Any idea how?"

"None whatsoever," I said. "At least, not yet."

He pulled a branch back for me to duck under. "May I make a suggestion?"

"Please do," I said, rising from my bend in a crackle of leaves and crunch of old seed casings. Lud, I was sweeping half the forest behind me with every step. I would have to do something about my gown.

"I think we should take off our cravats. They are too white and will be seen."

Not the suggestion I was expecting, but it was a good one: Weatherly's pristine cravat seemed to almost glow in the dim light.

"Excellent thought." I tugged at the starched cravat that finished off my riding ensemble, ripping it away from my neck with a swirl of cold air at my throat.

"Allow me, my lady." I handed over the length of linen. Weatherly carefully folded it and slid it into his greatcoat pocket. Always the quintessential butler. He removed his own cravat, a thoughtful expression crossing his face as he considered its length.

"I do have another suggestion, my lady," he said. "We should leave a trail for Captain Morland and his men to follow. It is not much, but it might help."

Ah, like the old German fairy tale. I nodded my agreement. "We do not have much in terms of weaponry either, but I do have this." I pushed my fingers up into my sleeve, found the hilt of the dagger in its sheath, and drew it out.

"Useful," he said. "May I?"

I gave him the weapon, and after a minute or so of shredding, we had our starched linen breadcrumbs. Weatherly returned the dagger to me. I slid it back into its sheath, then gathered up the hem of my riding habit—glad of the long knitted pantaloons that gave some protection and warmth to my legs—and led the way through a close stand of ash.

Even with the trampled track made by Mulholland and his

crew, our progress was hampered by the gloom and the terrain. The ground sloped or dropped without warning under its deceptive cloak of leaves and undergrowth, and twice I tripped upon a hole, only to be caught from injury by Weatherly's strong reflexes and quick hands. Occasionally a night animal would skitter out of our way, the sound clenching my innards. It felt as if it was taking forever to push our way through, and every minute that passed was a minute that could be Evan's and Mr. Kent's last.

In a patch of weak moonlight, I stopped to consult my fob watch, squinting to make out the face. We had been walking for twenty minutes. Dear God. I dropped the watch back upon its chain. A plan was beginning to form in my mind. A plan I did not like, but I could see no other way. I snagged another ribbon upon a twig and forged through yet another patch of dense hazel.

Just as I was beginning to fear we had wandered away from our goal, Weatherly stopped my progress with an arm across my path.

"My lady, look," he whispered.

Ahead—about three or four hundred feet—I saw a light and what looked to be a clearing with a flicker of movement between the eerily lit tree trunks. Then I heard it: the nicker of horses and the murmur of voices.

We had found them.

We both instinctively crouched. My heart pounded in my chest, my breath misting in small puffs before my mouth.

"I have a plan to get them out," I whispered. That is, if they were still alive, but I could not bear to voice that thought.

I outlined what each of us was to do, Weatherly shaking his head at each point. "No, my lady. That is too dangerous, especially for you. I heard what Mulholland said at the phaeton. What if—"

Indeed, what if, but I forced that possibility from my mind.

The question of how far I would go to save Evan was now squarely in front of me. And the answer, it seemed, was very far indeed.

"Do you have a better idea?" I asked.

He eyed me for a long, agonized second. "I do not."

I pulled the dagger from my sleeve again. "Then, take it."

Reluctantly, he took the knife from my hand. It seemed so small in his grip.

I consulted my watch again. If Julia had been successful, the army should be on their way. But would they arrive in time?

"Is everything clear? You know what to do and when to do it?" I asked.

Weatherly drew in a worried breath but nodded.

I rose, half-bent, and led the way. Although every impulse in my body screamed to run across the distance, to find out if Evan and Mr. Kent were alive, we moved slowly from a stand of ash to dense scrubby bushes to a huge oak, its trunk as wide as two men. Every step placed carefully and silently, the seconds ticking away. Sweat trickled down my back by the time we reached our goal: a clump of hazels that edged the clearing. We crouched again. For all our slow momentum, both of us breathed in shallow gasps.

In the clearing, a single lamp had been lit and hung from a tree branch, its light casting a warm glow on the grim tableau below. Mulholland stood with his back to us, his men in a loose half circle around two figures sprawled on the ground with their backs against a large fallen oak, their arms still wrenched back, hands bound behind. Both beaten: Evan with blood oozing from a cut near his temple, Kent with a bloodied mouth.

But both still alive.

Beyond them, near the far tree line, two of Mulholland's men were digging. Long, shallow indents in the hard autumn ground. For a second the shape did not have meaning; then I pressed my hand against my mouth to stop the realization escaping into sound. Makeshift graves.

I touched Weatherly's arm. Time for him to go. He gave a nod and then touched his chest, the flat of his hand covering his heart, his brown eyes on mine. How many times had I met those eyes, trusted the calm, shrewd cleverness behind them? Too many to count. I pressed my hand against my heart in return. Then my friend was gone. A silent shadow in a forest of darkness.

I took out my fob watch, fingers fumbling a little with the silver case, and watched the hands in the meager light.

Five minutes and then it would start.

The wait was excruciating, for both my spirit and the searing pain in my crouched thighs. Had I given Weatherly enough time to get into place? Would he be seen before I could act? What if Mulholland did not react as I thought he would? The tumult of doubt and questions and fear quickened my breathing. Good God, Weatherly was right. It was too dangerous. For both of us. And what if it did not work? We would all be dead.

Finally, the watch hand shifted. No more time for thought. Only action. I stood. Took a deep breath through the ache of over-worked muscles. And stepped into the edge of the clearing.

"Mulholland, you son of a whore," I yelled, "your prick is as small as your brain. You are a shag-bag, a worthless coxcomb. Not even a sailor would have your arse!"

All the men whirled around to face me. Yes, look at the mad-woman! I kept my gaze fixed upon Mulholland's stunned face, trying to search for movement behind him but, at the same time, not give the game away.

"What the hell?" one of Mulholland's men said. "How did she get here?"

I placed my hands upon my hips. "You are a scurvy, useless

piece of shit," I added at full volume, the last gleaned from a lifetime of eavesdropping upon grooms. "Your John Thomas is as poxed as your God-benighted face."

"Search the perimeter," Mulholland yelled. He swept an authoritative hand around the circumference of the clearing. "She won't have come alone." He pointed to the closest man to Evan and Kent. "You, watch those two."

Had Weatherly delivered the dagger? For a second, I found Evan's eyes, but we were too far apart for any communication other than his stiffened shock at my sudden appearance. And then Mulholland ran at me, faster than I had anticipated, arms pumping, every step promising violence.

I hoisted up my gown hem and turned, launching myself back into the undergrowth. I tried to retrace my steps, past the big oak, jumping over the dips and hollows I remembered, ducking the branches, hoping my footfalls did not plunge into a hole and send me sprawling. Every breath was hard and hot in my chest, a fiery agony of effort.

I heard shouts of triumph, a voice yelling, "We got the Black cove," and knew Weatherly had been found. Dear God. I bunched my gown higher, but holding it up hampered my stride, the hem snagging on a shrub. I staggered and wrenched it free. Too many seconds lost. He was gaining on me—hard breathing, the thud of feet, branches snapping. I ducked down and dug my fingernails into the forest floor, scraping up a handful of damp dirt. *Keep moving. Keep running.*

"Where are you, bitch?"

So close. Only a dense thicket of hazel and gorse between us. I stopped and held my breath, tucking in my chin to hide the pale giveaway of my skin.

"I told you what would happen if you followed me," he said,

his voice a caressing singsong that sent a chill across my skin. By the crack of twigs and the sound of his breathing, he was walking to the edge of the thicket. If he turned my way, he would see me.

Another step. The crunch of dried leaves. The smell of earth in my hand.

And then I saw his huge body, his teeth bared in predatory delight. "Got you."

He lunged. I threw the dirt, hard, enough of it hitting his face in a blinding spread. He reeled back, but not far enough, his hand grabbing the skirt of my habit as I turned to run, his weight and strength dragging me backward. Frantically, I twisted, punching at his face as he coughed, but he caught my wrist. I tried to wrench it free from his grasp, but he was too strong. I swung my other hand, fingers clawed to scratch, but his fist was faster, heavier. The pain of the punch exploded into my eyes, a burst of white agony that ripped away my breath and jagged through my head.

I buckled, falling, my momentum stopped by tight arms around my ribs. He hauled me upright, pinning me against his chest. My hands locked against my pounding heart, the smell of his sour, unwashed body thick in my throat.

"Now then," he said against my ear, his breath hot and fetid. "Let's see how brave you really are."

43

❦

I struggled against his tight hold, but he hooked his forearm around my throat, tightening the choke until I could barely breathe. The woods around me grayed into an air-starved blur as he half carried, half dragged me back to the clearing. I had not run as far from it as I had thought.

He dumped me on the grass in the middle of the circle of men. I gasped for air—hauling it into my aching lungs—then pushed myself upright, blinking to clear my sight, my jaw throbbing at the same rapid beat as my heart.

Two men at my left were holding Weatherly. Blood glistened on his chin, his mouth cut. I met his eyes: no longer calm and shrewd but wide with fury and fight. *Did it work?* He gave a slight nod. The dagger had been delivered.

Well, that was something. Not much considering the current circumstances, but something.

"No one else around?" Mulholland demanded, glancing around his crew.

One of the men, clearly second-in-command, shook his head. "Only these two."

Mulholland crouched in front of me, a knife in his hand. I stared at the ruby cabochon set into the silver mount and the elegantly engraved *EB*. Evan's dagger.

"Pretty, isn't it?" Mulholland drawled. "Just the thing a grand lady might give her lover."

Nothing got past him. I glared up at him.

"Seems you both care a great deal. Very sweet." He shifted his hand upon the dagger into a more businesslike grip.

"Where are your brother and sister, Lady Augusta?"

"They would not come," I said.

"Can I believe you?"

What would he have me say? No? I stared at him, trying to ignore the pain that dug through my head and the blade so close to my face.

He reached across and grabbed the back of my hair. One brutal wrench and my head was craned back, my scalp a handful of agony. He laid the flat of the blade on my cheek, point aimed at my eye.

"Where are your brother and sister?"

"They would not come," I repeated, my breath locking into my throat upon the words. All I could see was the point of the dagger.

He released me, my head jolting forward with the force. The blade was gone, but the relief was short-lived. He grabbed my jaw and dug his thumb into the damage already inflicted. For a second, white starbursts of pain blinded me. I gasped and grabbed his wrist, trying to wrest away the excruciation, but his grip was locked upon me and he dug his thumb in deeper.

"One more time, where are your brother and sister?"

"They would not come," I screamed through the vise of his hand.

He released me, the sudden absence of pain swaying me upon my hands and knees. Dear God, were Julia and Morland close? I tried to focus past the circle of leering men to the tree line. Did I see movement by the oak log? Was it two men struggling? I could not make it out clearly. I looked back to the ground, in case my focus drew attention.

"Your brother and sister are far more prudent than you, Lady Augusta," Mulholland said. He was back on his feet. "You are a fool for coming here. I told you what would happen." He looked around at his men. "I've always wanted to know if a lady's quim is any different from a whore's. Shall we see?"

Low laughter rippled around the circle. I forced back a surge of fear.

"I don't know, sir," one voice ventured. "She's noble. If we hurt her, the quality will come after us and it'll be the gallows."

"Didn't I tell you we're protected?" Mulholland said. "No one's going to come for us."

I tried to gather my focus. Keep him talking. "Who is protecting you? Is it Whitmore? I know he is part of the Exalted Brethren of Rack and Ruin."

Mulholland gave a low laugh. "You think you know so much. You don't know the half of it."

"What do I not know, then?"

"When to shut up."

He grabbed for me. I scrabbled across the grass, glimpsing Weatherly's fury as he fought against the two men holding him, but Mulholland was too fast. He caught the hem of my habit and hauled me back, slamming me onto my back, the impact driving all the air from my lungs. I gasped for breath, gathering all my strength to roll over, but a hand struck me in the chest, driving me back against the ground. Hands were hauling up my skirts, dragging them over my head, a stifling, blinding prison of linen and wool. Then a viselike hand grabbed between my legs, fingers jabbing into the knitted gusset of my riding pantaloons.

Fear and revulsion galvanized me—that primal female fury and terror that was made of teeth and claws and scream. I kicked and hit and scratched blindly, connecting in a drag of flesh and hard bone.

"Watch it, she's a fighter," a voice called.

"They've gone!" The voice was urgent. Not aimed at me. "Belford's gone."

"Jesus Christ!"

Mulholland's crushing weight lifted. I fought my skirts, finding cold air, then sky and moon above me. The sounds of men running. I rolled onto my knees, pushing myself upright in panting, staggering effort. Ahead, two men still held Weatherly.

I lunged forward, all my momentum suddenly and brutally stopped. A body slamming into mine. A choking arm around my throat again. The stink of Mulholland. He dragged me back against his body, the cold silver dagger across my throat.

"Belford," he bellowed. "Show yourself or she's dead!"

I dared not breathe, the steel of the blade already biting into my skin. Mulholland's men had taken up positions around the clearing, all armed, peering into the darkness for Evan and Kent.

An odd silence. All I could hear was Mulholland's breath in my ear, the heat of his fury exhaled against my cheek.

"Belford!" he bellowed again.

"He's in there!" one of the men at the far side of the clearing yelled. He fired into the forest. A single explosion and flash of light that flinched across my body.

"Advance!" a voice yelled, and then the clearing was full of men, soldiers, the crack of explosions, and flashes of light and smoke and bodies. The whir of rifle and pistol balls propelled through the air, chunks of bark flying and the screams of men, hit.

"Gus!" Through the smoke, Evan and Mr. Kent were running toward me, both with pistols in hand.

"Get your hands off her, Luddite!" Morland's voice yelled behind us. "I will shoot."

Mulholland wrenched me around to face the captain. Morland had a pistol pointed at us. "What?" Mulholland said, lowering the knife from my throat. "No. I'm not a—"

I grabbed his wrist and bit into his flesh as hard as I could manage through the pain in my jaw. I felt the resistance of flesh give way to the metal tang of hot blood. He screamed, the dagger dropping, and wrenched his hand back, a hunk of bloody flesh ripping under my teeth.

He grabbed me around the neck; then another gun exploded. Fired from somewhere behind us, the heavy thud of a ball hitting meat and muscle, driving us both forward a step. I smelled the sharp stink of spent powder, felt a wet spray of red matter, then heard the gargling rise of blood. Mulholland's hands dropped from my body.

I turned. He had crumpled to the ground, his neck a ragged, bloody mess. The last seconds of life were still in his eyes, and they were locked upon mine. Perhaps he smiled, or perhaps it was the oncoming rictus of death, but I saw something cross his face. A malign moment. And then his focus shifted beyond this realm and into death.

44

"Gus!"

I whirled around. "Evan!"

He was safe. I staggered into his outstretched arms. He pulled me in against his chest, but it was a fleeting embrace, for he set me at arm's length, wildly looking me over. "Are you hit? Are you hit?"

"No!" Although . . . was I? My jaw throbbed; everything was pain. But no, it was Mulholland's blood. Not mine. "It's his. It's his blood."

I looked down at Mulholland's staring dead eyes and felt my knees buckle. Evan caught me.

"Talbot," Captain Morland yelled through the drifting smoke, "get Lady Augusta out of here. Her sister is waiting on the road with a guard."

Evan and I looked at each other. He was still Mr. Talbot. Duffy had not told the captain the truth.

"Time to go," Mr. Kent said, running up beside us. "Talbot, help me carry Lady Augusta." He had heard Morland too. "Now, man!" He looked around. "Weatherly, your mistress needs you!"

Evan slung my arm across his shoulders, Kent taking my other side, and they half carried, half dragged me toward the edge of the clearing. I looked over my shoulder. Weatherly had ducked to the ground to pick up a pistol and was up again, following.

"I can run by myself," I said through the crack of rifles and screams of men.

And so we did. The four of us crashing through the forest, dodging branches, forcing our way through undergrowth, until the sounds and sights of the battlefield were at a safe distance.

"Stop!" I finally yelled as we wove our way through a stand of ash and gorse. "Stop!"

Kent, ahead by a few feet, grabbed hold of a tree trunk to stop his momentum. "What? What is it?"

Evan stopped beside me, panting. Weatherly spun around, checking for pursuit behind us.

"We cannot run willy-nilly like this," I said, realizing I was lisping through my throbbing mouth and jaw. I cupped my cheek in my palm, the light touch sending spikes of pain into my head. "You and Mr. Kent must get as far away as possible. As fast as possible."

Evan stepped up to me. "Let me look. Please."

I dropped my hand. "Is it broken?"

Tenderly, he pressed his fingertips along the bone, his face registering his apology as I hissed. "No. Thank God, and I think your teeth are intact, but you are going to have a hell of a bruise. Cold compresses and arnica balm."

"Yes, Doctor," I said, and touched his cheek, bringing his smile back. "But now you must go. Weatherly and I will return to the road and Julia will drive us back to Davenport Hall. The longer we can confuse Morland, the better. He said he left soldiers with my sister for protection. You cannot be seen by them."

"It was you who got Morland and his men to come?" Kent asked.

"We all did," I said, glancing across at Weatherly. "A group effort. Julia went back for the army."

"It was her ladyship's idea, though," Weatherly said.

"Astonishing," Kent muttered.

"She is always astonishing," Evan said. He took my hand and turned it, kissing the palm. "I wish I could kiss you properly, but I think you would probably faint from pain."

I tried to smile, but it hurt too much.

Kent looked across at me, his intensity reaching me even through the dim light. "You will give her my love? All of it."

"I will," I promised. "Get word to us if you can."

"My lord, take this," Weatherly said, handing Evan the pistol. "It is loaded."

"Good man," Evan said, checking the cock. He looked at me, his imminent departure upon his face. "Thank you."

"Just stay alive," I said.

"I do not know what or where we will—"

"I know," I whispered. "Have faith."

An odd thing for me to say, but I did have faith. In him and in me.

Mr. Kent looked up at the sky, clearly reading the stars. "We should go this way," he said, pointing deeper into the forest. He pointed in the opposite direction. "The road will be that way."

And so the four of us turned to the directions we were heading. I looked over my shoulder as Weatherly led the way out of the ash stand and saw Evan do the same. Both of us watching the other through the trees until we were no longer in sight.

*A*bout ten minutes into our stumbling walk back, Weatherly stopped and turned to face me.

"My lady," he began, "may I say something?"

"Of course," I lisped. "Always."

He was clearly agitated, his hands clenched before him. "I am sorry I could not get to you in time. I tried, but I could not free myself. Those men—"

"It was the plan," I said quickly, ignoring the pain that came with speaking. "And Captain Morland did arrive in time." I swallowed a sudden ache in my throat. "You did everything I asked, Weatherly, exactly as I asked, and put yourself in great danger. Thank you. Lord Evan and Mr. Kent would not have been saved without you."

"But I cannot help but think what would have happened if the army had not arrived."

"Well, it did not happen and Mulholland is dead." I gave a watery smile and sniffed back a sudden rise of tears. "Is it awful of me to be glad that he is dead?"

Weatherly nodded. "Absolutely, my lady, but we shall be awful together, God forgive us."

I laughed, a croaked, pained huff, but still a laugh, and it lightened the heaviness that I knew was going to haunt me. Weatherly always knew how to bring things to rights. Even so, the next had to be said, although I did not want to say it, for, in truth, I trusted him more than my own brother.

"If ever you do not want to follow me in these mad ventures, Weatherly, you must say so. Please do not feel obliged. You must do what is right for you. Do you promise?"

"I have always known that, my lady." He looked up at the sky, through the branches. "You are your father's daughter, and he was the best man I have ever had the honor of knowing." He smiled. "I think he would have enjoyed your mad ventures. He had a few of them himself."

"You must tell me one day," I said.

"No, my lady. Your father's secrets are as safe as your own." He turned, then looked over his shoulder and cast me a droll look. "I think I recognize this stand of ash."

"Indeed," I said, matching his tone through the teary thickness in my throat. "So different from all the others."

As it turned out, that stand of ash was not so far from one of our linen markers, and so our return to the road was reasonably quick. A good thing, too, since my stamina was fast collapsing under the pain, exhaustion, and nervous strain of the past few hours.

We stumbled out onto the road, our sudden appearance bringing the four soldiers guarding my sister upon us.

"Halt!" their leader yelled.

We stopped. All four rifles were aimed at us.

"It is my sister! My sister," shrieked Julia, still seated in the phaeton. "Do not shoot."

The soldiers lowered their guns.

Weatherly took my arm and helped me across to the phaeton. I looked up at my sister, who, upon finally seeing my state in the dim moonlight, gave a low moan of distress.

"You are hurt!"

"It is not as bad as it looks," I lisped, leaning against the dusty side of the carriage. I was feeling, suddenly, very dizzy. "But I wish to go back to Davenport Hall."

"Of course, immediately," Julia said.

"Forgive me, my lady, but I cannot allow that," one of the young soldiers said. "Our orders are to keep you safe, here."

Julia was in no mood for a boy to tell her what to do, even one with a gun. A heated discussion ensued, Julia insisting I needed medical assistance and it would be upon the British Army's head if I died, the soldier countering that he had his orders. It seemed my appearance, and the fact that I stepped into the undergrowth for a moment to retch, clinched the argument. A compromise was struck: the soldiers would escort us back to the hall.

Under the guard of the four men, we drove slowly back to the estate, Weatherly once again in the groom's seat and holding me upright by my shoulder. Since the soldiers were constantly in earshot and my swollen mouth made talking difficult, my report of the escape to my sister was necessarily short and somewhat in code. However, I did manage to whisper, "He sends all his love." I knew it was not much reassurance, but she smiled.

Through my exhaustion, I did wonder where Duffy had gone, why he had not revealed Evan's identity, and why he was not waiting with Julia, but it was too much effort to ask and she did not volunteer the information. Still, the fact that he was not haranguing me was enough.

45

The Davenport stables were still brightly lit when we arrived, the grooms jumping into action as the mismatched pair plodded into the cobbled yard. Weatherly climbed down from his seat and helped me from the high-slung carriage to the ground, the effort bringing a gray cast across my vision.

"My lady, take my arm," Weatherly said urgently. "You are very pale."

I leaned against his solid arm, thankful for the support. The activity around me had blurred, the sounds oddly distorted: a crashing clang, then muffled voices, then clanging again.

Charlotte's figure came into focus as she ran across the cobbles, emerald gown hitched above her ankles.

"Augusta, dear God, what has happened?" she said, taking my free hand. Her face loomed close. "We must get you upstairs. Julia, are you injured too?"

"No, I am unharmed," Julia said. "But we must get Gus to bed."

For a second my vision cleared. I blinked as Porty entered the yard, followed by the ever-curious, ever-intrusive Ermine and her husband.

"Lady Augusta, whatever have you done to yourself?" the Ermine asked in shrill condemnation, as if my injured state was somehow a character flaw. "You are so disheveled."

"What the hell is going on here, Charlotte?" Porty bellowed. "Deele said Lady Augusta and Lady Julia were keeping his sister from him. Where is she now? Where is Deele?" He stared at the pair hitched to the phaeton. "Good God, whose donkeys are these? Where are your bays, Charlotte?" He rounded upon me, his words literally hitting me in a spray of wrath. "What have you done with those horses? They are prime blood. You are taking advantage of my wife's friendship, Lady Augusta. This is not the behavior of a woman of your rank or indeed a friend of any—"

He was in a passion, all red face and bulging veins, and frankly, I was not up to listening to such venom, let alone feeling it land wetly upon my skin. I did the only thing possible under the cir-cumstances. I fainted.

I opened my eyes, an almost-resurfacing from somewhere deep and quiet. Dim light from the edges of a curtained window, my body warm beneath blankets, my hand held. I turned my head upon a pillow—an ache, distant but persistent along my jaw. Beside me, Julia atop the covers, her hand in mine, asleep. And Tully on my other side, in a chair, head back, a breathy snore breaking the silence. I closed my eyes, feeling the soft heaviness of safe slumber rise and carry me back into dark oblivion.

I woke again, this time into full consciousness and a sense of basic body urgency. The room was still dim, but Julia was not beside me. I tried to say her name, but it came out as a cracked groan.

Tully's face loomed above me.

"She is awake, my lady."

Julia's face appeared alongside. "Gus, how are you feeling?"

And then Charlotte's face, on a waft of her lily perfume, all three of them peering at me in a similar state of concern.

I licked my lips, trying to find some saliva with which to form words. "Pot," I managed.

Upon that statement of need, Julia and Charlotte left the room and Tully helped me out of bed to use the chamber pot. After I was much relieved, my maid helped me back onto the bed, plumped the pillows behind me, and pressed a glass of barley water into my hand. I took a long sip, feeling the cool liquid soothe my parched throat as she opened the bedchamber door for Julia and Charlotte to enter again.

"How long have I been asleep?" I croaked.

"A whole day and night," Julia said, sitting upon the edge of the bed. I heard the worry in her voice. "Your jaw is so bruised."

"It is not broken," I said. "Lord Evan assured me of that. Is there any news of them?"

Charlotte and Julia exchanged a look.

"I think your mistress needs something to eat," Charlotte said to Tully. "Go to Cook. Tell her I sent you."

She and Julia waited for Tully to depart; then my sister pulled out a letter that she had tucked into her white morning gown sleeve. "I received this from Sarah Ponsonby earlier today. By messenger."

She unfolded the paper and read aloud:

> *1st November 1812*
> *Plas Newydd*
> *Llangollen*

> *My dear Lady Julia,*
> *Lady Eleanor and I wished to express our pleasure at your recent visit and to convey the news that Lady Hester and Miss Grant have settled in very well. Lady Hester is*

particularly taken with our garden and I feel that her
connection to it will aid greatly in her recovery.

You will no doubt be pleased to know that Lady Hester's
brother and his friend returned that same morning and,
although a little worse for wear, are whole and well. They
have received aid from our mutual friends and have now
moved to a location more suited to their circumstances. Our
mutual friends have asked me to assure you and Lady
Augusta that all is in hand and they suggest that you return
to London as soon as your situation permits.

Julia, my friend, I believe you can trust this report of
their well-being as well as the source from which it comes.

You are always most welcome at Plas Newydd and we
look forward to the next time we see each other.

Yours in affection,
Miss Sarah Ponsonby

I looked at their expectant faces. "Lord Evan and Mr. Kent went back to Plas Newydd," I said.

I closed my eyes for a moment, taking in a full, clear breath. They were safe.

"Julia believes the mutual friends are Mr. Brummell and Lord Alvanley," Charlotte said.

"It cannot be anyone else, can it, Gus?" Julia said. "They have, for some reason, helped Mr. Kent and Lord Evan to safety. Charlotte is not convinced."

"Why would Mr. Brummell and Lord Alvanley help Lord Evan and Mr. Kent?" Charlotte demanded. "They would not risk it. They may be leaders of fashion and society, but that does not put them above the law."

"Even so, I believe they have helped them," I said. I had great faith in George's system of favors and his influence upon his friend Alvanley. "And now, it seems, they want us back in London." I frowned, remembering the intense conversation between Mr. Kent and Mr. Brummell at Plas Newydd. It seemed George was a man of many hats, and not only of the fashionable sort. "We should do as they ask."

"You are not well enough to travel today," Julia said. "Besides, it is Sunday."

"And you are, of course, welcome to stay here as long as you like," Charlotte said.

Julia glanced sideways at our friend. "That is not what Porty said last night."

Charlotte lifted her chin. "True enough. He wants you both out of the hall. He and the Ellis-Brants have gone to the hunting lodge and he has told me you are to be gone when he returns. As if I would drive you out!"

"You are a stalwart friend, Charlotte," I said, managing to smile through the pain in my jaw. "But I think we have intruded upon your kindness for too long. We must go back to London. I believe I want my own home, my own things around me. Is that silly?"

"It is not," Julia said. She took my hand. "Are you strong enough to tell us what happened in the forest?"

I took another long draft of barley water—savoring its soft, slippery sweetness—then reported the events at the clearing. I skipped a little over the circle of men and Mulholland's attack upon me; it would distress Julia and Charlotte, and I certainly did not wish to relive it. At some point I would have to think on it, perhaps even talk of it after enough time had passed, but not now. Otherwise, I reported it all, or as much as I could recall.

"That is quite some ordeal, my dear," Charlotte said softly, her head tilted to one side. I think she knew I was holding something back.

"Mulholland is really dead?" Julia asked. "I think you tried to tell me in the phaeton, but you were not quite making sense."

"Yes, very dead." I pushed away the image of his glazed eyes. And that last rictus smile.

"Who shot him?" Charlotte asked.

"I do not know. I was facing the other way."

"Well, it does not matter," Julia said briskly. She released my hand. "He is dead and now the matter is closed."

Julia was not usually so callous. And oddly, she would not meet my eye. It took me a few seconds to understand why: she did not wish to know in case it was Mr. Kent. The sixth commandment was "Thou shalt not kill"—heaven cried out for vengeance upon those who killed with intent, and all who helped them—and Julia lived by the commandments. I hoped Mr. Kent had not killed Mulholland, for my sister's sake. On the other hand, if it was Evan who had fired the fatal shot, that did not distress me at all.

"But the matter is not closed, is it?" Charlotte said. "Whoever is behind Mulholland is not dead."

"True," I said. "But we have a name. Charles Whitmore."

Charlotte shook her head. "I do not understand why Charles Whitmore would want Lord Evan dead. There is no connection. None at all."

"Nor, it would seem, to the duel and the death of Sanderson twenty years ago," I said.

"Even so, you have Whitmore's involvement from two sources now, so there must be something to it."

A silence fell as we mused individually upon the conundrum. I took a sip of barley water. I certainly had no answers, but another question came to mind.

"Where is Duffy?" I asked.

Julia sighed. "He has gone back to London. Apparently, he returned here after I left to fetch the army, and then set off at first light."

Charlotte nodded her accord with that report. "He was most keen to go and would not even stay for breakfast."

"I thought he would follow you to meet the army upon the road," I said to Julia. "Lud, what kind of brother is he?"

"Think on it, Gus. He is a magistrate. If he had met the army with me, he would have had to choose between betraying us or the law. So he chose to leave and not put himself in that position at all. I think, in his own way, he was trying to be a good brother."

"You are more generous than I am," I said.

A knock upon the door sounded.

"Come," Charlotte said.

I was expecting Tully with the food—which I rather wanted—but it was Hanford, Charlotte's butler.

He bowed and addressed his mistress. "My lady, a Captain Morland is downstairs and demands to see Lady Augusta and Lady Julia. He says he has the authority of the British Army and will not go until he has seen them."

Charlotte eyed me. "Shall I send him away? For all the army bluster, he is still the son of our friends and I am sure I can get him to leave."

It was tempting, but I shook my head, the action sending a shooting pain into my temple. "It will have to be done at some point—it might as well be now. Are you ready for it, Julia? You are the one who lied to his face."

"We all lied to his face," my sister said. "And I rather think we are about to do so again."

46

A cup of chocolate revived me enough to dress, but it took me an hour to ready myself for the interview. I craved a warm bath but made do with a carefully administered wash from Tully, who tutted as she navigated the sponge around the bruises and cuts upon my body.

Upon finishing my toilette, I looked at myself in the dressing room mirror. No wonder the Ermine had been so shocked at the sight of me: the right side of my face was deeply bruised and still a little swollen, the deepest blue and black upon my jawbone. I blinked, suddenly back in the forest, clawing at Mulholland's face, my breath hard and fast.

"My lady," said Tully, grabbing my hands, "what is it? Shall I fetch Lady Julia?"

"No!" I drew in a long, shaking breath. I was not in the forest; I was in the dressing room at Davenport Hall. I pulled in another breath, and another, fighting back the night and the trees and the hands. "I will be quite myself in a minute."

It took more than a minute, but eventually I stood and made my way to the corridor and collected Julia from her room, and together we descended the staircase to the drawing room.

"It reminds me of when we first met Mr. Kent," she whispered, outside the door.

"Well, do not fall in love with Captain Morland," I said.

"Very funny." But she was smiling. The first I had seen since I had woken up, and I was glad to see it.

She nodded to the footman. He opened the door and stood aside with a bow.

At the sound of our entrance, Captain Morland turned from the far window. He was in dress uniform, complete with sword, and holding something small wrapped in a cloth. Our eyes met, his shock at my appearance plain in his youthful, good-humored face. A good start. I added a slow, stiff gait into the room, but resisted tottering—one did not wish to overplay it.

"Lady Augusta," he said. "I am—I did not know how bad—"

He bethought himself of his manners and quickly bowed to both of us.

Julia returned the courtesy, but I said, "You will excuse me if I do not curtsy, Captain."

"Of course, my lady."

"You wished to speak to us?" Julia said, helping me onto Charlotte's damask sofa. I added a hiss of pain as I sat, which was not entirely fabricated.

Julia sat beside me and motioned to the chair opposite. "Please do sit."

"Thank you." He took the seat, back stiff and straight, his initial shock under control, for he studied us both with a return of his usual shrewdness. After what felt like a full minute of silent scrutiny, he placed the cloth-wrapped item upon the small table beside his armchair and said, "There are some matters pertaining to two nights ago that I have been sent to clarify."

"As you can imagine, it is not an evening my sister wishes to recall," Julia said.

"I understand, Lady Julia, but there are inconsistencies that need to be answered."

"Go ahead, Captain. We are, of course, happy to answer your questions, although I do warn you that I cannot remember much." I hoped the lie did not show on my face.

"It has transpired that the men who stopped you upon the road were not Luddites, as you reported to us, Lady Julia, but a thieftaker by the name of Mulholland—the man who held you at knifepoint, Lady Augusta—and his crew on the task to arrest a criminal."

I managed not to flinch at Mulholland's name. "A thieftaker?" I echoed. "He did not identify himself at the time, did he, sister?"

Julia shook her head. "No. With all your talk of Luddites in the area, Captain, we just assumed it was that desperate band of men."

"I see," Morland said, his eyes narrowing slightly at my sister's gentle invocation of his own warnings. "It has also come to our attention that the man calling himself Mr. Talbot is in fact Lord Evan Belford, the man Mulholland was seeking to arrest. He is wanted for absconding from a penal colony, highway robbery, and other crimes. He and his companion, Kent, a Runner who seems to have crossed to the side of lawlessness, are still at large."

"Really?" Julia said, her voice under careful control. "How shocking."

Still at large. I knew my sister felt as much relief as I did.

"You did not know?" Morland demanded.

"We did not," I said, arranging my features into some semblance of astonishment. "To think we dined with him and I rode at his side. Shocking. How did you discover such a masquerade?"

"It seems Mrs. Ellis-Brant realized who he was and reported the matter to my superiors."

Of course she did; it was going to be hard to resist slapping the Ermine when we next met. I glanced at Julia, but she was keeping a polite smile pasted on her face.

The captain leaned forward. "I find it hard to believe you did not know, since Mrs. Ellis-Brant told me you arrived here with Belford's sister and her companion, the two ladies traveling under assumed names."

Ah, the Ermine had done a very thorough job.

"Indeed we were traveling with Lady Hester and her companion, Captain," I said. Always best to stay as close as possible to the truth when lying through one's teeth. "There is a family matter between her and Lord Deele, her other brother, that we are not at liberty to discuss. But we did not know that Lord Evan had joined the party here at Davenport Hall as Mr. Talbot, and Lady Hester certainly did not tell us. He hoodwinked us all, but I can understand Lady Hester's reticence."

Morland sat back. "Can you, now?"

"Indeed. Family loyalties and so forth," I said, waving an expansive hand. It was time to bring this interview to a close. "We are of course shocked to hear that such a desperate man was among us, but we have no other information for you."

Morland, however, was not about to be so summarily dismissed. "Why were you in that clearing, Lady Augusta? It seems very odd that a thieftaker arresting a highwayman and an ex–Bow Street Runner would march one lady through a forest and leave the other on the roadside in a phaeton."

Well, that was a very good point. I glanced at Julia, then bowed my head theatrically under the weight of my ordeal. "I have no insights into the minds of such men, Captain. It was a terrifying few hours, which I can barely recall."

I risked a glance at him.

He met the glance with raised brows. Damn.

"I have no doubt your experience was terrifying, Lady Augusta," he said. "However—" He reached over and picked up the cloth-wrapped packet at his side. With a flick he unfolded its edges and held out the item to me upon the flat of his hand. A silver dagger, set with a ruby. "I found it in the clearing. Not the usual weapon of a thieftaker. Is it yours, by chance?"

The engraved cartouche was face down. Was it mine? Or was it Evan's? Either way, I wanted it back with a violence I had not expected. Yet, if I claimed it, what would this sharp mind before me glean from such an admission?

By all rights I should deny it. And yet . . .

"Indeed," I said, "it is mine."

The captain smiled and turned the dagger over. "Why, then, is it engraved with the initials *EB*?" He ran his forefinger over the letters. "Does it stand for Evan Belford, by chance? I saw him run to you in the clearing, call you by the name Gus, and embrace you. Moreover, you called him Evan and returned the embrace quite fervently."

I cleared my throat. "I have no recollection of such familiarity," I said.

"It is not a *B*," Julia said abruptly. "It is a *D*. It stands for *Ex Deo*. From God."

Both the captain and I stared at her, nonplussed.

"It is a *D*?" Morland said, peering at the cartouche. He frowned. "No, it is a *B*."

Julia leaned over, her fingertip tracing the engraved letters. "It is all the flourish around it. It is a *D*. I gave it to my sister as a gift."

I managed to nod. "And I will have it back, please." I held out my hand.

He hesitated, then flipped the cloth back over the blade and passed it to me. I felt the weight of it across my palm, an image of Evan's delight as he balanced it upon his fingers warring with the memory of its cold metal against my throat. If I had a chance, I would return it to Evan. But would I have that chance?

"Something is awry here; I know it." Morland's voice drew me back into the room. "Something unlawful, I think."

"But you are not the law, Captain Morland, are you? You are a soldier, and a very good one," my sister said, rising from her seat. The captain, bound by his sense of etiquette, stood too. "I thank you for coming to the aid of my sister. Without your gallant intervention, I cannot conceive of what would have happened. In our eyes you are a hero. We cannot add to our reports of the evening. It was a most disturbing time and our memories are clouded by the agitation to our delicate womanly nerves. Perhaps that is what should be reported to your superiors."

Captain Morland opened his mouth to protest, but then shut it again and smiled: the half smile of a man admitting defeat. "I rather think you and Lady Augusta have never had a clouded minute in your lives," he said. "It is obvious I am on a fool's errand." He turned to me, his voice sincere. "Lady Augusta, I am sorry for your injuries. I wish I had arrived earlier to spare you such hurt."

"You came at exactly the right moment, Captain Morland," I said, matching his sincerity, for he had, indeed, saved me from a much worse hurt. "Thank you."

"I will take my leave and wish you all the best," he said. "But in all seriousness, I know it is a *B*."

"It is a *D*," Julia said firmly. *"Ex Deo."*

"Yes, of course. For God. Let us hope he does not take umbrage at such an invocation of his name," the captain said dryly, and, with a somewhat ironic bow, made his exit.

47

We departed for London the next morning. Charlotte, bless her, gave us one of Porty's best teams for the first leg, as much to annoy him, I think, as to expedite our return home.

I wept twice upon the journey, both occasions in my sister's arms.

The first time, we cried together—in relief that Evan and Mr. Kent were still alive and free, and for the sobering fact that we did not know when or if we would see them again.

The second time the tears were mine alone. They had welled up from some deep and private part of me as we had driven through a dense forest, the smoky smell of November permeating the carriage cabin. Although my sister discerned a difference from our shared tears and asked me what was wrong as she stroked my hair, I would not tell her why I wept so hard. But I knew that I was, in part, mourning a sense of inviolability that I had taken for granted, and which I no longer held.

It took us three days to reach Grosvenor Square, by which time the bruises upon my face had shifted into the greens and yellows of slow recovery and the pain in my jaw had dissipated into occasional discomfort.

What bliss it was to be home. To greet our staff and eat Cook's fine dinner and to say good night to Julia upon the landing, each of us with our night candles, as we trod to our separate bed-chambers. And waking again after a sound sleep to Tully's cheerful "good morning" as she drew back the curtains, and dressing, and descending the stairs to the morning room for breakfast.

Everything as it should be.

And yet, we were a house in waiting. I could feel the silent expectation between Julia and me, as inevitable as our heartbeats, while we ate breakfast. *What next? What next? What next?*

"Shall I cut you some seed cake?" Julia asked, knife poised above the newly baked round.

"Yes, please," I said.

She cut into the cake. I had noticed that she had not brought down the little gold filigree box in which she kept her blue mass pills. Had she given them up? Good God, I hoped so. I took a sip of coffee, stifling the question upon my lips. It was her decision. But, Lud, it was hard not to ask.

After breakfast we moved into the drawing room, as had been our routine for years and years. And the silent expectation still drummed: *What next? What next?*

The answer came midmorning. Julia sat at the little writing table near the window, catching up on the invitations that had arrived while we were in Lancashire. I sat before the hearth reading *The Times*, hoping I would not find a report of a highwayman recaptured.

A knock upon the door brought Weatherly into the room, his expression troubled.

"Lady Augusta, there is a man at the kitchen door insisting upon seeing you. He has a letter that he will not give up to me. He says it must be delivered into your hands only."

"What does he look like?"

"He is dressed as a tinker, my lady, but his voice does not match his garb. Far too refined."

"And you do not recognize him?"

"I do not, my lady, but I would wager he is a gentleman."

Julia placed her quill back upon its rest. "I do not like the sound of this, Gus."

"Weatherly, tell Samuel and Albert to join us in here, and to be ready for the possibility of violent action. Then bring our visitor here."

"Of course, my lady."

Julia rose from her chair and came to sit beside me upon the sofa. "Violent action?"

I shrugged. "It has happened before. I wish to be prepared."

Our two footmen duly arrived, an air of suppressed excitement about them as they took up their positions inside the door. If nothing violent occurred, I suspected they would be greatly disappointed.

Finally, a knock upon the door and then it opened. Weatherly led a shabby man into the room, his coat smeared and dusty and an old tricorn upon grizzled gray hair. But all that could not hide the close-set eyes or the overly small mouth of Charles Whitmore.

I stood up, the force of the action bringing Samuel and Albert a step closer, and Weatherly looming behind our visitor. "Why are you here, Mr. Whitmore?"

"Mr. Whitmore?" Julia echoed. She rose from her seat. "Good Lord, why are you dressed in such a manner?"

"I am in disguise," he said.

"Clearly," Julia said. "I hardly thought this was a fashion choice."

"We know you are a member of the despicable Exalted Brethren of Rack and Ruin, Mr. Whitmore," I said, all my rage about Miss

Hollis and Jenny rising to the forefront again. "Women have died in that place. Give me a reason why I do not have you thrown out upon the street."

Samuel and Albert exchanged full glances and stepped even closer. Whitmore clearly noted their advance but did not blanch. More staunch than I thought.

"Lady Augusta, I ask you to read this before you take any action," he said. He thrust out a packet. "It is from a mutual friend. Please, it is important."

What mutual friend could we have? I eyed him warily but took the packet. There was no direction upon the front, but all three of its folds were sealed with a separate blob of red wax. A letter, then, from someone who wanted to make sure I knew I was the first to open it.

With three flicks of my thumb, I broke each of the seals and spread the single sheet of paper.

5th November 1812

> *My dear Augusta,*
>   *Behold, the favor.*
>   *Trust him. I do.*
>   *George Brummell*

"What does it say?" Julia asked, leaning over to read the short missive. "Oh Lud, so this is his favor. Are you sure he wrote it?"

I read the note again. It was, indeed, in George's hand. But a favor involving Charles Whitmore? And could I really trust a man who was a member of the Exalted Brethren of Rack and Ruin, even if George Brummell did?

"What is going on?" I demanded. "What favor does Mr. Brummell wish me to do for you?"

He looked pointedly at our footmen and Weatherly. "This must be a private conversation."

I glanced at Julia. She nodded. "You may go," she said to our footmen. "You, too, Weatherly. Thank you."

Upon their somewhat reluctant departure, Mr. Whitmore motioned to the sofa opposite us. "May I sit? It has been a hectic few days."

I gave a curt nod, although I sensed Julia's concern about his shabby self upon her sofa.

We all sat. Mr. Whitmore removed his greasy tricorn and placed it on the sofa beside him—Julia giving a soft cluck of horror—then clasped his hands together, his brow furrowed.

"I believe you know I am undersecretary of the Alien Office?" Julia and I nodded. "It is the responsibility of my department to ensure that foreign spies do not obtain information about England or smuggle it out of our country. As you can imagine, a crucial task during this drawn-out war with Bonaparte. It has also become our task to root out dissent among our own people."

"The Luddites," I said, with some accusation in my voice.

He inclined his head. "Indeed, and I understand your discomfort with the idea. However, it has come to our attention that a much more highly ranked problem has become embedded in our society. A person, or perhaps people—we are not yet certain—who have collected harmful information about highly placed officials and are using it to protect themselves and influence the outcome of government and military decisions. We know the identity of one of the perpetrators and we are now trying to discover how deep the rot has penetrated."

"That is indeed a grave concern," I said. "But what does it have to do with us?"

"You and Lady Julia, and also Lord Evan Belford and Mr. Kent"—he paused to allow his knowledge of our connection to settle—"have inadvertently become noticed by the architect of this villainous activity. As you are quite aware, he has already attempted to kill Lord Evan, and now he knows about your association with his lordship."

"We thought you were trying to kill Lord Evan," Julia said.

Mr. Whitmore gave a thin smile. "Quite the opposite, my lady."

"Who is trying to kill him, then? And why?" I demanded.

"Lord Milroy."

"Milroy?" Julia said. "He has the reputation of being devoted to pleasure and gambling and not much else."

I recalled my clashes with the man and the hideous wagers written in the Exalted Brethren's wager book. The kind of pleasure he took was in the pain and humiliation of women. And perhaps their deaths.

"I have heard whispers that he is a kingmaker and has some influence," I said.

"That is more to the truth, Lady Augusta," Whitmore said. "He takes great care to be seen living a rake's life of dissipation and indulgence but is, in fact, a very shrewd manipulator. We believe he is under the impression that Lord Evan saw something that would destroy his position in society. Lord Evan tells us that he cannot remember seeing any such thing, but despite Lord Milroy's self-proclaimed love of cards and dice, he is not a man who takes chances."

"You mean Lord Evan saw something at the Exalted Brethren of Rack and Ruin twenty years ago?" I queried. "It does not seem enough of a reason to order someone's death, the mere possibility that they have seen something." I felt a leap of logic. "Did Milroy orchestrate Lord Evan's duel with Sanderson?"

"Maybe so, though it would be a haphazard way to dispatch someone. I believe there is more to the story and I have tried to discover it, but to no avail."

"Ah, so you are not a member at that club by choice, are you?" I said.

He grimaced. "I am not."

"You are there to watch Lord Milroy."

He nodded. "I am."

A dangerous occupation considering the nature of Lord Milroy. Mr. Whitmore was, indeed, far stauncher than I had thought. Even so, maintaining surveillance upon an alleged spy did not grant amnesty regarding the other activities of the club. "Did you know about the women being murdered in that dreadful room downstairs?"

Mr. Whitmore sat up straighter. "I swear I did not. I have never been down there. It is for particular members only. I attend the club only to watch Milroy and his associates." He could see my distrust and placed his hand upon his chest. "I swear upon my honor, Lady Augusta."

"So that is why you have come to us dressed as a tinker," Julia said. "You think Milroy knows we are connected with Lord Evan and you cannot risk being seen here, visiting us."

Mr. Whitmore nodded, a wry smile upon his small mouth. "Lord Evan and Mr. Kent told me you were both clever."

Julia sat forward. "You are in contact with them? Are they well?"

"They are both well and safe. And mention of them brings me to the favor. The events in Lancashire have made it quite urgent that they disappear from England for some time for their own safety. As it happens, the Alien Office has an important mission in

France that needs attention. Lord Evan and Mr. Kent have agreed
to discharge this mission."

"What?" Julia said, her hands clasping in agitation. "You are
sending them to France? Into the war?"

"They have elected to go. Since Mr. Kent can no longer work
as a Bow Street agent and is clearly a man of worth, I have offered
him a position in the Alien Office. He has accepted and so now
works for me. In Lord Evan's case, he has been offered a pardon on
the successful completion of the mission, although I rather think
he would have accepted it without the reward."

"A pardon?" I echoed.

"A full royal pardon," Whitmore replied.

Good God, a royal pardon. All past deeds undone. The slate
wiped clean. With such an acquittal, Evan could live once more in
society.

I sat forward. "What is the favor you ask of me, Mr. Whitmore?"

Whatever he asked, I would do. Anything to secure that
pardon.

"You are to go with Lord Evan and Mr. Kent to France to
bring back someone who cannot fall into the hands of Bonaparte.
Mr. Kent was a cavalryman and campaigned in France, so he is
well qualified to lead you, and will have the details of the mission.
He speaks fluent French, as does Lord Evan. I believe you do so as
well?"

I nodded. "Every lady knows her French. It is drilled into us in
the schoolroom. How long do we have?"

"As long as it takes. The safety of the person in question is of
utmost importance."

"Who is it that we bring back?" I asked.

Mr. Whitmore shook his head. Apparently, that was information I was not yet to have.

"But why does Augusta have to go?" Julia asked. "If Mr. Kent and Lord Evan are going, is that not enough?"

"It is of the utmost importance that a woman of rank be part of the mission. The person cannot be retrieved without your sister's presence." He wet his lips. "It is not only Lady Augusta that we ask, Lady Julia. We also ask that you go, to serve your king and country. We cannot afford to send over only one lady in case she . . ." He stopped.

"Dies?" I supplied.

He ducked his head. "Quite."

"I do not wish to be a spy," Julia said. "It is a ridiculous idea."

"You will definitely not be spying," Whitmore said quickly. "That would be a death sentence if you were captured. We ask only that you go as what you are: two ladies of noble rank, who are attempting to travel through France to return to your home in"—he paused—"Sweden."

Sweden again. Evan had proposed to take refuge there with Hester.

"How are we to be Swedish?" I asked. "We do not speak the language."

"Your French will suffice and you will have legitimate papers. In addition, since ladies of your rank would never travel without servants, you may take two people, but no more, and you must trust them implicitly, for your lives could depend upon their discretion and resourcefulness. Lord Evan tells me you have a man who has proved himself most useful and trustworthy."

"Our butler."

"If he is to accompany you, he may know the dangers he may face, but not the goal. The fewer people who know, the better." He sat back. "Do you agree to go, Lady Augusta?"

No wonder George Brummell had refused to tell me anything

about his favor. It was rather more dangerous than those he had granted to me. Moreover, Whitmore's rather glancing reference to capture and death had not gone unnoticed. Still, I had made George a promise, and frankly, nothing was going to stop me from helping Evan obtain that pardon.

"I will go on one condition, Mr. Whitmore," I said. The inevitability of my agreement was not going to stop me from making my own demand.

He eyed me warily. "What is it you want?"

"I want the Exalted Brethren of Rack and Ruin shut down. I want that place gone before I go to France."

Julia angled a glance at me. The implacability in my voice had surprised her, but she had not seen poor Miss Hollis or Jenny.

Whitmore frowned. "But that is our main source of information about Lord Milroy."

"I do not care. If you want me to go to France, then it must be closed."

"Even if we do close it down—which is nigh impossible considering its membership—it will just move somewhere else, Lady Augusta. There are always clubs like it."

I knew he was right. There would always be such clubs catering to the baser nature, and there would always be brutal disregard for the lives and bodies of women. Still, I had to do something to avenge Miss Hollis and all those who had died or been hurt for the sake of men's lust and amusement.

"That is my condition, Mr. Whitmore. Do you agree?"

"You are set upon this?" he asked, his mouth set in grim lines.

"I am. It is not negotiable."

"Then I find my hand forced. I agree."

I sat back, triumphant. "Excellent. And that means I agree—I will go to France."

Perhaps now I understood why George thought we were cut from the same cloth, for I had to admit I was filled with rather too much elation at Whitmore's capitulation, and excitement at the thought of the mission ahead. A good deal of fear, too, of course, but far more excitement. At least for now, from the safety of my own home.

Whitmore gave a nod of acknowledgment. "I am relieved you will do so. Frankly, you are essential to the entire enterprise."

It occurred to me that Mr. Whitmore seemed to have no doubts about my ability to take part in this mission. I was, to him, a competent and required presence. Not a worthless, overbearing spinster or deficient female. Was this how men felt all the time? This intrinsic acceptance of one's significance? No wonder they walked through life expecting so much as their due.

"And you, Lady Julia?" he asked.

"I need to think about this," she said. "I cannot give an answer so quickly. There is too much to consider."

Whitmore had clearly not expected Julia to refuse an answer, for he turned to me. "Perhaps you could persuade your sister, Lady Augusta. I am sure you do not wish to go without her. As I understand it, you are a formidable pair and work most effectively when you are together. You would have a much better chance of success if you both went."

I looked at Julia, who had her mouth set at its most Colebrook mulish. It was true, we were formidable together and it was hard to conceive of doing this without her at my side. Until a few days ago, I might indeed have tried to sway my sister's answer. Perhaps even chivvied her into voicing it now.

"It is Lady Julia's decision, Mr. Whitmore," I said firmly. "She must choose her own path in her own time."

Julia looked sideways at me, her mulishness shifting into a small smile: *Behold the new Augusta.*

I returned the smile: *And behold the new Julia.*

She gave a small, perplexed frown: *I am not new.*

I raised my brows: *Are you not?*

"You have a day to think about it, Lady Julia, but no more." Mr. Whitmore stood and picked up his tricorn. "We have arranged a smuggler's boat from Walmer to take you across three days hence."

"Three days?" I repeated. Good God, how would I get everything prepared and travel down to Walmer in such a short time?

"Three days," he confirmed. "Lord Evan and Mr. Kent must depart the country as soon as possible." He placed the tricorn upon his gray wig. "Speaking of those gentlemen, I have two messages that I am obliged to pass on to you, for I gave my word." He drew a preparatory breath. "Lady Julia, Mr. Kent has bid me say, and I quote: 'On no account do as Mr. Whitmore asks, my love.'" He cleared his throat, clearly embarrassed by the final endearment. "And Lady Augusta, Lord Evan says, 'I will see you soon, Renegade.'" He reached into his grimy pocket. "He also asked me to give you this."

He passed across the item. A small glass pot of arnica balm, a written direction upon it in Evan's hand: *Use it.*

I laughed, perhaps more from the fact that I would see my love soon than from the pot of balm. "Tell him—" I started.

Mr. Whitmore stopped me with a raised palm and a shake of his head. "I am sorry, Lady Augusta, I cannot pass on a message. I will not see Lord Evan before he, and you, leave England. It is too dangerous." He turned to my sister. "We will be in contact soon for your answer, Lady Julia."

"And you will arrange for the Exalted Brethren of Rack and Ruin to be closed down before I go," I reminded him. "If you fail me, I will not step foot on that boat."

"I understand. I will send word when it is done." He looked at Mr. Brummell's note in my hand. "May I?" he asked, reaching for it.

In reflex, I passed it to him. He took the few steps to our hearth and threw the note into the fire, watching the wax spit and the paper curl into flame.

With that, he bowed and departed the room.

48

*ulia rubbed her hands together and walked to the hearth, although she could not be cold within the warmth of the drawing room. She took the iron poker from its stand and dug into the flames, where Brummell's note had burned.

"Well," she said. "That was rather unexpected."

I watched her as she placed the poker back into its slot and walked to the window, twitching a perfect curtain pleat into further perfection.

"You are perturbed," I said.

"Of course I am. Are not you?"

"Yes, indeed."

She shook her head. "I think we differ in our agitation, Gus. You crave this type of thrill, but I do not."

I opened my mouth to protest but shut it again. Perhaps it was a fair observation.

She placed her hands upon the windowsill, her head bowed. "I get so frightened. When you went into the forest, I could barely breathe the entire time for fear that you might never return. And when Mr. Kent was taken—"

"I get frightened too," I said.

How many times had I blinked past the image of Mulholland's

leering face in that circle of men or the sensation of his grabbing hands?

"But it is not only that," Julia said. "I may have stopped taking the blue mass pills, but I am still fatigued, still not well."

I bit my lip, stopping myself from commenting upon that happy decision.

"And we are at war with France, Gus," she continued. "We are not trained for such things. Moreover, we would be in the company of men to whom we are not married, whom we have no real claim upon."

"Except love."

She eyed me for a moment, silently conceding that claim. "Even so, it is just not done. We are Lady Augusta and Lady Julia. We do not sully ourselves with the matters and work of men. Especially such sordid work as the Alien Office. We would be two unmarried women in the company of two unmarried men, neither of them acceptable to our family or our social sphere. If it was discovered, we would be ruined. Beyond contempt. Or thought mad and pitied."

I had not thought of that aspect of the mission. Traveling with Evan in another country, in the guise of another woman. Another life and another set of rules without the eyes of English society upon me. An interesting prospect. Still, that was not Julia's point.

"You are right. It would certainly be unconventional," I said.

"Unconventional?" Julia gave a small laugh. "That is an understatement. The truth is, Gus, I am a conventional woman. Unlike you, I do not wish to flout society."

"By loving Mr. Kent, I think you already do."

She pressed her fingertips to her face and shook her head. "No, I have not stepped boldly into society with Mr. Kent. I have not shown my attachment to the world. I—" She stopped, turning to look out the window at some commotion below. "Oh no."

"What is it?" I crossed to the window.

A town carriage stood at our door. Duffy and Harriet had clearly just alighted, for their footman was folding up the step and closing the carriage door behind them. I grabbed Julia's arm to pull her away from sight. Damn, too slow: Harriet looked up and saw us at the window, raising a hand in greeting. We could not send Weatherly down to claim we were not at home.

"I suppose this visit was inevitable," Julia said.

"Inevitably irritating," I muttered.

My sister cast a critical look around the drawing room, then walked over to the sofa where Mr. Whitmore had sat. "Is that a mark? Harriet is always so . . . observant."

"No, there is nothing there," I said.

She eyed it suspiciously but accepted my verdict. A quick circuit of the room adjusted the position of a vase, tidied Julia's pen back into its holder, and wiped a speck of dust from the side table. Then Weatherly's knock upon the door sent us both to stand before our armchairs.

"Come," I said.

The door opened and Weatherly announced, "Lord Duffield and Lady Duffield, my ladies."

Harriet trod daintily into the room—again wearing her blue wool and ermine-trimmed pelisse but without the bonnet—followed by our brother in his customary Weston. His hat and cane had been handed over downstairs, but he still wore his caped greatcoat. All good omens of a short visit.

"Good morning, sisters," Harriet said, pausing ever so slightly for us to curtsy first. We obliged, then received her curtsy and Duffy's bow.

"Good morning, Harriet," Julia said with an almost genuine smile. It was more than I could conjure. "Good morning, Duffy. Shall I send for tea?"

"Oh no, not for me," Harriet said, casting a coy look at Duffy.

"Nor for me, Julia." He offered his arm to his wife and escorted her to the sofa. Harriet sat, but Duffy continued on to his usual position standing at the mantel. "We do not stay long."

I refrained from murmuring "amen" and took my seat, Julia claiming her own armchair beside me.

"You no doubt know why we are here."

"Absolutely not," I said, finally managing a smile through my teeth.

Duffy sighed. "You are going to be difficult, I see." He glanced at Harriet, who gave him an encouraging nod, her tightly tonged curls bobbing at either side of her face. "I am here because of the events at Davenport Hall. I can barely believe the behavior I witnessed, from both of you. Interfering in Lord Deele's affairs, taking advantage of Lord Davenport, and worst of all, associating—nay, worse than that—actively helping and consorting with a criminal and a man claiming to be a Bow Street Runner. It does not bear thinking about."

"You seem to have done quite a great deal of thinking about it," I said. "Although I wonder how you reconcile your part in the evening. Or should I say your lack of part."

Duffy glared at me. "What do you mean by that?"

"I mean you failed to help either Julia or myself. I asked you for your sword and you refused, and the least you could have done was to stay on the road with Julia. But no, you turned tail and ran."

Duffy drew himself up. "Are you calling me a coward?"

"That is your word, not mine," I said.

"Duffield did exactly as his duty required, Augusta," Harriet said, small mouth pursed. "He is a magistrate. Besides, he had more important obligations than to pull you out of your ridiculous situations. Duffield, tell them."

Duffy tugged at his waistcoat hem, regaining some composure.

"Harriet has told me that it is highly probable she is enceinte with the Duffield heir."

I looked at Harriet, who smiled smugly up at Duffy. I had to admit I did not know much about childbearing, but Charlotte had told me the way one knew one was with child. If my quick calculation was correct—barely four weeks had passed since the wedding—then that was very fast indeed.

"How wonderful," Julia said. "Congratulations."

"Are you sure?" I asked, perhaps a little too baldly.

"Gus!" Julia hissed beneath her breath.

"It is, indeed, early to be sure," Harriet acknowledged, some color mounting her cheeks, "but I am fairly certain it is so, and the situation, we thought, called for the announcement."

"Indeed," Duffy said. "We only tell you at this early point in our expectation because there can be no more of your foolish behavior. The Duffield heir must be born into a family of spotless reputation. There can be no more unnatural infatuations with criminals and the lower orders. No more careering around the countryside, brandishing weapons and lying to all you meet. You have already brought infamy upon the family, and frankly, I cannot see a way to fully contain what you have done. Not when Ellis-Brant and his awful wife—the worst gossip in England—witnessed it too. They saw you drive off with those men. Both of you, by yourselves, into the night. And you, Augusta, returning"—he gestured to my face—"beaten like some whore."

"Duffield!" Harriet protested primly.

"Apologies, my dear," Duffy said.

"Your concern for my well-being warms my heart, brother," I said.

"You have only yourself to blame, Augusta. As it stands, we must prepare ourselves for some scandal. Harriet and I, however, have determined a course of action that should preserve our family name and your reputations."

I looked across at Julia: *They have a course of action.*

Julia pressed her lips together: *We should listen.*

I narrowed my eyes: *Really?*

Apparently it was a list of things, for Duffy counted the first one off with a touch of one forefinger upon the other. "To begin, you must cut all ties with those two men. All ties. It makes me sick to think you have been in their company alone, especially you, Julia. I thought you, at least, understood your own worth, even if Augusta does not."

Julia shifted on her seat.

"Secondly, I have ordered the dower house at Duffield to be opened. We think it is best that you quit this house and London and live there from now on. You are well past the age to retire from society, anyway, and I am sure you will find enough families of good repute in the area for your social requirements. Finally, you must write letters of apology to Lord Deele for your interference in his affairs, and to Lord Davenport for the masquerade you enacted upon him and his guests. I have already written to him to say these events were prompted by mid-age megrims, and you should lean upon that explanation. Perhaps that will go some way to ameliorating the scandal."

"And if we do not?" I asked. I was rather proud that I spoke the words rather than shouted them.

"You have no choice, Augusta," Harriet said. "Duffield and I feel that our child must have aunts of impeccable reputation. If you do not follow our advice, we cannot allow you to be part of our child's life." She turned to Julia, a kind smile upon her face. "I am sure you do not wish to miss out upon the joys of being an aunt, Julia. I know you are fond of children."

We had all somehow ended up looking at Julia.

She took a breath—a quiver within it, for she did not like such confrontation—and stood. "Duffy, Harriet, thank you for coming today. I am so pleased to hear your good news." She lifted her chin. "However, Augusta and I will not be quitting our home and taking up residence in the dower house. We will not be writing letters of apology. And we will certainly not be cutting all ties with the men that we love. Quite the opposite. I will not be told where to live or how to conduct my life. And I will especially not be told whom I can love. Nor will Augusta." She turned to Harriet. "And shame upon you, sister, for using your unborn child as blackmail to force us into the lives that you want us to live for your own convenience. Shame on you."

Harriet gasped. "Duffield, surely you will not allow her to speak to me in such a way."

Duffy's face darkened. "Julia, Harriet is the senior in rank here. You must show her the respect she deserves. I thought you understood the importance of position and family."

"I do, Duffy. But I fear you do not."

"Julia, be sensible. If you do not do as we ask, I will be forced to disown you. I cannot have you and Augusta bringing more shame upon yourselves and our family. I will disown you! What do you say to that?"

Julia picked up the small bell on the table between us and rang it. Our footman promptly opened the door and bowed. "Samuel, please show Lord and Lady Duffield out."

Duffy drew himself up to the very top of his very average height. "I cannot believe you are choosing a life of scandal and degradation over your own family's wishes." He rounded upon me. "It is not like you to let Julia take the lead, Augusta. For once, you must pull her back from this precipice on which you both stand."

"In this instance, brother, Julia speaks for both of us," I said.

Harriet rose from her seat. "Duffield, they are beyond reason. Let us go."

Our brother drew in a long breath through pinched nostrils and stalked over to his wife. He offered his arm. She rose with great dignity and together they walked from the room, without looking back and without any farewell or courtesies.

I waited until Samuel had closed the door, then turned to my sister. I knew such a confrontation would have taken a toll upon her nerves.

"That was very brave," I said.

"I feel quite sick." She pressed her fingertips against her lips.

"Do you need something?" I started toward the brandy decanter.

"No, I will be quite well in a moment or so." A few steps took her to the writing table. She sat and slid a new piece of paper across the desk. "I think we should pack only those gowns that we commissioned from Madame Alisette: the ones fashioned in the French mode, and in the French silk. All our other clothes are far too English in style and will give us away." She picked up her pen. "I shall start making a list."

"You are coming to France?" I clapped in elation. "Even against Mr. Kent's advice?"

"I will not allow anyone to tell me how to live my life," she said. "I am going because I have discovered that I do not wish to be parted from my true family." She put down the pen again and held out her hand for me. I closed the distance between us and clasped her still trembling fingers. "Mr. Whitmore is right," she added. "Together we are formidable."

"And on occasion, ill-mannered too," I said, smiling.

"On occasion," my sister conceded. "But only under provocation."

49

Julia and I spoke first to Weatherly about the mission.

"Would you like to sit?" I asked him when we called him back into the drawing room.

"I would prefer to stand, my ladies," he said. He did so, before us, hands neatly behind his back, his full attention upon us.

"We have something to ask you, and please do not feel under any obligation to say yes," Julia said.

We outlined the plan to go to France with Lord Evan and Mr. Kent—as far as Mr. Whitmore's strictures allowed—and the dangers of moving through enemy territory. Throughout, Weatherly nodded, and I could see he had already made up his mind to accompany us. It was in the set of his jaw and the squaring of his shoulders. Even so, I had to make sure he understood the true danger of the mission for him, alone, before he made his decision.

"There is one further danger that you will face if you decide to come with us, Weatherly," I said.

"What further danger?" my sister asked me, for I had not mentioned it to her before Weatherly's arrival.

"Bonaparte's reinstatement of slavery, my lady," Weatherly said.

I heard my sister's intake of breath. "The fiend."

It was not recent news—the reinstatement had occurred ten years ago—but my sister did not follow politics or the subject of slavery laws with as much attention as Weatherly and myself. We had both assisted in Mr. Wilberforce's abolitionist efforts and, upon the news of Bonaparte's perfidy in 1802, had grieved for the many hundreds of thousands of people who would consequently be held in bondage.

"But you are a free man, Weatherly," Julia said.

"I am a free man on British soil, my lady. There is a legal assumption of freedom here. It is not so certain in France. Not anymore."

"It adds to the danger for you, my friend," I said. "I meant what I said in the forest. There is no obligation for you to accompany us on this mad quest. We will understand if you decline."

Weatherly acknowledged my restatement with a sober nod. "Thank you. However, your father saw something within me, my ladies, and offered me the chance to live like any other free British man. Upon my departure from his house to take up my position at yours, he asked me to ensure your safety and well-being. I gave my word I would do so." He gave one of his rare smiles. "So I will come to France, and I will ensure your safety."

"Oh, Weatherly, are you certain?" Julia said softly.

"I am."

"Thank you," I said. "And we will ensure your safety."

"Then we have every chance of success," Weatherly said.

The choice of our second servant had prompted some debate between Julia and me, for we needed a lady's maid and we both had stalwart, discreet women serving us. In the end we decided to ask Tully. Most lady's maids knew some French—it was a general requirement of the position—but Leonard, Julia's maid, only knew some French phrases, whereas Tully had learned the language at her Huguenot grandmother's knee.

We decided it was best for me to approach Tully alone, for we did not want the presence of both her employers to influence her decision. As I dressed for dinner that night, I told her about the mission and asked if she would like to accompany us.

"You are asking me to come with you to France?" Tully asked, looking up from pinning my bodice into place. Her large blue eyes had widened into round astonishment.

"You would be serving both Lady Julia and myself, and it will be very dangerous."

"Into France. Where the war is?" she asked. "On one of your adventures?"

"Yes. I cannot tell you anything about the mission, but it is for our king and our country. If you do not wish to go, then there will be no repercussions. Your position is safe. You are free to decline. Think on it carefully."

"I do not need to, my lady. I wish to come."

Although I was pleased by her enthusiasm, I felt it my duty to counsel caution. "Are you sure? It is a big decision to make so quickly."

"I am sure." She pressed her steepled hands to her small chin, suppressing, it seemed, an expansive celebration, for her eyes were alight with it. "Before I came here, my lady, I was a scullery maid, then a kitchen maid, and then a housemaid. It was all honest work, my lady, do not get me wrong. But it was small. I was small." Her steepled hands curved into the tight shape of a ball. "Then you gave me the chance to be your lady's maid, even when I was not the most qualified of those who came for the position. My world has grown so much." Her hands opened into a blooming of fingers. "I have been to so many places, bought disguises, even sewn a dagger sheath into your sleeve. Now you ask me to help you achieve something truly big in this world. Something important. Of course I will come."

I remembered back to my interview with Tully: the petite young woman with the sweet, round face who had stood before me, nervous but with a direct gaze and a hint of humor. Perhaps I had recognized her kindred, adventurous spirit, even then.

So, now we were six.

*T*he town of Walmer, situated on the little eastern foot of England, was a rather charming sea-resort town with a handsome Tudor castle and a nearby naval marines garrison. Despite the presence of the marines—or perhaps because of it—the town was also ideally placed for smuggling. Only twenty-five miles separated the shorelines of England and France.

Twenty-five miles that we would soon be crossing. At night.

I looked out of the carriage as we navigated a particularly narrow street, the windows of some of the higgledy-piggledy houses on either side already aglow with candles in the dusk.

Yesterday, in London, I had received a note delivered by a small boy who had run off before I could question him. The note was brief and unsigned:

> *Last night, 2 Bedford Street suffered a catastrophic fire.*
> *The house is destroyed. Fortunately, no one was injured*
> *within the house or in the dwellings on either side.*
> *May your travels be safe and successful.*

As we departed London, I asked John Driver to take us past Bedford Street; a little out of our way, but I had to ensure Whitmore was telling the truth. Sure enough, the home of the Exalted Brethren of Rack and Ruin was now, ironically, completely ruined. Perhaps it was a little ghoulish to take delight in such destruction, but I reveled in the sight of its blackened beams and crumbling bricks. The club would, I knew, eventually open its doors elsewhere. Still, if the delay of their hideous activities saved just one woman from a terrible death, then that was a victory. Just as importantly, its destruction proved Whitmore was a man of his word. And a rather creative thinker.

"I believe we have arrived," Julia said, as we turned onto Walmer's wider esplanade.

I looked out upon the long, flat sand beach, the white-capped sea and an indigo night sky lit by a bright waxing gibbous moon. A good moon to sail by. Some of the boats of the Walmer sailors—luggers and galleys, according to the seaside resorts guide I had consulted—were hauled up on the beach. Beyond them stood a distant forest of masts: ships waiting in the Downs, the area between Walmer and the treacherous Goodwin Sands, for safe passage. Even through the closed carriage windows I smelled the pungent odors of seaweed and salt and heard the screeching night call of gulls wheeling above.

The carriage traveled on a rough road alongside the beach for a distance, passing what was clearly the more legitimate side of the town's activities. Finally, we drew to a halt near a cliff. The carriage rocked; then Weatherly appeared at the door, huddled in his French-style greatcoat. Beyond him, Tully stood muffled in a new cloak and looking out upon the sea, one of my smaller travel boxes cradled in her arms.

"This is where we were instructed to stop, my ladies," Weatherly said, opening the carriage door.

"I must admit, I feel rather underprepared," Julia said to me as she took Weatherly's hand to descend the carriage step. "This may not be the wisest decision on our part."

"It is not wise in the slightest, dearheart," I said. "Are you regretting your choice?"

"I suppose there is no use for that now." She looked out upon the beach and the small group of men awaiting us next to a galley boat hauled up on the sand. Her face brightened into a beaming smile. "Look, there are Mr. Kent and Lord Evan."

I followed her down the carriage step to the road. Across the foreshore, I saw my love seated upon a large rock next to the galley with Mr. Kent standing at his side, both in heavy greatcoats and holding the brims of their hats against the cold breeze.

Upon seeing me, Evan raised his other hand in greeting, unfolded his tall, lean self from his vantage point, and started across the sand to meet me halfway.

I waved back, my own smile as bright as my sister's.

As Mr. Kent fell in behind Evan, I took Julia's hand and we forged our way through the scrubby undergrowth to the sand. The chilly wind upon the open beach blew with a great deal more ferocity than on the road, and we both gasped as it grabbed at our breath and wrapped our skirts around our legs.

"Good timing, Renegade," Evan called, treading with some agility over the sliding sands. "The tide is turning."

I stepped forward to receive his outstretched hands. The wind immediately caught the brim of his hat, and so I received only one hand. But it was enough, for it pulled me into a tight embrace against his chest. A rather similar embrace was happening nearby, although Mr. Kent had somehow jammed his hat on his head more tightly and had both arms around my sister.

"How is your jaw?" Evan asked, squinting down at my face. "Is all the swelling gone? No loss of sensation? Your teeth firm?" He laughed at my expression. "I know, I know. But I have been so worried."

I angled my chin for his scrutiny. "It is healing well, see?" I said.

"Then I can kiss you without causing any pain?"

"You can," I said solemnly.

He bent into a slight clash of hat and bonnet brims. With a smile, he pulled off his hat and tried again, his lips gently pressing upon mine. Definitely no pain. A great deal of pleasure, in fact. I leaned in closer, all of the past week rising within me into a fierce, heart-racing kiss that snatched at my breath far more thoroughly than any sea wind. The dark beach around us slid away into just the sensations of his smell and warmth and breath and the press of his need against mine.

"Gus!" Julia's voice, projected with a great deal of volume across the sand, wrenched us apart.

"What?" I blinked to see an old sailor a few yards away watching us.

"Tide's in, sir," he said to Evan with a nod. It was too dark to see his face, but I felt his amusement. "Got to load up quick or we'll miss it."

"Thank you," Evan said, but he did not release me from his embrace.

With another nod, the sailor trudged back toward the lugger. I looked across at Julia, holding Mr. Kent's hand, their heads bent together, intent upon their conversation. Beyond, on the road, Weatherly and Tully were unloading our luggage to bring down to the boat.

I felt Evan's arm around me: my safe harbor. Perhaps it was not the wisest decision to cross the channel into such a dangerous and reckless adventure. But under the circumstances—on a mission for England and with a pardon for Evan in sight—perhaps it was faith that was required, not wisdom.

And for me, that was faith in the five brave, loyal people by my side.

Author's Note

$\mathcal{T}$hank you for joining Gus and Julia on their new adventures. Some real Regency historical figures appear alongside our heroines, although I have taken some poetic license with their activities. It is always great fun to include real people and real events in the Ill-Mannered Ladies series. It does mean a lot of fascinating research, most of which doesn't (and shouldn't) make it into the story. So allow me to indulge my nerdy research obsessions with a bit more information about the historical figures and events that appear in this book.

GEORGE "BEAU" BRUMMELL

George Brummell, or Beau Brummell, as he was called, was the leader of fashionable life in Regency England. He was born into rather humble circumstances, with an unconventional mother who openly and rather scandalously lived with Brummell's father before they married. His father, a valet, rose in rank to serve as private secretary to the prime minister, Lord North, and the Brummell family lived for a short time at 10 Downing Street, which is now the residence of all English prime ministers. His father then managed to procure himself a baronetcy and so his children, George, William, and Maria, became part of genteel society. Through a dazzling combination of good looks, easy charm, impeccable taste, and quick wit, George Brummell rose to become the king of fashionable society. He was best friends with the Prince Regent and could make or break anyone's social standing with a lift of a quizzical eyebrow. His individual way of dressing for the times—in sober colors and fine, clean tailoring—has influenced men's fashions in such a profound way that we still feel it in the concept of the suit today. Like his friend the Prince Regent, he liked the company of older women and was the confidant of some of the Regency's greatest hostesses. He reigned supreme in society until he overstepped his own power at a ball he was hosting by making an insulting comment to the Prince Regent. Famously, when the Prince Regent approached him, Brummell asked Lord Alvanley, "Who is your fat friend?" While that actual comment might be apocryphal, whatever he said resulted in his being cut from royal favor, and his power waned until debt drove him from England. He died of syphilis in an asylum in France in 1840. He is perhaps the character with whom I have taken the most poetic license—there is no evidence that he was an agent or operative of any kind, although he did maintain a great deal of mystery about himself, leaving some tantalizing gaps for a writer to weave her story around him.

LORD ALVANLEY

William Arden—Lord Alvanley—was one of the leaders of society alongside his good friend George Brummell. Alvanley was considered to be the wittiest man of his time and also a man of perfect good nature, with a slight lisp that only added "zest and appeal" to his conversation (according to Captain Gronow in his memoir, *Regency Recollections*). In his younger years, Alvanley was a renowned athlete, and after his education he joined the Coldstream

Guards, where he acquitted himself with distinction. Upon inheriting his wealth and title, he embraced the lifestyle of the Regency dandy and spent his days pursuing pleasure.

THE BERRY SISTERS AND THEIR FAMOUS SALONS

Mary Berry and her sister, Agnes, were born in the Georgian era in 1763 and 1764, respectively. They were approaching ninety when they died in the same year, 1852, well into the Victorian era. The sisters were inseparable and lived fascinating lives. Mary was a writer and diarist, a keen reader, a daring traveler, and a talented conversationalist. Less is known about Agnes, but she was a talented artist and was noted for her pencil drawings. They held salons or, as they called them, "circles," inviting fashionable society and the brightest and most talented literati, actors, and politicians of the day. These were famous intellectual gatherings and were part of the tradition of the French salon, a space where mixed-gender gatherings were presided over by women. The Berry sisters became friends—in fact almost family—with Horace Walpole, the British member of Parliament and writer, and that deep connection brought them an inheritance and independence. More about the Berry sisters and the "salon" can be found in Susanne Schmid's excellent *British Literary Salons of the Late Eighteenth and Early Nineteenth Centuries*.

THE LADIES OF LLANGOLLEN

Lady Eleanor Butler and Miss Sarah Ponsonby, both born to aristocratic families in Ireland, ran away together in 1778 disguised as men and carrying a pistol and a small dog. They were retrieved by their scandalized families and separated. Both women, however, resisted the reproach of their families and the pressure to marry men of their own class and were eventually allowed to reunite and leave Ireland again, this time for North Wales. They settled at Plas Newydd with their faithful servant, Mary Carryl. As aristocrats, they did not work but relied upon gifts from friends and family—with whom they managed to stay on good terms—and lived a relatively modest lifestyle. Plas Newydd was on the main transport route to Ireland and so it became fashionable for society to stop and be entertained by the ladies, who had a reputation as excellent hosts and conversationalists. Their precarious financial situation was eventually alleviated by an inheritance from their faithful servant, Mary, and a pension from King George III, who granted it on advice from his wife, Queen Charlotte. The ladies always denied anything other than a platonic friendship and even threatened legal action against a newspaper that wrote about their relationship in an unflattering way. They are, however, widely considered to be an iconic historical queer couple and demonstrated to many women of their own time, and long after, that two women could flout convention and build a happy and stable home together.

The Luddites

The term *Luddite* now refers to a person who is afraid of or unwilling to use technology. However, the original Luddites were groups of working-class men and women protesting the advent of machinery in the UK textile trade that was making their skills obsolete and destroying their livelihoods. The name Luddite was taken from General Ned Ludd, or King Lud, a mythical figure who supposedly led the workers and whose name appeared on threatening letters sent to mill owners. The workers initially tried to air their fears and grievances through official channels but received little sympathy and no action. In order to gain some acknowledgment of their position and keep their livelihoods, they turned to breaking up the machines that were taking their jobs. Initially, great care was taken by the protestors to damage only the machines, but during 1812 and 1813 the outbreaks escalated into violence. The militia were called in, protestors were shot, and a mill owner was murdered on his way home from Huddersfield market. The government, terrified that a revolution like the "French Terror" was about to happen in England, responded with great brutality through the militia. In 1813, seventeen men were hanged (three for the murder of the mill owner) and seven men were transported. After such savage suppression, the Luddite movement more or less disbanded.

The Mercury Poisoning on the HMS *Triumph* and HMS *Phipps*, and Blue Mass Pills

The mercury poisoning on the HMS *Triumph* and HMS *Phipps* that Lord Evan mentions to Gus really did happen, although Lord Evan's correct conclusion about the poisonous effects of ingested mercury did not occur until much later in the history of medicine. Unfortunately, the mercury-based blue mass pills and other mercury-based medicines were still being used up until the late nineteenth century, and it is even thought that Abraham Lincoln suffered from medicinal mercury poisoning from blue mass pills, which greatly affected his health and mental state.

The Sex Clubs of Georgian England

The Exalted Brethren of Rack and Ruin in the novel is loosely based on the most famous of the sex clubs in Georgian England:

the Hellfire Club. An early version of the club was founded in 1718 by Philip, Duke of Wharton. It seems to have started out more as a satirical club ridiculing religion. It admitted both men and women as equals, which was unusual for the time. Wharton's club came to an end in 1721. However, in 1748, Francis Dashwood started another club, which had various names and would eventually become known as the Hellfire Club. Since then, quite a few iterations of the club have been documented, including one involving Lord Byron in the early 1800s. It was reported that the Hellfire clubs held meetings that involved orgies and sadomasochistic practices and celebrated pagan rituals dedicated to Venus and Bacchus. There were also whispers of Satanism and human sacrifice. However, those remain in the realm of rumor since a great deal of the information about the sex clubs, including Dashwood's and Lord Byron's, was destroyed during the Victorian era, often by somewhat horrified relatives of those involved.

JENNY

In the novel, the fictional character Jenny suffers the very real assault of non-fatal strangulation. Non-fatal suffocation or strangulation can cause delayed and long-lasting physical and neurological damage. If you or someone you know has suffered non-fatal suffocation or strangulation, please seek medical help as soon as possible.

Acknowledgments

As ever, huge thanks to my darling husband, Ron, to my friend Karen McKenzie, and to my parents, Doug and Charmaine Goodman. My wonderful stalwarts. Thanks also to Buckley, my dog, for insisting upon workplace health and safety via enforced walkie breaks and pat sessions.

I am so fortunate to have the support and talents of my fabulous agent, Jill Grinberg, and her team, who always have my back and love the Regency era as much as I do.

Thanks also to the lovely Kate Seaver, Amanda Maurer, and the team at Berkley, including talented cover designer Rita Frangie. Special thanks to Sveta Dorosheva, who created the sublime cover illustration. I am also indebted to my meticulous copy editor, Eileen G. Chetti, and to Anna Valdinger at HarperCollins Australia for her invaluable feedback and eternal enthusiasm.

Thank you also to Andrea Stringer, carriage driver and historic horse-drawn vehicle collector, who generously cast her expert eye over my horse-riding and carriage action.

Finally, my thanks always to Nicola O'Shea, who is the trusted first editor of my work.

This book was written on the lands of the Bunurong People of the Kulin Nation, and I wish to acknowledge them as Traditional Owners, and pay my respects to their Elders, past and present, and Aboriginal Elders of other communities.

The Ladies Road Guide to Utter Ruin

ALISON GOODMAN

READERS GUIDE

Discussion Questions

1. As twin sisters, Gus and Julia share a close bond, and each brings different but complementary strengths to their adventuring. What strengths do you think Gus brings? What does Julia bring?

2. Beau Brummell held an extraordinary amount of social power in the Regency era. He could ruin a person's social standing with a quizzical lift of his eyebrow or bring them into vogue by talking to them for fifteen minutes. In your opinion, what forms of social power exist today?

3. It is fantasy cast time! If you were casting the film of *The Ladies Road Guide to Utter Ruin*, who would you choose to play Gus, Julia, Lord Evan, and Mr. Kent? Beau Brummell? Hester and Elizabeth? Mulholland?

4. What are some of the rights that women have now that Gus and Julia do not have in the Regency era?

5. Who is more annoying, Duffy or Mrs. Ellis-Brant (the Ermine)?

6. Beau Brummell tells Gus that they are "cut from the same cloth." What do you think he means by this?

7. Regency-era clubs and societies often had very odd and convoluted names: for example, the Beefeaters Club and the Most Ancient and Most Puissant Order of the Beggar's Benison and Merryland. For a bit of fun, what would be your book club's Regency name?

8. Why do you think spies and the act of spying were considered sordid and disreputable in the Regency era? How are they considered now?

9. Do you agree with Gus that the Luddites may have had a case for destroying looms and other textile machinery as a way of protest?

10. Considering both the physical and social dangers of the mission proposed by Mr. Whitmore, do you think Gus and Julia should have agreed to go? What do you think about the condition that Gus placed on Mr. Whitmore's request for her participation?